The Curse of Babylon

RICHARD BLAKE

The Curse
of Babylon

HODDER &
STOUGHTON

First published in 2013 by Hodder & Stoughton
An Hachette UK company

1

Copyright © 2013 by Richard Blake

A CIP catalogue record for this title is available from the British Library

Trade paperback ISBN 978 1 444 70973 5
E-book ISBN 978 1 444 74705 4

Typeset in Plantin Light by Hewer Text UK, Ltd
Printed and bound by Clays Ltd, St Ives plc

Hodder & Stoughton policy is to use papers that are natural, renewable
and recyclable products and made from wood grown in sustainable
forests. The logging and manufacturing processes are expected to
conform to the environmental regulations of the country of origin.

Hodder & Stoughton Ltd
338 Euston Road
London NW1 3BH

www.hodder.co.uk

To my dear wife Andrea
And to my little daughter Philippa
And to my mummy

ACKNOWLEDGEMENTS

The couplet in Chapter 19 is from *The Review*, by Richard Duke (1658–1711).

The verse in Chapter 27 is from the *Epic of Gilgamesh* (c.1500 BC), translated in 1920 by Albert T. Clay, and published on the Project Gutenberg archive of public domain e-texts. Translation:

> May he make thine eyes see the prophecy of thy mouth!
> May he track out (for thee) the closed path!
> May he level the road for thy treading!
> May he level the mountain for thy foot!

The verse in Chapter 27 is from Homer, *Iliad*, Book I, 1–4. Translation: Thomas Hobbes (1588–1679).

The quotation that heads Chapter 42 is attributed to Tacitus, but is from Dio Cassius (c.AD 150–235), *Roman History*, book 59, c. 30 and translated from Greek by the author.

The poem in Chapter 57 is in Middle Persian (c.7th century). Author and translator unknown. Source: Wikipedia. Translation:

> I have a counsel from the wise,
> From the advice of the ancients.
> I will pass it upon you.
> By truth in the world,
> If you accept this counsel,
> It will be your benefit for this life and the next.

The quotations in Chapter 58 are from Herodotus (c.484–425 BC), *Histories*, Book VIII, c. 54 and Book VII, c. 223–4 – translated by the author.

PROLOGUE

Canterbury, Wednesday, 17 June 688

What do you say to a boy of fifteen when you're sending him to his death? The easy answer is you say nothing. After so many repetitions of the dream, there was nothing more to be said. I was staring into the face of someone who'd been dead over seventy years. He'd volunteered to serve. He'd then volunteered for nearly certain death. If that weren't enough, I had been only nominally in charge at the Battle of Larydia. I'd been a mile away when he went into battle. At the head of a frontal assault, I was hardly out of danger myself.

The easy answer never mattered. I looked into his eyes and saw him try for a nervous smile, then reach up to touch crisp and very dark hair. Another moment and I'd hear a voice behind me explain the plan of attack. It had all the boldness of desperation. We were three hundred men against forty or fifty thousand. Once the Persians were out of the mountain passes, nothing at all might stop them till they reached the walls of Constantinople. Hit them in the passes, though – and hit them in a manner suggesting we were the first wave of a bigger force – and they *might* crumple and make a run for it. But this part of the attack was the ultimate in desperation. Of the hundred men about to run down into the battle not one would return. A boy who was now shivering in the cold of a mountain dawn wouldn't live to feel the noonday heat.

I've said I wasn't there. I'd been watching events at the front of that gigantic invasion force. No place in this dream, though, for spying on Shahin as he put on his reluctant show. I knew that he was down in the pass, his back to me, ready to present a *certain object* to his master. I could almost see the cold glitter of the thing in its box, and the dark luxuriance of the box on a table spread with yellow silk. But almost seeing isn't actual seeing. I was dreaming of events above the pass. I focused once more on the boy.

Fifteen is no age for dying. I've had six times that and more, and I could live a little yet. Familiarity aside, what makes the dream bearable on every repetition is that the boy never sees me. Behind me, the voice was now going over the plan. It made no mention of wider issues. It was the sort of talk you'd want if you were ever about to attack a force inconceivably larger than your own – cover those beside you; keep in their cover; don't drop your weapon; don't stop for booty; listen for the signal to pull back; *and go to the toilet now!* That always got a big laugh. The boy was looking through me, at the owner of the voice. Also behind me, the little priest was holding up an icon of Saint Michael. He would soon claim that no earthly hand had painted it, and that all who fell this day would be received straight into Heaven, washed clean of their sins. That would be followed by a loud cheer. Then as the sun rose higher in a sky turning a painful blue, they'd get into position for their downward rush into the butcher's market.

And, all the while, I looked into the eyes of a boy whose mangled body I'd see later that day . . .

1

It was dawn already. My jailor was in the room. 'Get up, you lazy old bastard!' he shouted in English, pulling the blanket off me. 'Who should listen to you, blubbering away in your sleep, when every better man's already finished saying his prayers? Get up, and give thanks to God that you aren't yet in Hell!'

Unpredictable stuff, opium. You can hope it'll blot out all the discomforts of age and give you a good night's sleep. Mostly, it does. Then, every so often, it'll give you the sort of spiritual burp that leaves you wondering if you're not better off without it. I opened my eyes and waited for Brother Ambrose to come into what passes nowadays for focus. I found the gloom and the loud twittering of birds outside most provoking. But he'd not be nagging me this morning into my fine outgoing clothes, or stuffing me into that wheelbarrow again. That could warm my heart, if not my hands or feet.

'Haven't you been told, Ambrose,' I croaked, 'that the inquiry won't be resuming today?' He really should have guessed that much. He hadn't, of course. Are jailors always stupid? Or have I been invariably lucky in the various places of confinement I've known? I called on every ounce of strength left to a man of ninety-eight. After one failed effort, and one slight worry that I'd pulled a muscle, I sat up in bed and shuffled myself round until my feet were resting on the floor. 'You'll soon have your formal orders,' I said, now in better voice. 'You're to get all my stuff packed up and moved to the monastery round the corner.' I managed a toothless smile. 'Now, what have you brought me for breakfast?'

I watched his face turn from bafflement to a snarl of hate. 'Is that all you can think about?' he asked in a voice that was supposed to scare me. '*Breakfast?*'

'A very important meal,' I replied in a voice that I knew might send him over the edge. My head was clearing of the dream, and of the poppy fumes that had sent it. I looked about for my stick. Ambrose had knocked it out of reach, worthless pig that he was. My false teeth of ivory and gold were still where I'd left them on the bedside table. Those could stay put. But I did reach for my blond wig. I could do with that to keep the chill from soaking in through my scalp. And it was more provocation of my own to a man who, still spraying abuse at me with every breath, knew that such power of compulsion he'd had over me was now ended.

I looked at the covered tray the boy had brought up with him. The smell would have made a dog vomit. 'Ooh, nice runny cheese, if my nose tells right,' I said. 'The monks of Saint Anastasius won't spoil me like this!'

Ambrose pushed his bleary face close to mine. 'Don't think you've got away with it,' he snarled. 'You're a murdering bastard – and I've now found the proof.' He stopped, presumably giving me time to fall to pieces. Instead, I was coming properly back to life, and could feel my spirits rising like the sun itself at the thought that I'd soon be out of this ghastly place. I popped my teeth in and smiled. Ambrose stood up. 'There's a hole on the seventh stair down,' he gloated. 'It's a fresh hole. I wonder what was pushed in there, and *why*?'

Dear me – the low beast had finally done his homework! I couldn't have that. Nothing he said now could unstitch the deal I'd made. But he could still raise an unpleasant stink. He might even try his hand at blackmail. Yes, he was the type for that. I licked my upper teeth into place, and smiled again. 'Oh, Ambrose, Ambrose,' I said in my most emollient tone, 'this isn't a day for unpleasantness. We must soon take leave of each other. I like to think that, in spite of one or two disagreements, we have forged an unbreakable bond of friendship. Why not join me in a last shared drink?'

A *last* shared drink? There hadn't been a first! The way he'd been at my breakfast ale without asking, it was a wonder I hadn't seen to him months before. But it was nice ale, and he'd not pass up a last chance to thieve his half of it. Following his usual custom, he swaggered over to the window. He pulled its shutter fully open, and shouted something vulgar to anyone who might be passing by beneath it. This done, he hitched up his robe and began a piss that would leave a stinking puddle on the sill.

'I should have known you'd get off,' he said bitterly. 'Your sort always do. Lord High Bishop Theodore himself ain't nothing up against you people.' He'd splashed someone again. He leaned forward to look out of the window. 'What the fuck do you expect, walking so close to the wall?' he shouted. He turned bitter again. 'If there was any justice in this world, your penance would have been a flogging that broke every bone in your shrivelled old body. Theodore himself told me no less.'

His lecture and his piss would last a while yet. The door was barely ajar, and his boy was waiting outside. I shut my eyes and told myself that ninety-eight was no great age. I opened them and stood up. Avoiding the board that always squeaked, I crept over to my writing table and took a lead box from under a heap of papyrus too mildewed to be used. Back to the bed I silently tottered. I poured myself a cup of ale and, unable to see them as more than a blur, dropped two crumbling tablets into the jug. It was new ale, and the slight foaming of the tablets wouldn't show once they were dissolved. I took another look at Ambrose and added a third. I frowned at hands that wouldn't stop trembling. Thanks to that, I'd nearly added a fourth and fifth.

He was finished. Wiping pissy hands on his robe, he turned to face me. 'Right, Brother Aelric,' he called out with fake jollity, 'where's me drinkie?' I smiled again and pointed at the jug. I watched him drain it in a single gulp. He slapped it down on the bedside table and let out a long and appreciative burp. 'Fucking good stuff!' he said. 'Too good for an old sinner like you.' He thumped his chest and let out another burp. He put both hands on the table and screwed his face up. He now managed a long fart. 'Lovely tickling of my piles,' he explained. He noticed a stray sheet of papyrus on the table. 'Don't you write in nothing but Greek?' he snarled with a sudden return to the nasty. 'Ain't Latin fancy enough for you?'

Not answering, I smiled into my own cup. It was *very* good stuff, and it wasn't the ale I had in mind. Its first effects would be a slight fever before he turned in for the night. Considering his bulk, that might not show till morning. Not long after, the fever would take proper hold, and be joined by griping pains. Another day, and the pains would turn unbearable. Come nightfall at the latest, and there'd be a sudden and catastrophic voiding of blood and failure of every organ. Any Greek physician would know exactly what had been swallowed. In this dump on the edge of civilisation, death would be put down to a visitation of the summer pestilence. There would be much lamentation in public over the body, and much private rejoicing. Until he was replaced, there would be no more starving and beating of prisoners less fortunate than wicked old Aelric – no more compelled sucking off of his rancid member, no more stamping about the monastery by someone whose proper employment in life should have been pushing a dung cart.

I'll grant he'd kept some curb on his inclinations where I was concerned. I might nowadays be called Brother Aelric: no one dared, even so, to take me as other than the Lord Alaric. But some of his abuse had been most impertinent. More to the point, he was on to me. I couldn't have that.

Ambrose burped louder. 'Righty ho!' he laughed. 'Time to be off. I'm told there's a flogging to be done.' He snorted. 'That nutter downstairs has been playing with himself again. I ask you – wanking in a monastery!' He walked heavily to the door. He turned back to me before leaving. 'It don't matter shit who your relatives are,' he said, as if he'd been reading my thoughts. 'I'll make the whole world see you for what you are.'

I'd like to see him try, I told myself. But I made no outward answer. He gave me one last glare, before walking out and slamming the door. I waited for the sound of his key in the lock, then took out my teeth and got back into bed. 'Ho hum! Ho hum!' I heard him shouting on the stairs, no longer for my benefit. 'It's a bad world, I'll have you know – oh, a bad, *bad* world!'

I thought of going back to sleep. It would be Ambrose who supervised my packing later in the day. I'd need to be rested for that. I didn't want anything smashed or stolen. And I'd need to keep him from any search of my belongings. He might find my bronze cloak pin. That would be an embarrassment. But sleep was out of the question until I'd covered my tracks. I threw the blanket aside. Scowling, I looked at the wide-open shutters and climbed back to my feet. I filled the jug from my washing bowl. I swirled the water round and round, before tipping it from the window. I filled it again and let it stand. With the rest of the water I scrubbed my hands. General washing could wait till I was out of here. I might even demand a bath. I'd like a bath.

But, silly old me! I'd dropped my box of poison. Luckily, it didn't burst open. Instead, it bounced under the writing table. The act of bending down sent all the bones in my upper back into a popping sound that disturbed me. Rather than going back to bed, I sat down at the writing table and looked out through the window. Being locked away on the top floor had its advantages. It freed me from the inevitable smells of a city built without sewers. It gave me a better view than any of my jailers had. I looked east over the low huddle of roofs, some tiled, most thatched, to where the wall marked the city's boundary with the Kentish forest. The sun was fast rising above the topmost branches of the trees. I put up a hand to shade my eyes and continued looking south-east. Though far less dense and unbroken than it seemed, the forest stretched from here to Dover and the sea. Beyond that lay France and then Italy and Rome. Far beyond that lay the New Rome and its Empire which, for almost two lifetimes, I'd done more than anyone else to hold together.

I thought of my dream. You won't read about the Battle of Larydia in any of the histories. It had, even so, been the turning of the tide in the first of our two great wars of survival. It didn't let us clear the Persians out of Syria. It didn't stop them from taking Egypt. But all the shattering defeats we later inflicted on them had been made possible by what happened at Larydia. Because of that, we finally recovered our losses. Because of that, we made their empire into a protectorate. Because of that, when the second great war came along out of the blue, we, alone of those they attacked, held back the illimitable Saracen flood. Yes, we lost Egypt and Syria again – this time apparently for good. We may soon lose the African provinces. But, again and again since their first attack, the Saracens have smashed against the southern border of the Home Provinces. Each time, they've been thrown back, and with horrifying losses. So long as the lesson we learned at Larydia stays in mind, we'll keep the Saracens out.

I thought yet again of the boy. I had no reason to feel guilty. You can walk about Constantinople, staring at native and borrowed monuments to three thousand years of victories. Mostly, you can look away and ask what all those men fought each other for, and how their fighting and dying had added one grain to the sum of human happiness. The battle we fought at Larydia saved the Empire and its precious cargo of the only civilisation worth respecting. Or, if you want to be less pompous, that boy and all the others were fighting for their God and for their land. I did tell them that at the time. To be sure, they kept the land. No one there – on our side, at least – died in vain.

I thought forward to the end of our Persian War. I thought of how, with the Lord High General Radostes beside me, I was the one who identified the Great King's dismembered body. At last, his own people had turned on Chosroes, and had starved him and tortured him, and dumped him, still alive, in a field latrine. Over hills and fields, and skirting the edge of a baking desert, the General and I had ridden for days in hope of taking him alive. We got there just too late. His killers bought their lives from me with his crown. That I'd presented to Heraclius, and got a pat on the head for the effort. I'd then been sent off with it, to crown a puppet in the Emperor's name. I can't say an age of peace and plenty had followed our triumphal ceremony in Jerusalem. But our victory at Larydia did allow us to make the best of things.

I sat up straight and, as if made stronger by the rising sun, turned to my desk. I pushed aside the pens and inkwell and papyrus. With fingers that moved slightly later than I'd willed them to, I managed to get the cloth bag undone and took hold of what it contained. The first time I held this, it had been in one outstretched hand. Now it needed both hands, and a tensing of aged back muscles, to lift it into the sunlight.

I beheld the fabled Horn of Babylon. Men had killed for this. Men had died for it. Men had sometimes worshipped it as a god in its own right, and sometimes as a vessel of godly power. Who had originally made it, and when, and for what purpose, were questions I hadn't been able to answer when I was in a position to ask them of others. It was a waste of time to ask them now. All that could be said for sure was that, in its form, it had been made as some kind of vessel. You could argue whether its bowl had been made to hold wine or to collect blood from a sacrifice. I had no doubt it had been *used* for both.

I say I beheld it. Even if it didn't now have the colour and sheen of rotten teeth wet with spittle, I'd not have been able to see the marks that covered it inside and out – not with my old eyes. But, if I ran a thumbnail over it, I could still feel the mass of characters, each one resembling nothing so much as the footprint of a tiny bird on wax. I couldn't read them. Though men had done well out of claiming otherwise, I doubted anyone had been able to read them in the past thousand years. I doubted anyone knew the name of the winged god they surrounded. So much fuss over an object steeped in mystery!

I sniffed and looked up. I'd left a cup of barley juice on the table. Without my falsies to keep my lips firm, I slobbered much of this on to the blanket I still had round me. I must have made a disgusting sight, but the taste was strangely cheering. I could easily guess what fancies had drifted the day before through the mind of poor old Theodore. But the past only hurts you if you let it. The opium had betrayed me. Awake and in my proper mind, I'd make sure the past stayed exactly where it belonged.

I stared again out of the window. The steam that rose above the forest would soon clear. Whether or not it rained again, I'd make sure it was a lovely day.

2

I once knew a poet called Leander. He was an Egyptian and, like me, had learned Greek as a foreign language. Unlike me, he never learned it well enough to adorn even the lower reaches of its literature. He was a dreadful poet, and I can almost rejoice that, away from his native Egypt, books written on papyrus die within fifty years unless recopied. What brings him now to mind is his habit, when he wanted attention, of stopping whatever he was doing to cry in a grand voice: 'I can feel the Muse about to come upon me!' I'll not go quite so far as that. But I do feel that what began as one of my occasional diary entries ought to form part of a longer narrative. At the very least, since I've mentioned it, I should explain how I came to take possession once more of the Horn of Babylon.

This means the story doesn't begin on Wednesday the 17th, but on Monday the 15th. It had been another promising dawn, though Ambrose made sure to spoil it, by shouting and threatening me out of my bed. Still, teeth cleaned and polished and pushed well back, wig on the right way round, I think I looked rather good in my wheelbarrow. Even Ambrose didn't roar with laughter at my appearance.

We came to the point where the street leading from my place of confinement joined with the main square. 'Put me down here a moment,' I said to the boy who was pushing me. 'I feel the need of a rest before showing myself to the people.'

'You're late as it is,' Ambrose grunted with a nervous look at the sky.

I cupped a hand to my bad ear. 'I hear no complaints from those who are waiting,' I said brightly. To the boy: 'Put the handles down and fan me with your hat.' To Ambrose: 'You'd surely not want me to die before I can assist in Gebmund's inquiry.'

Ambrose took on the appearance of a caged animal when it looks through its bars. 'Inquiry, my cock!' he snarled. 'You're on trial for your fucking life!'

I gave him a flash of my nice teeth and added a look of faint senility. 'Oh, is that why I'm a prisoner?' I asked. I looked at the boy. If I wasn't mistaken, his spots were all inflamed. Either he was feeling the morning chill, or he was still hurting from the buggery Ambrose had inflicted on him while I was deciding which hat to put on over my wig. It was probably the latter. I leaned back on the filthy padding. 'Oh, let's just get it over with,' I sighed. I reached inside my woollen robe. I hadn't left my double strength oil of frankincense behind. I unstoppered the pot and shook some of it down the front of my robe.

I was halfway across the square, when the crowd outside the church struck up a respectable cheer. Rattled by the sudden noise, the boy twisted my wheelbarrow to give me sight of the crowd. I took off my hat and waved it. That got me a louder cheer.

'Not a word, you old fool,' Ambrose said into my good ear. 'If you cause another riot, it'll be the worse for you.'

'If you don't keep a civil tongue in your head,' I replied through a fixed smile, 'I may see to it that you don't have a head.' I leaned forward and jabbed my stick into the boy's stomach. 'Come on,' I urged. 'You mustn't keep the people waiting.' He gave me the stupid look of one who hasn't heard, but doesn't want to admit he wasn't listening. I repeated myself, now louder. He swallowed and dropped both handles of his wheelbarrow. Its impact had the blond wig straight off my head and into the dust. By the time it was recovered, I'd decided against putting it back on. Instead, I sat up and tried to look as dignified as a bald, shrivelled old thing ever can. 'Well, come on, boy,' I prompted. 'It isn't us they want to string up – no, not even Brother Ambrose today.'

Even as the boy got ready for one of his pubescent squawks, there was a loud groan, and the crowd took a collective step backwards and to the left. 'There he is!' someone shouted. 'Oh, but hasn't he got a nerve!' someone else said.

It wasn't that much of a nerve, to be fair. As the crowd broke into a low and disapproving chatter, I twisted round on my cushions and saw that Brother Aelfwine had followed us across the square. Flanked by his two elder brothers and any number of cousins and family hangers on, he had a strained look on his face even I could see. I thought he'd hurry past, so he could be in place before everyone else squeezed into the church. But he saw I was looking in his direction and hurried over.

'Greetings, Brother Aelric,' he said stiffly in Latin. Impassive, I looked back at him. I couldn't doubt he was a pretty lad – far too pretty for a monk. What else, though, could he be but pretty? Not only Kentish, he was of royal blood. Being both myself, however much decayed, I may be biased. But, now we've given up on putting butter in our hair and rings through our noses, you'll search hard to find a handsomer race than the better class of Kentishmen. No tonsure was enough to conceal his advantages of birth.

He leaned forward. 'Why don't you just confess?' he whispered. 'I'll see to it that Gebmund gives you his mildest penance ever. Family is family, after all.' He tilted his head at the crowd. 'Must we inflame the common people any further?'

'I have perfect faith that, when My Lord Bishop of Rochester has heard me, there will be no more talk of penances.' I said loudly in English. For just a moment, he looked me in the eye. Then he looked away and breathed something that I couldn't catch but got his flunkies into a dark mood. I was still trying to tell if the biggest of these wasn't one of the King's bastard sons, when I heard the doors of the great church open far across the square and, in a crowd of monks and deacons, Aelfwine's cousin and mine began a slow and almost visibly unwilling progress towards the place appointed for his court of inquiry.

Leaning forward on his big chair, Bishop Gebmund looked nervously round the church. 'For the benefit of our brethren from overseas,' he stammered, 'we shall conduct these proceedings entirely in Latin.' I blew my nose loudly enough to be heard at the back of the crowded nave. In all decency, he hadn't been able to keep the common people out. Looking surly, they sat cross-legged on the floor. One way or another, I'd find a way to keep them generally informed.

Gebmund got down from his chair and, trying not to breathe through his nose, approached the stone slab on which the body was laid. It wasn't so many days since I'd assisted the Deacon Sophronius across the threshold of death. But it was as if the gross corruptions to which he'd given himself up in life were now seeping out through every pore of his body. Or, if you want a less poetic explanation, a combination of nice weather and excessive corpulency had brought on a speedy dissolution of the flesh. A cloth over his middle to preserve the decencies, Sophronius filled the entire slab. His mottled left arm hung down its side. Just below his hand, a pool of slime was already gathering on the floor. I plucked at the front of my robe. I snuggled deeper into the invisible palisade of my oil of frankincense. Not so lucky, a young deacon opposite me turned green and began to swallow repeatedly.

'Dear Brothers in Christ,' Gebmund began after much clearing of his throat, 'I have called you here today to witness the full and fair inquiry that the Lord High Bishop Theodore and our Lord King Swaefheard have jointly commanded into the death of the Deacon Sophronius.' He paused and looked about. No one dared stand up and say that the Dear Departed was, in fact, another of our cousins, and that the illiterate drunkard who was currently head of the family had been bullied into allowing this public washing of our linen. Gebmund hurried back to his chair and went into a rambling account of how Sophronius had been found at the bottom of the stairs that led from my place of confinement, his neck broken in two places. He stopped again and waited for the usual pious words to go the rounds.

He started again. This time, his face began to twitch with the strain of what he'd been given no choice but to do. 'I don't think anyone would object if I were to announce a verdict of accidental death,' he said, plainly wishing that was just what he could do. 'Sophronius was a large man, and a fall down so many stairs could only have one outcome.' He shut his eyes. 'However, I have been informed that the discoverer of the body wishes to address the court.'

He opened his eyes and looked about again. 'Is Brother Ambrose with us?' he asked hopefully. Hope faded as a creature hardly less bloated than our dear departed Brother in Christ heaved himself to his feet. He'd been sitting close by the body and leaning out of sight to watch the dripping of slime. He stood forward and bowed. Gebmund turned his mouth down. 'Then I call on Brother Ambrose to explain his belief about the death.'

Ambrose struck a dramatic pose at the feet of the Episcopal chair. He looked about. 'I am Brother Ambrose,' he began loudly. 'I look after the deluded sons of the Church who have fallen away from their vows and must be corrected.' He stopped and looked up at the roof timbers for inspiration. 'Me Latin's gone off and hid somewhere it can't be found,' he said in English. 'Can't I do me bit in English?'

Put me in that chair and this would have been my excuse to call things off. At the least, I'd have adjourned them. After the briefest dither, though, Cousin Gebmund called for an interpreter and let the charade roll on. Ambrose had been put in charge of me last spring, he explained. Deacon Sophronius had ordered me to produce a long and elaborate report in Greek for the Lord High Bishop Theodore. I'd been confined to make sure I pulled none of my tricks. On the day the Deacon said he was to collect this report, however, he'd fallen down a staircase he'd used every day for months. Ambrose had found him at the foot of the stairs.

'The fucker had it coming to him!' someone shouted in English. There was a loud cheer from where most of the English observers were sitting, cross-legged on the floor. 'Where's all them kids gone?' someone else shouted. That got a loud groan.

Gebmund jumped up and banged his staff for silence. 'Do not interpret these impertinences for our overseas brethren,' he cried.

That got the French and Italian clerics murmuring among themselves. Gebmund coughed for attention. 'I am able to confirm,' he said, stammering again, 'that Brother Aelric's "long and elaborate" report in Greek turned out to be an essay in Latin on the rules of prosody.' All eyes turned in my direction. I plucked at my robe, releasing another cloud of perfume. I pushed my teeth back and smiled.

'I heard the Deacon shouting in anger,' Ambrose continued. 'I heard the Prisoner laugh and say something in Latin. Then I heard the door shut and the Deacon begin to come down the stairs. After six steps, he cried out as if in fear and fell all the way down. While I was trying to roll him over and perform the last offices, I heard a scraping at the top of the stairs and another laugh. Then I heard a soft closing of the Prisoner's door. When I reached his room, the Prisoner was smiling and looking at his face in a hand mirror. I say that Brother Aelric murdered the Deacon Sophronius.'

One of the foreign observers burst out laughing. Someone else got up and walked out in visible disgust. I composed my face into a look of mild outrage. It was an accusation with feeble support. On the other hand – let's be fair to Ambrose – he was spot on in the accusation. That was exactly how I'd killed the swine. I'd fabricated an argument with him and told him to fuck off. I'd counted his rather agitated steps outside my room and pulled hard on my cunningly hidden cord at number six. Sophronius had done the rest. The bronze pin I'd hidden away. The twine I'd cut into one-inch lengths and scattered, one at a time, from the window.

Gebmund finished his silent prayer. Getting up, he pointed at me. 'Brother Aelric,' he said, his raised hands shaking, 'this is a most serious charge against you. Have you anything to say in your defence?'

I didn't bother standing. 'The charge is self-refuting trash,' I sneered. I thought of the effect I wanted and let my voice rise to an aged whine. 'No defence is needed. I'm ninety-eight. I can hardly stand up and walk, let alone commit murder. How am I supposed to have killed Sophronius? While he's at it, my idiot of a jailor might also explain how a man half my age could then have hidden this "long and elaborate report" he claims he *heard* that I was writing. You won't find it in the room where I've been unlawfully detained almost since my arrival in Canterbury.'

Gebmund held up his arms to quell the chorus of protests and contemptuous laughter that followed my answer. His face hardened. 'Brother Aelric,' he said, 'if this is the only defence you are prepared to make, I must proceed to my verdict.'

That was what he'd been instructed to do – and he could reach any verdict he pleased, no matter how perverse it seemed on the face of it. My only recourse would then be an appeal to Rome. But, as I'd expected, the foreign observers were looking shocked. The natives too were getting restless. 'It's a bleeding stitch up!' an old man shouted in English. 'We know Old Aelric's innocent.' You don't always need to understand a language to know roughly what's being said. It was enough to start an increasingly obscene clamour. We'd have to be taken through a few niceties yet.

Gebmund bit his lip and waited for the clamour to subside. He looked once more at the putrid corpse. 'I must insist, Brother Aelric,' he said, 'that you should give a fuller explanation of your actions than you have so far. You might begin by explaining in what sense you have been detained, or how this might be unlawful. As an ordained monk, you have a duty of absolute obedience to those above you in the Universal Church.'

I blinked and looked at Gebmund. Had he really just fallen into that half-hearted trap? I rather thought he had. I relaxed. No need to unleash the biggest scandal in England since the last one. 'Help me forward,' I cried in English. 'I will address the court.' Half a dozen very big men came forward. Two of them lifted me from my chair, and carried me gently to the speaking place before Gebmund. It hardly mattered whether they believed I was innocent, or that Sophronius had only got what he deserved. They sat down at my feet, giving moral support with their presence.

I faced Gebmund. 'My Lord Bishop has stated,' I opened softly, though not too softly to be heard through the church, 'that I have been ordained into Holy Mother Church. Such might be my dearest wish. However, it is not yet the case. Anyone who wishes

14

confirmation of this may write to Benedict, the Lord Abbot of the monastery in Jarrow. He will answer that my sole duties are to teach the civilised languages, and such other subjects as may be required, to the boys and novices committed to his care.'

Gebmund's face set like mosaic tiles in concrete. 'This being so,' I went on, 'I retain my secular status, which is as a Senator of the Empire and a Member of the Imperial Council. I may have come home to England a few years ago on the basis of a slight misunderstanding that involved His Late Imperial Majesty. But this has been set aside by His Present Imperial Majesty. I am, therefore, exactly what I was before my sad but temporary eclipse within the Empire. Without the Emperor's express consent, I cannot be required to plead before any judicial authority of the Church. I certainly cannot be required to answer to questions set at the behest of a ruler who is subordinate to His Imperial Majesty in Constantinople. Indeed, since I may be regarded, for all practical purposes, as the Emperor's Legate in England, I possess full immunity in any civil or criminal matter. My immunity can only be lifted by a sealed decree of the Emperor himself.'

Among those who could follow me, there were cries of outrage. But these were heavily outweighed by more contemptuous laughter at poor Gebmund. It was coming in rather handy that so many foreign clerics were gathered for the moment in Canterbury. This would have to go by the book.

Aelfwine was on his feet. 'This is ridiculous!' he shouted. He ignored Gebmund's desperate banging of his staff. 'No, I won't be silenced! The Old One is lying.' He frowned and looked about the church. No less than Gebmund, he'd tried everything possible with Theodore to get this called off. Now, far less than Gebmund, he understood what I was about to pull on them all.

'What is this Empire he talks about?' he asked defiantly. 'There was a time when the Romans were supreme in the world. Their territory included all of England and more, and Spain and France and Italy, and Greece and Thrace, and Syria and Egypt, and Africa even to its interior. You still see in these places the statues of their emperors, in marble as well as in bronze. But Rome is now

15

fallen and humiliated. Its western provinces are taken by men like ourselves. Its eastern provinces are taken by the Saracen unbelievers. The little Greek who calls himself Roman Emperor rules from Constantinople over the Asiatic provinces and Greece and Thrace and fragments of Italy and Africa. He has no authority here.'

He sat down. Still on my feet, I suppressed a smile. If this were a script for a play I'd written, it could hardly go better. 'I cannot fault the young man's geography,' I said. 'Such a pity about his law and his history. The Empire may, for the moment, be mostly confined within what are called its Home Provinces. It is still, nevertheless, the richest and most powerful kingdom in the known world. Even the Saracens are compelled, from time to time, to pay tribute to the Emperor, if they do not want their shipping swept from the sea, or the realms they have stolen from him troubled by internal strife. As for those of us who are Christians, the position, in both secular and canon law, is plain. The Emperor is ordained by God as the Head of Christendom. He may not choose to exercise his prerogatives over the kings whose people have been allowed to settle in his provinces. These prerogatives exist, however, and cannot be abolished. Kent itself remains part of the Universal Empire. Is there any man here of sanctity or learning who will dispute my words?'

I sat wearily on the steps to Gebmund's chair. I was annoyed at how weak my voice had sounded towards the end. Still, I'd said my piece. Little as they'd understood me, my Englishmen stuck their jaws out and looked proud. The foreign clerics were doing their best not to laugh again.

Gebmund finally broke the long silence. 'This inquiry is adjourned until further notice,' he groaned.

3

Theodore, Lord High Bishop of Canterbury, managed a look of what, all considered, was impressive hate. 'I suppose My Lord Alaric may be seated,' he snarled softly in Greek. The room was bleak as ever – though, defying all medical opinion, the window was still unshuttered. It let in a breeze from the garden and a sound of birdsong. In the months since our last meeting, time had consumed the remaining flesh of Theodore's middle years, and his hooked Syrian nose was as prominent again as when he was a boy. I could see that Theodore was in no mood for pleasantry. The civility that had tinged our two earlier meetings would not be repeated.

'Sorry to hear about the latest seizure,' I said, also in Greek. I put on a look that might, by anyone who didn't know me, be taken as sympathetic. 'But I can't help reminding you of those little lectures I used to give on the benefits of regular exercise and clean living. Why, just look at us, Theodore. No one would ever think I was twelve years your senior.' I hobbled forward and sat in a chair that had been placed for maximum discomfort and general subordination. My walking stick fell on the floor with a high *smack*. The sound made Ambrose look round the door from where he was lurking. I ignored it and him. 'Any chance of a drink?' I asked in English.

Brother Wulfric looked at me, then at Theodore for instructions. But odd things, these seizures. This was poor Theodore's second. If the first had deprived him of movement in his right side, this one had taken all his English. I could wish it had taken his Latin too. Theodore opened and shut his mouth a few times. 'Oh, but don't trouble yourself,' I said, now showing off in Syriac.

I turned to Wulfric. 'He says to get me a pint of that French red you brought me last spring,' I said brightly.

We were alone – perhaps, bearing in mind the snoring sound coming from Theodore's mouth, *I* was alone. But, no – Theodore opened his eyes again and focused on me. 'Where is the report you were instructed to prepare?' he asked with laboured menace. His head sagged to the left and he fought for breath. He shut his eyes and seemed to pray for strength. 'Whatever chicanery you dare to employ in this world,' he went on in Syriac, 'can you not imagine the torments that await you in the next for the murder you have committed?'

I'd been made to leave my sandals at the door. I looked sadly at my feet. They'd benefit from the attentions of a pumice stone. But – such the indignities of age – I could barely reach nowadays to wash them. 'Sophronius got what he deserved,' I said. 'If there is a Hell, he's already burning there in your favourite lake of black fire. Besides, you just try proving that I did him in. That jailor you put up against me today made a right dickhead of himself. And Gebmund must have told you that his hands are tied. Don't assume you can scare me into doing your dirty work. I'm the Emperor's man till I die. That's one oath I won't ever break.'

We glared at each other until Wulfric returned, jug in hand. If that was a pint the boy was carrying, King Swaefheard had been playing with the Kentish weights and measures. But I smiled and nodded, and pushed my teeth back into place. I left him with the cup and took the jug. One of the few blessings of my advanced age is that it takes very little wine to get me tipsy. In the glory days of my youth, I could knock it back like beer and drink anyone under the table. Now, I sipped with moderate delicacy and waited for the delicious warmth to radiate from the pit of my stomach. Oh, but rotten luck – I'd been given some kind of heated slop that tasted of lentils! I resisted the urge to spit and tried to look grateful.

Theodore closed his eyes and settled back into his pillows. 'Don't you understand the enormity of your crime, Alaric?' he whined. 'You have murdered a deacon of the Church. You have committed a crime that cries aloud to Heaven for punishment. Are you not willing to make *some* atonement for this unspeakable sin?'

'Oh shut up, Theodore!' I answered. I turned to Wulfric. 'If you don't bring me something drinkable,' I said in my chilliest voice, 'I'll find someone in Canterbury to take you by the scruff of the neck and smash your teeth out against a shithouse wall. Now, wipe that insolent smile off your face and get out of my sight!'

I looked back to Theodore and smiled. 'Listen, my boy,' I said slowly and in Syriac, 'we both know very well that, seventy-six years ago, I got the Pope of that time to agree, by his servants and agents, that the Will of Christ might be an aspect of His Person, and therefore singular. This means that he also agreed that any claim that His Will was an aspect of His Nature, and therefore dual, might be a misunderstanding of the decrees of the Council of Chalcedon. It doesn't matter what side deals attended this agreement. What does matter is that, if the Monothelite position is heretical, Pope bloody Benedict of Blessed Memory was willing not to anathematise heresy. You allowed that bag of shite now rotting before our eyes to pressure me into lying my head off about what happened at the Closed Council of Athens. You people would then use this to embarrass the Emperor in his dealings with the Syrian Church. Well, I gave in last spring, because I was pressed, and because I hoped you'd snuff it before I needed to deliver. But you're still alive – sort of – and so I've had to remove the pressure by other means; and there's bugger all you can do put it back on me. If you try to push things any further, I'll raise a stink that will poison dealings between the Church and the Kentish Crown for generations to come. After a lifetime of knowing me, you should be aware that I can and will do that.'

He managed to raise his good hand for silence. 'Alaric,' he sobbed, 'you committed both blasphemy and treason this morning. I beg you to reconsider your remarks.'

'Tough titty, My Lord High Bishop!' I laughed. 'All I did today was let slip a dirty little secret your sort have kept from my people for a hundred years. When my royal kinsman Ethelbert was baptised all those years ago, he was told it was a step up in the world. He could get rid of his tribal witchdoctors and steal a march on his neighbours. No one told him, or any of his successors, he was putting himself under a theoretical jurisdiction from Constantinople that might one day be used to drive a wedge between him and his pious subjects. The next time you allow Gebmund to convene that fiddled inquiry of his, I will stand up and recite the relevant passages from Agapetus and a dozen of the Church Fathers, both Greek and Latin, until no one is in any doubt of the position held in Rome as well as in Constantinople. And I'll do it in English too!'

Wulfric came in with another jug, this one filled with rich, red wine. I thought of getting the boy to taste it. But I doubted if any of these scared old women would join poisoning to blackmail – murder was my speciality. I slobbered in one mouthful, and then another. So what if much of it ran out again? There's nothing so heady as wine drunk in triumph.

'Drop the whole matter,' I said with final emphasis. 'Give up on toadying to the Pope's advisers – they'll be humming a different tune next year in any event. Send me back to Jarrow. I'll shut up, and you can find someone here with a dash of learning ready to lie about the true relationship between King and Emperor.'

'Never!' Theodore whispered.

I got up, still holding my jug. 'Then I dare you to make Gebmund reconvene his inquiry,' I said. I pointed at Wulfric, then at my stick, and waited for him to make the obvious connection. I held my stick in one hand, and my jug in the other, and took a step towards the door. 'You know where to find me.'

But Theodore wasn't finished. Incredibly, he struggled and sat up. 'I curse the day I let you persuade me to give you refuge in England,' he cried loudly in Latin. 'It's only because you were born here that I didn't send you straight back to the Emperor – and – and – because of what we used to be to each other. Oh what a fool I was!'

'There's no fool like an old fool,' I sneered, 'And don't give me any of that crap about the "happy days of old". We both know how those ended. You're bloody lucky I didn't have you killed.'

He fell back in a faint that might shut him up for the rest of the day. I jabbed Wulfric in the chest. 'Show me out,' I said. 'He won't be needing you.'

4

Brother Jeremy picked at one of his spots and tried to think. 'But why did you have to *kill* him?' he asked. He looked at the blood under his fingernails. 'Also, I can't hide your report forever. Everyone knows how you used up every sheet of papyrus in Canterbury, and how more had to be brought over from France.' I pulled a face and carried on looking out of the window at the moon. No sneeze resulted, worse luck. I'd have to give him an answer.

'Because, dear Jeremy,' I said, leaving slight gaps between my words, 'Sophronius told me that, if I didn't finish his report, he'd have you flogged to death for that customs officer he said you killed in London.' I stopped his reply. 'It's a minor detail that I killed him as well as Sophronius. All that counts is that, since the Deacon couldn't have his report, it was him or you. Can I have some thanks for choosing as I did?

'As for storing the report, I trust you put it where I told you. It'll be safe enough there.' I looked out of the window again. I finished my wine and let out a long and subdued burp of happiness. If only wine jugs were made of glass, the world would look such a fine place through their bottoms.

Jeremy squeezed his eyes shut and made a supreme effort at rational thought. 'Can I ask, Brother Aelric, why we need to store the report? Why not destroy it? No one would ever see it then.'

I put my jug down. It spared me the temptation of hitting him with it. 'Can't do that,' I said firmly. 'It's a very fine piece of writing – yes, *very* fine: important source material for historians, and all that.' I changed the subject. 'But, Jeremy, you've taken my dictation in English. It really is time for you to climb down that ivy and run off to spread my news of today's proceedings. You can start in the alehouse beside the western gate.'

Oh, shit! Someone was coming up the stairs. 'Get under the bed,' I whispered. 'Try not to breathe.'

Of my three visitors, Ambrose was first through the door. 'Oh, but it's the greatest honour that ever was,' he bawled. 'To think our monastery's been chosen above all others in the land.' He staggered from the drink he'd been soaking up, and nearly fell over. He gave me a look of slow-witted confusion. 'Why are you burning lamps this time of night?' he asked. 'Don't you know the price of mutton fat?'

'Sod off, Ambrose!' I yawned. 'And shut the door, and let me hear you go downstairs.'

I ignored Gebmund, who was looking utterly crushed, but smiled into the angry though scared face of young Aelfwine. 'Greetings, My Lord Aelfwine,' I said. 'I take it you're standing in for Cousin Swaefheard. I've heard ever so much about him in the months I've been stuck in his kingdom. Diplomacy isn't one of his strengths. But I'm sure you can supply that in his place. Sorry we're right out of anything to drink – not that I suppose this is a family get-together.'

Aelfwine sat on my bed. Was that a yelp I heard? 'Why are you fucking us over, Aelric?' he asked. 'We've done nothing to you. Just confess to keep old Theodore happy. We'll see you right about the penance. You are family, after all.'

I told my shaking fingers to behave and turned the lamp full up. Aelfwine had a face like thunder. I smiled again. I waved about the bare room. 'Stop listening to silly old Theodore,' I said, 'and I'll stop making you choose between a massacre of King Swaefheard's loving subjects and having to explain to His Holiness in Rome why half of Canterbury is a pile of smouldering ashes.'

Gebmund found his voice 'Brother Aelric – My Lord Alaric: whatever it most pleases you to be called,' he cried in gentle panic. 'It has been brought to His Majesty's notice that you have information affecting the welfare of his kingdom. In the Church, or out of the Church, I really like to think of us all as one big happy family. We've come here in a spirit of loving concern to see how we can resolve any issues that might otherwise draw us into a more confrontational relationship. I – we . . .' He trailed off and looked miserably at the floor.

I'd been wondering when I'd get the representatives of church and state suing for peace. There's a time for subtle diplomacy, and a time for bluntness. Time, obviously, for the latter. 'I can prove,' I said, 'that, behind his show of holiness, our late Cousin Sophronius was up to his neck in a scam that could get the two of you run out of Kent.' I stopped and waited for Gebmund to take his hands from over his ears. 'For the past three years, he paid regular visits from Rome to Canterbury. Each time, he selected seven of the prettiest boys he could find and promised their parents a life for them in one of the papal choirs. However, he was packing them off to Spain for castration and sale to dealers who'd then sell them on to the Saracens. Instead of singing chaste hymns of praise to Christ and the Virgin, those who didn't die from the operation and of other causes have been performing lewd dances for the unbelievers, and having their mouths and bottoms used for various modes of sinful gratification.'

I stopped again and waited for the full horror to sink in. 'I won't claim that either of you knew about this, or that you were on the take. But it's a sure thing that you never asked Sophronius for news of the boys he was rounding up. Equally for sure, none of the parents has ever heard from their little ones. I was thinking to blurt all this out in the first sitting of the inquiry. I hope you'll agree that the submission I did make was far less unhelpful to your continued enjoyment of your cushy places in life.'

I'll tell you now, Dear Reader, in strictest confidence, I wasn't able to prove any of this. But I'd picked up a few stray facts from Jeremy's nightly reports, and had put an easy two and two together. I think I'd made them into neither five nor three.

'Have you told this to *anyone*?' Aelfwine asked. He looked thoughtfully at the pillow on my bed.

'No, my pretty young cousin,' I said at once. 'But, if you're thinking to bump me off, it will inevitably spread once I'm not here to control the flow of information. So why don't we agree, as members of one big happy family, on the findings and recommendations that Gebmund will announce in the next – and closing

– session of his inquiry? And the less attention you both pay to Theodore from now on, the better I think it will be for all of us.'

I won't bore you with how things continued. You can fill in the gaps for yourself.

I couldn't know it, but Theodore had another seizure that night. According to what I got out of Wulfric, it came on about the same time as Aelfwine was sending Ambrose off in search of something for us to drink to happy families. You can't fault his attention to duty, however. Soon after lunch the following day, he sent for me again.

Worn out from the excitements of my own life, I limped into the room and sat beside him. 'Oh, this is awful, Theodore,' I cried, feeling almost as saddened as I was trying to sound. 'Not another one, and so soon after the last! If there's anything I can do to help, just say the word. You're all I have left from the old days. We've had our differences, I know. Perhaps I have myself not been wholly without fault in our dealings. But let's put these behind us and try to think of the good things that remain in our lives.'

He opened his eyes. I thought for a moment he didn't recognise me. But he was only gathering what he had left of his strength. 'Gebmund came to see me this morning,' he said faintly in Latin. 'He explained that you've beaten me. You've always beaten me. You've always taken what was mine. You only let me win the Monothelite dispute when you no longer found it politically convenient to keep the Empire immured in the darkness of heresy. You have been the cloud that darkened my life.'

I snorted so loudly, I had to struggle with my teeth. Of all the passions, resentment is the most enduring. Love – even hatred – will often fade with time. Not so resentment. If his face hadn't been twisted into a snarl that reminded me of dead Sophronius, I'd have felt sorry for him. As it was, I gave up on the mockery.

'Theodore,' I said, leaning forward and speaking into his ear, 'you made yourself unhappy. Worse than that, you've spent a life-time trying to make everyone else unhappy.' I thought myself into the distant past. Yes, it was still in my head. I quoted:

O God of Love, who governs all
  With unimagined power;
Who sets the autumn leaves to fall
  And wither every flower –

Dear Lord, this humble praise accept,
  By us, Thy children, given,
And, in return, bless all – except
  Who lack a place in Heaven.

Let in everlasting torments
  Suffer, Lord, who give offence,
And us, Thy chosen instruments,
  Give ever, Lord, thy preference.

'You wrote that for me when you were twelve,' I said. 'There's more of it, and it gets worse. I should have seen then what a rotter you'd turn out. Don't blame me for the long shipwreck of your life. You chose your path. Don't blame me if it didn't lead to a bed of roses.'

'You lie, Alaric!' he sobbed. 'I was happy till you took hold of me, and tempted me with the filthiness of your corruptions. I know you think you've beaten me. But you'll see that I win at last.'

He closed his eyes for another rest. As ever, I thought he'd nodded off. But just as I was about to get up and leave, he came back to life. 'Bring it here, Wulfric,' he whispered in English. I perked up. This was interesting. I'd always assumed that what was lost in a seizure was destroyed. I now realised that the human mind was rather like a library. All that a seizure might do was to alter the catalogue – wiping, and sometimes restoring, entries and groups of entries.

I was still thinking that one over, when I felt someone tap me on the shoulder. It was Wulfric with a bag of something heavy. I took it from him, and stared at the elaborate knots securing it.

'No, Alaric,' Theodore urged. 'Don't look now. It's a present for you. Call it a reminder from the old days when we were together.'

He tried to laugh. 'Thanks to you, I've had not a single day of happiness since I was thirteen. Now it's your turn to suffer. You know that you can't give it back to me. The rules don't allow that.' He looked away from me and focused on the stained ceiling. 'Leave me, Alaric. I won't let you come here again. But enjoy the rest of your life. You deserve it.' He did now manage to laugh – a grating, wheezing sound that shook even those parts of his body that no longer moved at his command.

One thing I've learned to recognise over the years is when I'm really not welcome. I was out of that room as quickly as I could put one foot in front of the other. I didn't open the bag until Ambrose had locked me into my room.

And that's the end of the story. I'm now in the Saint Anastasius Monastery. I can go where I will, when I will. Brother Ambrose died the night after I'd finally moved out of his care. Even at a distance of two hundred yards, and through several walls, he kept me awake with his dying shrieks. I didn't attend the funeral. I'm told his replacement as clerical jailor is a man from Ireland who believes in reforming his charges though prayer and exercise.

But, as I write, I have the Horn of Babylon beside me on the table. It reminds me of an obligation freely assumed and still not discharged. I may have reached the end of the story I promised to tell you. I haven't touched the beginning. If I'm to do that, it means going back further than I have – very much further. You can forget last Monday, when I started these jottings. You can forget the Monday before that, and many thousands of other Mondays before that one. You can also forget the decrepit old thing scribbling away on his many sheets of papyrus, a jug of red before him and a quarter opium pill dissolving in his belly. If I really want to explain what's been happening these past few days, I'll have to go back seventy-three years, to Monday the 28th April 615. Put Aelfwine beside me then, and no one would have had eyes for him.

Yes, the proper start is that petitioning Monday in Constantinople, so very long ago . . .

5

The last owner of my palace had been unashamed in his taste for the violently obscene, and the mosaics of Tiberius on Capri could normally be trusted to keep me awake through the longest and dullest ceremony. But this wasn't a normal day. With no one to keep them under control, the eunuchs were running wild. Without missing a step, the Master of the Timings came back to the same square on the patterned marble and bowed low before my chair. He let out a sigh that verged on a squeal of joy, and spun round to face the assembled mass of clients and petitioning agents. Then he brought his staff down three times. As the echo faded of the last crash, he drew breath, once more defying the fog of incense smoke.

'*Let all be silent and hold his tongue,*' he cried in mellifluous, if oddly accented, Latin, '*for His Magnificence the Lord Senator Alaric, beloved friend of Heraclius, our great and ever-triumphant Augustus.*' I may have been the only man there who knew the old language of the Empire. Back in those days, however, there were still solemnities of utterance in Constantinople for which Greek just wouldn't do. After a long and dramatic pause, he turned and bowed to me. From a high gallery behind me, one of his underlings rang a golden bell.

I stood up. Anyone looking at me must have thought I'd got it made. Five years earlier, I'd rolled into the Imperial City on a very dodgy mission. But just look at me now. The gold brocade I had on was heavier than plate armour. Its colour exactly matched my hair, and the bluish-gold paint that covered my face was a tasteful contrast to both. My chair was of ebony, inlaid with ivory and more gold. Standing on a carpet of blue silk, on a platform six feet above the floor of the hall, I was the centre of attention – the earth around which all lesser objects were in orbit. Looking back across the seventy-three years that separate me from that last Monday in the April of 615, I really should have made some effort not to be pissed off.

Instead, I came as close as my paint allowed to glowering. I suppressed the urge to go into a choking cough and looked stiffly ahead. 'The request is excessive,' I said in a Greek from which all foreign trace had been carefully removed. I paused and tried to see without moving if the agent was looking crestfallen. He was – served the bugger right for puffing a two-line petition into a speech. I held the pause until my words began to sound final. 'However,' I went on, 'let his parish priest certify that he has indeed begotten twelve sons who are all alive, and I will grant Isidore of Zigana a *two*-year rebate of land tax, and a further ten-year *exemption*.' I sat down. The Listings Clerk scribbled a comment that would later be worked into a formal reply for carrying back to the farmer.

That should have been it. The Master of the Timings was already getting his staff ready. I couldn't turn and look, but I could hear the water clock gurgling in a manner that suggested a break from petitions. So why was that bloody agent still on his knees? He'd had my answer. His duty now was to get up and bow, and scuttle back to his own appointed square on the marble. Everyone else could then hop discreetly from foot to foot in the place he'd been occupying since dawn and wait for the bell to ring. Yet there he still was – not moving, arms folded across his chest. 'Will the rebate be in hard money?' he asked in a voice that still hadn't quite broken. There was a gasp of horror from the other agents. I thought the Master of the Timings would faint. I stared at the agent. Someone had just shovelled more incense into a brazier and it was impossible to see his expression. I'd already seen he was young for an agent. From my first glance about the hall, he'd stood out from the usual run of dyed beards and hard, glittering eyes. But, if his face was currently out of sight, his voice alone raised questions about what he was doing here.

29

I leaned back in my chair. I looked at my polished fingernails. 'From the second day of the second week of next month,' I said in a tone of polite menace, 'all silver payments to and from the Treasury are to be made in the new standard coins. Until then, the old coinage, of whatever quality, remains the legal standard. Had your client wanted to benefit from the decree, it was your duty to suggest delaying his petition.'

And that was him told. A couple of eunuchs appeared from nowhere and shoved him back into the crowd. Without waiting for the bell to ring, the Master of the Timings came forward and bowed. He turned and lifted his staff again. One deafening crash of wood on stone and a hundred men stretched out their right arms in my direction.

'*Long life to His Magnificence the Lord Senator Alaric!*' they chanted in their own attempt at Latin. '*Life, health, happiness, good fortune ever may he know – wise and generous-hearted, gentle, compassionate; most noble lord of all finances; benefactor; learned, beauteous, heroic . . .*'

Oh, forget that silly boy of an agent – this whole morning was like watching paint set. Normal petitioning days were over by now. Normally, we had an abbreviated opening ritual and then I withdrew to change into plain clothing. Upstairs in my office, I could read through all the petitions and see the agents one at a time. I could ask questions. I could explain myself. I could strike deals. Unless a matter needed further consideration, an agent could step out into the street with a sealed letter already in his satchel.

But I've said this wasn't a normal petitioning day. The Monday before had been Easter and there was a double load of work. Far worse, this was my first day of public business without Martin to hurry things along. He must by now be halfway up a mountain on Lesbos, and he'd be praying there till June. Today, so far as I could gather, while prancing in from their usual place in the Treasury Building, the eunuchs had spotted a dozen petitioners in their own right. Martin would have put them at the head of the list. They could have been dazzled by the opening spectacle, and sent on their way, preferably with whatever justice or favour they'd come to beg. No hope of that with the bloody eunuchs in charge of things. They'd jumped at the chance to lay on the full ceremonial. By the time I was carried into the hall, I could grin and bear it or cause a scene. I'd stood for the opening prostration and hoped the day's list wouldn't be too heavy. It had been, and was, very heavy . . .

The Master of the Timings was back in action. Next item was a break from petitions. 'A gift for His Magnificence!' he cried with slow jollity. He held up a box of painted wood that seemed to have been badly scratched along its underside. 'Behold the love and respect in which the Lord Senator Alaric is held by the entire universe!' he intoned. The response was a long monosyllable. It is best described as the sort of appreciative sigh you let out when something tasty is pushed under your nose. It began on the left side of the hall and moved, as etiquette prescribed, in stages to the right. Meanwhile, it was for the old eunuch to try, with decreasing elegance of movement, to get the box open.

Oh, bugger! I thought – *not a birthday present. And not in public!* My birthday had been the day before and I was hoping no one had noticed. Rotten luck I had to sit here now, getting ready to smile and nod at greetings that would soon be repeated across the City. Telling myself not to sneeze, and trying to ignore the tears that must be ruining my paint, I watched as elegance was abandoned and a penknife was used to prise the box open. I heard the groan of long nails levered out of wood. Leaning forward an inch, I caught a flash of coiled and polished silver. It could have been worse, I thought. If you must admit to a birthday, the presents might as well be worth having. I leaned forward another inch. Now fully open, the box was on the little table set before my chair.

I found myself looking into the old eunuch's glowering face. 'Can people not write messages in a *civilised* language?' he whispered. 'It shows such *disrespect* for My Lord.' He waved the lid under my nose. I glanced at the slip of parchment that was coming loose from where it had been stuck. I looked harder.

'I know your secret,' it said in Latin.

Though I kept my face steady, the shock was instant and over-powering. I turned cold all over. My heart beat faster and faster, and there seemed no limit to how hard it would eventually beat. There were dark spots before my eyes. A colder chill was radiating from the pit of my stomach. I looked again at the message and struggled to keep my legs from giving way.

'I know your *secret*,' it said.

Desperately, I fought for control. But cold panic now seemed to have spread through my entire body. In its suddenness and inten-sity, the attack was best compared to an orgasm – or, leaving aside any talk of pleasure, with the shock you feel between getting a possibly fatal stab wound and its actual pain. It can't have been more than a few moments that I stood there, looking at the little, stained slip of parchment. But I could have sworn at the time it was an age.

I barely noticed the muffled squeal the Master of the Timings gave as he pitched head over heels down the steps, or the bump of metal on carpet, and then its clatter across the marble. But, as if through a mist as thick as anything produced by incense, I did notice that the eunuch had collapsed and was lying, still on his back, with his mouth wide open.

6

That was enough to free me from the worst of the attack. I glanced up from the fallen eunuch. No one else had stepped from his appointed place. On every face I could see the kind of look that goes round at an execution, when the victim hasn't cried out for a while and it will soon be time for lunch. Someone stoked the brazier again and a cloud of yellow smoke blotted out the petitioning agents. Someone else in the gallery behind me began another rendition of all my titles and supposed attributes.

But the Master of the Timings wasn't dead. Before I could trust myself to end the audience and call for a doctor, he opened his eyes. With a soft moan and the writhing motion of a bug that's fallen on its back, he sat up and frowned. 'It must be something I ate!' he said firmly. He looked about and frowned again. 'Has nobody *any* respect in this modern age?' He pointed at the silver object where it had fallen.

The Listings Clerk hopped down the steps to retrieve it. He held it up and rubbed hard with his sleeve at the scratch it had taken from the floor. 'It *will* polish off,' he said with a desperate smile into my blank face. He buried it in a soft area of his robe and rubbed it furiously all over. 'It really will be as good as new.' I ignored him. I ignored the sweat that was still trickling into the small of my back. The break in proceedings had given me time to pull myself together. I said nothing and had my first proper look at the Horn of Babylon. It was untarnished then. Except for the scratch on its rim, it was still a fine thing to behold – no dent yet halfway down its length, nor any scratches deep inside its bowl.

Using his staff for support, the Master of the Timings got to his feet. 'Better give it back to me,' he said faintly. He took it into his trembling hands and looked for a moment as if he'd go over again. No problem this time, however. He cuddled it against his flabby chest and bowed to me.

'Who brought this?' I asked in a voice too quiet to show its tremor. I got nothing from the Master of the Timings. The Listings Clerk broke in with a kind of snivelled yawn. I let my eyes dart about the hall. The crowd had reappeared through the fog of incense and was showing its first sign that morning of active interest. But no one looked shiftier than usual.

I stood up and took the silver cup into my own hands. My legs were shaking and I had to steady them against the seat of my chair. But, as quickly as it had come over me, the attack was gone. Its afterglow was rapidly fading. It no longer felt as if I had a pint of vinegar swilling about in my stomach. My heart was steady again. With every heartbeat, my legs were shaking a little less. Everyone stepped one pace forward and went into a three-quarter bow. This was followed by another long blast of Latin. In hands that didn't tremble, I held the cup at chest height for everyone to see.

It's a birthday joke, you idiot! I told myself. And what else could it be? Though the Emperor hadn't chosen to notice, let alone object, I had been four years now on the Imperial Council, and I'd been Lord Treasurer for two years. All this and I was currently a day past my twenty-fifth – that is, I was one day into my manhood, as these things are counted under the laws of the Empire. Of course, it had been a quiet joke throughout the City. But, if an emperor doesn't notice or object, why should anyone else – in public, that is? I was only now eligible for the increasingly exalted offices I'd been occupying these past few years. Someone was having a laugh at me.

I looked for support at the bizarre and probably impossible act Tiberius was committing on the far wall with a dolphin. No support there today. I looked again at the cup. It screamed every possible expense, tinged with an odd sense of humour. Who could have sent it? Heraclius? This *was* the sort of joke Emperors played on their friends. But it couldn't be Heraclius. He had no visible sense of humour. Besides, he was a hundred miles away in Cyzicus, consulting some smelly old monks on pillars about how to beat the Persians. Even granting he'd discovered a playful side to his nature, he had other things on his mind. I gave up on questions. Doubtless, someone important would come up to me later in the day and give me a knowing slap on the back.

I felt a returning trickle of moisture into my mouth and was able to stand forward. By now, the adoration of my gift had run its course. I gave my present back to the Master of the Timings and sat down. I closed my eyes for a moment. When you have a Secret, of course, any mention of *secrets* will set you off. This was hardly the first panic attack I'd had in the past year. But it was the oddest. None other had faded so fast without opium or cannabis to knock it on the head. If only I could think what to do about their cause . . .

I leaned forward. 'Let's hear the petitioners in their own right,' I said to the Listings Clerk, almost forgetting to hush my voice. I glanced over to where they'd been placed at the back of the hall. Dressed in shabby brown, they had been gawping all morning at a slow, heavy ceremonial they'd never guess had been laid on for their benefit. They were already being brought forward, when the Master of the Timings staggered over and tapped one on the head with his staff. He hissed something frantic at the Listings Clerk and opened his mouth so wide for air that I thought his false teeth would crash on to the floor. 'I said to get those men forward!' I snapped. The Master of the Timings shook his head, and the Listings Clerk stepped sideways, knocking over a basket of documents.

'You can't hear unlisted petitions while there is any other business,' the Master of the Timings cried in a soft panic. 'It's listed petitions, then other business – and only then unlisted petitions.' He leaned harder on his staff and rolled his eyes back till only the whites were visible. 'It was ever thus,' he whispered.

'Oh, indeed, My Lord,' the Listings Clerk added in the tone of one who reminds a child that the sun doesn't set till dusk. 'It was ever thus – from the very creation of the world.'

'Then get on with it!' I groaned. I knew I was making one of those surrenders even emperors make when eunuchs close ranks. But it was that or let everything fall into chaos.

Looking relieved, the Master of the Timings turned and raised his voice. 'A letter from His Magnificence the Lord Senator Nicetas, Commander of the East,' he trilled in a fair approximation of his usual manner. A bearded messenger came forward and scowled at the pool of sunlight that was moving steadily down one of the columns. I'd been idly watching him all morning. He'd looked as impatient as I felt. He now took his place at a special lectern that set him at right angles to me and the crowd, and waited for the golden bell to be rung three times to indicate the quality of his employer. This done, he held out his knife and, with a dramatic flourish, slit the cords of the scroll he'd been wearing round his neck. He arranged his heavy features into a semblance of the charming as he read out the greeting and, after a pause for everyone to shout the praises of the Emperor's worthless cousin, went into the main body of the letter:

The Divine Plato it may justly be observed stands to be corrected inasfar into the mouth of Socrates he betook himself to present the notion that the art of impressing marks upon the skin of a beast or upon the woven mat of Nilotic reed, hasn't nay in any sense diminished the memoriative powers of mankind . . .

I tried for a look of reverential joy and thought about the work piling up in my office. At last, raising his voice in the customary manner, the messenger got to the letter's climax. This involved a line of Theophrastus falsely given to Hesiod, and a series of grammatical blunders gross enough to raise the thought that I was being insulted. But there was no insult. Like the Emperor, Nicetas had been raised in Carthage. They were both happier in Latin. And I'd had worse from natives. Indeed, this probably had been ghosted by a native. For all its faults, it did the usual job of a letter between persons of quality: *You are absent. But no separation can sunder those who are united in spirit.*

The messenger came forward and embraced my slippered feet. 'What's the message?' I whispered.

'No offence meant,' came the reply, 'but the Master's legs is taking a turn for the worse. Tomorrow evening's off.'

Mindful of how the egg underlay on my face was coming loose, I wiggled my toes to show the required desolation. 'Give my sympathies to the Lord Nicetas,' I replied without moving my lips. The man nodded. This was my first good news of the day. Nicetas might, this time, be festering to death. At the least, I'd been spared an evening of the poet he'd brought back with him from Egypt and was crying up as a second Callimachus. 'Tell him that I pray for angels to attend upon his bed of sickness,' I added. The messenger bowed, and walked backwards down the steps from my chair. I suppressed a cough and got up. There was a sound of shuffled feet and much brushing of sweaty hands on robes.

'Let the whole universe bear witness,' I began, 'to the learned eloquence of My Lord Nicetas. Truly, has such a letter been received since the glorious days of old?' There was an attempted murmur of admiration, though somewhat more coughing. I heard someone quote one of the more illiterate phrases. Someone else repeated it and threw in a loud groan of ecstasy. 'Let it be known,' I cried when all was silent again, 'that this most astonishing of letters shall be displayed in my hall of audience beneath the icon of the Emperor. Let it be shown there for all eternity.' There was a sound of clapping that began in the centre of the crowd and moved outward. It was followed by a variant on the standard acclamation, and then by another handful of incense, and then by helpless coughing. Still on my feet, I let out a sigh of relief. I'd just had an explanation of the cup and of its Latin message. Like his Imperial cousin, Nicetas had no visible sense of humour. But I could suppose he'd set Leander to work on an epigram to be recited at me the next time I had to attend one of his horrid *soirées*.

As I sat down, the Master of the Timings went into a sort of waddling dance with the messenger. It was all as should be expected – save that the eunuch kept missing his steps, and the messenger didn't give the customary embrace, but kept his hands clamped behind his back. Everyone else continued shouting himself hoarse in Latin and bells rang out repeatedly from overhead. I glanced at the back of the crowd. One of the older petitioners looked as if he'd died and was being propped up from behind.

I moved a hand to get the Listings Clerk's attention. For some reason, I glanced down at the litter of documents that hadn't yet been cleared away. Among various parchment scrolls was a half sheet of papyrus, cracked and then split where it had been folded over. I couldn't see the message. But the seal was plain. I reached down and snatched at the broken sheet and read its contents:

My Lord Alaric,

I beg to inform, further to your standing orders, that we have impounded a ship that foundered last night near the second mile-stone on the western road out of the City. It is registered in Tanais and stuffed with furs. We have reason to believe that no tolls were paid on its journey through the Straits from the Black Sea to the Propontis.

Again further to your standing orders, we have secured the area, and we await your personal attention.

It was signed by Lucas, Head of Customs Enforcement, and a standard Treasury seal covered the end of his name.

I forgot about my new cup. Furs from Tanais, and on the far side of the Straits, and untaxed – possible evidence of corruption in the Tolls Office? Even if it showed just negligence, I had more urgent work than sitting here in bored and largely ornamental magnificence.

'Why was this not given to me when it came in?' I snapped. '*When* did it come in?' The Master of the Timings shrugged and gripped harder on his staff.

'It wasn't delivered into *my* hands,' the Listings Clerk added in a voice that accused everyone and no one. I looked again at the message. It could well have been here since before the beginning of the audience. Just in reach, the two eunuchs were hissing at each other in the rapid and deliberately unintelligible chatter their sort used for arguments. I could have handed out two bloody noses – that, or I could have promised immediate transfers to some barbarian-ravaged border province. I did neither. I looked again at the seal, and how negligently it had been rammed into the unmelted beeswax. The whole production screamed urgency. How much time had been lost already?

I stood up. The crowd stopped its shuffling and coughing. 'This audience is at an end.' I said loudly. 'All unheard petitions are stood over to next Monday.' I looked round at the uncomprehending faces. As I made for the door into the private quarters of my palace, I made sure to snatch up my birthday present and greetings. Until I could find time for a proper look at these, they could be locked away.

I barely heard the dejection in the voice of the Master of the Timings as he got everyone ready for a prostration before my now empty chair.

7

It was one of those days in late spring when the sun is pitilessly bright. I stepped through the hidden side exit from my palace and hurried blinking into the first shade I could see. Back then, Constantinople still had a population of about half a million – possibly more, depending on how you counted the dwellings. That meant the City air could never be called sweet. But my palace was in one of the best areas, far from the slums and smellier workshops. Why, then, did this empty dead end of a street smell like a broken sewer? It was a change from the incense the Treasury eunuchs had been burning, but in no sense an improvement.

Oh, there was a body in the street! I hadn't seen it at first. But someone had got himself beaten to pulp and his belly slit open, and then dumped in a spot where the sun must have been cooking him since an hour after dawn. The bloody vomit he'd splashed over himself didn't help – nor the wide pool of blood that had already turned brown, and was attracting a solid buzz of flies.

Oh, but the nuisance of it! I'd got a body in a side street it was my responsibility to keep clean. There would have to be a letter about this to Timothy. For me, he'd squeeze himself into his official carrying chair and be straight over. Questions, endless questions – most of them irrelevant to the case, all of them intrusive – that would be our City Prefect. I clenched my fists and snorted. But I shut my eyes and waited for the flash of anger to fade. Making sure not to tread on anything nasty in my fine new boots, I went over for a look at the body. All I could see of the face was that it had been bearded. The rest was smashed in. The clothing suggested a vagrant. So, unless it had been taken, did the lack of any weapon. I bent forward and sniffed at the vomit. No smell of wine. I'd gone off to sleep the previous night to a distant sound of brawling. The most likely explanation was that some young men of quality had got fighting drunk and found a sleeping beggar to kill. It was coincidence they'd finished him off outside my palace. I hoped the bastards had got themselves covered in gore – that, after all, would be their only punishment.

I stood back from the body. Samo would be out here later for his daily check on how clean the palace and its surrounds were being kept. He could deal with this. I looked down at my boots. They were still unspotted. I lifted the front of my outer tunic. My leggings were as white as my boots and showed my calves to nice effect. Once that brocade had been lifted off me, I'd put on some lovely clothes. I couldn't see it but my cloak pin alone would get me the envy of anyone I passed. I looked up at the dark blue of the sky. Not long to go and the sun would be fully overhead. For the moment, I stood in the shade of my own palace wall and, after so much gloom and smoke, the sky was of the deepest and most astonishing blue. It was the colour I'd demanded – with moderate success – for my cloak.

I looked at the body again. If this was an impulse killing, why had someone broken all the fingers on the right hand? My spirits sank back to where they'd started. But I tried to lift them again. In even a well-policed city this size, you could expect a few dozen bodies most nights. These had to be left somewhere. Why not here now and again? I could have rolled the body over and had a proper sight at the clothing. But that would have spoiled my own. I'd seen enough. I stood upright and smoothed the front of my outer tunic. I had official duties, and was already late for them. I stood forward and crushed an engorged fly that had crawled a little too close by my left boot.

I turned and walked towards the archway that led into the Triumphal Way. I stopped in the shade and pulled the wide brim of my hat down another inch. Just a well-dressed man about his business, I slipped though the archway and turned right into the road that cut through the vast ceremonial district of Constantinople.

★　　★　　★

41

When barbarian kings or ambassadors are honoured with a tour of the City, they always start with the view along the Triumphal Way. This isn't the main street on Constantinople, or the longest. It is simply what its name suggests – a street that, deviating neither to right nor left, and cutting through two hills, and crossing one valley on brick arches, runs for a mile through the centre. That mile really is the most astonishing vista of glittering porticos and colonnades, triumphal arches and colossal statues and gilded inscriptions. Whether you look at magnificence that goes on seemingly without end, or at the swarming, chattering multitudes of the well-dressed as they go about their business, you'll think you're in the capital of an empire at the height of its glory. But that's always been the intention. You don't call a street the Triumphal Way and line it with monasteries and sewers. It was laid out so the Emperor himself could ride along it in his chariot of state.

Truth was, the Empire was on its uppers. The Persian War I've already mentioned had been going on for a decade. With Nicetas now in charge of the defence, we'd just lost Syria. Egypt would surely be next. The magnificence on view was all about the past – sometimes the distant past.

Grim thoughts to keep me company! Still, they kept me from visible impatience. The sun was about to turn beastly overhead and we were in the last rush before siesta time. There was no chance yet of a decent speed. Come the siesta, I'd be able to get a move on. The Triumphal Way would take me past Imperial Square and into Middle Street. From there, it would be another reasonably straight two miles to the Golden Gate, and another two after that to where Lucas would be waiting like a cat that's caught a bird for its mistress. Until then, it was a matter of threading my way through crowds that seemed to have all the time in the world, and avoiding the carrying chairs that crept or hurtled along in both directions.

I looked into the colonnade on my left. That was packed – you might have thought the shouting, jostling mass there was gathered to pass the time of day, not to get from one point to another without stepping into the sun. I reached up to check if my hat was still in place and stepped round a heap of replacement paving stones that would be set in place once the crowds had melted away. I thought again of Nicetas. It's only reasonable that an emperor should hand all the really plum jobs about his own family. But why make *Nicetas* Commander of the East – that is, put him in charge of the Persian War? Why then bring him back to Constantinople, while Heraclius was away, and make him Regent as well? The man wasn't fit for changing the straw in a public toilet. Any one of the statues I was passing would have made a more active Regent. In Syria, he'd run away from the Persians so fast, he hadn't even stopped by Jerusalem to snatch the True Cross to safety. The Empire was on its uppers, and there was a good case for blaming it on Nicetas.

Far ahead of me, there was a sudden disturbance. It looked like another carrying chair race. I didn't want to get in the way of that. I gave an involuntary look at the sky and moved towards the right-hand side of the road. I found myself looking at a big statue of Cicero. I could have looked at many other things. If I turned, I'd see the vast mass of the Great Church looming above all else in the City. Though not visible from here, the immensity of the Circus was a half mile beyond. I'd got chariot racing cancelled until further notice, but might be able to hear the faint cheering as one of the cheaper entertainments came to its end. But Cicero suited me better. I looked into the troubled, bronze face. What would *he* have thought of all this?

To be fair, his opinion might not have been the one I currently wanted. However useless Nicetas was, there was a limit to how much blame you could load on one man's shoulders. It wasn't just the Persians. Every other frontier was soft or collapsing. We were losing Greece to the Slavs and Avars. We'd mostly lost Italy to the Lombards. Our foothold in Spain was going to the Visigoths. Our control of Africa stopped barely twenty miles inland. You couldn't blame Nicetas for that. As for the Persians, with one partial exception, we'd found no one else able to stand up to them. If Nicetas was useless, he wasn't alone in his uselessness.

Thoughts of the 'partial exception' brought on a faint stirring of unease. This wouldn't ripen into another panic attack. But thoughts of that in itself deepened the unease. The two were obviously connected. If the one wasn't continually simmering away, the other wouldn't keep boiling over. I'd have to do something about the causes of the unease. But this was easier said than done. I turned my thoughts back to the safer matter of Nicetas and his nearly certain attempt at a joke. Should I take it as a good-humoured joke? Probably not. There was little humour of any kind about the Emperor's cousin. None of it was good.

The chairs had now hurried past and I set off again at a quickish stride. I passed the square in front of the law courts. The morning crowd of lawyers and their clients was fast dwindling away. The Monday property auction in the square was nearly ended. I counted five men – probably Jews or Armenians – putting up with the sun for a closing bargain. There was a general smell in the air of charcoal and of roasting meat. Unless you fancied a week of the shits, eating from the public stalls was off limits. But it was a fine smell and it reminded me I'd had nothing since breakfast, and little then.

My quick stride didn't last beyond the Belisarius Memorial, which blocks the whole centre of the road. Unless there's a procession or the chariots are racing, you don't normally see paupers in the better parts of Constantinople. The police have orders to keep out all but a few licensed and almost sanitised beggars. By day, the poor cluster in the dumpier parts of the City. By night, they sleep or swarm in vast and stinking slums even the authorities barely know. You don't welcome these creatures into your own world. They're ugly. They're light-fingered or plain violent. They smell. They carry the seeds of contagion about their unwashed clothes and bodies. Once past the massive statue of Belisarius, though, I found the way was blocked by a loose crowd of the unwashed that must have been a hundred strong.

'God bless the Lord Nicetas!' someone shrilled at me. The call was taken up in a ragged chant. 'My God preserve the Lord Nicetas,' he called again, 'who feeds the posterity of Romulus and the heroes of old.' I stepped out of his way and was almost knocked sideways by a wagon piled high with food. Drawn by white oxen, this had lurched, without warning, from one of the smaller side streets. There were four others behind it.

'Blessings on the Caesar Nicetas and his bread!' someone cackled on my left. I glanced round. A woman had left the throng and come over as if to intimidate me into agreement. I looked at her and tried not to shrink back in horror. You couldn't possibly have said how old she was. Mouth open in a dark and toothless hole, her face said extreme old age. Her uncovered breasts hung down in the most disgusting manner, and one had been honeycombed from within by a cancer. But her matted, lice-ridden hair was still black. She opened her mouth wider for a howl of triumphant laughter. '*Emperor* Nicetas won't let us starve!' she screeched. I almost believed she would step closer and try to touch me. I stared at the black and red mottling that ran upward from her wrists and shuddered. Woman or not, I would have gone for my sword. But a man with one eye and weeping sores on the visible part of his chest now appeared beside her and led her back into an army of living refuse that was growing from one moment to the next.

No wonder those chairs had been racing each other away from this lot. The smell and general danger aside, you don't hang about when a mob starts talking treason.

8

However, the poor hadn't been assembled here to talk treason. I'd no sooner gone round the food wagons when I nearly crashed into the seditionary theatre that was the gathering's real purpose. Two men in reasonably clean robes had taken their places on very high chairs placed about five yards apart. They were trying to look grand. In the eyes of their audience, they probably succeeded. I think I'd caught them close to the beginning of their act.

'So good, don't you think, Alexius,' the elder of them struck up in an affected voice, 'that My Lord Nicetas understands the duties of his class?'

'I couldn't agree more, my dearest Constans,' came the reply in a louder and still more affected voice. 'It's all so very unlike *another person* I could mention.' One look at these two troublemakers and I'd guessed what they were about. I gritted my teeth and waited for the inevitable.

It came from a scabby dwarf who'd been darting in and out of the crowd. 'So unlike that piece of barbarian shite the Emperor's allowed to steal our bread,' he gasped. There was a ragged cheer from everyone who'd heard this, and a louder cheer as the words were carried back and repeated for those who hadn't heard them.

Yes, I'd caught this at the beginning. Even as I tried to back away and continue about my business, the crowd shrank to a dense mass about the seditionaries. This left plenty of room for me to continue on my way. But Nicetas – more diligent, I might say, than in any of his official duties – was having me slandered to the mob. I'd be silly not to stay awhile and find out his line of attack. Cautiously, I pushed up the brim of my hat and looked

46

over the heads of the stunted, bandy-legged poor to where the seditionaries were settling into their act.

'It may have been wrong of him to stop the people's bread,' Alexius announced in a tone you might almost have taken as a defence of the Lord Senator Alaric. He paused and cleared his throat. 'But it was surely unpardonable to say there were too many of us in the City, and that not even a hundred of us were the equal of one dirty peasant digging in the fields.' This got a loud groan, followed by general denunciations of Alaric the Barbarian who'd halved the free distributions of food to the City poor, and who plainly wanted to end them altogether. You can be sure no one bothered complaining about the new entrance fee I'd ordered for the public baths. If one of these animals had so much as washed his face since Easter, I'd have been surprised.

Constans took a sip of wine and looked in my direction. I wasn't the only person of quality lurking beyond the crowd. But it wouldn't do for him to recognise the man he'd been hired to preach against. I pulled my hat down a little further.

Still looking at me, Constans laughed nervously, before going back about his business. 'I tell you, that barbarian is a snake in the bosom of the Empire. He isn't a Greek like us. He isn't even a Latin or a Syrian or Egyptian. He's a barbarian immigrant. He hadn't been here a quarter of an hour before he'd wormed his way into the Emperor's confidence. He's been turning everything upside down ever since. He's doing to us from the inside what his ancestors did as invaders to the Western Provinces. Unless *someone* stops him, he won't stop till he's pulled us all down to his own level.'

'Come now, my dearest friend,' said Alexius, when the chorus of hawking and spitting had died away. 'I'm sure the boy means well. It's just that he doesn't understand our ways. He's read a few books and thinks he knows everything. When he finally grows up, he'll surely accept the rightness of ways that were always good enough for our ancestors.'

'*Means well?*' Constans shouted in mock outrage. 'You're too trusting, Alexius. How do you think he pays the bills on that palace he was given? I tell you, he's on the take. Where else is all the money going? What's he done with all the taxes that come in from the provinces? They don't go on us, the Roman People, that's to be sure. What happened to the olive oil ration?' He raised his voice. 'Do you even remember that?' Loud groans. More repeating of the words. More groans.

'Never mind the oil,' Alexius broke in, still sounding even-handed. 'But I'll grant you have a point. What really matters is the army and there's been precious little money spent on that. If the Lord Nicetas had been given proper support, we'd never have lost Syria to the Persians. The Empire wouldn't have been cut in half. We wouldn't now be facing an invasion of Egypt.'

Oh, the fucking injustice of that! I really had to struggle not to kick my way through the crowd, to pull Alexius off his chair and wring his lying seditionary neck. But I did control myself. I also kept my face down when Constans called me a yellow-haired catamite, and someone with a Cypriotic accent accused me of conjuring headless demons in my palace to let loose in the City.

Yes, the *gross* fucking injustice! I'd put off the currency reform so money could be found for the defence of Syria. As if from nowhere, I'd squeezed out as much money for that as had been lavished in the old days on the combined land and sea operation to recover Africa from the Vandals. I'd given Nicetas the best-equipped army we'd sent out in a generation – and to hold a perfectly defensible province. The duffer had fallen into a trap an idiot child might have spotted and, a thousand years after Alexander had brought it under Greek dominion, the Persians were again masters of Syria.

One way or another, I'd have Nicetas for this. If I got any say in the matter, serving in a public toilet would be a soft option for the useless, blame-shifting bastard. For a moment, I thought of pulling my hat off and giving these flecks of stinking gutter scum a lecture on how to save an empire run down by a century of misgovernment. You can imagine this didn't involve piling still more taxes on those who grew food for the Empire and provided it with soldiers. But I kept my mouth shut. Someone in the crowd now began bleating how I'd used the whole Imperial budget to make solid gold statues of myself in the nude. If true, that would still have been a better use of the taxpayers' money than spending it on food to shove down his worthless throat.

Constans struck up again, now suggesting a petition to the Emperor when he finally decided to come back from consulting the 'holy fathers' in Cyzicus. They could ask for me to be dragged from my 'demon-haunted' palace and blinded and stuffed away in a monastery. There was a long groan of agreement from the crowd and a woman began shrieking as if about to give birth. Alexius disagreed, merely suggesting I should be taken back to whatever northern forest was my true home. There, I could be let loose to run about with the other howling savages. That got him a raucous laugh. I didn't like the repeated talk of demons. I'd speak with Samo, when I got home, about another change of the locks. I watched the two seditionaries smile at each other. You couldn't deny they were earning their fee for the day.

They now decided they'd finished earning it. As the crowd drifted in the direction of the food wagons, I walked slowly across to the wide steps that led down to Imperial Square. This journey was already taking longer than it should. I needed a short cut to the city walls.

Dignity almost recovered, I stood on the topmost step and took my hat off. I fanned myself and put it back on. The breeze was settling into a regular wind and the afternoon might not be quite so sweltering as I'd thought it would be. I looked at my boots. They could do with a light brushing but I'd avoided stepping in any of the filth that drops from the bodies of the poor. I'll not say my spirits were rising but it was a fine day for being out of doors. Nicetas was trying to do me over. Good seditionaries don't come cheap. He'd spent a fortune on a cup that would be an excuse for one of Leander's leaden epigrams. But I'd more than match that. I'd send the cup off to the mint and put notice of this into *The Gazette*. That would put a sour look on his face.

49

But all that could wait. Lucas was waiting outside the walls, and with evidence that might let me save still more of the taxpayers' money on salaries and pensions. I prepared to hurry down into Imperial Square.

'Might Your Honour be a gambling man?' someone asked in the wheedling tone of the poor. I paid no attention and looked up at the sky – not a cloud in sight, but the gathering shift to a northern wind would soon justify my blue woollen cloak. 'Go on, Sir – I can see it's your lucky day!' I looked round at someone with the thin and wiry build of the working lower classes. He looked under the brim of my hat and laughed. 'For you, Sir, I'll lay special odds,' he said. 'You drop any coin you like in that bowl down there.' I didn't follow his pointed finger. I'd already seen the disused fountain thirty feet below in Imperial Square. He put his face into a snarling grin. 'Even a gold coin you can drop, Sir. The ten foot of green slime don't count for nothing with my boy. He'll jump right off this wall beside you, and get it out for you.'

I was about to tell him to bugger off and die, when I looked at the naked boy who'd come out from behind a column. I felt a sudden stirring of lust. Like all the City's lower class, he was a touch undersized and there was a slight lack of harmony in the proportion of his legs to his body. For all this, his tanned skin was rather fetching. Give him a bath and . . .

Oh dear! He'd no sooner got me thinking of how much to offer, when he swept the hair from his eyes and parted very full lips to show two rows of rotten teeth. The front ones were entirely gone. The others were blackened stumps. Such a shame! Such a waste! So little beauty there was already in this world – and why did so much of that have to be spoiled? I could have thrashed the boy's owner for not making him clean every day with a chewing stick. I stood up.

His owner hadn't noticed. 'Oh, Sir, Sir!' he cried, getting directly in my way and waving his arms to stop me. 'Sir, the deal is this. You throw in a coin. If the boy gets it out, you pay me five times your coin. If he can't find it, I pay you five times. If he breaks his neck or drowns, I pay you ten times.' He laughed and pointed at the boy again. I didn't look, but wondered if I might make an exception. Bad teeth are bad teeth – but the rest of him was pushing towards excellent.

But I shook my head. I could fuck anything I wanted later in the day. Until then, duty was calling me again. Trying not to show I was running away, I hurried down the steps.

'You've a nerve, showing your face in public!' the old man croaked accusingly. I'd been aware of him – of him and all the others – as I hurried across the square. My main attention, though, had been given to an epigram about me scrawled on a statue plinth. It was in better Greek than your standard graffito and involved a play on words that joined the name Alaric with the use of powdered lark wing as an emetic. 'Not content with stealing half my pension, you're also putting both my boys out of work.' He stopped in front of me and stamped his foot angrily.

'I didn't expect to see you here, Simeon,' I said, taking my hat off in deference to his years.

'And if you had seen me,' he snapped, 'you'd have been back up those steps before I could say "knife".' There was a murmur of agreement from all the other old wrecks in the square. I sighed. Would I *ever* get outside the city walls?

But let me explain. Imperial Square takes its name from the ministry buildings that surround it on three sides – either that, or from the group of statues at its western end. This is a complete set of emperors, beginning with Julius Caesar and culminating with Anastasius, whose reign, a century before, had seen the last big wave of city beautification. The statues were ordered in a tight spiral, with Anastasius at the outermost point. The series could easily have continued – Justin, Justinian, Justin, Tiberius, Maurice, Phocas – who, like the other tyrants, would simply have had an unmarked plinth – and then Heraclius. But the money or will had run out and the series stopped with Anastasius.

From the depression it had worn in the paving stones, the ritual of the aged could easily date from the time of Anastasius. The idea was to begin with Anastasius and, touching every plinth in turn, get round the outside of the spiral to Julius Caesar in the smallest number of breaths. The lap was then to be repeated on the inside on the spiral back to Anastasius. When there was no chariot racing or executions to watch, you could lay bets on who would get round the fastest. Sometimes, the square would be filled to bursting with the idlest sort of rich. Mostly, though, it was just a few dozen old men, some walking briskly, others staggering. No doubt those staggering had once been brisk and, assuming they got that far, the brisk would eventually stagger. So it had been going on since time out of mind despite the sun or rain or snow. So, if not quite to the end of time, it would continue.

And I'd brought it to a pause. Simeon took a step forward. The rest of the aged formed into a decrepit mob behind him. 'Is it him? Is it *him*?' one of them was crying insistently. 'Is it the one the Devil has sent to destroy us?' I could have taken to my heels. But I'd pulled my hat off. The least I could do was be polite.

'Gentlemen,' I said earnestly, 'you have been repeatedly assured that the halving of salaries and pensions will be balanced by payment in the new and purer coinage. With the late fall in prices, I really don't believe anyone will be worse off than before.' That wasn't true – unless renegotiated, most rents would effectively double – and it got me a low jeer, followed by a moaning, varied chorus of disapproval that was more genteel only in its expression than the roasting I'd had from the vermin who clustered round Nicetas. From more than one mouth, I caught the word 'barbarian.' I pretended not to hear this and waved my hat for silence. 'Look, my dear friends, we're at *war*,' I went on in my reasonable tone. 'We all have to make sacrifices.' I caught Simeon's eye, and put a faint edge into my voice. 'Besides, your two sons are among the lucky third,' I said to him directly. 'They still have their positions.' I smiled and waited for the threat to sink in. And it was more than a threat. Now I'd been allowed to make a proper start, even Heraclius was asking how much of the administration he'd inherited from the past was needed. I'd been looking at the Food Control Office for two years – you could double manpower in the home fleet if you shut down that gigantic waste of space.

I looked up briefly at the sun. 'Now, gentlemen,' I said with what I hoped was a winning smile, 'I am on official business. I wouldn't wish to keep you from your exercise.'

'You won't get away with this!' an old man shouted after me as I set off again.

'You try stopping me,' I said under my breath.

'You're a cuckoo in the nest, Alaric,' Simeon shouted as I hurried out of the Square. 'I hope that assassin carves you up good and proper.' He drew a long and wheezing breath. 'God pays his debts without money – you mark my words.'

I pretended not to have heard.

9

A word of advice, Dear Reader. If you ever feel inclined to follow someone about in the full light of day, do not dress yourself all over in black. Unless you're in a place governed by odd sartorial rules, your victim will need to be blind or drunk not to notice you. My further advice is not to flit from tree to tree, or try taking shelter behind free-standing columns and street posts somewhat narrower than you are. Even if no one beats you up for looking dodgy, you'll be laughed at.

I'd been aware of the absurd figure behind me long before Simeon had tried to do me the goodness of a warning. He'd probably been following me down the Triumphal Way. I'd certainly heard him clattering down the steps to Imperial Square. He was now making a pitiful effort not to be seen as he tiptoed twenty yards behind me, turning to look at statues or inscriptions every time I found reasonable cause to look round. Sadly for him, we were fully into siesta time. The streets were empty of everyone but a few skiving clerks. It looked a very cheap assassination attempt. If this were another Nicetas effort, he'd exhausted his budget on silver cups and seditionaries. Or probably not: Nicetas was the sort of man who'd spend more on finding this incompetent than on getting the job done properly.

I slowed down and took off my hat again. I wanted to make sure he'd keep my hair in sight. We were entering the medical district and it wouldn't do for him to lose me in the drug market.

Indeed not. In all the years I knew it, there was never a siesta in the drug market. It was as crowded, as I walked that day into the square containing it, as the surrounding streets were empty. And why not? Along with all the worthless mummy dust and incantatory herbs, it's here that the only heaven we'll ever know is bought and sold by the ounce. I looked at the happy lunchtime trade. I breathed fully out and waited for a moment, before slowly breathing back in. Yes – it was the usual smell of opium vapour and the dust or steam from every other mood-altering substance known to man. Here is the one place where you can be awake and fully clothed and truly forget the horrors of existence. Here is a place where every species of physical and moral pain can be blotted out, and where every type and gradation of pleasure can be infallibly dispensed. I'll add that, if you can't make your own and you know the right people, it's a fine place for buying poison.

'Oh, My Lord!' someone brayed into my left ear. 'My dearest and sweetest young Lord!' The compounder's voice would have said Jewish, but for the inky skin of one whose ancestors had lived so long in the African sun that the colouring had become hereditary. Most who knew him struggled to recall his name. It was best to avoid trying to pronounce it. I turned to face him, and watched him sink to his knees. 'No one said *you'd* be coming here!' he whined up at me without moving his lips. He shuffled forward a few inches, nearly crushing the hand of one of the naked beggars who'd been trying to pick a blob of cannabis wax off the ground, and kissed the hem of my outer robe. 'I don't want any part of what's going on.'

I glanced about the busy immensity of workshops and sampling booths, and put my thoughts in order. 'I don't know what you're talking about.' I said softly. Two assistants came forward and helped him back to his feet. He struck up in a loud voice about a new kind of stimulant imported from a place beyond the knowledge of the geographers. As if from nowhere, another assistant stood forward with a tray of silver cups. I took one of them and twisted it between forefinger and thumb. Its contents had the sheen and solidity of quicksilver and a faint peppery smell. Though a stimulant was the last thing I needed this day, I nodded approvingly.

The compounder took the cup from me and leaned forward. 'I thought *you* would know the penalties for treason,' he said. He licked suddenly dry lips. 'I can't help you. No one can make me do that.'

I took the cup again and twirled its contents. I fought off a second, though slighter, panic attack. He'd been recommended to me shortly after I began my rise to eminence. He may have guessed, from the way I'd combined orders the year before, that I was not entirely correct in my dealings. But why start making a fuss *now*? I thought once more about my silver cup, doubts pressing heavy on what I could feel had been only a brittle certainty. It would have been useful to take him aside for questioning. A shame I was being followed. 'You want to pull yourself together,' I whispered. 'The penalties for treason only apply to those who get caught. You just fill the same order every month and send me the bills – and keep your speculations to yourself.' A look of confusion flickered across his face, before it lapsed into another happy smile. I put the cup back and said something loud and flattering.

I stopped at the last main booth to look at myself in one of the big mirrors young men used for practising how most elegantly to sniff vapour from a heated spoon. I moved into a shaft of sunlight and grinned uncertainly at my own reflection. Given my lack of beard, I'd have had trouble passing for twenty, let alone the thirty-five I'd implied without ever claiming to be. The dominant appearance though, for anyone able to see past the beauty, was of a man trying not to give way to an unease that was never far below the surface. Suppose that compounder's nerve snapped and he turned himself in to the Emperor? Whatever happened to him, I'd probably get off with being locked away in a monastery – Heraclius had lately shown a taste for punishments to fit the crime. But it would be as spectacular a fall as any in the Empire's ancient or modern history.

Pull yourself together! was the advice I'd given. Now, as I watched my face go into its usual blank politeness, I tried to take it for myself. I leaned forward and touched my fringe. I could see how, before stepping out, I'd left a streak of paint just below the hairline. I took a napkin and wiped this away. I patted my hair back into place. I stepped back till I could see not only my face but also the elaborate gathering of silk across my shoulders. Seven years earlier, I'd been stealing food from Kentish pigsties to stay alive. No one looking at me now could have believed that. I was doing well. Given time, the one cloud that might blot out the sun in my heaven would inevitably pass away. Till then, I had only to keep a stiff upper lip.

I stood as if smitten by the sight of my own pretty face. It gave me the chance to see more of my follower. He was a few yards behind me, and was flinching away from someone who'd not yet sold all his clothes to buy drugs and was turning aggressive with his begging bowl. Take off that black cloak and I really doubted if he was much more substantial than the unfortunate boy I'd turned down on the Triumphal Way. He might have a poisoned dagger. Then again, if he proved as skilful with that as he had with keeping himself out of sight, I was in sod all danger.

Still heading for Middle Street, I turned into a street close by what, before I'd cut off its funding, had been the Imperial School of Rhetorical Studies. The street was so unfrequented nowadays that grass had sprouted between the cobble stones. I turned left and quickened my pace. Another hundred yards and, looking back to make sure I was still being followed, I turned right into a lane that sloped steeply down.

I'd now entered one of those places where, unless to sleep, the street cleaners never went. And why bother setting them to work in there? The poor districts of Constantinople have few streets in the normal sense. They are best described as warrens of high wooden structures, grouped round interconnecting courtyards that are often pools of sewage and of other waste sent downhill from the shambles and tanneries. Here was one of the less salubrious districts. Though crossed by an aqueduct, it had no running water. It was home to the class of festering paupers Nicetas was courting. Its main difference was not to be exclusively inhabited by the poor. By night, these courtyards were lit by a thousand torches, and swarming with multitudes, offering or on the lookout for vicious entertainment. Was it stolen goods you wanted? Or brothels filled with limbless cripples? Or sacrifices to the Old Gods? Or fights to the death between renegade slaves? Or horoscopes cast? Or slaves illegally castrated for punishment or profit? Or the comforts of a hundred proscribed and ludicrous heresies? Did you want gambling, where losers unable to pay could be dragged off and carved into a mockery of the human form? Or did you just want to breathe the air of a place from which the Imperial Government had carefully withdrawn all hope, without bothering to provide even the basics of order? If you wanted any of this, you came here.

Not, however, at this time of day. It's often hard to say what the very poor do for a living. They still keep faithfully to the siesta. Excepting a few stunted children, who shut up at the sight of a stranger, and a sound of chickens and the occasional pig, you'd almost have thought the place abandoned. Even the dogs were asleep. Unless my follower got lucky, the worst I had to fear was the misfortune of stepping into one of those shining puddles. The sudden blast of what you stirred up could knock you backwards. I did avoid them. Scented napkin held under my nose, in I hurried deeper and deeper into this labyrinth of despair, all the time making sure to keep the sound of pursuit not too far behind.

I took myself into a courtyard from which there was no longer any exit. Imagine a mass of wooden fish boxes. Heap them up on a dockside and wait for the upper levels of the mass to lean over in an unstable equilibrium. Magnify the smell coming from them and you have some resemblance to where I now was. Time, I decided, to bring this chase to an end. I stopped and made a show of tipping more scent on to my napkin. After that, I walked noisily round a corner and got myself behind a door that had remained standing after the collapse of its surrounding wall, and waited. There was a distant sound of crying children and the unbroken squealing of pigs. The wind was blowing in my favour, and the main smell was only of brick dust and rotting timber.

For a moment, there was no other sound. The children and even the pigs had gone quiet. I began to worry that my follower had lost me. So much of a detour – and now possibly for nothing.

I relaxed, stepping down from a mud brick that had begun to crumble. I'd run through various options since coming into the poor district. All of them involved a violent interrogation. I hadn't supposed this most useless of assassins would simply get lost. Still unspotted by the surrounding filth, I could almost see the funny side of things. I was in the thin, western extremity of a slum that gradually widened until, bounded by the military docks on one side and the Jewish district on the other, it stopped just short of the Golden Horn. Unless he managed to climb one of the steep banks that kept the poor from offending the noses of the respectable, there was every chance the duffer would wander lost in here until he fell into one of the cesspools and drowned, or was knocked on the head. He'd never collect so much as a clipped copper from Nicetas.

I looked up at a sky that was as beautiful here as outside my palace. I felt a sneeze coming on. I blinked and blinked again. Yes, it was a big one. If I held back, but kept darting a glance at the sliver of sun peeping over the highest rooftop, it would be the next best thing you can manage, without drugs, to sex. Sad to think, I told myself, this would in all likelihood be the high point of my day.

No sneeze, however. Just as I blinked harder to see through the anticipatory tears, there was a single, shrill cry of fear from close by. It was followed by the sharp sound of collapsing masonry and a sudden manic barking of dogs. After another crash, I heard the laughter of many voices and another loud scream.

What a buggery day this was turning out! I put a hand on the hilt of my sword and peered cautiously from behind the door. I was completely alone. It was a neighbouring courtyard where it seemed a riot was brewing. I took out my sword and tried not to make any noise of my own while stepping from one dry patch of ground to another.

The sounds of masonry were easily explained. The Christmas earthquake that had got me and mine out of bed, and set every church bell ringing by itself, had levelled whole stretches of the poor districts. Nothing had been rebuilt yet. Few owners saw the point of rebuilding. The survivors had squeezed themselves into other accommodation. The courtyard where I'd taken shelter had been knocked about. This one bordered on one of the areas of total collapse. And here was my follower. He must have lost sight of me and taken a wrong turn. Hard to say whether he himself had been followed, or if he'd blundered into a meeting of armed trash. Whatever the truth, he'd made a rotten job of clambering over a heap of mud brick. It had collapsed on itself at first touch. Here, within the slight depression made by the falling of bricks and tangled in his cloak like a corpse in its winding sheet, my follower's only answer to the two men who were poking at him with bits of wood was much twitching and a few muffled screams.

I waited for a pause in the entertainment and cleared my throat. A dozen dark and rattish faces turned in my direction. All was silent. Someone had already killed one of the dogs, and was holding it as a trophy. The others had scurried out of sight.

'Oo you?' one of the younger creatures jabbered. He held up a three-foot length of roofing timber. 'Oo you?' One of the others gave my follower a kick, but dropped the block of paving stone he'd carried over to use for a killing blow.

They all stared at me for a long moment. They could have tried rushing me but I knew they wouldn't. I sheathed my sword. 'Piss off, the lot of you!' I said quietly. I inclined my head towards the one exit. I saw the glint of an iron knife. Not going for my sword, I frowned slightly and took a step forward. That was all it needed. Everyone knew the score. I was in my class, they in theirs. No one would lift violent hands against the irresistible and merciless force that plainly stood behind me. No one fancied being torn apart in the Circus by hyenas, or being roasted over a slow fire, or being deprived of sight and manhood and turned loose outside the city walls. I listened to the retreating patter of bare feet, then turned my attention to the struggling figure who remained.

I glanced up at the nearest building. I was aware of the scratching sounds the very poor make when something out of the ordinary has happened close by their homes. But no face showed itself from within the unshuttered squares of darkness. Taking my sword out again, I stood behind one of the many heaps of crumbled brick. I stared at the human bundle before me. Completely lost inside a cloak made light by the brick dust, it had stopped moving.

'If you're still alive,' I said in a conversational tone, 'you can get yourself out of that stupid cloak and stand up.' After a long moment, when I began to wonder if someone hadn't managed a killing blow, a white and trembling hand emerged through a rent in the cloth. It was followed by another. They failed to rip a larger hole and vanished again. Still swathed in the stained blackness, my follower tried to get up. After more struggling, there was a faint ripping sound and the cloak fell apart. Rolling free of it, my follower looked at me and struggled on to his knees, arms raised in supplication.

I stared across three yards of rubble into the face of the young petitioning agent who'd pissed me off that morning. There were fresh tears trembling on the lids of those grey eyes, and the freckles hardly showed on a face pale with fear. As I had back in my hall of audience, I waited until it seemed I'd say nothing at all. This time, however, there was nothing to be said beyond a statement of the obvious.

'A bloody woman!' I cried, aghast. Ignoring the possibility of a stain on my outer tunic, I sat heavily on another heap of bricks and dug my sword into the packed earth. Tearful, but not yet crying again, she stared silently back at me. I sighed and arranged my face into a less menacing smile. 'Well, man or woman,' I said, 'you have the most wonderful capacity for slowing me down.'

Still kneeling, she dropped her arms. She smiled nervously. She managed a sort of shrug. I stretched out my legs before me and crossed them at the ankles. I'd chosen those leggings well. They really were most elegant.

10

'Of course they were trying to kill you,' I said impatiently. 'You may have noticed their attentions were somewhat less than friendly.' Antonia, only surviving child of Laonicus of Trebizond, looked back at me in scared if slightly defiant silence. 'However, this brings me to my next question, which is how long have you been in Constantinople? Since you haven't yet got yourself raped or murdered, I don't think you can have been here long.' The tear that I'd seen welling beneath her left eye chose this moment to start its progress down her cheek. Without thinking, I reached into my inner tunic and took out a clean napkin. I passed it to her and looked down at the hilt of my sword. It had a solid, reassuring feel in my right hand. I could have written a short epic had I wanted to give the names and miscellaneous attributes of those whose lives I'd ended with its point or sharp edges. But it had no place here. I stood up, sheathed it and covered it with my outer tunic.

I sat down again and looked at Antonia. She'd controlled her tears. At this distance, and in bright sunshine, she was obviously a woman of about twenty. But it wasn't hard to see how in male clothing, and with her brown hair cropped short and with surprise on her side, she could have passed for a young man. I cast about for something more to say that didn't involve reminders of violence or death. 'It is not the custom for women to lay petitions on behalf of others,' I said with a haughty sniff.

'Is it the custom for women to do *anything* but shuffle between bed and cooking pot?' she answered, tears suddenly giving way to defiance. 'I've told you who my father was. If you don't want me to starve or sell my body in the street, what else can I do but take over his practice?' She stuck out her lower lip and seemed to be expecting an answer. I sniffed again and felt the ghost of my aborted sneeze. I suppressed it and covered the effort with a frown. Rotten luck, no doubt, that plague had taken her family on its last visitation. But that was no reason why an Imperial minister should make a laughing stock of himself by hearing petitions from a woman. I looked into her eyes, and changed the subject.

'Very well, *Antony* of Trebizond,' I said, going back to the matter in hand. 'You made a quick deal, once I'd hurried off, with those petitioners in their own right and promised you'd get an answer out of me before next Monday. So you followed me, waiting for the right moment to start another of your interminable petitions.' I stopped and smiled. 'Most enterprising, I have to say. Did you insist on payment up front? Or did you agree on payment by results?'

She swallowed and looked back at me. 'If those men had money to spend on agents,' she said in a voice that tried and failed to sound manly, 'do you think they'd have walked here all the way from Pontus?'

I lifted my eyebrows at the look of firmness she'd attempted. I also noted the wavering, ever so slight, of her Pontic accent. If she had been born in Trebizond, she'd spent part of her life some-where else that I couldn't yet place. 'So, because you're from the same province,' I asked, 'you took on their case for free? Is that how you plan to make your fortune?' Antonia said nothing. I thought again. 'How did you get a petitioning licence? Leaving aside the matter of sex, the Petitioners' Guild doesn't allow anyone under forty to approach someone of my eminence.'

'You don't look very old yourself,' she said with another stab at the defiant. It was no more than I deserved. I smiled and leaned back. I looked up at the bright, cloudless sky, and then hurriedly back at Antonia. She was on her feet and brushing dirt from her outer tunic. I looked at her trembling hands. They had the right proportions for a woman, but also the slight roughness of some-one who's done manual work.

'Taking your leave of the Lord Alaric?' I asked.

She pushed her lip out again. 'Since you haven't arrested me,' she said, 'I don't see how that's any of your business. I see I've been wasting my time on you. I'm going back to my lodgings.'

This was my chance to be rid of her. Instead, I pretended to yawn. 'Your cloak is ruined. The clothes you have on aren't for wearing in the street. You have no hat. You seem confident, even so, that you'll find your way back alone and in safety.' I shook my head and put a sad note into my voice. 'You need to have grown up in a nunnery to believe any of these things. If you've been in this city longer than a week, I'll be impressed by your luck.'

I watched her stiffen slightly. It was only for a moment. 'But you won't stop me from going if that's what I want?' she asked, looking carefully into my face. 'You won't *make* me stay?'

'Not at all!' I said with a reassuring smile. 'You are a free individual. It's your undoubted right to come and go as you please. I'd never dream of forcing my protection on someone who didn't want it.' I made my smile broader and waved her about her business. I looked once more at my gorgeous leggings and wondered what I ought to say next.

With a sharp intake of breath, Antonia put a hand to her belt. There was nothing where her purse might have been. She looked down and patted all round her waist. Not looking at me, she stumbled past me to where she'd been rolled about by the locals. Helplessly, she looked at the mass of shattered or crumbled bricks that lay about.

I got up. 'What is it?' I asked. Ignoring me, she bent down and poked at random under the heaps of masonry. 'Where did you last definitely have it?' I asked, trying to sound helpful. 'You could try looking underneath the remains of your cloak.'

She sat on a low heap of rubble. 'It won't be there,' she said in a voice of quiet despair. 'I can't go home without it. It was my rent money.' She looked about to dissolve into proper tears.

There was a sudden clatter of disturbed masonry to my right. The reply I'd been looking for died on my lips. Looking straight ahead, Antonia put both hands to her mouth. 'They're back!' she cried softly.

She was wrong. Every city has its human trash. In a city the size of Constantinople, there are many gradations of the human trash. The poor who'd followed Nicetas weren't the absolute lowest in the City. Nor were the rattish creatures I'd lately chased off. Once I could jolly them outside the walls to grow their own food, some even of these latter had a fair chance of returning to humanity. Or their children had. Not so the small, shrivelled creatures in dark rags who, with a soft scraping of hands and knees through rubble, had been creeping towards us – *these* were the lowest. Alone, I'd have given them one look, before running away. I'd seen a man die from a scratch he got off one of these. Maybe their touch – and, for all I knew, their very breath – carried contagion. It may well have been the puke-inducing smell of their bodies that curdled, when there was no wind to moderate the sun, into the miasma by which the summer pestilence was caused.

I waited a few moments after letting them see they'd been noticed. Slowly, I got up and, without going for it, let my sword show. That put an end to their present attack. One of them dropped his length of sharpened stick. Another stretched supplicating arms in my direction. One after the other, they took on the high and pitiful whining of those who've decided they're more likely to get what they want by showing weakness.

I looked slowly about me. I raised my arms in a gesture of peace. 'You beg the charity of His Magnificence the Lord Senator Alaric,' I intoned in my most hieratic voice. I reached inside my robe and took out a leather purse. 'Let it be received.' I poured its contents into the palm of my left hand. With a flick of my wrist, I sent twenty or so misshapen coppers towards the far end of the courtyard.

Not looking at the effect this created, I turned back to Antonia. 'Take my hand,' I said. 'There's no present danger. But the mood of the burrow people is changeable. Try not to look at them.' She got up and put her hand into mine. With one backward glance at where her fallen purse might be lying, she allowed me to lead her across the wide carpet of rubble. Together, we picked our way across the courtyard. Never once did the beggars look up from their frantic scavenging and their squeals of exultation whenever a coin came to light amid the filth.

At last, I was in Middle Street. From the poor district, it was a matter of climbing over another collapsed building, then of finding the one flight of steps that led upward to a street that, long since abandoned, still had the names of shops written in Latin. From here, it was a short cut through an alley. Middle Street itself was largely empty at this time of day. But it was a relief to stand on paving stones again and to breathe uncorrupted air.

I stood in the shade of a triumphal arch begun and never finished by the Great Justinian towards the end of his reign, and looked west at the looming mass of the land walls. 'I have business outside the City,' I said, breaking a long silence. 'I'll give orders in the guardhouse for you to be escorted back to your lodgings.' I stopped and tried once more to think through what else I had in mind. 'You can come and see me tomorrow morning and explain your clients' petition. They took you on in good faith. Whatever the irregularities, it's only fair that I should hear what brought them all the way to Constantinople.' I kept my voice neutral. 'Since they have no money, I will pay the customary fee. We can settle that in the guardhouse.'

I thought Antonia would reject an offer of outright charity. I bent down and, taking care not to rub it in, brushed a patch of brick dust from my left boot. I stood up again and stared in silence along the quarter mile of street that separated us from the walls. Much of it was waste nowadays. Here and there, though, you could see little fields laid out and planted with crops. They were a cheerful sight. They showed how at least some people in the City were standing on their own feet.

I stood up straight again and looked at Antonia. Her face wasn't a mask of happiness. But she was bright as well as proud. My offer could be seen as a professional courtesy. It had no obvious strings attached. She'd be a fool not to take it. 'Come and see me at the third hour of light,' I said. 'Give your name to the doorman. He'll know that you're expected.' She still said nothing. I stepped out of the shadow and didn't look round to see if I was followed. After so long in shade or comparative shade, the sunlight was dazzling. I wondered if I should give her my hat. No need. When I did look back, she'd been rather inventive with my napkin. It did suit her, I had to admit.

11

You will have noticed, Dear Reader, that this is a story of digressions. Some of these might usefully be pruned. This one, I think, is needed. When I speak of places and events inside Constantinople, it doesn't much matter whether you know the City. It is a very, very big city. Even after five years of exploration, driven by my own eccentric tastes and by professional duty, there were still courtyards here and there, and whole streets and short cuts between streets, that I didn't yet know. Don't worry if you cannot exactly place all that I describe inside the walls. Unless you know its general situation, though, all that I say regarding the outside of the City might as well be in the language of one of the peoples who live beyond the furthest limits of the East.

Let me say, then, that Constantinople, by universal acclaim the greatest city in the world and sole capital – now Rome itself was a pile of ruins effectively owned by the Pope – of the Roman Empire, sits on a blunted triangle at the far edge of Europe. Its apex looks east, across five hundred yards of water, to the Asiatic shore. Its north-eastern side faces on to the Golden Horn, a big sheltered harbour that makes the City a centre of all trade. Its western and only landed side is guarded by an immense double fortification, four miles long, built when Thrace was almost a garden basking in the Roman peace, but now tested in wave after wave of those barbarians who had overtopped every other city wall in Europe. Its southern side looks over the wide Propontis. Only the land walls can be truly called impregnable. The sea walls, though respectable by the standards of most other cities, are the last line in a set of defences that begin with control of the sea.

This brings me to the long straits that separate Europe from Asia. These begin with the narrow strait, twenty miles long, that runs more or less south from the Black Sea, past Constantinople and into the Propontis, which is an inland sea about a hundred and fifty miles from east to west and about fifty from north to south. From here to the Aegean is another narrowish strait about forty miles long.

Does it now make sense when I say that, having finally made my way into Middle Street, and from there through the most southerly gate in the land wall, I was now hurrying west along the coastal road that joins Constantinople to Adrianople and to Thessalonica and eventually to the port of Dyrrachium, from where the Adriatic may be crossed to the heel of Italy? Tough luck if it doesn't – because that's where I was.

Once again, I told myself I was a fool. I should have picked up this bloody girl with both hands and dumped her into the guardhouse. Thanks to Nicetas, my plan of having her escorted back to her lodgings had gone tits up before everyone could finish saluting me. 'Emergency orders, Sir,' the officer in charge had answered me. 'None of us to leave our posts. Can't go out from the walls. Can't go back from the walls.'

'Then stay here till I get back,' I'd said to the girl with a smile that tried to look both firm and reassuring. 'You'll be safe enough here.' Being the obvious point for any combined land and sea attack, the Golden Gate is almost a fortress in its own right. What I've called the guardhouse is a looming mass of stonework perched above a triple arch. It must contain three dozen rooms, some of them rather comfy. But there'd been no getting Antonia into any of them. Without actually refusing, she'd given me a look of combined disappointment and fear that had me speaking again before I could realise I'd caved in.

'You can wait here till I'm done with my business,' I'd suggested with a quick glance at the face of the officer in charge. 'You can tell me what those petitioners want while we go back to the centre. If their petition is reasonable,' I'd gone on without proper thought, 'you can break the good news to them in time for dinner.'

'No time like the present,' had been the firm and immediate response. One exchange had led to another, and I'd been faced with a choice between compulsion and surrender. It didn't help that compulsion would have made me later still for Lucas – and he and his men were just one final dash along the road on which I was standing. I'd pretended to ignore the mocking stares of the guards as, with an indifferent shrug, I set off along the road. Then, instead of putting my best foot forward and hurrying through the streams of traffic, I'd slowed to let her keep level with me and not run entirely out of breath, as she explained her clients' petition.

So far as I could gather, they were victims of a standard injustice. If only my sodding eunuchs had let them put their own case, I could have added those petitioners to my list of things to do the following day, and saved myself the trouble of listening to a panting explanation that broke down as often as Antonia had to save herself from tripping over in a pair of boots that didn't fit her.

Annoyed, I kicked a stone and watched it skip forward over the worn flagstones. It got the thigh of a carrying slave. It made a slapping noise that I could hear at ten paces. I waited for him to look round, so I could at least bow an apology. But he didn't seem to notice.

I stopped and put up a hand for silence. This time, I got it. 'Look, Antonia,' I said, 'the mode of address you picked up from the men in your family is purely ceremonial. All I need from you is the tax district where your clients are registered and the name of the local grandee who's ejected them. Everything else I can get my clerks to assemble for me into a brief report. Now, do please stop this babble of rhetorical devices that haven't moved anyone to genuine tears in seven hundred years and of legal tags that you plainly don't understand. All I want are the *facts*.'

And that's what she now gave me – and what facts they were! At once, I'd forgotten the injured slave. I think I'd forgotten Lucas himself. I took Antonia by the arm and led her to the side of the road. Not far off two miles we'd been walking. Only now had she got to the point that mattered. Had she only started with it, I'd now be shepherding her back through the City in search of her clients. 'Please, repeat that name for me,' I asked, keeping my voice neutral.

'Which name?' she asked.

I took my hat off and ran fingers though my hair. 'The name of the man who ejected your clients from the land they've been assigned,' I said, speaking slowly. 'He is the man who ensured they got no hearing in the local courts and against whom they've come to seek my help.'

I thought she'd said Eunapius of Pylae but needed it confirmed. Eunapius it was. I put my hat on again and fussed to get it back in the right position. It was one way to keep myself from jumping up and down and laughing. I made sure to darken my voice. 'I wish you'd begun with Eunapius. He complicates everything.'

I'd made my voice too dark and Antonia misread me. 'So, you won't help those men?' she asked, a tone of outrage coming into her own voice. 'They walked here all the way from Zigana, hundreds of miles away. They believed you were the only honest man in the government and that you'd help them for sure.' She tried to see under the brim of my hat. 'You do know that all the country people in Pontus pray every Sunday for your health?'

I began walking again. It was pleasing to know there were *some* people in this Empire who didn't hate me. I smiled and turned to Antonia. 'I will get justice for your clients,' I said. 'But you need to understand that I'm in no position to give it by myself.' I fell silent. That wasn't the way to explain anything to a woman. That needs simple words and some attention to making their sense clear. I gathered my thoughts.

'You are right about the land law,' I said. 'It has no exceptions in any of the Home Provinces. Every free householder in every country district has the right to enough land to feed himself and those who look to him. There are different provisions that cover the different grades of land and these have already caused much litigation. There are also varying degrees of inalienability and of the obligation to serve in the new militias. But no landowner is exempt. Any landowner who refuses to make such land available as my surveyors have determined he should, may be sued in the

71

courts. If he avoids judgment through bribery or nepotism, he may be charged with perverting the course of justice and tried in Constantinople.'

'Then what's the problem?' she asked.

'The problem,' I explained, 'is that your clients have come up against Eunapius of Pylae. He's in thick with Nicetas, who is the Emperor's cousin. Anyone else and I could write one letter 'asking' for the law to be obeyed. Writing to Eunapius would be a waste of papyrus. He wouldn't be scared by the implied threat of a tax audit. And you can forget about formal proceedings. He'd go straight to Nicetas, who'd run to the Emperor with a cloud of accusations against me and your clients. No, it's worse than that. While the Emperor's away, Nicetas might try his luck and directly order me to desist. He'd also go public. Set up that manner of dispute and there's no chance Heraclius would side against his own blood.'

'So, what *will* you do?' she asked. 'The men who walked here aren't the only victims. There are dozens of other families who have had their land taken back. There are also accusations of rape and murder against some of his men.'

Now I had the relevant facts, this was getting better and better. And I'd been under the impression that Antonia was an assassin hired by Nicetas to supplement his seditionaries! I'd said I'd have him for the trick he'd pulled on the Triumphal Way – and I would!

I stuck my chin out. Doing that, I'd been told, made me look older and more authoritative. 'Your clients must wait until the new currency law comes into operation,' I said. 'On that day, Heraclius is due to come back from his pilgrimage and I have a long private meeting booked with him. If I use the right approach, he'll issue a formal rebuke against Eunapius. There will be no going back on that. Until then, I want your clients to keep out of sight. If they're short of money, I'll give help through an intermediary. But they must stay out of sight. I don't want anything that will prod Nicetas into action.'

Now I'd got the whole story, I could finally be glad that we'd met. Here was an open breach of the law – probably documented, if I got someone to dig round the local archive – by a known agent and possible nominee of Nicetas. If I used this right, I could get the Emperor to slap his cousin down good and hard. I might not be able to stop his general campaign against me but I could shut off the stream of collusive actions in which Eunapius of Pylae always managed to be a first- or second-hand party.

'So, we'll have to see the Emperor' – she squeezed her eyes shut, evidently thinking back to what I'd said in my hall of audience – 'on the second day of the second week. Will I need special clothes to see him?'

I stepped off the road to let a wide cart rumble by. I frowned at Antonia. 'What makes you think *you* are coming with me to see the Great Augustus?' I asked with a lordly toss of my head. All I needed to do was get Heraclius on side, and then produce those rough-handed farmers to look noble and put-upon. I didn't need a woman there to babble away like a drunken litigant in person.

'Because it's the custom,' she answered. 'When a Minister needs special clearance to do something, the petitioning agent always goes with him.'

'Don't be silly!' I said with another lordly toss, this time nearly dislodging my hat. 'All else aside, *you don't even look like a man.* I won't ask how you got this far. But there will be no more of this ludicrous attempt at a petitioning career.' I paused and made myself look very firm. 'Tomorrow afternoon, I'm having you put on a fast carriage back to Trebizond.' I paused again for dramatic effect and found I was growing more out of love with myself with every moment I allowed to slip by. 'However,' I said, softening my voice, 'the lowest clerical grade in the tax administration is some-times open to women. Since I assume you can read and write, I will provide you with a letter of appointment to the office in Trebizond.'

I couldn't say fairer than that. Even if unwittingly, Antonia had done me a favour. I'd return it by keeping her and her mother from going hungry. She'd had her big adventure in life, and could look forward to telling her children and grandchildren how, for one day, she'd laid petitions before Alaric the Magnificent.

That wasn't how she saw it. 'It's not fair!' she cried. She stamped her foot. 'I don't want to go back to Trebizond – and you can't make me!' She sat down in the road and drew her knees up to her chin. I looked at her. *Couldn't make her* – eh? I was a member of the Imperial Council. If I wanted, I could drag her aside and rape her in full view of everyone else on the road. If she didn't know that, her father must have done a crap job of bringing her up. I smiled and said nothing as she repeated and varied herself on the matter of fairness. Now I'd got used to the short hair, I couldn't deny she was a pretty girl. But that only made it more important to get her out of a place like Constantinople. I really was doing her a favour.

I kicked another stone, this time making sure it skipped into the brambles lining the road. 'I could make you an inspector of taxes,' I said, trying not to think of the scandal that would cause in the Trebizond office. 'You couldn't appear in court yourself as a prosecutor. But you could employ a clerk for that. The other duties would make you a woman of some consequence.'

'I've told you, I'm not going back to Trebizond!' she snapped. 'I'd rather die than see that dreadful place again.' Someone on a donkey who'd just overtaken us looked back at this. I fell silent and thought about my silver cup. I wouldn't send it to the mint, I decided. I'd write a poem of thanks that would annoy Nicetas by outshining anything his own Leander could make up.

12

At last, we were at the second milestone beyond the walls. It was here that the road veered right to avoid some very hard rock that lay along the shore. This left about a half mile of shoreline invisible from the crowded road. This was where I should have been before the sun was high enough to be warm. Serves me right if Lucas was stamping up and down on the beach like an enraged bull, and if the desk in my office had already vanished under a burial mound of unanswered correspondence. I looked at the expanse of low crags. I'd heard – and I may have heard wrong – that this was the mouth of a river long since diverted to feeding the City water supply. What remained was an alternation of dark and jagged rock and low points between that ranged between smelly puddles and salt marshes. Beyond that, Lucas should still be waiting. I glanced at the first of the puddles, and wished I hadn't come out in such lovely boots. But I could be glad of my cloak. If the sun was just lately over its zenith, the northerly breeze had settled into a chilly blast. I let my sleeves down and pulled my cloak forward.

'Smugglers put in here at night,' I said for the sake of conversation. 'It's the final link in a chain of evasion that begins at the Red Sea. You land small high-value items here – incense or pepper, for instance. You then carry them under your clothing into Constantinople. It's the same with contraband like heretical books or magical paraphernalia.' Antonia nodded vaguely. I'd got her back to her feet by offering an illegal appointment to clerk of the fourth grade. Since then, she hadn't spoken.

I stepped off the road. 'Give me your hand,' I said. 'You'll tear your clothes if you fall.' She ignored me. I shrugged. We scrambled without another word over the first series of crags. I tore my leggings and put a deep scratch into my left boot.

'Is Tanais in Egypt?' Antonia asked as we finished climbing down. The road was now out of sight. We'd soon be looking down at the sea. I was glad she was out of breath. I reached my hand out again. This time, she took it. She came down beside me in a little shower of stones.

'Tanais is a city on the far shore of Lake Maeotis,' I said in a return of my lordly manner. What *had* her father taught her? 'The lake is entered through a narrow strait from the north of the Black Sea. Since you live in Trebizond, I really thought you'd know that. It's been there for over a thousand years,' I went on with a mild frown – 'very important for trade. The River Tanais leads straight into Scythia, and may be part of an alternative water route to a place called England.'

'Oh, you mean *Tanais!*' She sounded annoyed, and didn't seem to have picked up on the reference to England. 'So, why are we on this side of the City?'

I reached forward and steadied her as she slipped on one of the smoother rocks. 'That's the reason I'm here,' I said. 'In itself, smuggling is something dealt with by subordinates of subordinates. But I'm told the detained ship is from Tanais. That raises the question of how it got through the narrow straits past the City.' Yes, that was my concern. Now I was so wretchedly late, I was thinking about criminal charges as well as general sackings in the Tolls Office. I tried to look fierce. I was his Magnificence the Lord Senator Alaric, Lord Treasurer to Heraclius – but I wasn't above getting my hands dirty, or my boots scratched, to make sure I ran a department as efficient and incorruptible as everyone knew I was.

I leaned forward and put my hand on a convenient lump of rock. Unless those unusually active seabirds overhead were lost, it was one more upward climb and then a descent to the shore. I recalled from my one previous visit that this was a narrow bay with a flat and sandy beach. I frowned and pulled my hand back. I looked at my hand. I rubbed my fingers together and sniffed them. I used my other hand to get out the napkin I'd soaked in perfume. I cleaned myself and stared at linen that was no longer white but stained with congealing blood.

Eyes suddenly wide, Antonia didn't cry out. I tried for a smile. I wondered how long I had before she realised what a total dickhead I'd been.

There was a salty puddle at the foot of this depression in the rock, and I moved to a loose rock in an effort to keep my boots dry. I drew a deep breath and tried to ignore the sound of my own racing pulse. I took out the two halves of the papyrus sheet. The message looked absolutely right. It was in the right handwriting, and was expressed in the right stilted phrasing. I'd read it once in my hall of audience and got it straight by heart. Why was I fussing over a few spots of blood? Perhaps one of my own people had slipped here and cut himself. These rocks were buggery sharp. But it was more than a few spots of blood I'd just wiped off my hand. I looked up again and tried not to sneeze as I stared close by the sun. Those seabirds were very active. They might be feeding. Or they might have been disturbed.

I looked again at the message and blinked until my eyes had adjusted. Though possible, convincing forgery of a seal is difficult and therefore uncommon. But I held it closer and looked carefully at the wax. Was it my dazzled eyes? Or was there a slight variation of colour? I tried to reconstruct how the seal had been pressed into the wax. Shouldn't it have left a full rather than a partial impression?

Put me before some commission of inquiry and I'd have persuaded everyone of how reasonably I'd acted throughout – how any other reasonable man would have found himself standing just outside the jaws of a trap. I might even have got away with a commendation for how I'd spotted things just in time. In the private turnings of my mind, however, there was no denying I'd been a dickhead – a total and culpable dickhead.

I turned to Antonia, who seemed to have picked up on my mood. 'Listen,' I said, keeping all urgency out of my voice. 'I want you to get yourself as quickly and quietly as you can back to the road.' I slipped off my signet ring. 'Stop the first carrying chair that comes past with more than a dozen armed guards and give this to the owner. Tell him I need immediate support.' I stared her into silence. 'I may not need help,' I went on. 'You may find that you get to the road with me only a dozen yards behind you. But I do implore you to go.'

I turned away from her and took my sword out. Now I was looking, I could see where a stream of blood had run down from above to my right. If I stepped up to a narrow ledge on the rock, I could pull myself level with the top of the ridge. As I considered whether I should take off my cloak and outer tunic, I realised that Antonia was still behind me.

'Go!' I said, jerking my sword in her direction. 'If I need to use this, having you about will only complicate things.'

She screwed her face up as if to start another of her objections. Suddenly, she pointed. 'Look out – behind you!' she hissed.

I'd already heard the scrape of shoe leather on rock. All clerical dithering over, I pushed her close against the ridge and got a fighting grip on my sword. The armed man didn't have time to call out. He didn't have time to stop. I braced myself as we made contact. I think he was dead before his breastbone had crunched against the pommel of my sword. Certainly, I had my sword back out of him and cleaned on his padded tunic before he was fully down. Unspotted by his blood, I was ready to fight again.

There was no need to fight again. He'd been alone. The brief sight I'd had of his face told me street thug. His clothing and the cheap sword he'd been carrying said much the same. He hadn't been the sort who attacked without cover of darkness or plenty of support. I could guess he'd been running away and had found me in his path.

'Did you see where he came from?' I asked, very calm. There's nothing like a quick and almost elegant kill to settle your nerves. Whatever my internal commission of inquiry might eventually decide, we'd reached the point of emergency. I managed a smile as I asked again. He must have jumped down from the shore side.

Everything suggested that. But I needed to know beyond doubt. Not speaking, Antonia pointed at the shore side. She looked scared, but not on the point of collapsing in tears. I was casting about for the right form of words to get her scampering back in the direction of safety, when I heard a distant clash of weapons and a cry of what may have been pain. I now heard a much shriller cry, though also from a distance. There was a fight down on the beach.

Antonia found her voice. 'Alaric – My Lord,' she said with quiet intensity – 'can't you see this is a trap? Let's both get out of here.'

She was no fool. That much was clear. I frowned as if to let her know she'd spoken out of place. I turned and looked up again. If I went carefully, I could stop at a point from where I could bob my head up very briefly. There was a chance that Lucas and his men were waiting on the other side. They might have had trouble with some smugglers. The man I'd killed might have been running away. Or they might be in trouble. I had a plain duty to have a look. As for Antonia, I'd given her the chance to get away. There's a limit to the consideration you give women. I took off my outer clothes and arranged them where they wouldn't be blown down by the breeze. Keeping my sword in hand, I climbed noiselessly up a ten-foot incline of jagged rock. The plan was to put my head up and then straight down. I took a deep breath and held it. I pushed my head up.

I was looking down a long incline towards a rocky beach. Thirty yards out from the shore, there was a small ship at anchor. The message had told me there was a ship – though this one wasn't beached, and was plainly not a trading vessel. The beach itself was covered with a few dozen men who lay very still. I didn't bother wondering if they were dead. I could see the dark splashes on their clothes. Here and there, I could see the shafts of arrows. I could see at least one man still alive near the water. He was held down by a small man who sat on his chest, and was twisting with pain as another man did something to his feet. He let out a long scream and what may have been a claim of ignorance. It could have been a cord twisting tighter about a couple of toes with a stone between them. It could have been a knife point into the sole. Sensitive things, feet – you can carry a most effective torture chamber about with you if you know what to do with feet. There was a dead man to my right. He was the one whose blood had run down. There was another six feet away from him, this one with an arrow in his throat. So far as I could tell, none of the dead was from customs enforcement.

For someone who was planning to pull his head straight down, I'd seen rather a lot. But it hadn't been a quick look. I'd put my head up and found myself staring into the face of a man who was standing not a yard away. It was a dark and bearded face. Its owner was carrying a sword of his own. A couple of yards further down the incline, there were three other men. All were carrying bows. One of them had an arrow already in place. I stared into a face that passed quickly through blankness, to surprise, to recognition, to relief, and then to a final glow of something between cunning and triumph.

'Oh, Alaric,' he said in Persian, 'you won't believe how pleased I am to see you! We thought these wretches had already killed you, and were about to go looking for your body.' Shahin, son of Cavad, gave me a flash of teeth dyed red, and went into Greek. 'Will you come on board as my guest? Or must I have you clubbed into submission?'

13

'It gets chilly at sea, I'll grant. But, following your last escape, I'd be mad to leave you with even a scrap of clothing to cover your nakedness.' Shahin smiled and leaned back in his chair. The ship was pitching very gently and we both watched as a wine cup moved a few inches on the table. When all was still again, he got up and bowed to Antonia, who had sat through our meal in silence. He spoke again in Greek. 'It is against our customs to strip women – even when they drift into our clutches on the arm of Alaric the Faithless.' He managed to scowl and smile at the same time. He put his face so close that his beard seemed to tickle her nose – at any rate, she blinked and shrank back. 'But I promise you this – one move out of place from you and I'll give you to the crew to be gang-raped. After that, I'll cut your throat with my own hands. Do you understand?' Antonia swallowed and nodded. That wasn't good enough. 'I said, *do you understand?*'

'Oh, come now, Shahin dearest,' I drawled in Persian, 'the girl is worthless. I picked her up this morning in one of the poor districts. Instead of threatening to pollute yourself with her murder, just put her ashore. You might then explain what you want with me.' When you're in the charge of a man like Shahin, the best reaction to being stark bollock naked is to carry on as if fully dressed. I cleaned my fingers on a napkin and reached lazily for the wine jug. 'Go on,' I urged – 'this is a very little boat for carrying even the pair of us to Beirut. Three's a proper crowd.' I put my face downward and looked up at him. I thought about simpering but decided that could wait.

'Get on your feet, Alaric,' he snarled. 'I want to look on your naked body.' I raised my arms to wave them about, as you must when speaking Persian. But he rapped out an order in Syriac and one of his men stepped forward to put a knife against Antonia's throat. 'Not her throat,' he said with silky menace. 'Get ready to cut off the little finger of her left hand.' He smiled at me. 'Would you care to watch this, Alaric?' I looked briefly at the wine jug. It had been a meal without cutlery. But you can do a lot of damage with a two-pound weight of ceramic – or you could, so long as you didn't worry what Shahin's men would do next. I got up and stood away from the chair. Shahin waved at his man to wait before cutting. He kicked his own chair away from the table and stood up.

'Arms and legs outstretched, Alaric,' he said. He looked quickly at Antonia, who had squeezed her eyes shut and was biting lips that were as pale as her face. 'Look at him,' he said. Another order in Syriac, and her head was forced round so she had no choice but to look. Another of his men came over and ran his hands lightly over my body. I let myself grimace at his stinking breath, but tried otherwise not to look as close to shitting myself as I was.

'Isn't he lovely?' Shahin gloated. 'Did you ever conceive such beauty could exist in the male form? Is it not a beauty that the eyes can behold without ever being slaked? Have you yet known the force and passion of his embraces? I'm sure you thought your luck had changed when he chose you above other women.' He laughed softly and walked forward to kiss me on the lips. I tried not to gag as he forced my teeth apart with his tongue and licked the roof of my mouth. He took hold of my buttocks and ground his hips against mine. He pulled back and stared into my eyes. Then, as if understanding from the look in my eyes the considera- tion of risk and benefit that was running through my head, he darted back. He nodded and his man let go of Antonia's wrist.

He smiled again. 'You heard the promise I made to your slag,' he said. 'Well, I'll extend it to you, Alaric. If you don't do as I tell you, I'll do more than cut her throat. She'll die cursing the day you turned your lying charm on her.' The ship moved slightly in a combination of breeze and current and he sat down heavily. He turned an ill-natured stare on Antonia, who was still looking at me.

So far, she'd taken things pretty well – crying out with fear now and again but not completely breaking down in tears. But I could see in her eyes the expression of a condemned criminal who's managed to smile and even banter with the crowd that has followed him through the streets and who now stands before the execution stake and sees the glowing brazier and the irons and knives and other implements of death. It didn't help that she must have seen the same in my own eyes. Shahin looked on complacently. He giggled in his eastern manner and reached for the wine jug. 'You may sit down, Alaric,' he said with a return to fake jollity.

I allowed myself one sip of wine and smiled easily. 'You know, Shahin,' I said, back in Persian, 'you always did have a taste for the dramatic. But don't you think it would save time if you simply told me what you wanted?'

Shahin drained his cup and stared at the ceiling. 'Do you know what His Majesty did to my uncle after you'd given him the slip in Ctesiphon?' he asked, still in Greek. I raised my eyebrows. Knowing Chosroes in general, and knowing how eager he'd been to pay me back for wrecking a whole year of his war effort, I could imagine poor Bahram had been put to considerable discomfort. I hoped the exact manner would be left unsaid, or at least explained in Persian. But Shahin had settled into his excellent Greek and was in talkative mood.

'My uncle was taken into the Shaft of Oblivion. You know that place, don't you, My Lord Alaric?' I did. Two years back inside the Empire and I still sometimes woke in a panic when I took opium in the wrong mood. I kept my face expressionless.

'He was taken to the lowest dungeon. There, Chosroes himself was waiting, with his own hands to geld and blind the Lord Bahram's two sons – and with a delicacy that ensured their survival. This done, a coat of silk mesh was wrapped tight about his body. It was wrapped so tight that one-inch squares of his bare flesh projected through. Every day, the Great King returned to slice off more squares with a razor . . .'

'Oh, Shahin, Shahin,' I cried as he stopped for a very dark scowl at me, 'but I never realised Chosroes would miss me so!' I smiled brightly and pushed my chair back so he could see more of me again. It made sense for Shahin to take no chances with me. Even so, stripping me naked plainly served more than one purpose. He still fancied the arse off me and, even before his latest demonstration of interest, had been drooling over me all though dinner like a voluptuary in a slave market. Of course, he'd have to be mad to get alone into bed with me. Come to think of it, I'd rather have got into bed with the toothless boy – and you could forget about the bath. Still, it was worth trying to divide his thoughts. Shahin was no fool. He'd not mess up like poor old Bahram had. But lust had finally topped intelligence in Ctesiphon. So it might do here. Sooner or later, I'd find means of escape. In the meantime, I could try to find out how he'd come to be operating as a pirate within sight of Constantinople – and how he'd known when to lift His Magnificence Alaric straight off that beach.

But Shahin paid me no attention and finished his account of how the two ruined sons had screamed reproaches at their father until the blood poisoning got to them, and how Bahram had lived another month as a bag of screaming, maggoty slime. I felt sorry for the poor man, and wondered how many days it might be from here to Ctesiphon. No – I put that straight out of mind. I needed a clear head. I couldn't afford to think of that grinning fiend, slavering and scratching himself on a mountain of yellow silk cushions.

'Sad stuff,' I broke in again. This time, I kept Shahin quiet by reaching down and playing, as if absent-mindedly, with my foreskin. Antonia pretended not to notice. Shahin tried not to look too obvious as he leaned forward, but trembled so much, he spilled wine down his front. Bearing in mind how shrivelled up I was from horror and the cold, there wasn't much to see. Still, I tried to keep up the impression of a man at full ease. 'Oh, sad stuff indeed,' I repeated. 'But we can be glad you got off lightly. You only got sent to sea. I hope you're enjoying Beirut. The Aegean is a sight you Persians haven't had in a very long time, except as prisoners.' I gave him a sweet smile, and began stroking the ridges of muscle on my belly. 'Just a few thousand sit-ups,' I'd once told him between bursts of drugged buggery, 'and you'd have the same.' I hadn't mentioned his flabby thighs or the distasteful flatness of his buttocks, nor the absence of any neck or the lack of symmetry in his nipples. He seemed to have lost weight in the past couple of years. But that must have owed more to some falling out with the sea than to any change in his generally shitty style of life.

Shahin got up and licked very dry lips. 'I'm going out on deck,' he muttered darkly. 'The pair of you will, of course, join me.'

The sun was going down behind me as I looked at the masses of shipping that sailed to and fro in the Propontis, or were scattered at rest along the shore. We'd moved away from the place of ambush but were at anchor again perhaps a few miles to the west.

Shahin leaned on the rail and looked sulkily at an armed convoy of grain ships. 'Our empires have been at war for years,' he spat. 'All trade is at an end with us. The tax gatherers take barely a half of what they're owed. You'd never think it was *your* empire that was losing.' He slumped forward on to the rail and continued watching the endless lines of shipping. I could have given my lecture on how a skilled boxer rolls with every punch he can't parry and nurses his strength for the eventual fight back. Though past its best, the empire I helped rule was still vast enough to absorb even the hammer blows of an invading army. And I would, in the financial sense, nurse it back to a health that would surprise everyone. But Shahin was now up again and his face was taking on a nasty smile.

'Oh Alaric,' he smirked, 'we're not a quarter mile from the shore. I should be careful that you don't step over the side. Haven't I seen you swim a hundred yards under water before needing to come up? On the surface, I've never seen a man swim so fast. You could be ashore before we'd even got our boat ready to go after you. Or you could make for one of the other ships. What trouble you'd make for us then! You know we had orders to take you alive – the best we could do was pull up our anchor and trust to our sail.' He took me by the arm and led me across the little deck to look at a pleasure boat that was scudding by almost within hailing

85

distance. Leaving me alone there, he turned and went over to where Antonia was held by a leash attached to a leather collar about her neck.

'Will the Lord Alaric make a successful dash for freedom – and leave this delightful young creature in my charge?' he jeered. 'Will you do to her what you did to Bahram?'

'Jump, Alaric,' Antonia shouted. 'Don't worry about me – just go.' Her keeper pulled the leash tight and her words ended in a squawk. He pulled again and she went down on her knees. Before she could steady herself, he landed a kick where she'd tied her breasts flat, and looked about for approval as she brought out a cry shrill with pain and fear. He kicked her again and watched her squirm at his feet. He shouted an obscenity in Syriac and uncoiled a whip from about his waist.

I got to him as he had his arm raised. I took him by the wrist and pulled his arm sharply back and to the left. I felt the click of his dislocated shoulder before he could realise what I'd done. I silenced his scream by twisting his arm another half turn and sending him into a spasm that checked even the working of his lungs. But I made sure, as he hit the deck, to smash the ball of my foot into his throat. I'd disabled this piece of human offal for life in perhaps a dozen heartbeats. Another half dozen and I'd have ended his life. But I left him and grabbed Antonia. I was inches from throwing myself over the side with her, when two men took me from behind. They got me on to my back and another put a sword to my throat. Someone else threw himself across my knees.

'No violence!' Shahin called in Syriac. I stared up into his gloating face. 'Whoever harms the Lord Senator gets impaled.' The sword vanished. My legs were free. I ignored the hand that Shahin offered and got to my feet. I turned to Antonia and helped her up. Someone else had got hold of her leash but was making sure to leave plenty of slack. She had her eyes closed and seemed to be making a big effort not to cry.

'Keep quiet and do what they say,' I said firmly. I couldn't tell if she'd heard me.

'Oh, Alaric, Alaric, I knew it was a good idea to keep the girl alive!' Shahin cried, triumphant. 'You'll not get away from us so easily this time.' I repressed a shudder as he rested a hand on my shoulder. The sun was halfway to the horizon and I shivered in the continuing wind. I allowed myself a final look across to the shore, then stood against the outer wall of the deck cabin. It still had some heat from the sun. 'I'm going to enjoy this voyage, Alaric. I'm going to enjoy it almost as much as I'm looking forward to the closure of a business everyone had thought would remain forever open.'

'Do I get *any* clothing?' I replied. 'Or are you proposing to keep me naked all the way to Beirut?'

'I'm having the pair of you tied up in a locked cabin,' was all Shahin replied. 'Shahrbaraz will decide what to do with you.'

14

We were alone in the blackness of the hold. I'd lost track of the time. From the steady creak of ropes and timbers and the regular motions of the ship, I could suppose we were under sail. That meant it wasn't yet dark outside. Perhaps we'd be spending the night in some quiet inlet on the southern side of the Propontis. Or perhaps not.

'Alaric, who was that man?' Before Shahin had done with feasting his eyes on me and gone out, taking the lamp with him, I'd seen Antonia tied to the far wall in the cabin. The first effort I'd made at comfort had gone nowhere. Since then, lost in my own thoughts, I'd barely registered her gentle sobbing. Now, she'd finally pulled herself together. Though her face was eight feet away from mine, her voice seemed much closer in the dark.

I made my lower jaw stop shaking. 'It's a long story,' I began. That was as far as I got. We'd been locked away below the water-line and I was frozen through. That, and I was rapidly falling apart. I'd arched my back and smiled wantonly at Shahin before he withdrew. With just Antonia for company, I could spare myself the strain of concealing what I really felt. Even those few words and my voice shook out of control. I squeezed my eyes shut – it made no difference whether I had them open or not – and felt tears running down my face. I twisted round and wiped them on my shoulders. I sniffed and tried to make it sound as if I were taking in the smell of tar and stale water.

'Why didn't you leave me here?' she whispered. 'You could be back in Constantinople, directing the capture of that man.'

'Because I didn't,' I said. That was all I might have said. But I felt some obligation not to go back to my own thoughts. I sat up.

'I had no idea the day would end like this,' I managed to say with an approach to lightness of tone. 'But I do most humbly apologise for having brought you into this nightmare.' Yes, I should have had her taken into custody at the Golden Gate. Better still, I should have had a look at that dodgy seal before it was absolutely too late. I'd brought this on the pair of us. 'I got you into this and I'll get you out. I'm sorry,' I ended before trailing off.

There was a long silence. Then, after a funny whimper, 'What will happen to us?' Antonia asked. I blew warm breath over my nose and put my thoughts together.

'If we don't get away, it will be bad,' I answered. We'd reached the point where false assurances would have been worse than the truth. 'But let's try putting what has happened into some kind of order,' I went on in a voice that was unlikely to travel though the locked door. 'I got a message very early this morning to come outside the walls. The obvious intent was to murder me. My eunuchs and you unwittingly conspired to slow me down. By the time, I arrived at the appointed place, my killers had themselves been killed.

'Questions: Who was trying to kill me this morning? Who was able to forge a more than reasonably convincing message? Why did Shahin turn up and stop the murder? How did he know I'd be there? Generally speaking, what is a Persian ship doing unobserved in our home waters?'

I thought again. 'I kept mentioning Beirut to our friend. That's where the Persians have their Aegean naval base. However, he mentioned Shahrbaraz. He's their best general. We tried to bribe him last year into revolting again Chosroes. The last I heard of him, he was hovering somewhere east of Armenia – we were expecting an attack on your own province. It's possible he could have got from there to supervise a naval assault on us. But I don't think he has. It's question enough how Shahin got into the Propontis from the Aegean. It staggers the mind how he got here from the Black Sea and is now proposing to go back there. How on earth could he have got past Constantinople?' How indeed? Forget smugglers and a bit of corruption – this implied treason close to the top.

Antonia broke the silence. 'I ran – I mean, I left Trebizond at the beginning of the month,' she said. 'There was no talk of a Persian fleet in the Black Sea. And where could it be based?'

Good question. Most likely, though, we were headed for the Black Sea. I began shivering again. Ever since I'd heard the name Shahrbaraz, I'd been in a state of horrified despair. So long as I thought he was operating out of Beirut, I'd told myself I had ages to find and use the right opportunity to get away. A dash through the Black Sea to one of its most eastern ports was something else. A man far thicker than Shahin could be trusted to keep me trussed up and helpless. I went back to thinking about suicide. The messiest lurch into the blackness of death beat the reception I could expect in Ctesiphon.

'When they found I was a woman,' Antonia said, 'they stopped searching me. But I've got a knife.'

I swallowed and counted downward from five. 'And can you get to it?' I asked, no longer caring if my voice shook.

'They tied my hands behind my back,' she said. I gritted my teeth. As if I hadn't known that already. The best way to magnify despair is to season it with hope. Far overhead, there was a shouted command in Syriac. It was too distant for me to catch any words. But it suggested the sun was finally down and we we'd be putting in for the night. Where? I wondered again. And, unless at least three ministries were riddled with treason that couldn't be kept secret, what story was being told to cover the ship's presence here?

Yes, I was thinking again as if I were in no danger and was gathering information for later use. It took my thoughts off what might be planned for me. And this general turn of events did have its interesting side. I thought again about the timings of my progress that day through Constantinople. No delay at all and I'd be dead by now – well, dead unless those killers had been complete duffers. If only Antonia had slowed me down more than she did, Shahin would have been gone by the time I got to the little bay. It was bastard luck, I thought, to have got there almost but not quite too late enough to find a pile of dead bodies. If I ever got out of this, I could work up a nice speech about the role of contingency in human affairs. Yes – *if only* . . .

I was so wrapped up in my own thoughts, I didn't at first notice the gentle but persistent scraping on the far side of the cabin or the squeaks of suppressed pain. 'What *are* you doing?' I finally asked. The answer was more scraping and what sounded like a piece of furniture tumbling over. I waited for what seemed a very long time. As I was about to ask again, I heard a quiet sob.

'I've got my hands from behind my back,' she said. 'But I can't lean forward to get to the knife.' For the first time, Antonia broke down and cried. It was now, I could hear, that the full disgusting horror of everything had reached the core of her mind. We'd reached the same point of despair. The only race from here involved whose bowels would give way first.

The muscles all about my ribcage were twitching and I knew my voice would shake no matter what control over it I attempted. But I took a deep breath and stopped worrying what my voice might say about me. 'Antonia, *where* is your knife?' I asked. I waited for another long shudder to pass. 'If you've managed to twist your hands from behind you, can you also push yourself across the floor to me?' I struggled for a tone that was calm but authoritative. 'Where *is* your knife?'

She began a stuttering answer that went nowhere. I waited. 'In a belt about my right thigh,' she finally managed to say. Her tone indicated she'd say more. Either she'd spoken oddly or she changed her mind. I heard a renewed scraping as she set about getting as much as she could of her lower body into the middle of the cabin. My own hands were tied behind me in a complex arrangement that didn't compress the flesh, and there was a rope that held them to my bound feet and was looped through a metal ring fixed into the wall. I found, if I twisted on to my stomach and bent my knees, that I could push my head and upper body towards Antonia. It took much scraping and a progressive tightening of the bonds about my wrists and ankles but I finally made contact with her clothing. I then realised, with a jump of the spirits, that we'd both been squeezing ourselves along paths that didn't cross. One moment, I was bumping my nose against a piece of cloth that might have been a discarded rag. Another, and my face was resting on the warmth of her lower belly and hands, close together, were dabbing about in my hair.

'I can't get my clothes loose,' she said. 'Where are your hands?'

'I left them against the wall!' I answered with a nervous laugh. And, much more of this strain, and there they'd drop off. But I arched myself back and began a shuffling move down Antonia's body to where, just below her knees, I'd find the hem of her petitioning robe. From here, it was a return upward into still greater warmth. I'd expected the knife would be on the outside of her leggings. What use, after all, of a weapon that could only be got at by stripping off? Of course, it was underneath the clinging wool and linen mix. It would have been no more useless in a street fight if she'd left it under her bed. But this wasn't a street fight and, pushing myself towards the cord that secured her leggings about her waist, I felt more positive than at any time that day since jumping out of my cold pool. She'd tied the leather in a neat bow that I was able to pull straight apart. I took the leggings between my teeth and began pulling them down. It was harder than it sounds. At last, though, my face was resting against her undepilated nether parts.

I heard her voice, muffled by two layers of fabric. 'It's about the *right* thigh,' she said sharply.

'Er, yes,' I replied, trying to sound natural. I'll not go into the details but one inward breath and a hot flush ran upward to my chest. If getting into bed with Shahin had required a double helping of the green beetle juice, this *was* a drug. Despair and cold forgotten, I took another breath and I thought I'd go off on the spot. But I put the throbbing ache in my groin out of mind. 'Right thigh it is,' I whispered, my mouth very dry. So far as I could tell by brushing over it with my lips, the knife was about four inches long and was held in a sheath that was buckled on the inside of her thigh. The belt was just a little too tight for me to pull it down past her knee. I could choose between chewing through the leather and using my tongue and teeth to get the buckle undone.

Antonia tried to sit up but the stretched ropes held her upper body tight. 'What's wrong?' she asked.

I smothered the giggle I hadn't managed to keep from breaking out. 'If any of my eunuchs had told me I'd be doing *this* before the day was out,' I answered, 'I'd have sacked him on the spot.' I flicked my tongue against the buckle. It had the taste you'd expect. 'In all my time as Lord Treasurer, I've never so far shaken hands with a petitioning agent.'

Antonia said nothing but I felt a slight tremor in her body that might have been a laugh. She spread her legs another couple of inches so I could have a better go at the leather. I squeezed my buttocks together and tried not to groan as I poked forward with my tongue.

15

Antonia could have saved me both time and a pulled muscle in my tongue if she'd explained the double loop in the buckle. But, with much poking and biting, I did finally get there. I'd almost got the thing apart when there was a sudden bump against the side of the ship. It caught me off balance and my lower face was jerked into the moist space between her thighs. For a moment, I thought someone had come into the cabin and was beating us apart. But there was another impact of wood against wood and, unbalanced again, I was knocked as far to the right as Antonia's robe and my own bonds would allow.

The ship had struck something. Were we sinking? With a lurch into panic, I thought of water pouring into the cabin from every direction. I was squirming back into position when the ship steadied and I heard a babble of Syriac. We'd made contact with another ship. My panic took a different turn. Shahin had given every indication that we were here for the night. But was there now to be a change of plan? Would the cabin door soon fly open? Was the plan for us to be moved to another ship for the run past Constantinople?

I gave up on delicacy and got myself back in place. I pushed and bit and pulled. It was no time before I had the buckle undone and was shuffling backward into the cold air. Like a dog returning a thrown stick, I pushed my head forward again until I made contact with Antonia's hands. She took a while to get her own wrists free. After that, it was very fast. She pressed her body against mine as men shouted overhead.

'Do you know what they're saying?' she asked.

'Too fast and too many voices,' I said. It was nice to sit here, free and no longer chilled from all directions. She kept her body against

94

mine. I put an arm about her and squeezed gently. It fell gradually silent overhead and the squeaking of timbers resumed, though in an oddly restrained manner.

Nice as it was, we couldn't sit here all night. I got up unsteadily. I could stand with my head pushed forward. I felt my way about the walls of the cabin. I've said we were below the waterline. The only way out was through a locked door, which I was about to push gently against when I heard the faint sound of a man droning away in Syriac. I held my breath and listened. It was, so far as I could tell, just one man. He was more than halfway through a long invocation of the Virgin that included an aggressive statement of the Monophysite heresy.

I thought quickly. I felt my way back to Antonia. 'Can you speak Syriac?' I asked. She couldn't. I thought again. Greek wouldn't do for what I had in mind. I doubted our guard would understand. He'd only call for help. He might call for help in any event but I had to try. 'Then repeat after me,' I said, 'one syllable at a time.' It took repetition after repetition to get her able to speak the sentences and to sound as if she understood their meaning. At last she got there.

'The Lord Alaric has bit open a vein,' she called out in a scared voice. 'I fear he is dying.'

For a moment there was no response. Had the man heard? Had he gone off for help without making a noise. Then, as I was forming another and still more urgent sentence, I heard a key pushed into the lock. Almost before I could get myself in position, the door opened an inch and a bar of lamplight shone into the room.

'I no longer hear his breathing,' she said. 'I feel his blood soaking my clothes.'

'I have a knife with me,' the man warned. 'You be very careful.' Cautiously, he pushed the door wider apart and stepped through it. 'You'll be careful if you know what's good for you.'

And careful I was. I made sure to stand well back as I snapped his neck from behind. I scooped him into my arms and held him till his legs had stopped kicking. I carried him over and dumped him where I'd been tied. He landed in a heap and settled with his

95

head flopped over to the left and his mouth sagging open. I turned and looked out into the now-empty space between the hold and the ladder that went up to the deck. The lamp could stay where it had been left – it sent in enough light for what I needed – but I picked up the knife.

I turned to Antonia. 'Take everything off except your leggings,' I said. I thought of the wool they contained. 'No, take everything off. I'll help unbind your breasts.' She looked nervously back at me. Now we had some light, she was able to see my continued state of arousal. 'Don't worry about that,' I said dismissively. 'I've just killed a man.' I felt a sudden stab of concern. 'You *can* swim?' I asked. She nodded. 'The sea will be cold. But you need to be able to move.' She nodded again. Relieved, I helped her out of her clothes and took my knife to the linen bandages that had been compressing her since morning. I then cut the leash from her collar. Unable to look away, I stared at her smooth, naked body. I shut my eyes and found I could still see her. 'We have to keep very quiet,' I said, my teeth chattering – though not, this time, from the cold.

The sun was down in the south-west and its long afterglow had almost entirely gone as we crept on to the deck. Just in time, I heard the grunting of men who strain over something heavy, and got the pair of us against the deck cabin. We were both shivering in the frigid air. But we stood in the shadows and, so long as we stood still, there was no reason to suppose anyone would see us without thinking it a trick of the light. The Syrians were complaining about the dangers of a night passage. If I'd bothered to tune myself to their particular dialect, I might have learned something. But, if quieter, there was a more insistent sound of Greek. As I worked out that it came from round the corner on my right, the last afterglow of the sun went out. One of the Syrians brought out a piteous moan about having to stow supplies without a lamp. Another joined in. I reached out for Antonia's arm, and shuffled carefully right.

Soon, we'd step into the cold sea. How, without light, we'd find our way to shore was a nagging worry. I'd come out on deck with the vague idea of taking something that floated. We could hold on to that till morning and hope we hadn't drifted too far out or away from the shipping lanes. For the moment, it was worth hearing what those low and now almost-whispering Greek voices were about. Sure I'd not be seen, I put my head forward and listened.

It was Shahin speaking. 'My dear Simon,' he said in the low voice he only used when fighting back the terrors, 'if you're telling me the blond boy has the cup, and actually *touched* it, can you explain how he's alive and in apparent good health?'

A few feet beyond where he stood, there was a scrape of finger-nails against a bearded face. This was followed by a sharp and anxious intake of breath. 'I've told you, My Lord,' the man called Simon replied in a native though faintly southern Greek, 'he was only the third to touch it. There may have been some loss of potency.' He scratched his beard again. 'But never mind this. I nearly had it! And I'd have it now if you hadn't interfered this afternoon.' He stopped and gave way to a nervous cough. I could tell nothing from his outline against the starry sky. But there was something about his voice that sounded familiar. Hadn't he brought me that purported letter from Nicetas? With Shahin, his accent was broader and his voice more wheedling. But it was him. He must also have brought the fake summons from Lucas – he'd slipped it into the mess of other documents at my feet and waited for me to notice it. Worth asking, though, was why, if he was a principal in whatever matter this was, he'd acted in person.

Simon spoke again. 'The plan was to get the barbarian some-where quiet and beat sense into him. If that didn't work, his muti-lated body, dumped in a public square, would have caused enough chaos in his household for my man to slip in and recover the cup. I ask again, My Lord Shahin – *why did you interfere?*'

Shahin's answer was one of the imitations of farting that Chosroes used to enjoy, and that might have saved him from the Shaft of Oblivion. 'You should remember your place, Simon,' he grated. 'The rules of this game are that *I* give the orders. *You* obey them. It's enough that you missed the cup when you assured me you virtually had it. You're now telling me that Alaric beat you to it. Well, you can put yourself back into that boat and go looking for it. If you don't have it by the time you see Shahrbaraz again, don't expect me to put in a word for you.'

Simon coughed again and twisted round in the gloom. I thought for a moment he'd seen me. But he was looking east and I was in darkness. 'I've already set another plan in motion,' he said. 'I'll have the cup before midnight. I do urge, however, that we go downstairs and cut Alaric's throat. My people are already getting nervous. Once they know he's involved, I can't speak for their loyalty.' His voice took on a pleading tone. 'Kill him. Give me the body. Kill the girl too. She's a nuisance for other reasons.'

There was a brief silence. Then Shahin yawned. 'You don't lay hands on the blond boy without my written agreement,' he snapped. 'The girl is useful to control him. Now, go and find me that cup. No cup, let me remind you, no deal.'

In the final glimmerings of light from the sky, I saw Shahin step across to the rail and lean so he could stare down into the boat that had brought Simon out from the City. Simon followed. They began discussing the preparedness of the 'chosen ones'. I could have stayed where I was, waiting to learn who these 'chosen ones' were and what they were expected to do. But I'd heard enough. Because we were passing into a darkness barely moderated by the stars and a thin sliver of moon, I only had to keep the pair of us from making a noise. I got myself in front of Antonia and hurried to the other side of the cabin wall. Bad luck that I bumped straight into one of the Syrians. Without any noise I'd troubled to hear, he'd got himself in my way. The first I knew of him was when his bearded chin made contact with my chest.

The bad luck, I should explain, was his. I still had a knife in my hand. Even as he drew breath to call for help, I took his beard in my left hand and pulled sharply up. I rammed the knife into the right side of his neck and pulled outward until I'd severed his windpipe. I silenced his last bubbling breath by clutching him to my chest. I held him tight as his blood sprayed warm over me, then laid him quietly down. I stood upright and wiped blood from my eyes. I looked down. So far as I could tell, the front of my body was covered in blood. It was a sudden and welcome barrier against the night chill. It made me more invisible in the dark.

Antonia was already round the corner on the far side from where Shahin was giving instructions to his Greek traitor. If the tiny moon was behind us on the right, this meant that we'd be looking west, which was the direction in which it seemed best to try swimming. I rounded the corner and, all else forgotten, I stood beside her and looked in astonished silence.

Though in darkness, we were already passing along the narrow strait that would take the ship into the Black Sea. Not three hundred yards away, Constantinople was a blaze of artificial light. I could clearly see the shape of the Great Church, and of the other high buildings. I could follow the whole line of the sea wall from the beacons that burned every twenty yards along it. It was the most astonishingly beautiful sight. I don't think any other city in the world could match what I saw. If a man saw nothing else, this alone was enough to tell him everything he needed to know about the size and glory of Constantinople.

Passing so close by the City that a man on board could almost cry out to another man on the walls – and by night – was as audacious as anything I'd yet seen from Shahin. But it made perfect sense. You can't expect to last long in your enemy's home waters by skulking from inlet to inlet. Anyone looking out from the walls able to see our shape would assume we were hurrying past in the dark to avoid payment of tolls.

I pulled Antonia closer. 'Do you see that gap in the lights?' I asked, pointing. 'It should be the Emperor's private harbour. Swim towards the left-hand side. I'll be close behind you.' She twisted free and pushed herself harder against the wall. She whimpered something that I couldn't make out. I took her firmly by the arm and led her towards the rail. 'We'll jump together,' I urged.

'Not thinking to leave us so soon, Alaric?' I heard Shahin say from my right. Someone beside him pulled the cover off a lamp and I saw the gleam of a sword in Shahin's hand.

16

'I told you to kill him while you could,' Simon cried. He was holding the lamp at waist level. It was easy to see that he was indeed the man who'd brought me the alleged letter from Nicetas. He'd changed out of his fussy robe and was wearing a turban that made him look faintly oriental. But the squint and the bearded face were unmistakeable.

Shahin lowered his sword. 'There will be no killing tonight,' he said. He stepped forward. 'Alaric, things are not entirely as they seem,' he continued in Persian, 'Let's go below to discuss matters like civilised men. You have my personal guarantee of safety. The Great King himself has commanded not a hair of your head to be touched.' He smiled. 'Come, dear friend. Come down and have a wash. You can even put your clothes on.'

As he handed his sword to one of his Syrians, I felt two men take hold of me from each side. 'You can cover the lamp,' he said in Greek to Simon. 'We can't risk being seen from shore.' He stepped past me, on his way into the deck cabin.

I'd got this far. Nothing short of overpowering force would get me below again. I untensed my body and raised my arms as if to begin pleading. Of a sudden, and relying on the blood that still made me slippery, I twisted free and rounded on the men behind me. One got my knife into his stomach. The other saved himself by sprawling backwards. I tore Antonia from the man who was trying to drag her away from the side and pulled her towards me.

'You're going nowhere!' Simon shouted triumphantly. He stepped towards me, and I saw the glitter of a knife in his raised hand. I think I heard a shouted order from Shahin.

'Fuck you!' I snarled. Ignoring his knife, I shoved his left hand hard against his body. That was the hand in which he still carried his lamp. Soaked in oil, his robe caught fire. He jumped back and dabbed at himself, shrieking as yet only with fear.

I hear the rasp of a sword and, in the light cast from Simon's burning robe, saw a man lunge at me. I went for him with my knife and, with a crunch of iron against teeth, got him through both cheeks. As he fell down in a sobbing scream, Antonia was pulled from my bloody left hand.

'No killing!' Shahin bellowed above the babble of shouted Syriac and the screams of those I'd injured. 'Just keep hold of the girl.' I turned away from the huddle of armed men who were now retreating from me. Someone had Antonia from behind and was pawing at her breasts. 'Put the knife down, Alaric,' Shahin took up again in a loud and desperately calm voice. 'Put the knife down, or she gets her face carved off.'

Someone had put Simon out and we were down to the light from the sky. But I saw the light reflected in the little knife Antonia had brought with her on deck. She sagged suddenly forward and twisted partly free. I watched as she brought the shining steel up and thrust it with desperate and unerring strength into the man's right eye. I'd underestimated her in a crisis, I thought approvingly.

Even before the screaming man hit the deck, I had Antonia's arm again. I threw my knife at someone who was hurrying forward to clutch at me. I took her in both arms and threw myself backwards over the rail. A moment later, she and I were coming up for air in a sea that was like black and liquid ice.

'Get the boat – the boat!' I heard Shahin roar above the babble of shrieks from the ship. 'I want them both alive.' I caught hold of Antonia's hair and pulled her close beside me. She'd got herself afloat but was crying out from shock and the cold. She wasn't up to much directed effort. I looked about for the lights of Constantinople. They seemed much dimmer and more distant at sea level.

Swimming with one arm, I dragged her forward until we had to be out of view from the mirrored lamps that Shahin's men had now brought up on deck. 'Get on my back,' I gasped, taking in a mouthful of salt water. 'Put your arms about my neck and hold on.' I stretched my arms into a wide arc and kicked in the direction of the shore. Shahin had seen me swim the Euphrates in July. That's wholly different from sea swimming at night – sea swimming at night with two arms clamped round your neck. But thoughts of Chosroes were a useful spur. By the time I stopped to see if we were still going in the right direction, the babble of shouts on board the ship was already a few hundred feet away. So far as I could tell, they still hadn't got Simon's boat or their own into action. I took a long breath and struck forward again.

Antonia loosened her grip on me. 'Let me come off you,' she cried in soft panic. 'I can swim by myself.' I slowed again and looked up to tell her not to be so stupid. One look at the shore and I realised what she was getting at. The long strait past Constantinople has a top current and an undercurrent. Their relative strength varies according to the time of day. No one with any sense ever tries to swim there. The currents are too dangerous. Even as I made for the shore, I could see it moving further and further to my right. If we didn't get a move on, we'd be swept into the wide Propontis.

'Keep hold of me,' I said in a voice that shook with cold and a fear I couldn't control. 'One big effort and I *can* do this.' I wasn't sure I could. But it seemed a fair guess that she couldn't and that she'd vanish the moment she let go of me. I looked again at the now fast-moving lights on the wall and pointed myself right. Leaving Antonia to hold on as best she could, I strained every muscle as I darted forward. Now I was swimming diagonally with the current, low waves kept sweeping over me. I thought once I'd have to stop to cough out a whole lungful of water. But I kept thinking of a boat rowed by terrorised Syrians, hurrying to get in front of us. I thought of Shahrbaraz and the very stiff bow he'd give me as I was shoved forward into his presence. I thought again of Chosroes. And I thought of the swirling, limitless waters of a Propontis that might begin only a hundred yards to my left. Antonia moving her own body in time with mine, I called on every reserve of strength and swam toward the lights.

I was still swimming when Antonia slid off me and stood up to her waist. I felt cold where she'd been against my back and tipped myself upright. After a boyhood spent swimming in the Channel off Richborough, it was no surprise how warm the sea now felt on the rest of my body – nor how cold I felt out of the water. I crouched down, with my head out of the water and my feet bouncing on the smooth boulders placed all about the sea walls to stop any ship from landing. From what I could see of the wall, we weren't far from the Golden Gate. When I did finally stand up properly, I should be able to see the night beacon on top of the Marble Tower.

Antonia splashed down beside me. 'I think they're coming after us,' she breathed through chilled lips. I nodded. I'd expected no less. I turned and looked out to sea. The light that was coming closer might be from one of our own patrols. But I didn't think it was. I shook more water from my ears and tried to listen. The voices were too deliberately low for me to hear other than they weren't Greek. I felt Antonia take me by the wrist and pull me behind a large boulder. I slipped lower into the water and stared at the crescent moon. We'd got away! There was now the matter of getting back inside the City. I was knocked out. Now I'd stopped moving, the sea was feeling cold again. The wind would make us colder. It would be at least half a mile to the nearest gate and that would be barefoot over ground that some very clever engineers had made difficult to cross in shoes. But sod all this – we'd got away.

'Alaric!' I heard Shahin call from perhaps a dozen yards away. I froze with the shock of his voice and sank in up to my neck. He went on in Persian: 'Alaric! I know you didn't drown. You're here somewhere and listening to me. There are matters we need to discuss. I have a deal I should have put to you over dinner. You must believe I am your safest option. Come out and join me in this boat. Bring the girl or leave her. She's no longer important.'

He drew breath to say more. But I didn't hear. As he'd been calling out to me in a language she didn't understand, Antonia was pulling me behind a clump of boulders where the water shelved to about nine inches. At once, her cold lips were pressed against mine, and her body was joined to mine. If I've suggested I was wholly worn out from that wild dash through the sea, I'd be exaggerating. I had energy enough to go with Antonia into a world of intense and sustained pleasure, and to stay there for what seemed a very long time.

I moved away from her for the last time and realised we were both up to our waists again in the cold sea. Her face drained of expression, Antonia was staring up at the moon and the wide carpet of stars. 'You didn't leave me,' she said in a wondering voice. 'You're the first man I've known who didn't betray me.'

I thought what reply to make. Even then, I was a man who could speak and write to effect in many languages. I might have told her things that a poet would have envied. But the time for words was drifting by. What to say, though? Women are strange creatures. When you aren't completely certain what to tell them, it's best to say nothing at all.

I got up and climbed on to one of the larger boulders. I put down a hand to pull her beside me. We sat together in silence. Though I was chilled through from the sea and from all that had gone before that, the City wall was shelter from the wind. Without that, the night was what in England would have counted as sultry. I could remember a night rather like this in Cornwall when, to the distant sound of hunting horns, I'd been diverted from stealing sheep to the final and glorious loss of my virginity. I hadn't been at all cold then. I'd soon warm up now. I listened for any sound of voices. I heard only the soft chirruping behind me of the night insects. I stood up and looked across the sea. The moon lit up a long streak of water. The stars gave all else a dim and silvery glitter. On the far side of the strait, there were individual gleams of light from the palaces and the better remnants of what had once been the Asiatic suburbs of Constantinople. So far as I could tell, the sea was empty.

Antonia stood up and looked across the sea. After another long silence, she turned to me. I saw her eyes glitter in the starlight. 'Alaric,' she said. I waited for what she might have to say. She looked away. 'What happened?' she asked in a voice no longer charged with significance. 'What did those men want?'

I put my arm about her and I felt a tremor run through my body. It went on a long time, and ended in an explosion of unseen light deep within my chest. Not caring whether she could feel anything of this, I smiled and continued looking out over the faintly glowing sea. 'I currently have no idea,' I said. 'But I do plan to find out.' I pulled her closer. 'It's treason and with Persian support,' I went on. 'You can be sure of that. The question is how something this big can go on in broad daylight, apparently unseen by the Intelligence Bureau.'

'Could it have been Eunapius?' she broke in with an eagerness she didn't try to hide. 'Could it have been him and the Emperor's cousin, Ni – Nicephorus?'

'Nicetas,' I corrected her. It was a good question. 'Did you notice the Greek beside Shahin?' I asked. 'He was the one with the lamp. He spoke at this morning's audience.'

She nodded. 'He came up to me when I was with my – *my clients.*' She paused for me to register the slight but defiant emphasis of the words. 'He pointed me in the direction you'd gone and told me to stay out of sight until I could surprise you outside the walls. I think he'd guessed I wasn't a man.'

I stared at the crescent moon until the urge to burst out laughing had passed. '*She's a nuisance for other reasons,*' Simon had said. What could that have been if it wasn't connected in some way with Eunapius?

I shivered slightly after so long without movement. I reached up to brush a hand over very hard nipples. I noted the immediate response in my groin. But this was something I must and could control. 'I won't rule Nicetas out,' I said cautiously. 'But I can't see him as a traitor. Besides, all that's happened today needed fast communications, not to mention a capacity for decision that I haven't seen in Nicetas or any of his creatures.'

'And where do I stand in this?' she asked as if she hadn't heard me. Once more, her voice had taken on a wondering, almost a dreamy tone.

I looked at her. She had the pale glow of the city walls behind her and her face was in comparative darkness. The moment for speaking had passed beyond recall. 'Let's get inside the walls,' I said. I turned and climbed down from this boulder on to another. I helped her down beside me and looked over at the walls. I'd seen the white dust of a path. If we could get across an expanse of smaller stones, and then a mass of brambles without cutting ourselves, we might soon be able to present ourselves in reasonably good order before the Golden Gate.

17

'You have seen naked men before?' I asked impatiently. Now we'd rounded the corner where land and sea walls met, we were back in a chill wind.

The guard's mouth twitched slightly. 'Never a naked Lord Treasurer, Sir,' he said. I scowled. But he'd had his fun. His face vanished from the inspection window ten feet above. A moment later, I heard the scrape of bolts in the tiny door beside the main gate. A few moments more and I was sitting with Antonia in what seemed an astonishingly warm room, a cup of wine in my hand.

The guard finished shaking the dust from two dark cloaks he'd found in a cupboard. 'It's a proper relief to see you, My Lord,' he said. 'We'd been fearing the worst ever since your clothes was found close by them dead bodies. There's talk of sending a fast galley off to tell the Emperor.'

'Then we can be glad his communion with the monks of Saint Vesalius will not now be disturbed,' I said. The last thing I fancied was a summons along the straits to Cyzicus, or – much worse – a sudden return by Heraclius. Whatever else he did, he'd drag me into a church and keep me there praying and fasting till I wished I was still with Shahin.

The guard sat down before me. He dropped his voice. 'What *was* you doing out there, if you don't mind my asking?' He looked from the corner of his eyes at Antonia, who'd wrapped herself in one of the cloaks and was looking ready to fall asleep. 'She's a nice bit of tail, Sir,' he whispered. 'But you can't have been fucking her all afternoon and evening. And what about all them bodies? Most of them was shot with arrows. Also, didn't I see you go out through my gate with a young man?'

I finished my wine and pushed the cup forward for a refill. I'd made my promise to Antonia. Now was the time to keep it. 'When you send in your report,' I said, 'I'd like it to say that I turned up alone at your gate and fully clothed.' The guard frowned. I looked about the room. 'There's been much speculation about the design on the back of the new silver coins. I'm sure you'd like to be among the first to see the design for yourself – shall we say enough copies to fill that leather bag over there?' The man pursed his lips. Then he nodded. I smiled wearily at him. 'I'm glad that was so quickly arranged,' I said. 'Now, if you can find two suits of plain clothes for the pair of us, we'll be on our way.'

The guard shook his head. 'Can't do that, Sir. It's quiet enough out here. But the mob's taken over all the central streets and is celebrating your death. You'll have to wait while I send off for an armoured chair to get you home.'

As if on cue, I heard a distant sound of cheering. It came from deep within the City, and reminded me of the solid roar a winning charioteer gets in the Circus.

You never realise the full convenience of a secret entrance to your palace until you need to make a secret entrance. A hundred feet each side of the main entrance, the Triumphal Way was packed with the City trash, dancing round bonfires, or just cheering themselves hoarse at their apparent liberation from my spending cuts. But I was snug inside the thick walls of my palace before most of the household could know that I was alive, let alone insist on embracing me, one after the other.

'I didn't believe any harm had been allowed to come to you,' Theodore said, once he'd got over the shock of seeing me in the chapel. It was a double shock, I might say – seeing me, *and* in the chapel. Pale and sad, his face wavered in the light of many candles. 'I prayed before the icon of Saint George. It has never let me down.' He got off his knees and embraced me. I can't say our relationship had ever been affectionate. It hadn't been that sort of adoption. Still, I liked to think there was a certain regard between us. I kissed his greasy forehead, noting how he'd shot up in the past few months. If he didn't come up to my chest, he was no longer short for thirteen.

I looked about the unfamiliar room. With Martin away, the boy must be lonely in here. Oh, but silly me – you're never alone in a House of God! 'Where is Maximin?' I asked.

'I had him put to bed at the usual time, My Lord,' Theodore answered. 'I told the nursemaids to say nothing without my permission.' I nodded. Looking at his sallow face and lack of bodily shape, no one could imagine Theodore was other than adopted. But, as well as much holiness, he had a frequently sound judgement. It compensated for the holiness. It even compensated for his lack of attention to personal hygiene and his absolute refusal to contemplate stripping for daily exercise in the gymnasium.

I looked again about the chapel. No wonder I'd nearly passed out on entering. The boy had five sticks of incense on the go. Should I tell him this stuff cost more than its weight in gold? 'Where is Father Macarius?' I asked instead. Since I'd been nagged into hiring a chaplain, I could go through the motions of annoyance that he wasn't beside Theodore to pray for my safety.

'He's giving comfort to the eunuch who was struck dumb this morning,' Theodore said. He saw the blank look on my face. 'It was after you went out,' he explained. 'The older eunuch – the one with the fine voice – died suddenly of a bloody flux while easing himself in the latrine. His assistant fell down shortly after, and may not see the morning.'

That was a shame and an oddity. I would have asked more, but I noticed the boy was now looking past me. 'Ah, Theodore,' I said, turning to wave Antonia forward, 'this is . . .'

'I am Antony,' she said, stepping forward with outstretched hand. 'Your father saved me from the bandits. I am eternally grateful.' She pulled her military cloak into place and tried for a manly smile. I pulled a disapproving face at her. Keeping her any longer than tonight in male clothing hadn't been on my list of things to do. If she thought she could run a petitioning business from the Lord Alaric's palace, she could think again. But she ignored me.

'Your father is the bravest man I've ever met,' she added. 'You must be terribly proud of him.'

'Our guest will be staying with us till further notice,' I sighed. This wasn't the time or place for complications.

Oh, bugger! I'd no sooner let this new moment for truth go past, when I turned back to Theodore and saw how red his face had gone. The redness was followed by a look of exalted longing. 'I am delighted to make your acquaintance, Antony,' he croaked. He put out a shaking hand and bit his lip hard as she took it. He looked down at the mosaic floor. 'Shall I arrange a temporary bed?' he whispered. 'Or has Samo already been informed?'

I glared again at Antonia. I was already feeling nostalgic for a household in which the only females allowed were there to cook and clean and generally do as I told them. I'd put off one complication and raised another. I could still have taken charge and made a joke of telling Theodore about our little deception. But his face had settled into the look of rapturous agony you see described in Sappho and Catullus. Theodore *had* been growing up, I could see. It was time for me to attend to the next stage in his education. But that wouldn't begin with a brutal and public disabusing.

'Samo will attend to everything,' I said. I pretended to misunderstand Theodore's look and smiled. 'Now, do go down to the kitchens and find Samo,' I said. 'I sent him there to arrange celebrations for the household. It may be worth reminding him of the need to keep every man sober who can handle arms. If word goes round that I'm alive, the mob may take a battering ram to the main gate. I'm sure you remember how much it cost to replace the bronze facings there after the last riot.'

'You may leave us,' I said in Lombardic. 'Ask Samo to attend on me alone at dawn.' The young slave bowed and, having dimmed the lamps, padded out. I shut the door behind him and almost fell out of my clothes.

I sat down and watched Antonia tug at the unfamiliar laces of her own clothes. She'd seen the massive luxury of my palace and my own absolute mastery within it. It seemed no more to throw her than the sight of my naked body had earlier in the day. 'What is to be my status here?' she asked in a tired but businesslike tone.

'My steward has his orders,' I said, avoiding the main question. She frowned slightly, before coming forward to let me help her from her under tunic. Naked, she sat down beside me. She put up a hand to arrange hair that she realised too late was no longer there. She frowned again and seemed about to ask another pointed question. Beyond a certain level, the real purpose of luxury is to intimidate. I couldn't doubt it had failed with Antonia.

I thought whether I should put my arm about her. I decided against. 'Until I can puzzle out today's events,' I explained, 'I do think you'll be safest inside these walls. Your own living and sleeping quarters will be ready by morning. You can send off to your lodgings for anything you want here with you.'

She lay back on the bed and looked thoughtfully up at the ceiling. 'There's nothing I particularly want,' she said. 'I'd like to send some messages. But I'm sure you'll urge me against that.' She pulled at the silk covers. 'Can I take it that the slaves you assign me aren't the talkative sort?'

I got into the bed with her and moved a few inches towards her. 'This is a household of many secrets and of many corresponding layers,' I said. 'Until further notice, most of the slaves will know you as Antony. Those who attend on you as Antonia will say nothing.' I snuggled closer and wondered if sex was out of the question. Even as I reached for her naked body, though, she was asleep. I moved towards her and took her in my arms. Without any sense of change, fierce and joyous lust had given way to an odd happiness. I buried my face in the salty taste of her hair. Before I could fall to wondering about all that had happend, I was myself asleep.

Bathed in sweat, heart still pounding from the horror of my dream, I woke in a completely dark silence that suggested the dawn couldn't be far away. I was still holding Antonia. She'd moved in her sleep and her own arms were tight about my chest. I shut my eyes and willed myself to sleep. But, though I'd had one of those nightmares where the details fade like the morning frost in Kent, enough sense remained of its overpowering fear and helplessness to keep me awake.

I untangled myself from Antonia and went over to wash myself in scented water. I caught a flicker of light from the balcony window. I slipped through the curtains and pulled the glazed door open. I went out into the renewed chill of night and looked down over the Triumphal Way. No longer celebrating, the mob was still far below, still blocking the entire width of the street before my ceremonial entrance. Resembling nothing so much in size and shape as animal droppings, I could see the dark bodies, stretched out and sleeping beside the dying bonfires. In the morning, these parodies of the human form would shamble off to whatever they did by day – or, if they didn't wake in time, would be flogged about their business by the Prefect's deputy. Shortly after, I'd have it formally announced that I was alive. What details my announcement would carry I hadn't yet decided. There was no doubt, however, it would set off a chorus of lamentation in every district where the inhabitants didn't work for their daily bread.

I leaned on the pitted marble and looked across the dark city to where it merged into the greater darkness of the sea. The street lighting had long since been left to burn itself out. But, here and there, in high towers or in the windows of palaces as immense as my own, there were the bright points that indicated some late activity. I breathed in and smiled. Somewhere out to sea, Shahin might by now have drunk himself to sleep. No doubt, he'd remit all the floggings and impalings he'd promised his crew in return for their silence over his failed capture of the Great King's only successful enemy. I thought about Simon. I had told myself to keep it all out of mind till morning. But, as I stood up and walked back inside, I could feel a connecting thread begin to run itself through some of the facts of the past day. I listened to the slow and regular breathing that came from my bed. Thinking about anything at all should be left to the morning.

I was looking at the dim shape of the bed, when I heard a familiar cough.

'I was in no doubt you'd survive the murder attempt,' a voice called out from behind a screen. 'It must have been a close shave, though, if, having brought a woman back, you just fall asleep and babble half the night in what sounded like Syriac but wasn't.' I hurried across to the bed. Eyes still closed, Antonia had rolled over to my side.

'Don't worry, dearest Alaric,' the voice said again. 'The girl's fast asleep. You should be more concerned about the inability of your barbarian sots to notice the man who broke into *our* palace this evening.' He laughed and there was the loud click of a box closing. 'I kept him alive a while for questioning. Among much else that made fuck all sense, he spoke about a cup. Would you believe he was here to steal a cup from you? 'I regret that the only place I could hide the body was under your bed. But please don't think ill of poor old Uncle Priscus for that.' He sniffed up whatever powder he'd chosen and followed this with a long groan of ecstasy.

'Do tell me about this cup,' he went on at last. 'I really am all ears.'

18

It may be age, or opium, or the nature of what I'm trying to explain, that requires this to be a narrative of digressions, and that these often involve abrupt shifts of time. However, Antonia won't mind if she's left sleeping, unmolested, in my big and wondrously soft bed. Priscus can nurse his box of drugs. The mob – well, let the mob drowse over dying bonfires, and enjoy the immemorial privilege of making trouble: I'm not revealing much if I say it was a privilege with a longer past than future.

You, my Dear Reader, I'll simply assure that this is the last of my deviations. So let us leave the world of 615 – the year when Alaric the Farsighted brought in the new silver coinage – and go back two and a half years. We go back to the December of 612, a week after I had returned with Priscus and various other companions from nine months of adventuring in the outer provinces of the Empire.

'Oh, come on, Martin,' I said. 'It's stopped raining and we'll be ever so early if we carry on by chair.' I jumped down and, avoiding the other traffic, hurried across the road into Imperial Square. I looked up at the sky. We'd had heavy rain since dawn and Martin had insisted on a covered chair – 'You can't think of turning up on foot!' he'd said, aghast. But the clouds were now rolling by. We might even have a spot of sunshine to light up proceedings in the Senate House.

I turned back to Martin. 'As your former master and as your only friend,' I said firmly, 'I command you to climb out of that chair and walk for one mile with me. Our fine outer clothes can stay in the chair. So can your writing things. That's quite enough weight for the poor slaves to carry uphill. Now, you come over here and take a little health-giving exercise.'

The oiled curtains twitched and then parted. Slowly, and with a glance at the sky and a hurt look at me, Martin waited for one of the carrying slaves to bring round the little steps that were for the use of invalids and the aged. Avoiding a puddle, he stepped down beside me. As he did, a gust of wind took his hat and carried it a dozen yards into one of the bleak flower beds. With a laugh, I ran after it. As I brought it back, Martin was patting the last of his hair back into the elaborate weave that, in poor light and seen only from the front, gave the momentary impression of a man who wasn't actually as bald on top as a boiled egg.

I took him by the arm and led him towards the Imperial statues and a ritual of the aged that had been only delayed by the rain. He came to a sudden stop and looked at the wide steps that led up to the Triumphal Way. I could almost hear the scream inside his head of 'a hundred and twenty steps!' He walked over to a stone bench and flopped down. He pulled his hat harder on to his head and, glaring at me from under its brim, looked very like a donkey that has shed its load and is refusing to walk another inch.

I stood before him. 'Just look at these men,' I said, trying to hide my annoyance – 'every one of them old enough to be your father and fit enough to be your son!'

Martin stopped trying not to wheeze from the hundred yards we'd just covered on the flat. I sat beside him on a dry part of the bench. I put a hand on his shoulder and dropped my voice. 'Listen, Martin,' I said urgently, 'you've heard the doctor. If you don't take action now, your heart really will go pop.'

That only got me one of his despairing looks. 'Does it matter?' he asked. 'We're back in the spider's web. We'll never get away now.' He put both hands over his eyes and rocked back and forth till the rolls of fat on his body set up a rippling of his outer tunic that I found distressing to watch.

I got up again and stood over Martin. 'You prepared the reading text of the speech I've written,' I said. 'You know perfectly well that we don't need to get away. We're in the clear.'

I might have pointed out that we'd effectively been prisoners since leaving Alexandria. There had been no chance of escape from the Viceroy's ship, nor – unless, that is, we fancied the certainty of barbarians on land and pirates at sea – anywhere to run to from Athens or from Corinth. I didn't want to think when was the last time we hadn't been travelling about in a gilded cage. I was sure this approach would only send Martin into an attack of the vapours that would keep him here for the rest of the day.

I took him by the hand and pulled him to his feet. 'Look around you!' I hissed. 'Look at this great and wonderful city. Look at its clean pavements and magnificent buildings. Think of its libraries, filled with every book ever written that is worth reading. Think of its comforts, of its delicacies. Think of our own leading part in its defence and improvement. If none of this strikes you as worthwhile, think at least of the oath I swore to Heraclius. Greeks may break their oaths. You know that we don't. Now, stop this lachrymose bleating about the joys of omnipresent dirt and squalid poverty. We were both happy enough to get away from that. And, if you see Ireland through rosy window glass, that isn't how I see England. *I'm never going back!*'

I let my face relax. I linked arms with Martin. 'Now come on,' I said soothingly. 'I'll help you and we'll do the stairs a dozen at a time. We're not in any hurry. There's plenty of time to rest between exertions.'

'You're looking pleased with yourself,' Priscus said, catching me unawares. 'Did you stop by a brothel on your way here?' He'd put on his purple-edged toga over his uniform as Commander of the East. On anyone else, the resulting mix would have looked absurd. Now that illness had stripped away nearly every ounce of flesh from his body, the extreme padding suited Priscus.

'Yes, *very* pleased with yourself, if you don't mind my saying,' someone added from behind in the drawl of a court eunuch. 'After all, it wasn't *you* who got past my guards to the Emperor. It wasn't *you* who put his side of the story. For which of us three, I wonder, has that closed carriage been parked behind this place of deliberation?'

I didn't turn. 'Piss off, Ludinus!' I said. 'Or do you fancy an accidental cup of wine down your front?' I stared past Priscus to where Martin was nagging some slaves to get my ivory stool the right way round. As they lined it up again, he looked about the wide space between the semicircle where the Senators would sit and the Imperial Throne. Unable to see that I was watching him, he stuffed another honeyed oatcake into his mouth. 'A moment of the lips, a lifetime on the hips,' I'd announced when the first tray was uncovered. A waste of breath that had been. I turned to look the Grand Chamberlain in the face.

'Though he may possess two objects that bring more trouble than joy,' he went on, 'the Commander of the East has all the faithless treachery proverbially ascribed to my own species.' He stepped back and tried for one of his dramatic poses. The movement of his outstretched arms sent off a miasma of rose perfume that blotted out the general stink in the room of stale sweat soaked into wool. 'According to my report of the audience,' he sniggered, 'the Lord Priscus is to be godfather to the Emperor's son. He got this by feeding the man a pack of lies and even blaming dear young Alaric for the massacre *he* unleashed in Alexandria.' His jowls wobbled and his mouth fell open to show a double line of stained and broken teeth.

Priscus fought to suppress one of his coughing fits. The last one I'd seen, a few days earlier, had involved a gush of foul-smelling blood. Ludinus stared complacently at him. 'So much ambition in a dying man,' he said in a bleak and almost uncastrated voice. He looked again at me. 'If Caesar makes you a junior professor of Greek in Catania, you can thank my intercession,' he said. 'If it's blinding in a monastery, Priscus managed just a little too well to spread the slander you made up about my dealings with the barbarians. I can promise that I will see to that!'

Someone whose face showed more than a few hundred years of marriage between cousins now took Priscus by the sleeve. His eyes caught mine for just a moment, then glazed over as if I'd been about to ask for a loan. As they went off together into the main crowd of Senators, I heard the beginning of a fawned request for preferment. That left me alone with Ludinus. It was unwelcome company in itself. It also reminded me that I was as much an outsider in this place as he was. Those little cold looks we'd been getting from men who wore their Senatorial robes as easily as if they'd been born in them weren't only for a eunuch promoted beyond his physical right.

Without troubling to excuse myself, I turned and walked away from Ludinus. I almost knocked into someone who'd stepped in my way. I nodded an apology and found myself looking into more glazed eyes. Behind me, there was one of those tidal movements you get in gatherings of convivial humanity, and I heard someone let out a barking laugh. 'Couldn't agree with you more, Rufus,' it may have been the laughing man who spoke. 'The only way to get the common people working at all is to keep them hungry. Take the goad off their backs, give them land – and it's *our* land, mind you! – why, isn't that just a recipe for idleness? As for arming them – well, I ask you why we're bothering to fight the Persians, when we're at risk of being murdered in our beds!' I turned and found myself looking into a mass of suddenly blank faces. I continued looking and a couple of men brought out the shifty, speculative smiles of those who are willing to keep all options open. Everyone else, without openly shunning me, always managed to be looking the other way as I passed by. Someone had been busy with his tongue, I could see.

Trying to seem genuinely interested, I stood where the sequence of wall paintings began. This was the Senate House and it was decorated without concession to the artificiality of the order it housed. The pictures were all of events in the history of the *Roman* Senate. Here were the Senators, calmly awaiting massacre by the Gauls. Here was Cato, demanding that Carthage should be destroyed. Here was the formal condemnation of Nero for treason against the State. The captions were in Latin, though most had recently been supplemented by Greek translations. I looked hard at the final painting, in which the Great Constantine was managing to speak at the same time to the Senate Houses in Rome and

Constantinople. In each place, the Senators were reaching out to those in the other. They were embraces of shared blood and history, of common loyalty to the Roman State – embraces that ultimately had stood for nothing in Constantinople when it proved convenient to wave goodbye to the Western provinces.

Priscus put a bony hand on my arm. Then he leaned his remaining weight on me to steady himself. 'The old eunuch's a liar,' he said wearily. 'I fucked him over with Heraclius beyond hope of repair. I showed the severed finger and everything.' I said nothing, but moved Priscus towards our own ivory stools. So long as I didn't let my arm shake, it might look as if he were leading me to my place. 'You don't believe that I've shat on you, Alaric?' he asked, still weary, though with a trace of concern. 'We always knew it had to be me who saw the Great Augustus first. I *am* head of the old aristocracy. Not even the whole tribe of eunuchs could deny me an audience. I told Heraclius the complete truth – well, I told him the truth as you wrote it up once we'd left Alexandria. You keep your land law. I go off to keep the Persians out of Syria.'

I pretended to fuss with my toga. It gave him cover from the main crowd of Senators as he drank one of his potions from a glass bottle. I had no doubt this would perk him up in time for the audience. How much time he'd have after that was anyone's guess.

'How many times have I tried to kill you?' he asked, his spirits already rising. My tally was eight. But I said nothing. Some of these probably counted as misplaced signs of affection. For others, I could doubt where to draw the line between outright murder attempts and conspiracies just to get me out of his way. Priscus smiled. 'Something I want you always to know, Alaric, is that our personal interests and our beliefs about what is good for the Empire are as one. *We stand or fall together.*'

I looked down and smiled at him. 'My thoughts entirely,' I said.

I was wondering what more to say, when, with a sudden whoosh of stale air, the doors flew open and the first of the heralds came in with their silver trumpets. All about us, the babble of laughing conversation died away and every man who wasn't already there made a dignified scurry for his seat.

19

At a hidden command, the trumpeters let out an ear-splitting blare of sound. More came in behind them, and then I saw the gold armour of the Emperor's personal guard. With more trumpet blasts, they marched steadily down the aisle that divided the Senators into equal blocks and stood to attention in the semi-circle we'd vacated.

He might have been a statue, for all he could move his face under its double layer of gold leaf. But I could hear the smirk in his voice as the eunuch chosen by Ludinus to stand in his place waved his staff of office at us. '*Long may our Great Augustus reign!*' he shrilled in Latin.

'*Long indeed and well may He reign!*' we called back in unison.

The eunuch was drawing breath to lead a more complex acclamation. It came out as a long squeal of shock. I ignored the elbow the Priscus jabbed in my side and looked steadily at the eunuch. I didn't need to see that Sergius was out of prison and dressed once more in his patriarchal best. 'Oh, for one look into that black heart!' Priscus breathed. 'Oh, the despair that must be welling up inside it!' But that was something I could see. Ludinus was a few places from the front on the other side of the aisle. I had an unbroken view of his suddenly strained and sweaty face. Without moving my head, I flicked my eyes about the room. Most faces carried the sort of look you see on men who are watching a slow collision of chariots in the Circus. They'd guessed there would be some change of Imperial favour. They hadn't expected a revolution.

Sergius stepped past the eunuch and raised his arms to Heaven. 'Glory be to God in the Highest,' he cried in Greek, 'and to His

Servant Heraclius, whom He has sent in goodness and in love to rule over the Roman People.'

As if this were a ceremony established since time out of mind, Priscus and I raised our arms. 'Glory, glory, glory be to God in the Highest,' we responded, also in Greek, 'and may victory and all good fortune attend Our Lord Emperor Heraclius, and His Heirs and Successors by Law appointed.' We waited for every other Senator to turn astonished heads in our direction. As we raised our arms again, the chant was taken up by two hundred voices. There was the crash of a cymbal just outside the door, followed by more trumpeting.

'He hasn't washed since the fall of Caesarea,' Priscus said without moving his lips. 'Be warned he smells like the bedding in a doss-house.'

In another break with protocol, Heraclius came in on foot, Sergius walking backwards before him. He'd also set aside the normal olive wreath for these events, and with it the last scrap of pretence that the Emperor was one temporarily important Senator addressing his colleagues, and was wearing his biggest golden crown. As he passed by us into the semicircle, the pair of us drew breath and cried in Greek: 'Praise be to the Lord Heraclius Faithful in Christ!' We paused and, with another loud drawing in of breath, led the whole Senate in the new acclamation. We continued with it until the Emperor had gone up the steps to his throne and the long train of his purple robe had been tucked out of the way. Now Sergius fell to his knees before the throne. 'We salute the Lord's Anointed,' he intoned, still in Greek. This, at least, was the signal everyone knew. We fell forward into our long prostration.

Afterwards, perched on my ivory seat, I looked across the room at Heraclius. Never mind his abstinence from soap and water – he was looking old in the light of day. He was bald. He was fat. His beard was more grey than golden. Above the beard, his face carried the look of a gambler who knows he's on a losing streak and doesn't know how to change it.

He kicked impatiently with both feet until he'd got his long silken train loose. I'd told Martin to prepare the reading copy in big letters so Heraclius could see his speech without having to lean forward. But he leaned forward anyway. '*Conscript Fathers*,' he began in Latin. So he carried on for a few sentences. After this, to general relief, his text switched into Greek. Martin had written out the accents for all the longer or less colloquial words. Here and there, he'd added a marginal gloss in Latin. I'd given the text to Heraclius the afternoon before and I knew that, if he'd not been able to memorise it, he'd read it through several times. And he had. At his age, there was nothing he could do about his strong Western accent but I could make sure he sounded competent in Greek.

It was a long speech. The year since he'd last called the Senate together had been crowded with events. If none was cause for celebration, custom required many of them to be noticed. I listened, at every pause wondering if he'd carry on along the path I'd laid out for him or if he'd go off on some possibly fatal deviation. After every pause, I heard my own words read back at me. There was the earthquake and tidal wave in the Black Sea, the raising of the dead in Petronella, the loss to the Persians of our last outpost in Cappadocia, the defection to the Persians of a mountain race whose name I'd left out because the Emperor couldn't pronounce it. No mention of the bloodbath Priscus had unleashed in Alexandria, or of my own unwitting contribution to making it inevitable. Nothing of how we'd saved Egypt from the Persians. Nothing of our saving Athens from the barbarians, or of the triumphant though closed religious council I'd run there. I'd left them out of the speech and no one had thought to put them in. It went on as predictably for me as a lesson read out in church.

We were at the key passage. 'Come forward, Priscus, my beloved Commander of the East,' he called. Once or twice during the unfashionably direct and uncluttered prose Heraclius was reading, Priscus had given me a funny look. Now, without looking at me, he got up and walked towards the Throne. 'Priscus, I resolved when my son was born that there was one man alone in the Empire who was fit to be his godfather. That man was our greatest general – our shield against the Persian menace – and last posterity of a family that, in every generation since the most ancient days of our

Empire, had distinguished itself alike in the council chamber and on the field of battle.'

All about, I could hear the collective wiping of sweaty hands on togas. I swallowed and tried not to look at Priscus. He was kneeling with both arms stretched forward and I knew he was struggling not to cough. 'A few words of advice, however, I ask from my Commander of the East. When a man insults his Emperor, whom does he offend?' At once, the soft, collective rustle ceased and the room was quiet.

Priscus waited until his fit was past and he had full control of his voice. 'Who insults his Emperor surely offends God who has appointed the Emperor,' he managed to answer in a voice that I could barely hear. I darted my eyes to the right. A look of panic on his face, Ludinus was clearly wondering how far he'd get with his monstrous bulk before he was caught in a noose of silver chains.

Heraclius continued: 'And if a man, through cowardice and negligence, loses one of our choicest provinces to the enemy, and rages like a ravening animal through the second city of our Empire, should he receive a lenient sentence?' There was a long pause, then Priscus answered in a cowed stammer that I couldn't hear. By now, Heraclius was on his feet. Still reading from his text, he raised his voice. 'In every evil the Empire has suffered, you were involved as author or accomplice. You betrayed your lawful Emperor, Maurice of lamented memory, and helped bring to power Phocas the unmentionable tyrant. The Tyrant gave you his daughter in marriage, in spite of which you betrayed him to me. You have failed to defend the Empire. You have butchered its citizens. You were a bad son-in-law to one Emperor. You are a bad friend to another.'

In a movement I hadn't scripted, he snatched up all the pages of his text and threw them straight ahead. Priscus raised his hands up to protect his face and toppled forward. Heraclius stepped over his fallen body and looked about the hushed Senate. 'I declare Priscus guilty of high treason,' he shouted. 'I dismiss him from all his offices. I degrade him from the nobility of the Empire. I confiscate all his goods. I sentence him to be immured for the rest of his life in the Fortified Monastery outside the walls of Constantinople.'

As Heraclius stepped backward until he was just a yard or so in front of me, cries of horror broke out from every corner of the room. A few dozen men rushed forward and stood in a ring about Priscus. '*Accursed be the traitor!*' they shouted in Latin. *Let his name be forgotten. Let his final days be short and filled with bitterness.*' One or two of the men shuffled close to the Emperor and held up their ivory nametags for him to note and remember. Above the increasingly shrill and demented chorus of hate, I heard Priscus break out in a coughing fit. Then I heard someone clear his throat and spit. I heard more hawking and a long groan, as if someone had kicked the fallen man.

'You certainly know how to keep everyone guessing,' Ludinus said beside me. 'For just a moment there, I thought you were going back on our deal.' His face creased into a smile of relief. Trying not to ruin its double layer of paint, he dabbed at his face.

I looked over his shoulder at the two Imperial Guards who'd appeared and were awaiting my command. 'The Emperor has found you also guilty of high treason,' I said, looking at my fingernails. The smile froze on his lip. 'We decided you weren't worth a public denunciation. But the particulars will be shown to you in writing. Their burden is your conspiracy with the barbarians to destroy the cities of Attica.' Without moving my head, I looked up at him. 'If you make any fuss in here, Ludinus, I'll have your legs broken where no one can hear you scream. Your sentence is that you are to be taken to Athens, where the survivors from Decelea have been settled, there to serve in the military canteen. If you breathe a word of your real identity, or try claiming that you acted on orders from the Emperor, I have no doubt the unfortunate Deceleans will visit on you the punishment that you deserve.' I nodded at the guards. 'Take him away,' I said softly.

I remained on my stool. I stretched my legs and stared at the silk leggings below the lifted hem of my toga. I didn't watch as Ludinus was bundled out of the debating chamber – though some of the more reflective Senators had, and were now turning their hard, calculating faces in my direction. The eunuch had deserved his fate. Murder is murder and his hands were red with the blood of thousands. That besides, he'd been a fool – a fool for letting me charm my way past him to Heraclius, and for not having a competent spy in hiding whom I couldn't then corrupt. I felt more pity for squashed bugs than for this broken eunuch.

A couple of monks had joined Sergius, bowls of steaming water in their hands. Razor in his own hands, the Patriarch was pushing through the ring of Senators. Once he'd tonsured Priscus, the denunciations would cease. Priscus would then be a monk and entitled to some formality of consideration. The man would also have been ruled, by law and by public opinion, incapable of any return to favour. I could have pushed in behind Sergius and watched the infliction of this final punishment. It was richly deserved. From the day he'd got up and walked, Priscus had led a life of the utmost beastliness. Compared with him, Ludinus was clean.

But I didn't watch the humiliation. Paying no attention to Heraclius, I got up and walked from the room. I hurried though the main hall, crowded with carrying chairs and gossiping slaves, outside into the cold air. I walked a hundred yards along the Triumphal Way and stopped by the terrace overlooking Imperial Square. It was coming on to rain again and I squeezed myself under cover of a bronze Achilles that had been snatched from a derelict temple on Seriphos.

Through a mist of rain that blurred its outlines, I looked over the City. Justice aside, I'd landed an astonishing double blow. A Greek might spend his entire adult life plotting to achieve less than Alaric the underaged barbarian just had. At the next meeting of the Imperial Council, there would be no more Ludinus to spray out policies almost designed to bankrupt the State and impoverish the people. There would be no more Priscus to lead resistance to my creeping demolition of the land-owning nobility. There'd be me and there'd be Sergius. So long as we continued to agree on what was needed, Heraclius would poke his tongue between his teeth and write the lawful form of words on whatever sheet of parchment we chose to set before him.

I was thinking, though, of Priscus, Commander of the East. As well as snake and general obstructer, he was also the Empire's only competent general. He hadn't lost Cappadocia. If Heraclius hadn't turned up and demanded a battle, the blockade of the Persians in Caesarea would have finished the war on our terms. If I still couldn't understand the details of a campaign that involved endless marches from nowhere to nowhere, and that took in half the East, I'd believed Priscus when he said he could have defeated the Persians with never more than a skirmish. I'd now ruined him. The Empire he'd wanted to save would have been an oversized desert, squabbled over by tax gatherers and parasitic landlords. But what use would my alternative be, if it was swallowed up by the Persians one battle at a time?

I turned to stare at the Great Church. Fat lot of guidance that gave me. Once more, though now with rising guilt and misery, I went over reasonings that had seemed quite clear so long as I thought I was for the chop. I'd saved myself at the expense of men who had no claim on me – who had no abstract claim whatever to consideration. But what of the Empire and of its toiling millions I was supposed to be defending? Our fates were connected – but at what price?

I heard a shrill cry to my right. It was Martin, running towards me as fast as I'd seen him move in years. Outside the Senate House, several dozen men in togas were milling about, regardless of the rain.

'Aelric, Aelric,' he gasped in Celtic, too knocked out to address me in any civilised language. 'The Emperor was looking for you. He's granted you everything he confiscated from Priscus.' I went forward to catch him before he collapsed and helped him beneath the cover of an upturned shield. I perched him on the rim of a water basin and waited for him to finish struggling for breath. I noticed he was crying. 'Aelric, before he was taken out in chains, Priscus called to me in Slavic. He said that he'd been straight with you and that you'd made a terrible mistake.' Not speaking, I looked at Martin. Priscus would say that, I told myself. In a race of men who lied with as much compunction as whores or street beggars, he was the greatest liar I'd ever met. Priscus was a shifty, murdering degenerate. But there was now enough doubt in my mind to finish my decline into self-disgust.

I helped Martin to his feet and got him to a passing chair that was for hire. I had no choice but to stay and receive the gesticulating sycophants. They'd all now seen me and were scampering forward with arms outstretched, regardless of how the rain was spoiling their togas. I smiled and pretended not to notice as the best men in Constantinople kicked and punched each other for the right to be first to throw his arms about the knees of the new and undoubted favourite.

Was not of old the Jewish rabble's cry –

I quoted softly in Latin –

Hosanna first, and after Crucify?

The following spring, news came back that Chosroes had illuminated Ctesiphon for three days to celebrate the fall of Priscus – and then for another three when he heard that Heraclius had recalled Nicetas from Alexandria to be Commander of the East. With this came a report from one of our spies that General Kartir had been ordered to prepare a direct stab at Constantinople. He was to lead a small and highly mobile force through the mountain passes, before sweeping along the southern shore of the Black Sea. With our main forces already committed in Syria to face Shahrbaraz, we had nothing to put in his way. Heraclius responded by shutting himself away in his palace on the Asiatic shore. I sweated. I dithered. I did everything short of pray for guidance. What are you supposed to do when interest and duty so plainly collide? At last, I put out an announcement in the Emperor's name that I was being sent off to Rome to negotiate a loan from the Pope. That night, not telling even Martin what I was about, I set out alone.

I didn't see Constantinople again until the late October of 613.

20

Expressionless, the Abbot stared at the seal I'd affixed to my warrant. 'I don't recommend seeing him alone,' he said in the cold voice of a jailor. 'That he tried to kill a man is beside the point. The sin he has committed against God is not something to be specified in writing.' He continued looking at the seal. 'This is not a fit place to contain such evil,' he muttered.

I shook my head. The man had wasted enough of my afternoon already. 'You summoned me here on his behalf,' I said. 'I see no point in being here unless we can speak alone.'

The Abbot looked closer at the impression I'd made with the Great Seal. If I was here at his request, the warrant I'd thought to bring along gave me unquestionable authority to demand anything I cared. In silence, he made an entry on to a parchment roll, every sheet of which was stitched together and numbered. I wrote my name where he pointed and took in the other entries on the page. I was signing near the bottom. The top entry was dated six months before and recorded a visit sanctioned by the Emperor. The entry immediately above mine went some way to explaining why I'd been called here. I waited while the Abbot went over to a cupboard and took out a single key. 'He's been given the room in the tower,' he said to me as he walked towards the door of his office. 'I have no authority to search you, My Lord. But you will be aware of the rules governing his confinement.' I shrugged. We both knew the rules didn't apply to me. But he was doing his job, and I'd play along.

In silence, he led me past an outer chapel into the main part of the Fortified Monastery. I passed down long and gloomy corridors heavy with the smell of human excrement. Most of the cells appeared to be empty, though here and there I caught faint sounds of praying or of senile or insane giggling. I could have sworn I heard a baby cry somewhere. I could have stopped and listened but didn't. In a shorter corridor terminated by a bolted iron gate, one of the cells was open. I looked in as I passed. It was a large room and furnished in a manner that, before time and the damp had got seriously to work, had been lavish. One monk sat on a rickety chair, putting books and smaller objects into a crate. Another monk was dabbing the stone floor with a mop. I saw no evidence of a living occupant.

The monk who went before us unbolted the iron gate and bowed as we went by him on to a wide spiral staircase within what I guessed was a much wider tower. We stopped halfway up at a wooden door. The Abbot took out his key and poked it into the lock. He opened it and stood back to let me go in before him. 'Brother Gondo will remain outside,' he said. 'If he hears your voice raised, his orders are to summon the guard. I advise you to remain outside the white line that has been drawn on the floor.'

At first, I saw nothing. The darkness of the corridors and stair-case had been moderated by a brace of lamps. Here, the fading light of a winter afternoon was almost wholly shut out by a curtain that hung before the one small window in the cell. I waited for the Abbot to come in behind me and took one of the lamps for myself. I pulled the wick fully up. I waited for the pale and flickering light to show me what I was looking for. After a long silence, I found the malefactor stretched out on a stone ledge that served him for a bed. I thought he was asleep but he was only wrapped in a wool-len quilt against the cold. He opened his eyes and looked at me. He sat up and glowered. Behind me, the Abbot cleared his throat. 'Brother Priscus,' he said in a curiously soft gloat, 'your request has been heard and granted. But though it has been suspended, so you may speak collectedly with the Lord Alaric, your daily whip-ping will resume tomorrow.' With that, I heard the door swing shut behind me.

I stood just outside the white semicircle drawn on the floor and looked at Priscus. Ever since Martin had opened and read out the

Abbot's letter – and fallen into a heap of sobbing misery after a second re-reading of it – I'd been going through possible openings to this conversation. Priscus had committed people to worse than this and for less. Our first ever meeting had involved my arrest, followed by promises of torture. Now the tables had been irreversibly turned, I could have opened with any number of self-righteous lectures. Instead, I looked at the bald and shrunken scarecrow huddled in his own filth. 'Hello, Priscus,' I said softly, 'I'm given to understand that your head is filled with all manner of insane fancies and that you barely survived a suicide attempt.' I stepped forward across the line. The look he gave didn't indicate he'd get up and kiss the hem of my robe. I wondered if he'd spit in my face. 'I'm surprised to see you alive at all,' I added – 'let alone so comparatively well.'

He swung himself stiffly into a seated position. 'I knew you'd come,' he sneered in Latin. He kicked the stained quilt on to the floor and stretched his legs. 'No cups, I'm afraid. But there's a jug on that table. The horse from which its contents were collected seems to have been drunk at the time.' He let out a cold laugh. I waited for the coughing fit. Nothing. If he'd put on no new flesh, three seasons of enforced holiness in the damp seemed to have arrested a decline I'd been sure would carry him off in months. He stood up and waved his left arm. The chain that connected his manacled wrist to an iron bracket on the wall rattled. 'It means stepping well within range of wicked old Priscus,' he said with one of his nasty grins. 'But, unless you've brought your own refreshments, that's a risk you'll have to take.'

I took up the jug and carried it over to where Priscus had sat again. He laughed bitterly and raised the jug to his lips. Then he caught sight of the icon of Saint George on the far wall. He put on a look of patient humility and handed the jug to me. 'Do sit beside me, My Lord Alaric,' he said with another of his grins. 'I do have fleas. But I'm sure you were used to those in Britain, or wherever it was you were born and dragged up.'

I sat down on the ledge and nerved myself for a mouthful of the thin yellow liquid. I felt something behind me, and twisted round to see a familiar wooden box. 'It may have soothed your conscience to keep me in powders and potions,' he said. 'But I'm not inclined to blame you for that.' He took the jug from me and drank. He smacked his lips and reached for his box. 'Won't you join me in a pinch of blue powder? It goes well with the wine. If I take the first pinch, you can be sure the second won't poison you.' I knew Priscus well enough to be sure of no such thing – if he wanted, he could poison a man by kissing him. But I didn't suppose he'd brought me here to kill me.

'I gave instructions for you to be treated well,' I opened in a voice that I couldn't force into the tone I wanted. 'Why did you try to kill the monk Nicetas sent to see you?'

Priscus wrinkled his nose. 'Would you believe me if I said I bit his finger off because he spoke disrespectfully of you?' I'd spoken in Greek. He stayed in Latin and nodded slightly towards the door. I took a small pinch of the stimulant he was offering me. I put it on my tongue and washed it down with another mouthful of wine. I had specified comfort for him. No doubt, that's what he'd been given till he upset Nicetas.

'The man offended me,' he went on. 'He was here to explain how, in your absence, the new Commander of the East was about to become a second Alexander. I was more interested in where you'd been and for so long that you'd lost the advantage you got from fucking me and the eunuch over. Of course, fathead Heraclius tells everything to his cousin and he'd told enough to his confessor for me to get the drift of things. I'll be surprised if the story isn't all over the City.'

He took another drink. He smiled. 'When I was first brought here, I could hardly believe you'd done what you did. You were Alaric, the silly young barbarian. Then astonishment ripened into hate and I went three times a day into the chapel to implore God for your destruction. But, if I won't say I'm a reformed character, I've had time enough in this place to reflect on things. Whoever it was Ludinus sent to whisper in your ear only told you the truth.' He laughed nastily. 'I won't lie to you – not at this stage in proceedings. I really thought it was all settled for you to be sent here, not me. And I was planning to have you blinded as well as locked away.' He sighed. 'But I'll bet you've forgiven me. So long as you come out on top, you're not the sort who bears grudges. About the only thing that makes you endurable is your lack of belief in God.'

I said nothing. A flea had hopped on to the white silk of my outer tunic. I took it between forefinger and thumb and popped it with my nails. I wiped the blood on a napkin. Priscus sighed again. Beneath his sneery façade, he seemed almost as embarrassed as I was. 'But, you might tell your dear old friend Priscus the details,' he took up again with forced jollity. 'I get bugger all excitement in this place.'

I stood up and lifted a corner of the curtain. The giant walls of Constantinople were about a half mile to the east. Between there and this place lay the ruins of one of the suburbs that, in better days, had spread far beyond the walls. Barely any light had come into the room. But Priscus was squeezed against the wall, hands pressed over his eyes. I let the curtain drop. I went to where I'd put the lamp and moved it closer to the bench. Despite the heavy clothes I had on, I could feel a damp chill soaking through. I was sure I could hear the squeaking of a rat. I sat down again beside Priscus. 'I'm waiting, Alaric,' he jeered. 'I've heard something dismissive of what you did in Persia. I'd like to know exactly what happened.'

He sprawled on a pillow black with grease from his scalp and listened as I felt my way into a story that I hadn't come here to tell, and that still managed in places to bring a scared lump into my throat. A few times, he stopped me to ask a question about persons or places. But he listened mostly in silence as I spoke until the faint glow of light on our side of the curtain had faded and we were in darkness but for the wavering gleam of the lamp.

When I'd finished my account of my last days in Persian territory – speaking a different language and giving a different story to every picket that stopped me – he got up and walked to the farthest length his chain allowed. He turned and made a bow that I thought for a moment was ironic. Then he was back beside me and reaching for his box of drugs. He watched me take a small pinch of his orange powder and waited for its effect to begin. He put his face close to mine. For the first time since we'd met, his breath smelled only of rotting teeth. 'You know, dear boy, I decided to kill you after your first proposal of a law to dispossess my class of its land. I went out with Heraclius when he needed a piss during the banquet after that Council meeting. I just happened to be carrying the right poison in a flask about my neck. I found myself alone with all the boots and I could tell yours from their size. Five drops in each and you'd have fallen dead some time the following day. Everyone would have agreed it was a heart attack. Instead, I stood looking at those boots till Heraclius had put his catheter away. I never had such an easy chance again.'

He stopped and gathered his thoughts again. 'Listen, Alaric,' he whispered, 'if Heraclius will never understand the brains and courage required to keep the Home Provinces safe, *I do*. Give Uncle Priscus your hand. He'd like to touch a man who at last has become his equal.'

I could have laughed at him. Perhaps I should have got up and crossed to the other side of the white line. I could have called an order to the monk praying in a scared voice outside the door. I could have walked out. I could have hurried through the ruined suburbs. If the Military Gate was already locked and barred, I could have ordered it reopened. I could have let my eyes glaze over every time I found myself looking at the Fortified Monastery.

Instead, I gave him my hand.

21

So was resumed what you might call our friendship. On the first Friday in every month, I'd slip outside the City and walk alone through the ruins to call on Priscus in the Fortified Monastery. After my first visit, I'd given orders for the whip to be put away and for him to be moved into better quarters. There, we'd spend the evening drinking wine and sniffing drugs and talking over the state of the Empire. It was an odd relaxation from the cares of office. Perhaps I should confess it was a support for those cares. Beyond torturing householders in fallen cities into screaming where they'd hidden their savings, Priscus knew nothing of finance. The delicate web of dealings I was beginning to map out in earnest, one touch on any part of which would be felt in all the others, was as great a mystery to him as colours are to a blind man. But show him the correlation of forces in the Imperial Council and he had the feel of a master for how to break up hostile combinations – who should be bribed, who blackmailed, who should be quietly entrapped, without showing by whom, into boys or heresy or financial losses to the Jews. My survival so far in the councils of the Empire – indeed my achievements in the demented snake pit that was Ctesiphon – showed some understanding of the courtly arts. What Priscus now taught me was of a wholly different character. Even when I had no taste for following his advice, it was useful to know what others might be planning against me.

Martin stopped before a statue that showed Polyphemus in the act of eating a man. 'Aelric, I still don't like this place,' he whispered in Celtic. 'The very walls pulsate with evil. Can't we just move back to the smaller palace you were given?'

I frowned and looked at the statue. Though not from the very best age of Greek art, it was a fine composition. Its provenance carried it through a line of owners and dealers that led back to the demolition of Hadrian's villa outside Rome. It might have been commissioned by the Emperor himself. I waited for a couple of slave girls to walk past us in the corridor. One of them looked back at me and smiled. I smiled and nodded. That was tonight sorted, I told myself with a thrill of lust I took care not to show.

I turned to Martin, whose face had taken on a greyish colour in the light from a glazed window. 'Bricks and marble do not pulsate with anything,' I said with greater patience than I felt. 'Now, I'm the Lord Treasurer. I can't be expected to slum it in a residence stuck between a monastery and an ivory warehouse. I need a big audience hall and room for offices. I need somewhere in which I can show off to all who attend on me.' I could have gone on to say that I needed somewhere with walls thick enough to let the Emperor's Lord High Economiser not be torn apart by the mob. But I smiled and reached out to my bedraggled secretary. 'Oh, come on, Martin,' I said. 'We've finally got the place spotlessly clean – and you have said how you love the rose garden.'

We continued together along the corridor. The door to my office anteroom was ajar and I heard Samo inside let out one of his moderately drunken burps.

I sat at my desk and stared at the sullen boy. The look in his eyes had already taken Martin's thoughts off invisible horrors. He was sitting on my left and giving nervous glances at the iron sword on my desk.

I looked up and down the semi-literate scrawl on the wooden board that had been taken from about the boy's neck. 'Your name is Rado?' I asked in Slavic. He stared back at me, his eyes showing their first trace of humanity since he'd been made to stand before me. I let my face break into a smile. 'I speak several languages,' I said – 'most of them rather well. However, the working language of this palace is Latin. Do you know any Latin?' His eyes darted sideways at Samo, whose chair creaked with every movement. He focused on me again and nodded.

I looked again at the wooden board. 'You were found trying to run away on a sprained ankle after the failure of your tribe's raid on Rhodope.' The boy nodded, but made no other answer. I got up and went to stand over him. He stank like a dead fox. His hair was still plastered with something that made it white and spiky. I guessed its natural colour was light brown but this was only from looking at his eyes. 'Your people have colonised some high mountains,' I said. Breathing through my mouth, I walked round him. He had the wiry look you get in mountain races. At the same time, he had the makings of something rather more harmonious. My agent had been in Rhodope at the time of the raid and had been able to get first pick of the human debris left after an unusually firm defence of the city. This boy had been his only selection. I stopped in front of him. He was too young to have suffered the scarification that made adult males of his race useless for anything but working in the mines. In its few moments of relaxation, he had a pretty face.

'Take off your clothes,' I said in Latin.

'You'll have to kill me first!' he snarled back in a voice that wasn't quite broken. He looked at the sword and tensed his muscles as if to make a lunge for it.

I shook my head at Samo to stay seated. I picked up the sword by its blade and handed it to the boy. As I'd expected, it was too heavy for him to do other than let its point bump on the floor. Leaving the sword in his hands, I pulled out a low stool and sat before him. 'Listen, Rado,' I said, now back in Slavic, 'you were held in the slave pens of Rhodope for several days before the road was declared safe enough for travel. I'm sure that let you see how the other captives were made ready for servitude. Did my agent beat you? Did he starve you? Did he cause you to be raped? Did he force you to eat his shit or to assist in killing the injured boys of your people? According to the note that came with you, he bound up your ankle, and packed you off to me.'

I paused and continued looking at the boy. The agent knew my instructions. Despite the unpromising snarl on the boy's face, he probably hadn't failed me. 'You are my slave,' I said softly. 'I haven't had you broken to slavery. But a slave is what you are. You are a two-legged beast as much in my absolute and unaccountable power as a pig bought in from the market to serve at my dinner table.' I smiled again and waited for my words to register in his head. 'Here is the deal, Rado. You can be trained as a dancer for my guests and perform such other duties as are assigned to you. You will be taught the rudiments of Greek and be baptised into the Christian Faith. It goes without saying that I expect obedience at all times. I also expect personal cleanliness. In return, you will not be beaten. You will not be chained up at night. You will, moreover, train in the use of that sword and you will keep it sharp and within reach; and you will use it as required in my defence or in defence of this palace. You will receive my absolute trust. Most of the time, you will be holding that sword when my back is turned on you. On the Emperor's birthday, I free one fourteenth of my slaves, and send them into the world with my blessing and a gift of money.

'You can accept this deal. Or I can send you to one of the slave markets in Constantinople, where you can hope for – and almost certainly not find – a better master. How do you choose, Rado?'

'Do you give me any choice?' he asked bitterly.

I smiled again. 'Of course not,' I said. 'But I always like to ask.' I stood up and took the sword from him. 'So do untie that tunic, Rado. It's filthy as well as torn. It can help feed the boiler that provides water for your first-ever bath.'

I flashed a happy smile at Martin. He might think this palace accursed and claim there were shadows moving just out of his direct view. There were upwards of a hundred other people here who counted it their lucky day when they were brought through the gates. And every night because of that, I slept soundly in an unlocked room.

'Alaric, I'd like to ask you a question,' Priscus announced one late afternoon. Outside, it was raining and the barred window had no glazing to keep out the chill. After a fair beginning, the conversation had languished. All Priscus could bring out was another of those ghastly anecdotes that showed what a good idea it had been in general to lock him into this cage. As for me, I was depressed by news of another campaign mishandled by Nicetas – this one had let a Persian army deep into the Home Provinces and, only after much loss of life and property, had a confederation of my local militias eventually forced a retreat.

I looked away from a stain on the table cloth that reminded me of a map of Britain. 'By all means,' I said, trying for an interest I didn't feel. I was thinking of an excuse to make a dash back inside the City before the rain came down in the volume that, before it darkened, the sky had seemed to be threatening.

'The philosophers and priests teach that it doesn't,' he said after fumbling with his wine cup. 'But do you think the end *ever* justifies the means?'

I put my own cup down. 'Yes,' I said. By tacit agreement, we'd long since given up on trying to deceive each other. If we were lurching into a symposium, we might as well both be honest in ways that would have shocked Plato. 'The end does justify the means if a number of conditions are satisfied. First, the end must be worth achieving as reasonably understood. Second, the means chosen must be reasonably likely to achieve the end. Third, they must be the most economic means available. Fourth, they mustn't involve reasonably foreseeable costs that outweigh the expected benefits of the end. Answer yes to all of these, and the means are justified.'

Priscus smiled. 'A good philosophy for a saint or a villain,' he said. 'In Persia, you lied and killed and betrayed. Because you then kept telling yourself how it would keep your beloved farmers digging their fields in peace, I don't suppose you have any trouble, now you're back, in thinking yourself an honest man. I'm sure you still think yourself a better man than me.'

'Fewer bodies,' I answered, 'even allowing for age. Less enjoyment, too, in producing them.'

He arched his eyebrows. 'Dear me, Alaric – so little understanding of your truest friend!' He stood up and, as if from habit, went over to put his ear close to the door. 'Listen,' he went on, 'if I've usually killed *with* pleasure, I'd like you to tell me when I've ever been known to kill *from* pleasure.' He stopped and sat down with a sudden loss of energy. 'What I did outside Simonopolis got me black looks from all and sundry in the Imperial Council. But I lifted the siege with fifty dead on our own side. The Avar horde I sent streaming back towards the Danube left ten thousand of their own dead to be fought over by the crows. Compare that with the irreplaceable armies Nicetas is about to piss away in Syria.' He poured himself more wine.

'If you're wondering what's put me in the mood for moral philosophy, be aware that today is my sixty-eighth birthday. You may think this a very advanced age. I never believed I'd make it so far. But you'll pardon me for wondering how I shall be seen a hundred years from now. That I ended up in this place will be less important to the historians than what else I did.' He got up again and beat his chest. The response was a dry cough that terminated in itself. He laughed. 'I also can't help wondering if I haven't been reserved for some final achievement.'

He laughed again. Visiting time would soon be over. I'd have to hurry if I wanted to get back before the guards I'd bribed at the Military Gate went off duty.

22

It was Good Friday in 614. I'd spent all afternoon with Heraclius and everyone else of importance in the Great Church, listening to a mournful sermon from the Patriarch. The sufferings of Christ had been his overt subject. Every mind, though, had been on the news, drifting in with every post, of the catastrophic defeat Nicetas had managed for us in Syria. After that it had been a gambling party, where I'd stripped a couple of young heirs so naked their fathers would have to come begging my indulgence the next morning. Then it was home for a nightcap of triumphant sex with pretty young Eboric and his brother. All was as it should be when, at some time in the deepest part of the night, I was woken by a cold and bony hand clamped over my mouth.

'Not sleeping with a knife under your pillow,' Priscus wheezed. 'is an affectation I beg you to reconsider.' He took his hand away. I sat up and blinked in the light of the dimmed lamps. I looked about, trying to make sense of things. I was in my own bed. The boys must have gone back to the slave quarters.

I got out of bed and stood facing Priscus. 'What the fuck are you doing in my bedroom?' I demanded.

'Dearest Alaric, it did used to be *my* bedroom,' he said. 'I see there are ways about this building you still don't know. You evidently don't know about the *very* secret entrance. It's as dusty as when I last used it.'

I began to feel panicky. Visiting a traitor in his place of confinement was something you promised not to do again if it came to the Emperor's attention and he chose not to be pleased. Harbouring one at home was treason. Priscus reached for one of the darker bed covers and threw it at me. 'Come over here and look,' he said.

We went together to the balcony window. Even before he'd got the door open, I could see the glow of fires that blazed from a dozen points beyond the land walls of the City. I leaned over the balcony and looked right. It seemed the abandoned suburbs were a sea of flames.

'While the cat's away, the mice will play,' he jeered. 'It may be purely opportunistic. It may be that the alliance you broke up between them and the Persians has been revived. Whatever the case, an Avar raiding party has made its way into Thrace, and is killing and burning right up to the land walls.' I followed his pointed finger to the north-west. The wide splash of bright fire could only have been the Fortified Monastery. He sat down on the floor and went into a coughing fit that owed more to the smoke he must have inhaled than to any return of his sickness. 'Don't ask how I got out,' he said weakly. 'I came into the City with the last crowd of refugees before the gates were closed again. Where else could I have gone after that but to the home of my beloved friend Alaric.'

As he spoke, there was a sound of shouting deep within the palace. Priscus climbed to his feet again and pulled out a knife already dark with blood. I heard the door fly open in the big ante-chamber to my bedroom and felt my heart jump into the back of my throat. But it was only Martin. 'Aelric, wake up!' he cried in Celtic. 'The Barbarians are breaking into the City. Everything's on fire.' I shoved Priscus behind a curtain just in time. I was no sooner away from the window when Martin burst in, a lamp in his shaking hand.

I took hold of him and led him out on to the balcony. 'It's only a raid, Martin,' I said soothingly. 'No one can break through the walls. We're perfectly safe.' He stared for a long time at the distant fires and his shoulders sagged with the relaxing of tension. 'It really can't be more than a few hundred men on horseback,' I urged. 'They'll be gone by morning.' I took him back inside. 'Now, go down to the nursery and make sure the maids don't start a fire as they run about. I have work to do in here and I don't want to be disturbed.'

I locked the door behind him and walked slowly to my bedroom door. 'There's food and drink out here,' I said. I turned up one of the lamps and sat down. Limping from a sprain I supposed he'd picked up on his dash for the walls, Priscus came forward and took the wine I'd poured. 'Now you're officially dead, you are free to go where you will,' I said. I could have kept up the pretence, with talk of gold and horses. But my heart had sunk back to its normal place and now somewhat lower.

'You owe me, Alaric,' he said. 'Where do you expect me to go in my condition, but home?'

'Don't be absurd!' I snapped. 'You can't stay here.'

'And why not?' he asked. 'My grandfather built this palace almost for the purpose of hiding people. There are rooms and suites of rooms you'd need an army of surveyors to find. You can get tubby Martin to look after me. You know he'll never grass us to Heraclius.' He slumped down in his chair and looked old. 'Oh, go on, Alaric,' he whined. 'You do owe me – and you know I'll soon be dead. Let me die in the place where I was born. You've taken everything from me. You've even taken my child. Give me back at least this much.' He dropped the pretence of feebleness and looked steadily into my eyes. 'I claim from you the hospitality that no barbarian can refuse and still think well of himself.'

'And if our positions were reversed?' I asked.

Priscus shrugged. 'You do ask some silly questions, Alaric,' he said. 'If our positions were reversed, you'd already have noticed the poison in your wine and I'd be wondering how best to get rid of your body. Now, since that isn't the case, let's proceed to business.' He finished his wine and raised both arms. 'As God is my witness,' he went on in Lombardic – the closest language he knew to my own – 'I swear that, if you give me refuge, I will never shit on you again, but will truly and faithfully serve you as my lord.' He put his arms down and returned to Greek. 'Refuse my fealty and I beg you to kill me on the spot. I'd rather be dead than dragged off to another monastery.'

I looked for a while into the darkness of my wine cup. 'You can stay the night,' I sighed. 'That's the limit of what custom lets you claim. And, since you've mentioned young Maximin, do bear in mind the danger your presence brings on his head as well as mine.'

'Absolutely!' he said, almost hiding a smile of relief. He looked about the room. 'Any drugs here you fancy sharing with me?'

The Avars left with the dawn. Once it was clear they wouldn't be back, Heraclius had the Military Gate unbarred and rode out with the whole Imperial Guard for company. Uncomfortable on horseback, I went with him from one heap of smoking ruins to another, mostly religious houses that had ignored the general retreat of population within the cover of the land walls. I counted four dozen bodies in the ruinous streets, all of them hacked about most horribly.

Heraclius stopped his horse beside one of the few Avar bodies. This one, so far as I could tell, had drunk himself paralytic on stolen wine and not been able to resist when someone had cut his throat. 'There will, of course, be a full inquiry,' he cried in a voice that accused everyone about him of some dereliction. I didn't see how that could include me. If I'd set up the Intelligence Bureau once he was Emperor, he'd long since taken it under his own control. For all he might sack and disgrace a few underlings, there really was only one person to blame for the failure of the usual warning systems. The raiding party had got itself through a hundred miles of increasing Imperial control. Why had no one reported its presence? More likely, why had no one paid attention to the reports? Already whispered voices would be asking what use there was in an Emperor who couldn't safeguard his subjects even within sight of the capital. Forget the siege the Persians were tightening about Jerusalem – the smoke of burning monasteries that had billowed half the morning over Constantinople would normally have been enough to spark a murder plot or calls to abdicate. Because, by general agreement, Heraclius was the best Emperor we were likely to get, there would be neither. But the whispers would go on nevertheless.

Heraclius looked up from the dead barbarian. 'Lessons *will* be learned,' he cried in a firmer voice. The rest of us nodded and set up the buzz of agreement that might have greeted a plan to rebuild our forts on the Danube.

He dismounted at the smashed-in gate of the Fortified Monastery. 'Barbarians don't like to go inside a walled compound unless they know there is another way out,' he said as if he'd been the first to notice what every inhabitant of the European provinces had known for two centuries. This time, we simply nodded. Undoubtedly, the Fortified Monastery had almost lived up to its name. If the gateposts hadn't been allowed to rot through, the building could have held out. As it was, the intrusion had been brief enough to let most of the monks and inmates survive.

To the plain relief of his carrying slaves, Timothy the City Prefect got down from his chair. He waddled forward to a spot where he blocked further progress through the gateway. 'Oh sad day, indeed!' he cried with a melancholy wave at the remains of a monk who'd been nailed to the gate, then disembowelled. 'But sad beyond reckoning for our young colleague, Alaric,' he went on, coming straight to the point. He arranged his flabby face into what anyone who didn't know him would have thought a pitying smile. 'Is it not here that the Lord Treasurer was a regular visitor to the cell of the fallen traitor Priscus?' He waited for a dozen disapproving faces to fix themselves on mine. 'I am told they had quite resumed their old closeness.' He broadened his smile. 'Please, dearest Alaric, accept my sincerest condolences on your loss.'

I could almost feel the Emperor's blank stare at the back of my neck. 'We haven't yet taken a roll call of the survivors,' I said quickly.

Still looking at me, Timothy nodded. 'Of course not. And was not Cousin Priscus always the survivor? Did he never tell you how he was the only man alive out of Mantella after it fell to the Slavs?' He paused. 'That was where he first established his reputation for selfless heroism.' I looked briefly at the dead monk. How long had he outlived the ripping open of his belly? I wondered. A shame it hadn't been Timothy. Not that the barbarians would have got very far with him. His weight would have pulled him off the nails and it would have defeated our own executioners to find his entrails among the fat.

Someone came forward with a list of the survivors. Heraclius blinked short-sightedly at the impression of the names on wax. 'I want to look inside,' he said. With odd nimbleness, Timothy bounced on to a heap of fallen brickwork and we all passed through the gate.

The Emperor grunted and waited for me to reach out a hand to help him over the charred body of another barbarian. I could see the head had been knocked in from behind. I avoided making it obvious that I knew my way through the chaotic but largely intact front offices of the monastery. We stood together in the chapel as someone went ahead into the central courtyard to get all the survivors lined up for a prostration. I helped him balance himself on a scorched chair so he could stare out unobserved at the faces of the living.

'So Priscus is finally answering to God for his crimes,' he said softly. I said nothing, but looked across the room at what had to be the body of the Abbot. He lay face down before the altar. Anyone who turned him over would probably find his face was an unrecognisable mass of charred meat. But I didn't need to lift the remnants of his cloak to see the shape of his body. It was enough that I recognised the hilt of the knife that had been rammed into the right killing spot between his shoulder blades. 'I did think of pardoning him and sending him off to lead the armies in Syria.' He paused and began to look into my face, before his eyes darted away again. 'But that would have upset Nicetas and the whole Church. And would it have made any difference? It was surely the Will of God that we have lost Syria.'

'Blessed be the Name of the Lord,' I said. It was best never to say anything more to the point when the Emperor was going into one of his sad moods. I thought about the burned-out cloakroom beside the main gate. That contained several bodies that I could hope would never be recognised.

I helped him down from the chair. He did now look at me. 'Alaric, I give you the job of arranging for the burial of the dead. Please also speak in my name to those poor souls in the courtyard.

145

As an act of clemency, I release all surviving prisoners. As Lord Treasurer, you will make what provision you think proper for their needs. Tell the monks this building will be repaired by Christmas. They can remain here to await such other prisoners as I may condemn in the New Year.'

I bowed and listened as he picked his way back out of the monastery. I only stood upright when I heard the ragged cheer from the sightseers who'd followed us out of the City. It wouldn't be long before Martin came in to see if I had any instructions for him. Before I went off to break the happy news to the survivors, we had various matters to discuss in Celtic. If he chose to collapse before me in a sobbing heap, I could let it be known he'd been overcome by the horror of a looted House of God. Even among these generally timid Greeks, Martin was noted for the infirmity in his upper lip.

23

I think that's a natural end to my digression. Let's return, then, to the main narrative. Thirteen months later, Priscus – no, the digression is ended: don't ask me to explain how one night had stretched to nearly four hundred – stood up from a long inspection of the sleeping Antonia. 'Not bad looking, if that's the sort of thing you fancy,' he conceded. 'But, if you intend holding on to her, your brains really have migrated to your ball bag.' He looked again at her closed eyes, and carried his lamp out into the antechamber. I followed him, closing the door as I went.

I suppressed another yawn and looked about for something to put on. Away from the endlessly shifting winds, though, it was a hot night. Besides, it was only Priscus with me. I sat down at the little table where he'd placed his lamp and waited for him to finish making sure that the main door to my sleeping quarters was locked. As silently as a cat, he came back to the table. Still silent, he stared at the wooden box I'd taken from the secret cupboard in my dressing room. At last, he sat down. He pushed the lamp to the edge of the table to get a proper look at me.

I smiled into his cold eyes. 'Whatever you're on tonight,' I said with another and this time unsuppressed yawn, 'I could fancy a bit for myself.' He fished about in his tunic, before tutting softly and reaching behind him for a glass bottle. He put a drop of something sticky on my forefinger and watched as I licked it off and took a sip of wine. Unlike most of his potions, this one had no immediate effect. I didn't question, though, it would perk me up.

'Very well, dear boy,' he said smoothly, 'I will summarise today's events. Do stop me if I get something wrong. But you're the one who's always insisted on getting the known facts straight before trying to move beyond them.' He moved the lamp back to the middle of the table. 'Your face has gone very pale. But I think you'll be surprised at this latest blend. It shouldn't even give you a headache tomorrow.' He smiled brightly and continued in what I could see was a mocking parody of my own manner.

'You were presented with a silver cup this morning by some person or persons unknown,' he began. 'Someone who announced himself as a messenger from the useless bastard Nicetas then appears to have slipped you a message, in correct form, to go off to a quiet spot outside the walls, there to be murdered. He was delayed in getting the message to you and you added to the delay by shambling about the City like a blind pilgrim. By the time you did get there, whatever ambush was arranged for you had been rumbled by Shahin, who is, by the way, one of my second cousins on the Persian side. Once you'd got yourself free, you overheard a conversation that revealed treason in high places. You also learned that Shahin is eager to lay hands on your silver cup. The girl you'd picked up along the way in your usual careless manner may indicate a connection of this plot with Nicetas.'

He stopped and scratched his scalp. 'Oh, but I'm losing track of things. Why don't you carry on? You do these things so much better.'

I closed my eyes and stretched deliciously. He'd been right about his latest potion. Without ever announcing themselves, its effects had stolen over me as Priscus spoke. I fussed with the lamp until the flame came up brighter and took out the cup. 'Though in good shape, this is very old,' I said. I ran a thumbnail down the tiny lettering that covered it inside and out. 'I saw characters a bit like these on some of the older monuments in Ctesiphon. They'd been pulled from the ruins of Persepolis and Ecbatana, and I was told they dated from the first Persian Empire – the one Alexander conquered, that is. No one can read them any more.' I stopped and thought. 'But I think they look more like the inscriptions I saw in the much older ruins of Babylon. No one can read those either.' I looked harder at the cup. I was surely right. The picture, amid the writing, of a winged lion with a man's head had a definite look of what I'd seen in the desolate silence that had been Babylon. I looked closer at the tiny face and a faint recollection of horror drifted through the back of my mind. This was my first real inspection of the cup. How could elements of it have featured in my dream? I pushed the question aside. I was drugged, and might be confusing present impressions with memory. Otherwise, hadn't I just said I'd seen images like these before? I offered the cup to Priscus. 'Any thoughts?' I asked.

He sat back in his chair and put his hands out of sight. 'Don't pass it to me, dear boy,' he said, raising his voice before dropping it again. 'Shahin thinks it's bewitched. It's killed at least one eunuch who touched it. Sneer at me if you will, Alaric – I haven't made it this far in life to be carried off by some wog curse. You touch it if you will. But keep it away from me.' He laughed nervously and scraped his chair slightly backwards. 'Have you considered, Alaric, why the box was closed on every side with such long nails? *I don't believe it was meant to be opened.*'

Anyone who'd rubbed poison over the surface of the cup was probably an amateur beside Priscus. But I let a short and pitying smile stand in place of the obvious arguments. I put the cup down before me and ran my fingers over it. 'I'd guess, from its probable age and good condition,' I said with pointed nonchalance, 'it was dug out of a tomb. It has the general appearance of a drinking horn used by the Persians and probably by those who ruled the East before them, at formal occasions.' I stopped and picked it up again. Even empty, it seemed too heavy for actual use. Also, the lettering showed no sign of the differential wearing you get when an object is routinely handled. I twisted the cup to see more of the inscription. It wasn't possible to tell where it began, or in what direction it was supposed to go.

I sat forward again. 'I found a body on my way out,' I said, returning to less impenetrable facts. 'It was dumped beside the private entrance. I'll take your word that you didn't leave it there. It may have no connection, but I'm told the cup was found pushed under the main gate. The nice box in which it came was scratched on one side. Let us assume that this man had been running away with the cup. He needed to get rid of it before he was caught. Perhaps he needed to get it to *me*. This is only a surmise, but it would explain the sudden and elaborate plot to get rid of me. The cup had been left in a place from which it couldn't be recovered at once. So a murder plot was ordered as well as a burglary.'

I stretched. More than my thinking faculties had been revived. If Priscus hadn't been sitting opposite, I'd have been more than half-inclined to go off and slap some life into Antonia. No chance of that, however. Priscus took his eyes off the cup. 'Treason on this scale, dearest Alaric,' he said with a return of his mocking tone, 'and you knew nothing till its projectors hit out and nearly killed you?'

I shrugged. 'I have spent the past six months absorbed in bullion ratios and other calculations,' I said defensively. It was a feeble answer. Heraclius had taken the Intelligence Bureau out of my hands but I should have been aware of at least one Persian ship in our home waters. I shrugged again, now adding a fierce scowl. 'What have *you* heard?' I asked.

Priscus smothered a smile and looked into my eyes. 'Alaric,' he said, 'you know our agreement was that I should never go outside the walls of our palace. What could I possibly have heard that you didn't tell me yourself?'

'Let's stop playing games,' I said with a genuine scowl. 'What, if anything, have you picked up on your nocturnal wanderings through the City?'

'Nothing, my dear,' came his maddening answer. 'If I'd heard cousin Shahin was about, I'd have told you at once. If you don't believe that, let's agree that Nicetas is somehow involved. Do you suppose the thought of him in a dungeon, maggots wriggling in the suppurating flesh of his legs, wouldn't have got my tongue wagging?' It was a decidedly Greek answer – argue from probabilities, rather than swear to facts. But they were strong probabilities. I looked at my wine cup. I hadn't realised how empty it was. Priscus noticed, and reached for the jug.

I put the silver cup back into its box. That morning, I'd thought the box was ebony. In fact, it was quite ordinary wood, painted a shiny black. You could see that from the scratches on the under-side. Careful not to knock it on to the floor, I reached in for the parchment slip that carried the only writing I could understand.

'The misshapen *S*, and the spelling mistake *sekretum*, indicate a Greek who is unfamiliar with Latin – or, at any rate, with written Latin,' I said. 'But why go to the trouble of Latin at all?'

Priscus raised his eyebrows. 'I bet you nearly shat yourself when you saw the message,' he said. '*I know your secret!*' He giggled and swilled wine about his mouth. I frowned, but didn't rise to the challenge. I stared at the neat slip of parchment. Why Latin? Except the two characters not found in Greek were uncertainly written, the message was smooth and unblotted. It couldn't have been written by a man who was on the run and desperate to tell me something. Had the message been meant for me? If not me, for whom?

I got up and pulled gently at one of the shutters. I'd expected to see the eastern sky ready for the pale glow of dawn. Events and whatever I'd taken, though, had jumbled my perceptions of time. The sky was still dark. 'What did you learn from the man you questioned?' I asked.

'Much less than I can teach you about him,' Priscus sniggered. 'When Heraclius gave you this palace, your first act on taking possession was to free all my slaves and kick them into the street. Some of them you would have found more useful than the slobs you stuck in their place. Regardless of that, you never considered that one of them might one day be found useful by somebody else for gaining entrance. The man under your bed was called Marcian. He had a talent for snooping that I often found useful. He got past your useless household and made his way here. When I caught him by accident, he was picking the locks in your office cupboards. Despite my best efforts, he told me fuck all. He was looking for a silver cup, he told me. That was it.'

I rubbed my eyes. Priscus had lied about the headache. His drug had worn off as quickly as you might snuff out a lamp. I stood up and stretched. 'Since I don't fancy sleeping with your latest victim under my bed, how do you propose getting rid of him?'

Wearily, Priscus raised his left arm. 'How do barbarians dispose of rubbish in the towns they've settled?' He asked.

I shut my eyes and breathed slowly out. Antonia had rolled across the bed, but was still fast asleep. 'How did you keep him quiet while you did *that* to him?' I asked as quietly as I could manage. If I'd been more my usual self, I'd have been struggling not to vomit. Priscus grinned back at me in the gloom and muttered something about a 'trick of the trade.' I swallowed and pulled the dead man fully clear of the bed. Priscus didn't offer any help and I didn't ask. Instead, I got the body by its shoulders and tried to keep the leaking areas from touching the floor as I got it over to the balcony. Priscus was there already and draped a towel over the ledge. I shook my head and lifted the heavy corpse into my arms. I threw it straight over and watched as it tipped over and then over again, before landing with a faint but audible splash on the granite pavements of the Triumphal Way. It landed about a dozen feet from one of the sleeping figures and almost on top of one of the dying fires. I looked cautiously down. If anyone had noticed the new arrival, no one bothered to move.

By the time I turned, Priscus had already used the sponge and washing water left by the bed to clean up the bloody trail across the floor. I used the towel and what was left to wash the slimy blood from my own body. Over the edge went the sponge and towel. Over too went the remains of the water.

The dawn was still nowhere to be seen. But I now felt as if I'd gone the whole night through and longer. 'Go back to your attic,' I said to Priscus. 'We'll take this up again when we've both had some sleep.'

Reluctantly, he got up. 'And the cup?' he asked.

'It goes back in a secret place only you and I know.' I said.

Priscus arranged his face into a bleak smile. 'Your trust in my honesty is an inspiration that I will do my best to keep in mind,' he sneered. I smiled back at him. Priscus was a champion liar in a race of liars. I'd seen fear in his eyes, though, even he couldn't fake.

24

After a mostly wet April, the winter roof was now off my gymnasium. Once I'd finished scraping off the thick coat of sand that was stuck to my oiled body, I could hurry off to the bathhouse. After that, I could make a start on the morning's work and deal with whatever accumulation had been carried over from the previous day.

Glaucus pointed at an unscraped area on my lower back. 'A civilised man ties a cord over his foreskin,' he said shortly.

He was starting an old argument. I twisted round with my strigil and got nearly everything off with a single stroke. 'The ancients wrestled with other free men,' I said lazily. 'Young Rado, on the other hand, would feel put out if I didn't shoot all over his chest.' I smiled at the boy. He'd almost got himself clean enough for the steam room. He smiled back and flexed himself most charmingly. But for the pale faces already looking through the doorway, I'd have suggested another grapple in the sand.

The old trainer frowned at the stiffy that had popped up again. 'I have repeatedly told you,' he said, 'exercise is *not* an opportunity for sex,' he said. I could have told him to address that remark to the ancients. Why else do it in the nude and end it so often with wrestling? But Glaucus was Glaucus, and he'd said his piece. 'I've given you lighter weights,' he said going back to my earlier question, 'because I don't like the way your biceps are growing. For the same reason, I refuse you any breakfast. Your shoulders are already on the outer borders of harmony with your lower body. Just because you are a barbarian is no reason why you should look like one.' He stood back and stared at Rado. 'You can interpret the same to him. If he pumps himself up any more, you might as well complete his ruin as a dancing boy and cover his body with tattoos and get him kitted out as a bodyguard. From what I hear of yesterday's adventure, you're a fool to go about alone in the City.'

I bowed. 'It is as you say, Glaucus,' I said meekly. I suppressed the memories he'd stirred of the previous day. I did it too late. My foreskin rolled fully back, exposing the pink of my glans to the morning sun.

Glaucus came out with something unflattering and walked slowly round me, grunting and poking at me with his cane. 'The purpose of training,' he said as if telling me for the first time, 'is not to make yourself look like a human bull for two seasons, before running to fat. It is to keep the body in balanced proportions throughout the whole term of life. Hair goes. Teeth go. Get it right early enough and good muscle tone lasts a lifetime.' He stopped and looked angrily into my face. 'I have told you many times, a depilated crotch is unattractive. It gives an impression of effeminacy. You waste your time in modelling your speech on the correct elegance of the ancients, if you cannot leave your manhood clothed with its natural modesty.'

I bowed again and thought of the all-over kiss of silk undergarments. 'I crave indulgence for the weakness,' I said. Saying no more, I joined Glaucus in a probably illegal genuflection before an empty niche.

'Your *kava*, Sir,' young Eboric said behind me in Latin. I nodded and continued taking the salutes and greetings from the multitudes who passed back and forth along the Triumphal Way. It was one of those glorious mornings the spring gives only occasionally to Constantinople. The sun shone clear on my right, but a cool breeze from the north took away all but a hint of what it might do later in the day. The roofs of the lower City shone a cheerful red or glittered like jewels on velvet. The seabirds called and circled overhead.

And here I was, alive and well, and bathed and oiled and perfumed. Dressed in a white outer tunic crossed by bands of shimmering green, I stood at ease on the front steps of my palace.

There could be no doubt of the previous day's horrors but I was almost ready to believe the lying account of my capture and escape I'd dictated in the steam room. It was already set up on its easel and attracting a most flattering number of readers. I was alive and well, and Shahin and all his friends could go fuck themselves.

Not even Timothy's presence could sour the morning. 'Duty presses, dear boy,' he said again, 'Duty presses. Can't possibly step inside.' Even so, his cold unsmiling eyes were looking past me into the darkness of my entrance hall. Of course, a man of my quality deserved no less than the City Prefect in person – though his local deputy would have been more welcome.

He turned and looked down the steps to where my easel had been set. 'Shocking story,' he went on – 'perfectly shocking. These bandits were never so bold when I was your age. A man could ride halfway to Thessalonica before hitting serious trouble.'

I sipped delicately at the contents of my glass beaker and continued looking into the street. Was that Eunapius of Pylae down there? His head and shoulders were hidden behind the easel. But there was surely no one else in the City with that combination of emaciation and fussy taste in clothes. From what I could see, he was reading my account to a crowd of his parasites and to the general trash who couldn't read for themselves. I looked harder. I frowned. Several of the listeners were breaking into a shambling dance. I was sure I could hear a low titter. I pretended not to notice. 'The street cleaners have done a good job,' I said, looking back at Timothy.

I'd caught him in the act of picking his nose. He moved a fore-finger that had been poised an inch from his mouth and wiped the bogie into the off-yellow banding of his robe. 'It was the least I could do, my dear fellow,' he answered. 'I had them out with the dawn, scrubbing and cleaning. I was here myself to supervise. We had to flog a few of the stragglers awake. A couple of dead, too, we had to carry away.' He pointed to a brown patch where two of the public slaves were still at work. The lower part of his face took on a sad smile. 'You should have seen what had been done to the poor creature we found there. Animals in human form – no, demons out of Hell – some of the humbler people of this fair city.' He looked carefully at my face.

'Any reports of an older body found in the area?' I asked with a slight wrinkling of my nose. 'My own slaves found a dried blood patch in the side street round the corner. If you have found anything, I feel a certain obligation to pay for its collection.'

'Your goodness, young Alaric, is proverbial,' was Timothy's answer. Without giving more of an answer, he turned to feast his eyes on Eboric, who was waiting quietly for me to finish my *kava*. 'As, if you'll pardon the compliment, is your taste in slaves.' His lower jaw sagged open, giving full view of his teeth. 'Where does one lay hold of such freshness and elegance?' he cried with sudden enthusiasm. 'Speaking for myself, I find the markets in this city a continual disappointment.' He leaned forward and stroked the boy's cheek. 'So fresh, so elegant!' he repeated. Eboric shrank back and turned appealing eyes on me. I gave him the tiniest reassuring nod.

'I take a personal care in the training of my younger slaves,' I said, staring into a face visibly consumed by lust.

Timothy settled his features into a look of only moderate satyriasis. 'If you'll pardon an older man's advice,' he said, now in a patronising tone, 'your way with slaves has provoked a certain degree of adverse comment.' He continued staring at Eboric. 'You don't make a human being into a slave by the mere facts of capture and sale. Taking anyone into your house who hasn't been broken by the dealers to servitude is rather like taking in a dangerous wild animal. Having more than a few slaves of the same nation compounds the risk. You'll never sleep soundly. You'll never rely on them in a crisis – you mark my word.' Still looking at Eboric, he controlled himself. He leaned close to me. 'To see the boy naked would not displease me, though,' he whispered from the corner of his mouth.

Eboric and his brother had been glorious finds after the repulse of a Lombard attack on Naples. Leaving aside their own dignity, I'd be buggered if I so much as considered sharing either of them with anyone – certainly not the tub of rancid fat that was His

Magnificence Timothy. I gave my empty cup to the boy. 'Tell Cook you've earned a very big spoonful of honey,' I said in his own language.

The same thought in our minds, Timothy and I watched him scamper up the last flight of steps to the entrance. He'd outgrown his tunic again and it barely covered his upper thighs. My attention was pulled away from those endless bedtime romps by a low groan of horror from the street behind me. It was followed by a faint babble of insults.

'Some of your Jewish friends, I think,' Timothy said, now in accusing tone. 'If you can bear another friendly word of advice, they're all Persians at heart. Your good nature was surely misled when you persuaded the Council to advise Heraclius against enforcement of the conversion law.' I nodded vaguely. I could have asked what use there was in making things worse than they already were. But we'd had that argument already. It was a nice morning, and my Jews were here. I stared at the three uncovered chairs that were making their way past the big statue of Poseidon. There are many reasons for employing Jewish financial agents. One is that they don't waste time when you call them to an emergency meeting.

I watched ben Baruch and his cousins carried towards the lesser entrance to my palace. 'I imagine there's something they want,' I said dismissively. Not quite truthful, that. I was about to call in some favours. Another reason Jews are worth employing is that they're often a good substitute for the Intelligence Bureau. If there was anything I needed that morning, it was a bit of intelligence.

I took off my hat and smiled my thanks at the slave who was setting about me again with his fan. 'Withdraw five baskets of the new coin from the consignment for the Lord Exarch of Ravenna,' I said. 'Exchange it for gold at the bank of ben Baruch and give it to the envoys of the Chagan. Give them also three pieces of purple cloth and an appropriately altered copy of the letter written earlier this year to the Grand Chieftain of the Malakioi. The oral message to give them is that the Emperor would look benevolently on their crossing the Danube, so long as it was for an attack on the Avar encampment outside Sirmium. A further payment will be made in copper on the standard scale for every Avar scalp presented by the next embassy sent to Constantinople.'

I waited for the clerk to finish making notes on wax that was probably melting in the heat of my official garden. 'Send notice of my decision to the Lord Caesar Nicetas,' I went on with a sigh. 'Draw attention to my compliance with the Emperor's Standing Order made on the Feast of Stephen in the second year of his reign. Make sure to get a receipt from the Lord Caesar's secretary.' A useful requirement, that, as the notice wouldn't be read by His Magnificence the Lazy Turd. I thought about the depleted shipment of silver to Ravenna. I hadn't made any definite promise to the Exarch of how much subsidy he'd get. But the shipment I was now making was barely more than a token of our continued interest in Italy. 'Tell the Lord Exarch,' I added, 'that he is at liberty to approach His Holiness of Rome for another contribution to Imperial defence. He is permitted, in return, to overlook the Pope's dealings with the Lombards in respect of their withdrawal from the Septenna district of Etruria.' I put my hat beside me on the stone bench and closed my eyes. The sun was turning hot enough for August. 'Bring me the draft of the letter to the Exarch. I will expand on it in my own hand.'

Another clerk stepped forward with his own load of correspondence. An earthquake had damaged the running track in Aphrodisias. Would the Emperor pay for its repair? 'No,' I said. 'The general remission of taxes to the Home Provinces is the only help we can presently give. Diverting money from the war effort is out of the question. Find the letter I wrote last month to the town council at Nicomedia on a similar request. Adapt it and bring it to me for checking.' There was a new paragraph I had in mind about the joys of voluntary effort in an age of lower taxes.

'Your son, Theodore, craves a moment of your time,' one of the clerks suddenly intoned.

I opened my eyes and focused on the boy. 'At your age,' I said, going into Syriac for privacy, 'you should be wearing no clothes at all on a day like this. But you might at least take off that bloody cloak. Do you want to be ill again?' He bowed and said nothing. I gave up on the next sentence I was forming. If overdressed, Theodore had put on cleanish clothes. He'd even washed and combed his hair. I wondered if I could manage a paternal smile. Best not, I thought. I had a dozen clerks watching me with close attention. 'What is it?' I asked, trying instead to sound friendly.

'I have a favour to ask of you,' he mumbled in Greek.

I got up and put my hands on his shoulders. Even through four layers of wool, I could feel how bony they were. Why would the boy not give himself to Glaucus? There were limits to what could be done with a body so naturally unpromising but daily training would put something on those bones. It might also open out his lungs. I smiled into his sallow face, and felt the usual wave sweep over me of pity mingled with guilt. I should have sent him home to Tarsus. I could easily have paid for one of his dead father's neighbours to take him on. But I'd felt so sorry for him in Athens, once his stepmother was gone.

'Ask your favour,' I said loudly. 'The answer must surely be yes.' There was an approving murmur from the clerks. Theodore opened and closed his mouth. He turned a shade of pink. He looked round at the clerks.

'My Lord,' a new voice called behind me, 'the map is ready for your inspection.'

I looked away from Theodore. 'Ready so soon?' I asked. The drafting office must have been working night shifts to get that ready. I looked again at Theodore. He was no closer to making his request. 'I'll be up in my office,' I said generally. 'Join me after a half-hour break by the sun dial.' I took Theodore by the arm. 'Come on, I said. 'We'll talk indoors.'

After so long in bright sunshine, it was a matter of feeling my way to the foot of the backstairs or waiting for my eyes to adjust. I chose the latter. Even this far, a brisk walk had left Theodore wheezing slightly. 'How is that eunuch who was taken poorly yesterday?' I asked.

'Father Macarius was with him at the end,' came the answer in Theodore's mournful voice. 'His skin turned the colour of lead and he cried out that the Devil had taken his soul.'

'Oh, surely not!' I said in a voice of what I hoped was firm piety. Obviously, I thought about my cup. Unlike ceramic or wood, you can't impregnate metal with poison. Both eunuchs had pawed all over the cup. One of them had polished it on his robe. That would have removed anything nasty smeared over the surface. There had been nothing left for me. I made a note to have a proper look at the thing once I was completely alone.

25

I looked up from the squares of starched linen that covered half the floor in my office. 'My compliments to the entire drafting office,' I said. The young clerk nodded and tried not to look as pleased with himself as he deserved to feel. I took another step back to admire the neatness with which numbers had been turned into blocks of colour. If the basic idea was mine, the Treasury officials had eventually taken it up with an enthusiasm that made its final shape their own achievement. I took a step left and wondered if there had been some defect of scale in showing the Italian provinces. Also, was Syracuse really so far south of Corinth? It didn't matter. It might even be useful to give Heraclius something he could then correct in some unimportant detail from his own knowledge. What did matter was the correspondence of numbers with colour. That, I could see, was wholly correct.

I smiled at the clerk. 'Do please arrange for five copies on one-third scale,' I said. He nodded again and scratched my instruction on his waxed tablet. 'Oh, and please ask the chief drafting clerk to abstract the main figures from each report and tabulate them on a standard sheet of papyrus. I'll need eight copies of that.'

We'd given special attention to the Home Provinces. I bent low over a band of pink that began in the foothills of the Taurus Mountains and terminated just short of Halicarnassus. More than ever, the patches and banding of different shades of the same colour struck me as the beginning of a new way of looking at everything in the human and the natural world.

Behind me, Theodore was recovering from the wheezing attack that running up six flights of stairs with me had brought on. I heard him shift weakly on the chair I'd given him. Was he about to start coughing again? It was a bad sign when he coughed. I felt another stab of guilt. But he didn't cough.

I straightened up and continued looking at the solid edging about all the provinces so far lost to the Persians. 'Go down to the garden and join the others,' I said to the clerks. I moved backwards to look at the long purple streak surrounded by uncoloured linen that was Egypt. 'Tell everyone to start the half-hour break again,' I added. I suppressed a yawn and glanced at a covered jug of wine. No breakfast, Glaucus had said. That also meant no drinking. I turned my attention to a lead box of stimulants I'd left on my desk. I walked over and opened it. I pulled a face at the acrid taste of the pills. There was a jug of water beside the wine. I'd have to make do with that.

'You are looking well, My Lord – I mean, *father*,' Theodore opened nervously. 'I expected you would want to rest after the terrible events of yesterday.' I smiled, and waited for the slight agitation caused by the pills to blot out the hunger pangs. The formalities over, Theodore stood before me and opened and shut his mouth a few times. I could see his nerve had failed him again. Much longer and we'd run out of time. But I kept up the smile till my face began to ache. He looked for a while at the one main document on my desk. This was a folded sheet of papyrus covered in map coordinates. It must have meant as much to him as the characters on my silver cup had to me.

'What is that?' he suddenly asked, turning to stare at my big map of the Empire.

'It's a population map,' I said. Our best relationship had always been of master and student. Our closest moments had been over Latin grammar and Greek prose composition. I now took the easy option and got up from my desk to lead him over to the patchwork of linen squares. 'Our last complete census returns are from the third year of Phocas,' I began. 'That was only a decade ago but there have been continued losses to plague and the disruptions of war. What we've done is to correct the last full census in light of the partial returns we got last year. We've then compared the result with the returns from the last year of Anastasius, which was nearly a century ago.'

His reason for breaking into my day set aside, the boy stared at the Syrian provinces. He looked at Africa, then at Italy. 'I don't understand the meaning of the colours,' he said. He looked again at Africa. 'I thought Carthage had many more people than Rome. Yet the areas about both are the same colour.'

I nodded and guided him to a spot on the floor from where he could easily see the whole map. 'I'm not trying to show numbers of taxable units,' I explained. 'What the map shows is the differential loss of population since before the Empire fell on hard times. Black shows no loss at all, or an increase. Pale blue shows a loss of more than half. Green shows losses of more than three-quarters. You'd see the meaning of all the colours if you could refer to a guidance sheet that isn't yet finished.'

Theodore looked again at Syria. 'How long did it take to prepare?' he asked.

'Oh, it took months and months,' I said with an airy wave. And that was no time at all, considering the magnitude of what had been done. I'd had to create almost a new class of officials to deduce population from the indirect evidence of the returns and then to compare three sets of figures, each of which had been collected in different ways. Would I find anyone, outside the circle of those I'd trained or inspired, able to appreciate how I'd carried light into regions of knowledge no one before had known to exist? Probably not, and I doubted Theodore would be among them. But my stimulant pills were doing their job. Here was the best audience I had.

Theodore was looking at the black and pale-blue banding that covered Africa. 'And these numbers?' he asked, beginning to sound oddly interested.

I stroked my nose. 'Those refer to more detailed maps that show the differing qualities of land in each province,' I said cautiously. I looked at the boy. His courage must return soon. I thought of putting a comforting hand on his arm. But it sounded so unnatural that I dropped the idea. 'Come and sit with me on

163

the balcony,' I said. 'Join me in a cup of lemon juice, and take in the beauties of Constantinople.'

The windows of my office faced west. Since the sun was still somewhat below its zenith, we could sit in shade. The view from here wasn't so spectacular as from the other side. It was still plain, however, that you were looking over a city of barely conceivable wealth and magnificence. Looking only at the vastness of the land walls, two and a half miles away, no observer could mistake this place for one of those mere agglomerations of humanity that you read about in the farthest East. I settled myself into a chair lined with padded silk and poured two cups of the thin yellow liquid that would have to do in place of wine.

'I won't trouble you with false laments about the burden of work,' I began. 'But I do regret that I have been so busy since Christmas that we've hardly spoken.' I raised a hand to cut off his formulaic reply. 'You were a boy for so long after you came under my protection that I now have trouble accepting how close you have approached to manhood. It is my duty, as your father, to take a close interest in your plans for the future.' I stopped. The sense of failed paternal duty was beginning to crush me. Perhaps, though, I should leave this till Martin got back. He was so much closer to Theodore than I had ever been.

I was still thinking what to say next – it should have contained something about Antonia – when Theodore broke in. 'What is the purpose of your big map?' he asked.

I tried not to brighten at the change of subject. I failed. I put my cup down and stared at the roof of the Law Faculty's library. I'd passed many useful afternoons in that cavernous repository of oppression and chicanery. My duty was to speak to him as father to son. I took the easy way out.

'The clerks who worked so hard to produce it still don't understand the purpose of the map,' I said, again cautious. We were alone, but I still looked about from habit. 'What it does is pull together a series of conversations I've had with the Emperor during the past four years. You will be aware of the Empire's difficult situation. The cause everyone talks about is the Persians. However, the military defeats we've suffered should really be seen as symptoms of a weakness more fundamental than a lack of competent generals.'

I drank slowly and gathered my thoughts. Theodore had asked his question and would get an answer. It would be an excuse for seeing how well I could summarise a long and difficult – and, at all points, controversial – argument. 'The Empire, as it stands, cannot be defended,' I began. 'Its frontiers are too long, its enemies too numerous, its resources too limited. The loss of population that began with the arrival of plague seventy years ago has set a gulf between ancient and modern times. Italy and Africa can't be made to pay for their own defence. Any tax gathering at all only makes things worse. It's the same with everywhere between the Danube and Corinth. Egypt and Syria remain in better shape. But the decay of the Greek population in those provinces has allowed the emergence of dominant classes alien in language and heretical in religion. It's no surprise that Syria fell so easily to the Persians, or that Egypt will soon fall.

'This leaves us with the Home Provinces – that is, Thrace and Asia Minor. These are both Greek and Orthodox. They form a natural and defensible unit as the hinterland of Constantinople. They have not suffered a catastrophic decline of population and are potentially as rich as they were before the Empire fell on evil times. So long as they are not called on to pay for the maintenance of a world empire, there is no need to subject them to massive and destructive fiscal oppression. We have the makings about us of a wealthy and powerful nation – mistress of the seas and in control of every trade route by land. Everything else should be quietly abandoned. Our new neighbours can be loosely controlled by diplomacy and an occasional show of force. All that we hope to get as tribute we can get by trade.'

I waited for the enormity of what I was suggesting to sink in. 'So you *do* want to break the Empire up,' he said softly. 'Father Macarius says that's what everyone believes. Are you also planning another land confiscation?'

165

'I wouldn't call it *confiscation*,' I said, making a note to get rid of that bastard priest at the earliest opportunity. 'The *redistribution* law Heraclius made four years ago has done much to stabilise the Home Provinces. Giving untaxed and inalienable plots of land to those who work on the land is rapidly turning bondsmen into citizens and – bearing in mind the consequent militia duties – even into soldiers.

'But it has so far been a limited scheme. It has barely touched the larger estates. Except in the maritime provinces, the new land-owners have retained significant legal obligations to their former landlords.' I paused and darted a glance into Theodore's face. Was that hostility I saw? I blinked. I looked at my polished fingernails.

'Injustice aside,' I said firmly, 'we can't afford to let two thirds of the useful land in the Home Provinces be owned by families that render no tangible service to the Empire. A nobility is useful as a repository of culture and as a higher administrative and military class. But we need to reduce the size and wealth of the nobility we have. Smaller amounts of landed wealth should be held on the understanding that they have public duties attached. Everything else should be handed over to a much-enlarged class of independent and armed farmers.'

There – I'd said it all in surprisingly few words. Perhaps Theodore was worried about it as a native of Syria, and because of what it meant for the gigantic landholdings of the Church. But he dropped the matter. 'I've had a letter from Lesbos,' he said. 'Martin says he misses us, but feels increasingly purified by his vigils at the shrine of Saint Deborah.' I looked solemn. The reason I'd given in so easily to his request for leave was that Saint Deborah had been martyred three thousand feet up a mountain. So long as it didn't kill him, the daily climb would certainly shake some of the weight off him.

Theodore's courage now returned. 'My Lord – I mean, Father – I believe you are to attend a poetry recital this evening.' I nodded. I'd sat down on my garden bench determined to cry off that ordeal. The first new letter my clerks had opened, though, was an undeniably genuine note from Nicetas. Dripping concern for my safety, he'd renewed his invitation in terms it would have been insulting to refuse. Theodore got up and walked jerkily inside. When I caught up with him, he was staring at the map coordinates on my desk. 'I was wondering if it might be possible to come with you to the recital,' he whispered. 'You have often said I should acquaint myself with the secular arts.' He ended with a pleading look into my eyes.

'I'd be delighted if you were to come,' I said. That wasn't quite true. But getting him home to bed would be an excuse for leaving before Nicetas and his poet became too unbearable. 'Of course, you'll need a bath and your finest clothes. It's to be a late event, and will go on till midnight. My own chair will be waiting down-stairs at the second hour of darkness. Speak to Samo, and he'll arrange a place beside me.'

'Thank you, Father!' he cried. I told Antony you'd let us go along with you.'

Us? My smile faded like colours left out in the sun. I'd assumed Antonia would still be asleep. What was she doing up and about? 'Young Antony will be staying with us for a while,' I said smoothly. 'Though he will be joining us for meals, he does have duties that will keep him largely to his own quarters, or with me. I'm not sure if he has any time for poetry recitals.'

'Oh, but he said he'd *love* to hear the works of a poet attached to someone as important as the Emperor's cousin,' Theodore cried with desperate enthusiasm. 'After I bumped into him in the main garden, we spoke of little else.' I watched his face brighten and go though as many colours as my map. Anyone else of his age I'd long since have taken to a brothel and given over to slaves who would tease out exactly what it was he fancied. With Theodore, I still hadn't got round to discussing the mechanics of the fleshly sins his favourite authors denounced so roundly.

I could have said no. I was lord and master of all I surveyed. I should have said no. Every hypothesis I formed about the previous day somehow involved Nicetas. He'd done nothing to contradict that. I'd never yet had a note in his own hand, nor in his native Latin, and there had been more than a hint of the slimy beneath its tone of gushing friendship. But I couldn't remember the last time I'd said anything to please the boy. I remembered the promise I'd made before all my clerks. 'Very well,' I said – and I regretted the words at once. 'We'll all travel together in the big chair.' He was beginning to tremble with excitement. Taking Antonia about in public hadn't been on my list of things to do. She'd probably spend the evening gawping at Eunapius of bloody Pylae – I set aside the ultimate horror that she'd ply for business. But the Lord Senator had spoken and wouldn't go back on his word. I led the boy to the door. 'Do ask Samo to step in and see me at his convenience,' I added, not exactly pushing the boy from the office but making it clear that I had other business that wouldn't wait.

Alone, I picked up the sheet of map coordinates. They described various landmarks and villages in relation to their distance and direction from Laodicea. After so long living with all this, I had only to scan the neat tables of numerals and fractions, and then shut my eyes to see the map take shape. Instead, I dropped the sheet and closed my eyes to think of Antonia. Theodore had said she was up and about. If I hurried down to the garden, she might still be there. I was getting up from my desk – and finding that my own hands were beginning to tremble – when there was another knock on the door.

Either Theodore had run all the way down to the main hall or Samo had been coming up on business of his own.

26

After that promising northern breeze of the morning, the afternoon air was still as inside a church. I emerged from the Treasury
archive where Lucas had his office into the baking and mostly
empty semicircle that lay at the southern end of the Circus. My
next appointment lay within a district of narrow streets that was a
survival from the ancient Byzantium. The quickest route was a
turn to the right and a walk past a junction of many sewers that
was presently unroofed. I shaded my eyes and looked across at a
sundial. I'd spent less time with Lucas than expected. I turned left
and made my way towards a long covered passageway that would
take me under the building that connected the Circus to the
Imperial Palace. From here it would be a longer walk, but through
streets that nearly always picked up some breath of air from the
sea.

Just before the covered passageway, I had another change of
mind. The sea walls were a few hundred yards behind me. You
couldn't go very far west along them. There were two harbours
where the walls gave way to other defences. But it was a nice walk
to the east. You had the sea on your right and could look to your
left over the public gardens of the Imperial Palace. There would
certainly be a breeze up there. Half a mile along, there was even
an eaterie on top of one of the towers that sold passable wine. I
had a little time on my hands and I could do worse than spending
it in solitary thought.

My meeting with Lucas had been a matter of drawing one blank
after another. Though excellent in its own terms, the Treasury team
I'd assembled under him was a poor substitute for the Intelligence
Bureau. Following an anonymous tip off, he and his people had got

to the beach before the blood was set on some of the bodies. Still smelling of urban filth and seawater, all the clothing had been carried into his office for me to poke through with a stick. No sign, though, of the forged note. I did recall having dropped this before Shahin had me tied up. Now, together with the alleged message from Nicetas, it had vanished. I'd given Lucas instructions for every ship to be searched that was passing through the straits without putting in at Constantinople. I could at least disrupt what looked like an excellent communications network for Shahin and whatever other Persian ships were operating in our home waters.

It was also the most I could do. A cup of wine while staring over the sparkling water of the straits might settle my thoughts for what should be a more productive meeting with my Jews. They'd had time enough to make their enquiries. It wouldn't be too soon to drop in on them for a private talk.

As I turned, I found myself looking at a man I was pretty sure I'd seen by the entrance to the Treasury building. He stared back at me just a little too long, before giving a ceremonious bow and stepping out of my path.

Armed guard set over me by Lucas, or hired assassin? There was a quiet scraping of shoes behind me. I stepped quickly against a wall and went for my sword.

'Please, My Lord, we are not here to do you any harm.' My drug compounder spoke with urgent politeness. He looked nervously round and spread his arms in a gesture of peace. 'You came to me yesterday with a request for help. I am now compelled to grant your request.' He stepped backwards into the shadow of the covered passageway. 'It will take up but an instant of your time,' he added.

I let my right arm relax and stared back at him. I'd assumed he was fussing about Priscus the day before. Perhaps he had been and still was. I stared at the scared look on his face. I'd never thought of him as having any existence outside the drugs market. 'What help have you in mind?' I asked softly.

He managed one of his oily smiles and looked about. 'My Lord Alaric,' he said with a sudden coming together of his faculties, 'I understand that you currently possess the Horn of Babylon.'

I reached up to adjust my hat. It kept him from seeing how tense my face had gone. 'If you are referring to twelve inches of coiled silver that other men have shown willing to kill to get for themselves,' I said with a forced easiness of tone, 'the answer may be yes.' I looked sharply right as some children ran down a flight of steps from the sea wall and began chasing each about the big open space. I relaxed again. 'Do you want it?' I asked.

'No,' he said. His body trembled with a spasm of fear. 'I never want even to see it. But if you will come with me, you may learn much about it.'

I looked at his grey and sweating face. What did he know about my silver cup? How had he known about it the previous day? I made up my mind. 'Where?' I asked. Not speaking, he pointed into the darkness of the passageway. It was two hundred yards long and the sort of place you advised newcomers to the City not to enter. Here, I had the plain advantage. If I chose, I could arrest him and his assistant and hurry them off for interrogation with Lucas. Or I could walk past him with a curt instruction to call on me the following day. Whatever he was doing away from his usual place, however, it was hard to imagine the compounder had come out to harm one of his best customers. He looked scared and I doubted he was scared of me. I stepped away from the wall. 'You go first,' I said.

I hurried blinking into the square dominated by the Great Church. Within the urine-soaked depths of the covered passageway, where men preached heresy above the moans of copulating slaves, the compounder had persuaded me into a hooded cloak that gave me a faintly monkish look. 'We *mustn't* be followed,' he'd squeaked, pulling my hat off. The hood now drawn over my hair, I waited beneath the shadow of a victory monument while he finished climbing the hundred steps that connected two levels of the City. Pushed from behind by his assistant, and wheezing from exertion, he staggered into the light, and leaned against the monument. When he was able, he got out a glass bottle and sniffed a vapour that reminded me of roasting *kava* beans. It revived him, though it turned his face a deathly shade of grey. 'I was mad to let you talk me into this,' he whispered in Syriac to his colleague. 'It'll surely get us killed.' He'd spoken in a dialect mostly used on the Persian side of the Euphrates. I pretended not to understand but was glad of the heavy sword I'd put on to replace the one lost to Shahin.

We walked across the square, the Great Church on our right, towards a brass statue of Saint Peter. Just beyond this stood a line of several dozen carrying chairs. We were deep into siesta and no one was expecting passengers. Ignoring us until our shadows loomed across them, slaves and owners alike were playing dice and drinking.

'Three men your size?' asked the owner of a chair that had been picked at random. He laughed. 'You'll need more than one chair if you don't want my slaves to go on strike.' The compounder silenced him with a quarter *solidus* that would have been more impressive if it hadn't stuck to the palm of his trembling hand.

While the owner borrowed more slaves to join in the work, I found myself looking at Saint Peter. This was a statue that would make any Lord Treasurer mindful of his safety. It was about these brass legs that one of my predecessors had flung his arms for sanctuary when the mob caught up with him. Phocas himself had been put to death in a reasonably civilised manner by the new Augustus. His ministers weren't so fortunate. The Lord Treasurer had been torn apart but kept alive long enough to see various body parts draped upon the statue like barbarian wedding gifts on a tree. It had been necessary, once order was restored, to take the statue down for a long soaking in vinegar.

For all the grim reminder, I was the least visibly scared of the three passengers who eventually set off in the chair. With much bumping and scraping, as even the additional carrying slaves couldn't keep us more than a few inches above the road, we crept along. At first, the compounder insisted on having the curtains drawn tight about the chair. Soon, however, the heat inside was heading towards the critical and the smell of unwashed bodies and farty breath was beginning to turn my stomach. He didn't complain when I lifted the flap beside me. This let me see that the owner of the chair was leading us past the old Admiralty building. After this, we stopped and the owner came back for further instructions. The compounder pulled his own curtains open and looked out. Once it was clear we hadn't been followed, he sat back heavily. Sweating uncontrollably, he got out another gold coin and named a place inside the poor districts – close by the place where I'd taken up with Antonia the day before. He cut off the obvious objection with more gold and pulled his curtain back into place.

'If I asked where we were going,' I enquired politely, 'would you be able to answer?' The compounder shook his head. My sword in its scabbard was pressing against my thigh. Would it get me out of any trouble I might be heading towards? As the carrying slaves got into their stride and lifted us higher above the pavement, the compounder unstoppered his glass bottle again and sniffed at its fumes until I thought he'd stop breathing. I'd have no trouble from him, I thought.

'Wait here for us,' the compounder pleaded. 'We shan't be long at all.' He mopped his forehead and ran a dry tongue over dry lips. 'I'll pay you double what I've given you so far,' he added. After a brief hesitation, the owner nodded and pulled out a short sword. The slaves already had their knives out. This 'moment of my time' had already extended itself to an hour.

My boots crunched on disintegrated bricks as I skirted heaps of filth too rancid to be scavenged away. We were moving into an area where no outsiders ever went for amusement. If I was right about the geography, we'd soon be in a place where the authorities never went without very good cause and then with a few dozen armed men for protection. As we emerged from one of the bigger courtyards into the semblance of a street, we stopped before a heap of dead and decomposing rats. Now I didn't need both arms to keep my balance, I took out a bottle of perfume and emptied it into a napkin.

'It's in here, My Lord,' the compounder whispered. He nodded at the narrow entrance to another courtyard and, within that, to a door that hung open in a high wall of surprisingly decent brick.

The other buildings were of the usual rickety timber. I thought again of the geography. Before renamed Constantinople and made the Empire's eastern capital, Byzantium had been given walls adequate for keeping out most barbarian raids. These walls were long gone. But, here and there, deep inside the modern City, traces remained. This could be one of the towers.

The compounder grabbed at my arm as I stepped sideways for a better look at the building. 'I crave your indulgence if anything you see or hear might contravene the laws of the Empire,' he said, looking nervously round the empty yard. I said nothing. I'd once heard it seriously argued that the laws didn't apply in these districts.

27

In a fog of smells that, despite the napkin pressed to my face, could have made a muckraker puke, we moved up one flight of irregular stairs. From here, it was an unlit passageway. Behind every door that we passed, I heard a scurrying that put me in mind of rats, but was more likely to be the human residents. We stopped at the far end of the building. This would have been the outer wall of Byzantium and there was no entrance here. We took another flight of stairs back to ground level. Hidden as if by accident behind a pile of building materials covered with the dust of generations, a solid door was set into a solid wall.

The compounder knocked three times. Someone on the other side knocked once and then again and a small hatch was drawn open. The compounder leaned closer so he could be seen. For added security, he said his name. As the door creaked inward, I suppressed a flash of sudden panic and stepped into an interior that seemed to be in total darkness and smelled like an opened grave.

'Please feel welcome here, My Lord Alaric,' the compounder's associate said, speaking for the first time, and in a strongly Syrian accent. 'Be assured you are among friends and that no danger can come to you.' By the dim light that came from the corridor, I could see I was in a curtained sliver of what may have been a large room. Whoever had opened the door was out of sight behind the foul and shining curtain.

The compounder pushed himself through the door, leaving me no choice but to stand against the curtain. 'I assure you, My Lord, you are in no danger,' he said, drawing the bolt shut. So many assurances of safety. I tried not to listen to the voice inside me that said to pull the bolt open again and make a dash for the light.

I looked past the compounder and willed my throat muscles to work properly. 'Where's your friend?' I asked.

'Keeping watch outside,' the compounder answered. I suppressed another flash of panic. If this was a trap, it was unnecessarily elaborate. Avoiding the curtain, I pressed myself against a damp wall and let the compounder run his hands over that horrid cloth in search of an opening.

Through the curtain, I was in a room about the size of a large holding dungeon, though somewhat higher. It was pointless to wonder what had been its original purpose. Whatever that had been, its current purpose was decidedly more exotic.

'You have brought him to us?' the most decrepit-looking of the three old men quavered in Syriac. 'You have brought us the seventh outsider to approach you after the breaking of the sun upon your face in the place of your business?' He got stiffly up from his place beside his colleagues and peered at me from within the wide circle of candles.

'As you directed, O Master,' the compounder answered in a voice that seemed likely to tremble out of control, 'I have brought the Lord Alaric.'

Oh dear! I thought. I'd assumed he was fussing about Priscus. If he believed I'd been in the drugs market to see him, his had been the bigger misapprehension. I kept my face steady and waited.

Without rising from his place, another of the old men looked at me. 'The stars assured us the thief was an older man,' he quavered, also in Syriac. 'It was an older man, and a darker, who was seen carrying it from its place of safety,' He reached out a bony hand to help him see past the candles. 'Is this not a young barbarian? Has he brought it with him? If not, why has he not brought it with him?'

The compounder went forward another step and bowed. 'Just as you told me a man would seek me out, Master, so came the Lord Alaric to me yesterday, seeking help. I have done as you directed. I can do no more.' His voice caught and he began a sentence in Greek that trailed off before it could make sense.

Still on his feet, the first old man pointed at me. 'Come forward, young man,' he said in Greek. 'Do you truly possess the Horn of Babylon?' He raised both arms in a dramatic gesture, the black folds of his robe stretching out like the wings of a bat.

The stone floor had dipped in places and every depression was a puddle of slime. Avoiding these, I walked forward to the edge of the pentagram that I saw had been chalked just beyond the circuit of the candles. Even after the door was closed, I'd seen how the candles continued to flicker, but hadn't used up the stinking air. From where I now stood, I could see a small window on my left. The main hole in its shutter was blocked with a sheet of oiled parchment.

'I do possess the object of which you speak,' I said, making my own attempt at the dramatic, 'and would learn whatever can be said about its current significance.' I stepped forward a few paces and tried to avoid showing my interest in the window.

The old man who hadn't yet spoken put up an arm for attention. 'Has My Lord *touched* the Horn of Babylon?' he croaked. I think I was supposed to give way to terror at this point. I folded my arms and tried not to look impatient. Aside from the nonsense they speak, the problem with astrologers is that they can beat eunuchs every time for stretching out the most commonplace utterances. 'Have you taken it from the box in which it was to be insulated forever, and touched it with your bare hands?' he elaborated.

'I have touched it,' I said, sounding earnest – *I, and whoever last polished the bloody thing*, I might have added but didn't. I ignored the nervous looks and the quiet muttering of the old men. 'Is this a matter I have cause to regret?' I asked. 'I know nothing of your Horn. It was brought to me yesterday, wholly unsought by me.' I paused and waited for the muttering to die away. 'What *is* the Horn of Babylon?' I asked with sudden firmness. If I wasn't to be here till nightfall, I'd have to move things along.

The old man who was standing tottered forward to the nearest of the candles. He stared at me for a long time through dull eyes. I met his look and hoped he wouldn't begin chanting incantations, or try for a conjuring trick with the candles. That sort of thing could soak up time beyond reckoning – it certainly would if this old fool set fire to his sleeve. But he only wanted to see me properly. Though he was five feet away, I could smell the filthy clothes he wore as if we were in bed together. I was almost glad of the otherwise overpowering background smell.

'Does My Lord know the story of how, in ancient time, King Cyrus took Babylon?' he shrilled. I knew the account given in Herodotus. I'd heard a few doubtful supplements to this when I was in Ctesiphon. Obviously, it was time to hear it again. I remained silent. 'When the city fell to the Persians,' he said, dropping his voice to an aged whine, 'the last King of Babylon was too busy digging in the foundations of his palace to lead a defence. After the last moment for victory had come and gone, he found what he had been told to seek. This was a sacrificial vessel made not by human hands. It was sent down from the skies by the ancient gods of his country. Anyone who kept it close would infallibly get his heart's desire – but, in return, would be deprived of all human happiness.

'The Horn was possessed by Cyrus. After its loss by his successors, it was possessed by the Alexander known as the Great. After him, it passed into the hands of those who desired other than worldly power. It is now sought again by those whose power is, or would be, of this world.'

'And who might those be?' I asked, perking up. The room fell silent. I was aware of a fly at the window. It could have flown straight out by going through a gap in the frame. Instead, it was beating itself against the oiled parchment. Now there was no other sound in the room, I could hear a child saying something in Armenian. It came from a few yards beyond the window, which must be into one of the courtyards. An adult was responding, though in a voice too low for me to hear what was said.

'Can you explain why Heraclius is Emperor, and not Nicetas?' the old man asked. I tried to make sense of his tone. Was this meant to lead me to enlightenment? Or was he after some from me? His Greek was too oddly accented for me to tell.

'The story is well known and true in its essentials,' I said, keeping my voice even. When the old man said nothing more, I gave way to the inevitable. 'Thirteen years ago,' I summarised, 'the Emperor Maurice was deposed in a bloody *coup* – the first break in legal continuity for about three hundred years. He and his five sons were murdered, but it was at first hoped that Phocas the Tyrant would stabilise the frontiers. When he failed to do this, he kept power by launching a reign of terror that squashed all opposition.' I thought of Priscus, who'd been the most enthusiastic officer of the Terror – in which capacity I'd first encountered him.

'Eventually, his purges and inability to keep out of war with the Persians, and his inability to beat them in war, provoked, or enabled, the Exarch of Africa to start a second revolution. The Exarch put forward two alternative rival Emperors – his son, Heraclius, and his nephew, Nicetas. The deal was that whichever of them got first from Carthage to Constantinople and deposed Phocas would be Emperor. Nicetas came by land but got stuck in Egypt. Heraclius came by sea and had a smooth crossing. There's more to the story, if you want to look at the details. But that is broadly what happened.'

The old man leaned forward. 'So Heraclius is Emperor simply because he got here first?'

'Yes,' I said. Of course, there was more to it than that. Heraclius, if sickly, wasn't an invalid. Heraclius wasn't completely incapable of taking decisions. The old men were cackling away again in Syriac. One of them now switched into a different language, his voice rising to an ecstatic babble:

> *Ta-ak-bi-a-at pi-ka li-kal-li-ma i-na-ka*
> *li-ip-ti-ku pa-da-nam pi-ḫi-tam*
> *ḫarrana li-iš-ta-zi-ik a-na ki-ib-si-ka*
> *šá-di-a li-iš-ta-zi-ik a-na šêpi-ka*

He ended in a long fit of coughing. 'Well spoken, my brother!' one of the others called out, 'The ancient words of the Horn are filled with wisdom – if only we could understand them.' Once again, I thought of the time. I could stand here as some kind of supplicant, and get nowhere very fast, or I could take a chance.

'I understand that Heraclius has been consulting you.' I said. I looked at the suddenly shocked and silent faces and tried not to burst out laughing. Had these transparent frauds been the best our Great Augustus could find? 'He wanted your help to win the Persian War,' I improvised with more confidence. 'You procured the Horn of Babylon and assured him it would bring him victory. It was then stolen before you could give it to him. You have brought me here because you need it back. You need it because, when he returns to Constantinople, he will not be pleased to learn that the object you have told him is of the utmost power is now in other hands – other deeply unfriendly hands.'

I smiled and moved my weight to my right leg. There was no doubt I'd cut out hours of dancing round the subject. Just before Christmas, Heraclius had burned two astrologers alive in the Circus, and had afterwards given a pious lecture to the mob on the Satanic nature of horoscopes. All that showed, of course, was that he believed in astrology. No surprise, then, he was now wasting the poor taxpayers' money on some for himself. He was credulous without limit. The real wonder was that, after four years of military failure, he'd stopped at consulting the stars. Why hadn't he also tried sacrifices to the Old Gods, or conversion to the fire worship of the Persians? Perhaps he had.

I went back to the question I'd been asked. 'Where does Nicetas fit into this?' I asked. I waited for an answer. Where *did* he fit in? Had his people stolen the Horn? I could assume there was some connection between him and Simon. I'd overheard Simon confessing that he'd missed getting the cup for himself. Who had got to it first? What had Nicetas wanted with it? Did he want its power for himself? He was another superstitious fool – though too besotted with his monks to risk his soul with magic. Perhaps he'd wanted to use the cup and other evidences of blasphemy to blackmail Heraclius into abdicating. Or perhaps he'd simply wanted to spare Heraclius from the sin of astrology. But Shahin – where did *he* fit in?

So many questions, though where to begin? One of the old men now found his voice again. 'Has the young barbarian read the words?' he asked the compounder. 'Can he be aware that whoever reads the words engraved by unworldly hands upon the Horn of Babylon will start a process that cannot be stopped and will end in the collapse upon itself of the entire universe?' The compounder let out a terrified yelp and rocked back and forth in terror. Evidently pleased, the old men went back to their own conversation.

This would never do. I clapped my hands together. When the room was silent, I walked over to the curtain. Looking as outraged as I was impatient, I turned back to face everyone. 'Whether or not you claim the Emperor as your master,' I cried in Syriac, 'you are all traitors by your own confession. You are traitors and blasphemers. I think we all know the penalties.' That got their minds off the end of the universe. Most Greeks never learn Syriac. These men had taken it as read a barbarian wouldn't know it. Crap astrologers that showed them to be, I might add. I walked back to the middle of the room. 'If you want me to walk out of here and never come back, I suggest you should put yourselves in order and start answering my questions.'

'My Lord is right in the essentials,' one of the old men allowed, still in his own language. 'But you must understand the danger in which you have placed yourself. The Emperor provided us with a box to shield him from the power of the Horn when it was given to him. You have touched the Horn with your bare hands. This is not safe for anyone who lacks the necessary training. None shall know happiness, though he get his heart's desire . . .'

'Oh, shut up and be seated!' I snapped. 'I'll have no more of this nonsense. The stars tell us nothing. The Horn of Babylon is a piece of silver looted from a tomb. You've already admitted you can't understand whatever's written on it.' I looked from one shaking face to another. 'If your methods gave true knowledge about the world, I think we'd have seen better results after so many thousands of years.' There I stopped. I hadn't time or patience for lectures on the nature of true science. I'd softened them for questioning and I'd now have some answers. 'The Horn of Babylon,' I said, 'is wanted by a man called Simon. I want to know what connection he has with the Emperor's cousin. I also want to know to what extent both these men are connected with the Persians, and why.'

I could say what I wanted. Fat chance I had of getting it. There was a loud cry of warning that came through the window. It rose to a shrill scream before suddenly ending. It was followed by a wild scraping of boots and a shouting of orders and by a firm banging of sword pommels on wood.

28

I turned and pulled the curtain down. In the light from the candles, I could see that the door's one bolt wouldn't stand a hard shove from the other side. I looked about for something to wedge against it. Even before I could give up on that idea, someone banged loudly.

'Alaric,' Simon shouted, 'I know you're in there. I've given orders that you aren't to be harmed. Put your sword down and stand away from the door.'

'O Reverend Masters,' the compounder begged, 'let me stand within your pentagram of safety.' Not speaking, the old men moved to its centre and clutched at each other.

I didn't ask for permission. I stepped over the chalked line and kicked one of the candles over. 'You can have this back in a moment,' I said, picking up its iron holder. I carried it over to the window. I heard a scrape of many feet outside the door. 'I've got my sword ready, Simon,' I shouted. 'Whoever comes in first gets it in his guts.' That would buy me a little time. I swung the candle-holder against the shutter. The whole rickety thing fell outwards and I blinked in the sudden brightness. It was a small window. I'd have to go out diagonally. Men were banging on the door and shouting. The men in the room were deep in argument over who had a right to be within the chalked line on the floor. I put my hands on the frame and heaved myself through into the daylight.

The bottom of the window was level with the ground and I came out on my hands and knees. 'There he is!' someone shouted from my left. I jumped up and went for my sword. Picking their way forward over the broken ground and forming a loose crescent as they came, there were a dozen men who hadn't gone with

Simon inside the building. He may have been telling the truth. Perhaps I wasn't to be killed this time. If so, I could make a dash forward and cut my way to freedom. But these were big men and they were armed. Mad as it seemed, the only escape was back inside the building.

'Don't read the inscription, Alaric!' I heard one of the old men shout feebly from the room. The next sound had to be the compounder's dying scream. For another few moments it would be chaos in there and more men would be hurrying down to join it. I waved my sword at the nearest armed man and stumbled back inside the building.

I nearly bumped into someone at the top of the first flight of stairs. He had time to fall back and pull out his knife. Before he could shout for help though, I'd got the point of my sword under his chin. I pushed until it hit the back of his head. I pulled it free and stepped over his twitching body. From the far end of the corridor came a noise of approaching boots. 'Remember, I want him alive!' Simon shouted. 'I don't care if he's wounded. But I want him alive.' It was worth hearing that. But there were men behind me now and I'd soon be caught from both sides. I tried to keep my feet from making any noise and darted up the next flight of stairs.

Most buildings in the poor districts are designed for rapid escape – that, or the inhabitants prefer to avoid stepping into those stinking puddles when calling on their more distant neighbours. On first entering, I'd instinctively looked for and seen the slender walkway of planks held together with rope that connected this building to another across the yard. That's what I was now looking for. At the top of every flight, I expected to see a hole knocked into the wall and my means of escape. Below me, I could hear a sound of smashed wood and of screams mingled with loud shouting. Simon was dividing his forces with a search of the whole building. No one yet behind me, I raced higher and higher upward in the stone tower. I found nothing until the topmost flight of stairs. This ended in a wooden door. I sheathed my sword and hurried towards it.

Just in time, I realised I'd overshot the walkway. I'd almost over-shot the roof. I threw myself back from the dazzling sunshine and a wild fluttering of birds. It was only because the door was unlocked that I hadn't smashed through it and plunged sixty feet to my death. I gripped the doorframe and looked down into the yard.

'He's up there!' Simon shouted. He'd left the building and, shad-ing his eyes, was looking up at me from the courtyard. 'Look – he's on the roof!' He laughed happily and, making quickly for the entrance to the building, rapped out a stream of orders that I couldn't hear. Behind me, there was already a clatter of boots on the stairs. The walkway was ten feet below me and another eight to my right. I hadn't seen it on my way up because it led from one of the lodging rooms. I ran fingers though my hair and tried to think. Trying to jump from here was a desperate last resort. I was some way from that. I looked at the crumbling roof tiles I'd have to crawl across to be able to jump down to the walkway. Keeping hold of the doorframe, I leaned forward into nothingness and twisted round to see how easily I could heave myself on to the roof.

A few yards behind me, someone shouted a warning. I turned and drew my sword again. He dodged my main blow but I managed a slicing cut to the side of his neck. With a scream of horror, he fell back, clutching at himself, blood spraying from where I'd got him. He was a big man and his body blocked the way for the other two men who'd come up with him – not that either who stood back from the twitching, blood-soaked thing I'd thrown at them seemed inclined to try his luck. Keeping my sword ready, I pulled off the cloak the compounder had given me and threw it at the men. I thought longer than I should about my outer tunic. It was of cotton, brought all the way as a made-up garment from India, and dyed a lovely blue. Its price would have paid any rent in this district for a hundred years. But I took it off and threw this down as well. I sheathed my sword and blew a kiss at the two men. Before either could make a dash to stop me, I'd sprung with a force and agility that would have made even Glaucus cheer and was spreadeagled, face down, on the roof.

Or would Glaucus have cheered? I had intended one roll to the left, followed by an easy jump down to the walkway. When you're still feeling the rush of a quick kill, everything looks possible. I'd made my calculations and I had no reason to doubt them. But I've never been one for heights and, for one sickening instant, I felt myself gather speed as I slid down the roof. With a ripping of silk on wooden holding pegs, I stabilised. But this only gave me the time to go into a full panic. My stomach had turned to ice and my limbs felt as if they'd turned to stone.

One of the men pushed his bearded face above the doorframe to see where I'd gone. 'Come back, you fool!' he shouted. He stretched a hand forward and scrabbled on tiles about nine inches from me. Deep inside the building, someone was shouting for Simon.

I wanted a triumphant cry of 'Fuck you!' All I managed was a faint squawk, followed by another wave of panic as the man pulled his hand back and I saw what seemed to be my one chance of staying alive move out of reach. He stretched forward again, this time only dislodging one of the tiles. I saw it slip out of sight. What seemed an age later, I heard it strike something solid in the yard. I pressed my sweating face closer against the roof and forced myself to think. Now, the tile peg that had got itself tangled in my inner tunic snapped and, if I didn't move yet, I had the awful feeling that one breath would send me on my way. Willing my wrist not to move, I dug the fingers of my left hand underneath one of the tiles. It snapped halfway up as if it had been made of dried mud and slid down with a clatter, ending in a silence that set off a dull roaring in my head. I controlled myself and got my fingers under what remained. This time, it came fully away, and there was a three inch gap where the tile below didn't cover. I plunged my whole arm down, dislodging more tiles, until I was clutching at one of the more solid battens. With another ripping of silk, I pulled myself into a sitting position and recovered a semblance of nerve while staring across a sea of other roofs, until the view was blocked by the clouds of steam that rose above the tanneries.

'Fuck you!' I did now cry. 'If you want me, you come and get me.' No answer. In place of another grab at me, there was a splintering of wood in the room directly below me. I looked forward. I was just about level with the walkway. If I dithered here much longer, those big men would grab hold of my legs and pull me back inside. I bit my lip and edged forward to where the tiles were unbroken. My stomach was twisting into funny knots and I wondered if I'd find the nerve to jump straight down. Once I was away from where I'd been able to hold on, though, it was like going down a children's slide. Gathering speed, and attended by a clatter of more dislodged tiles, I was over the edge before I could realise the full madness of what I was doing. After a moment of nothingness, I hit the walkway chest first and with a loud smack that trailed off into an echo that reminded me of a plucked harp string.

The walkway had no upper ropes for holding on. Using it was a matter of acquired balance. On instinct, I'd spread my arms and legs as I hit. Now, fighting for the breath that had been knocked out of me on impact, I joined my hands underneath the slats and got my feet together. More shocked than scared, I held on grimly and waited for the whole slender things of rope and rotting wood to stop swaying like a branch in the wind. 'Stiff upper lip – stiff upper lip!' I kept telling myself, for some reason in English. It didn't work. I wasn't as high up as the windows of my sleeping quarters. But there's a difference between standing on a rising sequence of brick arches that have survived a century of earthquakes, and looking through the two-inch spacings between wooden slats that are only eighteen inches long and half as much wide. I clutched harder and was aware of the still-dancing image, so very far below, of men who ran about, shouting and pointing up at me.

But I heard more shouting behind me, and I forced myself up on hands and knees to crawl across the void that separated me from the far building. Other slats disintegrated as I passed over them. I thought, the whole way, I'd tip over or go through. I focused on the slats a foot in front of my nose and did my best not to see the impossible distance they kept me from falling. Men shouted from the building I'd left. Because no one dared follow me, the cries grew fainter as I made my way steadily forward. Below in the yard Simon was in sight again and was ordering men into the far building.

I'd not be staying in the far building. I pushed past a couple of curious boys and an old woman, who'd woken from their siesta, and made for the next walkway. I was already a quarter across it and wondering if the next building would allow a choice of further escapes, when on the far side two men with the dark beards of Syrians stepped forward from the shade and raised their swords in silent warning.

I turned back. I was still on the last slats when another man appeared in front of me. 'You're going nowhere, my lad!' he snarled. He spoke to an accompaniment of approaching feet on the stairs. 'You'll come quietly if you know what's good for you.' He would have spoken more. But I now had my sword out. As he went for his own, I lunged forward and ran him through in the lower belly. I got up unsteadily, grabbed him by his beard and kicked him downstairs. Screaming and tumbling head over heels as he went, he crashed into more men who'd been hurrying up to join him. I was having a good day with the body on the staircase blocking move!

I turned back to the walkway. One of the men at the far end had a better sense of balance than I had and was already halfway towards me. I wheeled about and looked frantically for some other escape. I could go up the last flight of stairs to the roof but I didn't expect there to be any way off that. I could hear more men coming upstairs to join the two who were untangling themselves from the dying man I'd thrown at them. I went down a step and slashed at them with my sword. They fell back and looked round for the approaching support. I put my sword away and jumped back to the entrance to the walkway. I bent down and took hold of the two ropes that secured all the slats. I lifted and pulled them, and watched the Syrian I'd surprised throw himself forward to catch hold of the walkway. I pulled again and sent an undulating motion towards him. He missed his hold and fell headfirst, screaming all the way. He landed in a mass of filth and, alive though injured, cried piteously for help. His colleague stepped back to safety and waved his sword again.

'Simon wants me alive,' I said softly in a voice that shook like sobs. 'He wants me alive.' I waited for the swaying walkway to stabilise, then made myself get down again on all fours and crawl carefully forward. The seam of my inner tunic had split and its silk was slithering down my forearms. If only I'd been brave enough to lift my hands off the ropes, I'd have pulled it free and sent it billowing towards the ground – even in the state I'd put it, it was another windfall for some lucky pauper.

I was ten feet away from the building I'd left, when I heard Simon's voice behind me. 'And does My Lord think he'll get very far?' he sneered.

29

I stopped and sat astride the walkway. As Simon barked an order at the man far behind me, I swung my legs until no one with any sense in his head would have dared follow. The ropes creaked alarmingly and there was a sound of snapping wood far behind me. I pretended not to hear this. 'Hello, Simon,' I said with a bright smile. 'Do you fancy joining me? You get a lovely view from out here.'

He looked at the swaying walkway and moved back a step. 'You can't stay on that thing forever,' he said with a nasty smile of his own. 'You might as well make it easy for all of us. You have the power to make this a very civilised transaction. If you come over and take my hand, you can seal a note to your secretary telling him where the *object* is and directing him to bring it to us. You can then go free. If you want to make it hard for yourself, I can send a message of my own – wrapped about your left hand.' He brought out a villainous laugh and looked round to make sure his men had heard him.

'Either way, you'd have to wait for a reply,' I said. 'You see, my secretary's on Lesbos at the moment. I doubt he'll be back till June at the earliest.' I pulled off the rags of my inner tunic and used it to wipe my sweaty face. I looked at the dirt and another man's blood that I left on it. I found a cleaner patch of silk and wiped again. Like a spider at the centre of its web, I felt the walkway shake slightly behind me. I kicked my legs and leaned sideways and back. There was a cry of alarm but no horrified wail. More to the point, the shaking stopped. I looked at Simon. I could have sworn he'd gone up the night before like a bundle of rags soaked in pitch. Such a pity he'd been put out in time! Then again, his beard was singed right out of shape and there was none of it left under his chin. He wasn't dead or even seriously injured. But I could hope he was in roaring pain under his robe.

'Tell me, Simon,' I asked, 'how you forged that note from my own people so quickly and so convincingly. I'll grant I was stupid not to have had a closer look. But it really was an impressive production.'

'You don't owe Heraclius your life,' he said. 'You don't owe him anything. Come off that thing before it collapses.' I smiled at him and set the walkway swaying again. He scowled, then rearranged his face into a smile of his own. 'See reason, Alaric,' he pleaded. 'Once he's back from Cyzicus, do you think the Emperor will be grateful for any of this? You know things you have no business to know. Consult your own best interest, and join us.'

At last the man had come out with something worth listening to. What *was* I supposed to do with the cup? 'Here you are, Caesar,' I was supposed to say when Heraclius got home. 'Here's evidence of the one crime that could get you deposed. And, by the by, I think Nicetas has been plotting to get the Purple for himself.' At best, that might get me a room of my own in the Fortified Monastery. At the worst – well, if he was no Phocas, Heraclius did order summary executions now and again. And who would dare put in a good word for me? Who'd want to?

On the other hand, why shouldn't Simon go back to Plan A once I'd given him the cup? The only doubt would be whether he or one of him men would put a knife into my back. But I did listen while he explained the obvious. I glanced down at the yard, and found myself begin very gently to waver.

Bloody fool Simon, though – he'd not seen the effect of his words. While I still sat looking down, and feeling progressively more queasy at the distance between me and the ground, he went and spoiled the effect. 'I saw you touch the Horn of Babylon yesterday,' he said with an upward stab of both arms. 'Did the old ones tell you what that means?' He laughed and stared away from me. 'I'll tell you what it means. You have six days before the full horror descends upon you. Give it to me while you still have time.

You can't wait for Heraclius to come back. You must pass it to someone else before the seven days' grace is up.'

'Oh, fuck off, Simon!' I laughed. 'I'd be more touched by your concern for me if you didn't so plainly want *the horror* for yourself.' Was that another faint tremor behind me? Just in case, I bounced up and down. I focused on the bearded faces that looked nastily out from behind Simon and hoped he didn't notice the terrified fart that my innards managed despite the lack of breakfast and lunch.

Simon let his arms fall back to his side. 'You can't sit there all day,' he sneered. 'Yes, even barbarians must eventually understand when they're trapped.' I shrugged and looked once more into the yard. Except for the man I'd knocked off the walkway, and who still had enough strength in his shattered body to wave at the dogs who were quietly closing in on him, everyone was up here and waiting at each end of the walkway. The sun was beating down on my bare back. Forget spiders and webs – much longer out here and I'd dry up like a slug in the afternoon sun.

I took my sword out and waved it, with a look on my face of careless happiness. 'I may only be a barbarian,' I said. 'But you're a bloody traitor. One of these days, I'll finish the job of burning you to death. You'll be tied to a stake in the Circus and whoever lights the pitch barrels heaped beneath you will be cheered on by a mob of seventy thousand. If you've heard about the law I persuaded Caesar to issue last year, about strangling victims before the flames reach them, be assured you'll get the full old-fashioned service.' I raised my voice. 'You'll all burn as traitors.' I smiled at the nervous rustle of clothing behind Simon. 'You'll never spend a clipped penny of whatever the Persians have promised you.' I repeated myself in Syriac.

'My Lord Alaric assumes he will somehow remain influential in the counsels of the Empire,' Simon replied with gloating ill humour. 'You'll find the Emperor himself isn't that steady on the throne. I can see no place for a meddling barbarian in a government committed to peace and a restoration of the proper order of things.'

Ah – something else worth hearing. This was turning out, all considered, a most productive afternoon. 'Do you really think Nicetas will be grateful for any of this?' I asked. This time, though, Simon kept his mouth shut. I smiled again. Now everyone was looking at me, I might as well put on a proper show. I got unsteadily to my feet and braced myself against the renewed swaying of the walkway. I looked along its length and up and down the wall of the far building. I looked at another walkway that passed underneath mine at a right angle twenty feet down. I shut my eyes and thought. I turned and walked six feet closer to where Simon was standing. So long as I kept telling myself I was only six inches off the ground, I was surprisingly steady.

'I thought you'd see reason,' he gloated. Without turning, he ordered one of his men to reach forward and take my hand. But he'd broken too soon into his triumphant smile. I sat down again and waited for the renewed swaying to stop. I leaned forward and, paying no attention to arms that fully outstretched could pull my hair, sawed halfway through one of the supporting ropes, then halfway through the other.

'What are you doing, you fool?' Simon cried. 'You'll kill yourself.'

I looked up and smiled again. 'Oh, I'm conducting an experiment that will leave one of us very disappointed,' I said with fair success at a nonchalant tone. 'Since I think mathematically and have a good eye for distance, I rather think it's you who'll be disappointed.' I slashed quickly at both ropes and twisted about to hold fast on to one of the bigger and more solid slats.

The terrifying sense of having stepped off a cliff ended when my severed walkway hit the one below in a sudden change of direction that almost shook me loose. It buckled and arched, and picked up speed again as I saw the darkness of the first-floor window come closer and closer. With a burst of exhilaration, I realised I'd be spot on. I reached a low point about six feet from the ground, before swinging slightly upwards and slowing. I let go and, not so much as scraping myself on the window frame, landed on my feet inside the room. I steadied myself and sheathed my sword. It had been a perfect escape. Even if he'd been up to dashing straight after me, Simon would take ages to get down here. The one man on the top floor would be taking his life in his hands if he came downstairs at more than a crawl.

I went through the motions of brushing dust from what little clothing I still had on. 'Perfect, my dear boy – perfect!' I said aloud in Latin. I went into Greek: 'Sometimes, I amaze even myself!' I bowed to a wall of mud bricks. The thought then hit me of everything that might have gone wrong. And, from the moment I'd been approached by the compounder, *anything* could have gone wrong. It had been a continuing miracle that I wasn't the poor sod, bleating out his last on that dung heap. Having no audience now to think less of me, I wondered if I'd fall down and vomit. But I heard a whimper, and reached for my sword.

For some reason, I'd assumed the room was empty. It wasn't. Once my eyes were adjusted to the gloom, I saw a vastly obese creature, wallowing in straw as he was serviced by a couple of child prostitutes. He struggled to sit up, and the turd one of the children had deposited on his chest slid down, to be squashed beneath a fold of his belly fat.

'What is the meaning of this?' he demanded. 'What are *you* doing here?'

I peered harder at the man. 'Why, hello, Timothy,' I said. 'I didn't recognise you without the wig.' I realised I was standing on the outer garment of his Prefect's uniform, and stepped on to the rough boards. I glanced out of the window. Simon had gone from where I'd last seen him. I thought about asking for the loan of Timothy's cloak. My leggings were gone below the knees and their backside felt wholly ripped out. He'd probably refuse. I dropped the thought. My boots were sound. All else was secondary. I went for the door. 'I'll see you tonight,' I said without turning.

30

The only question worth asking about the carrying chair was how long its owner and his slaves had waited before buggering off. I couldn't blame them in a place like this. I looked both ways along the narrow street before deciding to go left. Far away, I could hear Simon's voice raised in wild shouting.

I'd rounded a corner when some piece of trash about my own age tried jumping me from above. 'Oh, ho ho!' he roared, nearly landing on my shoulders. I stunned him with the pommel of my sword and kicked him out of sight into a doorway. I didn't check if he was breathing. I didn't look about to see if he'd had friends. I'd have given more attention to scowling at a dog. Oddly cheered, I hurried forward. Unless I was mistaken, it couldn't be more than a few hundred yards to the western side of Imperial Square.

It was a shame about the compounder. He'd been dragged into this against his better judgement. If I hadn't taken my detour the previous day, he'd still be in the drugs market, innocently selling his wares. I tried to feel sorry for the old astrologers but failed. Besides, they might still be calling nonsense at each other from inside their pentagram of safety. I stopped in the silent street and looked at the contents of a chamber pot someone had flung from an upper window.

At whatever cost in frayed nerves, I'd found out something. I didn't know how or why it had come to me but the cup had been awaiting collection by Heraclius. It had been stolen by Simon. What he had to do with Nicetas, and what Shahin was doing in our home waters, remained unclear. I bent and stared closer at the excrements spread out before me. They were wormy and streaked with blood, and had the squashy look you get from eating porridge rather than bread. How had the compounder come to his misapprehension – the correct misapprehension, I should say – about the cup and me? I hadn't exactly flown from my hall of audience to the drugs market. Even so, I couldn't believe word had been carried to him any faster than my own movements. How many other people knew I had the cup? Excepting Simon, those who'd seen it at the audience surely didn't know what it was. Could I get away with holding on to it till Heraclius came back from Cyzicus, then leaving it in the place set aside in the Imperial Palace for anonymous gifts? Or should I tell everything to Heraclius and hope for the best? He had no one else who could balance the Imperial budget and otherwise tell him what to do.

So many questions. I sighed and straightened up. I skirted the mass of drying filth before me and walked quickly away from the cloud of flies that rose up from it.

No sound of a chase. The sun had moved far from its zenith and I shivered slightly in the shade of the street. The excitement of the escape was gone. What I'd done to that spotty, stinking creature far behind me was fading. I began to worry again about all that might have gone wrong, and about the inexplicable chaos I'd been plunged into by the presenting of a silver cup. With a determined effort I dropped that line of thought. It was replaced at once by thoughts of Antonia. What moisture I had in my mouth appeared to evaporate. I drifted back to the horror of those walkways. I felt no doubt they'd join the Shaft of Oblivion in my worst poppy-fed nightmares.

There really had been no sound of a chase. But I'd been listening for big men, whose boots scraping on the compacted earth would give them away from several hundred yards. A barefoot rabble of the locals was a different matter. I came out of my scared reverie to see that the street was blocked in both directions. If I'd missed the patter of bare feet on earth, I should have smelled the approach of their clothing.

'He stole the people's bread!' a woman shrilled from behind one of the crowds.

'His head's weight in gold, we was promised,' a man called from within the crowd.

'God bless the Lord Timothy!' the same woman replied. 'He'll see us right.'

Both crowds took a step forward. I looked about for escape. Unless I could jump ten feet and grab hold of a smashed balcony, there was no easy way out. There was another collective step forward, and a wizened youth took aim at me with a stone.

I reached for the purse that still hung from my belt. I held it up for all to see. 'You want gold?' I shouted. I undid its laces and emptied the purse into my left hand. I jingled several dozen new-minted *solidi,* and held one up for inspection. 'You want gold?' I turned and made sure everyone could see the value. Timothy could round up a mob and promise what took his fancy. Any one of the coins I had in the palm of my hand would keep all these animals fed for a month. 'If you want gold, there's plenty here.' I threw it as a glittering shower over the crowd that blocked the way from where I'd come. It dissolved at once into a snarling, ravening pack. The other crowd lurched forward, screaming and trampling on the fallen, to get its own share. It was the burrow people all over again, if somewhat more expensive. Not everyone joined the rush, but I'd levelled the odds. I got out my sword and went straight at them.

This killing had neither elegance nor equality. I stabbed. I slashed. I took the top off one man's head. I got another in the bladder. Someone who came at me with a knife got his head half-sawn off. I took hold of someone else with my left hand and smashed his brains out against a wall. It was over in barely any time at all. So far as I could tell, I was through without a scratch. I didn't wait for the shout of baffled rage behind me to begin. I didn't look back at the bloody carnage I was leaving. I held up my sword as if it were torch carried by night before a rich man's chair and ran for my life.

It was dazzling sunshine in Imperial Square. The mob didn't dare follow me into this place of civilised order and I passed the continuing ritual of the aged at no more than a brisk pace.

'You worthless bastard!' one of the old men shouted in my direction. 'I hope your suffering hasn't even begun.' It might have been Simeon again. This time, I didn't stop and try reasoning with anyone. The sun was behind me and I could feel a worrying tightness in the skin of my upper back. Watching my shadow go before me, I walked past some boys who were playing with a ball.

'Is that you, My Lord Alaric?' a voice called from my right. I made to go for my sword, then realised I was still carrying it. I snorted and put it back into its sheath. Little wonder those boys had kept out of my way.

'Hello, Ezra,' I said, trying my best to sound as if I were still arrayed in silk and cotton. I'd been eyeing up the young Jew for the better part of a year and he was a welcome, even a cheerful, sight. I raised my hands in the gesture of greeting usual among his people. I saw in time how bloody they were and the black incrustations under every finger nail. I let my hands drop down and shrugged.

'Your chest is looking very red, My Lord,' he said after a long pause. 'Should you be walking round with so few clothes?'

'Slight trouble in one of the poor districts,' I explained with a vague wave. Suddenly struck by the thought of dark, stinking bodies creeping along behind me, I turned round. It was just boys kicking their ball at each other. Beyond them, a dozen of the aged staggered in the sun about their endless circuit. 'I might ask, my boy,' I added in my best patronising voice, 'what brings you so far from the Jewish quarter and alone.' I stared into his face. I was sure he fancied me but had never tried anything. You can't tell with Jews – they gave us all our modern ideas of sexual propriety but have many others they haven't shared.

He looked away. 'My uncle sent me with a message to your palace,' he said. 'I believe it was about the rent collections near the Saint Andrew Monastery.'

The Saint Andrew district? Did I own properties there? I wondered. I'd bought up patches of the poor district facing the Golden Horn. I owned five blocks that were rented out to the better sort of artisan, but these were almost in sight of my office windows. Then I remembered. I'd lately won some property from an old fool who believed praying over his dice was better than reasoning from the frequency with which any combination of numbers was likely to come up. This had to be one of them. Since I already must have looked out of my head, I'd not make a total fool of myself by arguing with a Jew about what I owned.

I smiled at Ezra and led him towards the big flight of steps. 'Any chance you could pay for a chair to take me along the Triumphal Way?' I asked. He stopped, his face gone suddenly pale. I thought I'd shocked him by asking for the loan. But I followed his horrified look into the shadowy space between the steps and the embankment. Head smashed in by the impact, the naked boy I'd seen the day before was draped over the rim of the disused fountain. Except there was nothing left of his face, you'd not have thought he was dead. He might have been resting in the sun. Far above, his owner was looking down with arms raised in lamentation.

It wouldn't do to sit down and vomit – not here, not looking like this, not in front of a Jew. I swallowed hard and turned back for another look at the Imperial statues. 'Do be a love, Ezra,' I whispered. 'You're wearing far too many clothes for a day like this. You could lend your uncle's protector that grey cloak you have on.'

I watched the boy step back and unfasten his cloak pin. There was nothing athletic or otherwise attractive about his posture. Another year at the most and he'd be trying for a silly beard and probably filling out from the ghastly food Jews think it their duty to eat. But he was a pretty lad for the time being and he had the makings of considerable beauty. If only he'd put himself in my hands . . .

But he wouldn't. Just in time, I stopped myself from repeating how little beauty there was in the world.

There's nothing like the privacy of a closed carrying chair for getting over a long fit of the terrors. By the time I pulled the curtains aside and set foot on the steps at the main entrance to my palace, I was looking almost carefree.

The slaves who were hurrying down towards their filthy, blood-stained master wouldn't have expected any less of His Magnificence.

31

I looked up at the bathhouse ceiling and counted slowly to twelve. That should give Antonia time to dry the tears she was squeezing out. I looked down again. 'There is no taxpayer in Zigana called Isidore,' I repeated, this time with an implacable frown. 'Your alleged father, Laonicus,' I went on, 'left a wife and two sons. The wife is in receipt of a small pension bought from the Treasury by Laonicus before he died. This is still being paid. Both sons continue their father's practice but concentrate on laying petitions before the Master of the Offices.

'Almost everything you told me yesterday is a lie. I won't press you for the full truth all at once. But I'd like at least to know your real name.'

She looked at the waxed tablet where I'd let it fall. Giving up on tears, she smiled shyly. 'You say *almost* everything I told you is a lie?' she asked.

'Yes!' I snarled. I stopped and controlled my voice. Eboric couldn't follow what we were saying but was watching the argument unfold with shy interest. 'The agent I sent to their lodgings told me your "clients" vacated this morning. Their unpaid rent was settled to the end of the month by someone who didn't give his name but whose description matches Simon. I should imagine they're on the road back to Pontus and that you told me the truth about their complaint.

'Now, what is your real name? You might also tell me something of your real business.'

She sat down on one of the stone benches lining the wall and smiled at me again. Trying not to show exactly how angry I was, I finished towelling off the excess oil from my chest and loins.

Pretending to ignore her openly approving look, I dropped the used towel into a basket. On getting back, I'd measured myself just enough opium to settle my nerves from the fright Simon had given me. I should have taken a great deal more.

'My name really is Antonia,' she said at last in a voice that no longer tried to be other than aristocratic. The faint tinge of something else had also vanished. 'And I did spend a while in Trebizond. But please don't ask anything more. It's all become such a mess and I need to think about it first.' She leaned against the damp wall. 'You are a very beautiful man, Alaric,' she said suddenly. She stopped herself and sat forward. 'Look, I can imagine what you're thinking. But I have nothing to do with Shahin or Simon or whatever happened to you today. I got myself past your eunuchs yesterday on a whim. Among other things, I wanted to see how well I could pass as a man. I then got a little carried away with the success.' She smiled yet again. 'You could try thanking me, though,' she said.

I sat down on a stool opposite her. 'Thanking you for what?' I asked with a flattening of my voice. Her answer to this would determine whether I put her into a closed chair and turned my back as she was carried off only she would know where.

'For slowing you down, of course,' she said. I relaxed but covered this by picking up a small mirror and looking at my face. 'Without me, you'd have fallen straight into Simon's hands. I imagine getting away from Shahin was much easier.' Before I could break in, the smile went from her face. 'Where is your wife?' she suddenly asked.

'I don't have one,' I said. Confused, I looked harder at my face. I'd never seen it alternate like this between pale and red. 'Both my sons are adopted,' I explained. 'Maximin's father is – er, was – someone who used to be fairly important. You should have guessed, from his age and appearance, that Theodore wasn't mine.' I stood up and walked about the room. I was supposed to be asking the questions. Perhaps I should have taken less opium rather than more. I turned back to Antonia. 'Why were you walking about the garden?' I asked in a voice that nearly sounded accusing. 'I did tell you to keep out of sight.'

'I should keep out of sight?' she said with what may have been a genuine loss of temper. 'Have you seen the eyes on one of the disgusting pictures in the rooms you've given me? They're holes that someone can use for looking in. Are you going to tell me I imagined the footsteps I heard behind the wall?' She dropped her voice. 'So I shouldn't go into the garden to get out of this labyrinth of corridors and rooms bigger than a church? The maids you've given me don't know any Greek. Your steward is a drunk who couldn't take his eyes off me when he found me having a bath. And you tell me I should avoid Theodore. He's the only normal person I've met in this place.'

She stopped again for breath – or to cover a fit of the giggles: the loss of temper hadn't been genuine. Time for me to pull the conversation back to the course I'd laid down for it. 'Why did you encourage him to insist on going out tonight?' I asked. 'Theodore never goes out unless it's to church. He's never shown the slightest interest in secular poetry. I'll have to accept that you've been using me in some stupid game. I suppose latching on to me was a change from your normal – and no doubt vicious – entertainments. But why rope in poor Theodore? I do think less of you for that.'

Sure I'd finally got the upper hand, I stood up and scowled at her, hands behind my back. 'Now, Antonia,' I said sternly, 'I don't choose to wait till you've made up another pack of lies. I want to know who you are. You can begin by telling me who your father is.'

Antonia sat back and laughed softly. She looked at Eboric. 'What were you doing with that boy when I came in here?' she asked. Before I could think what to roar at her, Eboric got up from where he'd been sitting against the wall and bowed. It was a graceful, even a charming, gesture. No one could really hold his lack of clothing against him in a bathhouse and Antonia gave him a charming smile in return.

The smile stayed on her face when she turned back to me. 'Is there any young slave in this place, Alaric, who is actually ugly?' she asked. 'Are there any of them, male or female, with whom you haven't had sex?'

Oh, the outrage of it! She hadn't been here a day and she was already commenting on my household management. No – never mind the outrage of it: there was the irrelevance.

But, even as I bent down to look her close in the face, I heard a scraping of shoes in the outer room. Antonia stiffened slightly then, keeping her back to the door, was on her feet and looking into a pot of setting depilatory pitch.

'I was told you were down here, Antony,' Theodore said with a strained laugh. He came fully through the door and caught sight of me. He bowed briefly before looking away from my naked body. His eyes fixed on an image of Pasiphae having sex with the bull. He pulled them away and found himself staring at something even I'd for a while thought outside the normal range of taste. Served the boy right, I told myself, for having lived here over two years and till now avoiding comforts a civilised man enjoyed every day. I was deciding how to speak with him about the inadequacies of cold washing water as a substitute for the real thing. But he'd turned to Antonia and I could see he was going weak at the knees. I couldn't see his face. Could I complain if it had gone bright red?

'We were discussing what clothes Antony should wear tonight,' I said in a jolly voice too loud for the room. 'His luggage was taken yesterday by the bandits.' Theodore turned back to me, this time ignoring the sin of unashamed nakedness. What he would certainly have called a further and graver sin was presently under control. I hoped he wouldn't ask for any advance on the vague story I'd given about our meeting while in captivity. But that was easily handled. How was I to explain things when, sooner or later, Antony became Antonia? The staff I'd so carefully assembled wouldn't so much as blink if I turned into a swan and began propositioning the kitchen maids. If one of my guests changed sex between dinner and breakfast, no one would mention it outside the household. I'd need a bloody good explanation, though, for Theodore. Perhaps I should take him aside now and tell him what I'd had no proper reason for keeping from him the night before.

It was too late. The boy was smitten. From the look on his face, he loved Antony with total boyish devotion. If I told him anything without careful preparation, he might never get over the shock. I walked past Antonia for a towel and tied it about my waist.

'I came down,' Theodore said in a voice that seemed on the edge of trailing off, 'to ask if Antony would like the green silk you gave me for my birthday. Siegmund is sure it will fit him.'

I nodded. 'I'll call the tailors in tomorrow,' I said. 'For tonight, though, I agree the green silk will go nicely with his eyes.' I looked into Theodore's closed and faintly suspicious face. I'd barely started my interrogation of Antonia but Theodore wasn't moving. I got up. 'I have important business,' I said with an involuntary glance at the mirror I was still holding. 'If anyone needs me, I shall be in my office.'

I paused for the clerk to soak more ink into his pen. It gave me time to complete the passage I'd been forming in my head. It was a nuisance that his weak chest had kept Sergius in his Nicaea residence far beyond the passing of winter. Until he returned, the usual understandings we could reach together without too many words had to give way to a careful balance in writing between clarity and circumlocution. I took a deep breath and looked for inspiration at an ivory of Cupid making love to Psyche.

'As for the insistence of the Lord Bishop Longinus on a duality of will in Jesus Christ,' I dictated, 'this may not as yet be unorthodox, and the chapter in the decrees in the Council of Chalcedon to which he continually refers may not contradict him in their plain sense. Nevertheless, he has been made unofficially aware of the preliminary questions agreed at the closed Council of Athens. Even if he has not spoken out in public against a single will, I find his general attitude unhelpful. We are at one in asserting that such preferments between sees are a matter for the Lord Patriarch, and not for the Emperor or his ministers, to decide. It is, however, my personal opinion that the excellent missionary work overseen by Longinus among the Slavs should not be interrupted by his translation to a bishopric deep within the Home Provinces.'

I paused again and leaned back in my chair. 'Put that between the eleventh and twelfth paragraphs of my letter to the Patriarch,'

I said. The clerk bowed and brought his waxed board over for reading. I scratched one word out and put in another. It made no change to the overall sense but avoided a distasteful clash of consonants. I looked over the whole addition and smiled. If he thought he could poke his nose into matters of church doctrine best left with me, His Grace Longinus could go jump a foot in the air. I'd not have him yapping at me from a place as central or as cushy as Stauropolis. He could stay put in Larissa. Given luck, one of the barbarians he was trying to convert would knock him on the head. Unless he's made his position clear in writing, a dead martyr is always better than a live troublemaker.

I got up from my desk and carried a letter over to the window. The daylight was going, and someone in the Food Control Office had been showing off how many words he could cram on to a half sheet of papyrus. I looked at it and sniffed. I went with it to the clerk's writing table. I dropped it in front of him. 'Proposal rejected,' I said. 'I wrote a memorandum last August on the futility of price controls. Find it and adapt the relevant passages into a reply. Also, I want the man's head of department in this office on the third hour of light on Friday. Tell him to bring a complete listing of his clerks and their functions.'

I was pulling a face over some spelling mistakes in another document when the door opened and Theodore and Antonia crept in. I blinked and looked at Theodore in the fading light. Though I'd set half a dozen slaves on forcing him through the faster actions of the bathhouse and on getting him dressed, he still managed to look dirty. Antonia had been unjust about Samo's abilities. She'd been got up as the most astonishingly lovely young man. I looked at her and my heart beat faster. I looked at Theodore and realised again that he was totally and irreparably lost. I could have fancied Antonia in either sex. This silly boy would never have looked at Antonia. How long before he started feeling guilty about his passion for Antony? I felt a stab of pity, then of guilt. If I explained the whole plot to him when it was over, I might bring him to a reasonable view of things. I knew I wouldn't. How long before Martin was back? He'd have sorted this in no time.

'You look very fine, father,' Theodore said stiffly. I glanced down at my senatorial toga. After six hundred years of changes in manners and faith and language, you might call it an affectation still to be dressing up like Cicero. But I was undeniably a noble sight. The purple stripe suited me no end. I felt almost happy to look at it. I was too young for the Senate, and I might be expected to cheer and clap tonight at an epigram on the fact by that worthless arse-licker Leander. I'd bear up in the knowledge that I looked absolutely lush.

'The chair is waiting downstairs in the hall,' Theodore added. 'Do you think it would be an easier balance for the carrying slaves if Antony and I sat together opposite you?'

I nodded gravely. I hadn't expected him to notice how heavily armed the slaves were. In his present state, he might not have noticed an earthquake. It had its uses. One of his many points of resemblance to Martin was a dislike of violence. 'Your consideration for others does you credit in this life,' I answered, 'and will surely be rewarded in the next.' I glanced at Antonia. She was looking troubled. Well she might. But for her, Theodore would be settling down for his evening prayers.

32

After a supper that might have been put together from the lefto-
vers of his feast for the rabble, I was stuck in the place of honour
beside Nicetas. His legs, swaddled in more bandages than I'd seen
on Egyptian mummies, were propped on two ebony footstools,
and I had the best smell in the room of flesh that any competent
doctor would have uncovered in half a wink and left to dry out.
Though it had been dark for hours, the night was sweltering. No
hint of a breeze came through the open windows and the forest of
candles that burned overhead completed the resemblance to a
steam room. It could have been worse, I'd thought, as a semi-nude
black girl came over to stand beside us with a fan. She was a better
sight than the hard, scowling faces the rest of the audience had
turned in my direction. It then did get worse. One politely lecher-
ous look from me and she'd shuffled behind Nicetas. I was left
with nothing else to do but try for a look of awed enthusiasm and
pay attention to the latest masterpiece by Leander Memphites.
Oh, for another quarter pill of opium to replace the one that had
so completely, and so long ago, worn off.

It still could have been worse, I kept assuring myself. Leander
might have composed five books in praise of Nicetas rather than
just four. And we were approaching the climax of Book Four –
that is, I hoped we were. Leander had dropped his usual simper
and was steadily raising his voice till his Egyptian accent showed
through like the sweat on the underarms of his tunic. Yes, we were
getting there. After a worrying descent of his voice to describe and
praise the main churches in Carthage, he ripped his tunic open
from the neck downward to show an unshaven and distastefully
flabby chest and, his face taking on the look of a man who's trying

to defecate and knows that he won't, moved into an exultant squawk:

> As in some stadium ancient, behold a beautiful athlete.
> See the Lord Nicetas! Splendidly onward he rushes,
> Kicking the dust to clouds, as his feet, so fleetingly sighted,
> Spring on the ground and are gone. See, following after,
> Barely giving contest, how his opponents falter,
> All their long strides failing, as, claw-like, agony catches
> Hold of their chests. See him alone in the heat of the
>   morning
> Make for the finish. Lord Nicetas – Swift as Achilles . . .

So he carried on through another hundred lines or so to the end, before lapsing into a simper for the burst of applause that Nicetas led.

'Blessings on Leander,' a fat eunuch shrilled, 'wondrous servant of the Muses.'

'And blessings on Nicetas,' came the chanted response from the rest of us, 'great and victorious hero – the New Belisarius!' The great and victorious hero raised his walking stick for another round of applause. This given, there was a determined rush for the wine tables, and I found myself alone with Nicetas and his poet.

'Don't you think Leander is magnificent?' Nicetas grated. It was hard to know if this was a question or an accusation. Coming from Nicetas, it was probably both.

'I've never heard the rhythm of hexameters made so obvious,' I answered cautiously.

'Exactly!' he cried with an emphatic snort that ended in a cry of pain as he moved and one of his legs dropped off its stool. 'If you ask me,' he went on in an ill-natured mutter, 'I'm sick to death of those rules about long and short syllables. I can't hear them in Latin or in Greek, though I was flogged every day for years. You'll agree that Leander has much improved on the ancients. I've always wondered how they could sit through the poetry of their own age. I certainly can't abide it.' He raised his voice again. 'What this Empire needs is a renewal of the arts. How can I inspire men to win battles when they have no poetry ringing in their ears?'

'Absolutely! Well said!' Someone behind me cried through a full mouth. There was another cry of agreement on my left. I nodded politely. The true answer, of course, was that our armies were more likely to win if he wasn't leading them. But he'd put on an almost convincing show of concern when I was made to explain the previous day's murder attempt on me. Who was I to cast the first hard look of the evening?

'My Lord's patronage of the arts is an example to us all,' I said. Nicetas glowered at me, before prodding Leander with his walking stick. This got a quiet repeat of the running track passage. In a break for Leander to sip delicately at his wine cup, I clapped very softly, and smiled and nodded. 'Would My Lord excuse me a moment?' I asked. 'I must see how my son and his friend are getting on.'

Theodore was enjoying himself. I'd heard that much from a dozen yards away and in spite of the mass of sweaty bodies that separated us. 'You see, it's absolutely necessary,' I heard him call at the top of a still-unbroken voice, 'to regard Our Lord Jesus Christ as both Man and God and joined together in a Perfect Union. To see it otherwise is not merely heresy but also an inability to recognise the promptings of reason.' I embraced Paul, first deputy of the City Prefect, and, avoiding being dragged into conversation with his increasingly doddery father, came upon Theodore beside one of the wine tables. He'd got Antonia wedged against a column. He also had her by one of her sleeves. His tendency to spray saliva when excited was on full display.

'I trust you're enjoying the recital,' I said. Theodore nodded eagerly without taking the cup from his lips. The front of his robe was already stained and sopping wet. He looked into his cup. Before he could open his mouth to speak, a serving slave had noticed and was giving him yet another refill. 'Should you not be mixing that with three parts water?' I asked with vague concern. The wine I'd seen poured was a very dark red. Even I didn't knock it back like this – not in public, anyway.

'But it has the most refreshing taste,' came the silly answer. 'The Lord Eunapius assures me the taste is ruined by water,' he added in a voice that ended in a slur. He let go of Antonia and moved to take a step forward but clutched at the table for support. Time, I decided, to take him by the arm and get him out of the room. I'd left our chair in the main courtyard. I could sit him in it and rely on the carrying slaves to keep him there till he passed out. But I was looking at Antonia. Her own cup in hand, she seemed to be glowing from within. I tried to think of a careless remark and found that my chest was beginning its funny trick with light. Taking both arms from the table, Theodore tottered closer to me. 'Antony says the poetry was the finest thing he'd ever heard,' he said thickly. He burped, opening a pathway between my nose and the contents of his stomach.

I heard a sneering laugh behind me. 'Then I will say that your son's friend has taste as well as elegance of form.' I turned and made myself smile at Eunapius of Pylae. He licked his lips just as more white lead slid off his cheeks. He washed it down with another mouthful of wine and continued staring at Antonia. 'Did I hear right that young Antony is from Trebizond?' he asked with an upward motion of his eyebrows. 'You will surely be aware that I have estates close by there. How could I possibly not have come across so fine a young man as Antony?' The faint and satirical emphasis he put on *man* set me thinking. Either he'd seen straight through her disguise or he knew something.

Eunapius grinned and shuffled closer to Antonia. Looking surly, Theodore managed to get himself between them at the last moment.

'My dearest friend, Eunapius,' I said, leading him as if without thought into the crowd of braying Senators, 'I've been thinking hard, ever since our last meeting, about your suggestion of mixing copper into the new silver coins. Do you really think a mixture of two-fifths would not be noticed by the people?' He looked suspiciously back at me. I was saved from listening to more of the stupid idea he'd been putting to Nicetas by the arrival of a spotty boy, who pushed a message into his hands. We were in a place of comparative darkness and Eunapius had to move the thin sheet of wood close to his face to read what it said. I played with a fold of my toga that had come loose and pretended not to watch a face that had gone suddenly tense.

He scratched the fingernails of his right hand across the waxed surface of the message. 'I'll answer this in person,' he said to the boy. He looked at me and put a crooked smile on his face. 'My Lord will forgive me,' he said, 'if business calls me temporarily from the finest conversation I have yet heard in this most glittering event.' He twisted round to see where Antonia had gone. Listening to more of his slurred chatter about the Council of Chalcedon, she was quietly steering Theodore away from the wine table.

I watched Eunapius pick his way through the room. It was a long exit. He left no one important unapproached. In every ear he whispered something of about the same length. Nobody, however, seemed to be that friendly in return. He smiled and fawned and ran his fingers over woollen senatorial sleeves. The best he got in return was the distant politeness you show to someone you might know, but whose face you can't quite recall. At last he was between the two black eunuchs who guarded the door and the room seemed to brighten by his leaving it.

No chance yet of my own exit. I had my sleeve grabbed by someone who rambled on about a set of trusts into which he'd conveyed his property – something to do with stopping his son from giving it away to the Church. Because of that, he'd taken a bad hit from the land law and been compelled to give two-thirds away, rather than the half normally required. I listened with a pretence of sympathy. If I'd been able to understand his account of the trusts involved, I might even have suggested an approach to the Treasury for an *ex gratia* compensation payment.

'Don't talk to me about the Gracchus brothers!' someone snarled softly behind me. 'They were men from our own order. They never tried to strip us naked. If you must talk about the olden days, this young fucker's another Spartacus. It's now or never – now or never, I tell you.' He gave a yelp as if he'd been punched in the stomach. The conversation behind me fell silent, before taking up again as a bored discussion of the improved strain of silkworm some missionaries had carried back from the East.

I lifted a cup from a passing tray and, like a man coming up for air, stood back from the bore who'd now taken hold of my sleeve and didn't seem inclined ever to let me go. I was surrounded by several hundred men who looked to Nicetas to stop me from drying up all the teats on which they and their ancestors had been sucking since time out of mind. They could talk themselves hoarse about the Gracchus brothers. The Senators who'd faced down that threat to their landed position had been men of quality. Grasping, cold-blooded bastards to a man they'd been, but no one could deny they'd made Rome great in the world. These Greeklings in fancy dress hadn't a day's military service between them. All two hundred of them, I had no doubt, prayed nightly for Heraclius to grow sick of me. I had no doubt either that every one of them would shit himself if I showed him so much as a clenched fist.

I smiled at the bore. He was almost making sense about his trusts when the Lord Timothy came in sight. 'Lovely to see you, dear boy – lovely to see you,' he boomed, holding up two cups of wine as his excuse for not shaking hands. His wig was in place, and his false teeth. 'So sorry not to recognise you today,' he lied – 'fish out of water and all that.' Cold dislike in his eyes, he pushed out his lower set of teeth. He ran his tongue along the golden ridge, before sucking them back into place. 'I believe your appearance among them always occasions a certain disorder in the poor.' He stepped closer. 'Such a shame, I like to say, that we cannot all get along together.' He twisted down to blow his nose into the shoulder of his toga. He looked up and smiled. I caught sight of the dried dirt under his fingernails. 'I really must have you for dinner one evening,' he said with a snigger. He moved off, cups in hand. 'Yes – I'd like you for dinner,' he called over his shoulder.

Still listening to the man with the trusts, I looked over at Nicetas. Surely, he *couldn't* fancy himself as Emperor? If he was too stupid to realise how stupid he was, he must know what trouble he'd raise within his family from deposing a cousin who'd showered him with favours. If not that, even he must be aware of the lack of correspondence between the glorious creature of Leander's poem and the bloated invalid whose only victory in the Syrian campaign had come about when, incoherent from the pain of a septic haemorrhoid, he'd let his hairdresser give the orders.

And where did the Persians come in all this? I could imagine most things of Nicetas. Treason wasn't among them. Was he an unwitting puppet? Was Shahrbaraz pulling the strings from out of sight? That would make sense of the generally swift and ruthless unfolding of the previous day's plot. The benefit for the Persians would be the most incompetent fool as Emperor since – I had to stop here and think: in ancient times, Didius Julianus had bought the Purple at auction, but had been done away with too quickly for his full uselessness to be revealed. The only risk for the Persians was that there'd be a vacancy for Commander of the East and this might accidentally be filled by someone who knew what he was doing.

I thought about my own place in things. The previous day Simon had worked a miracle of organisation and put himself personally at risk. Did he suppose I knew about the cup and that I'd call on its awesome powers? Did he think I'd drop everything and take a fast ship to the Emperor in Cyzicus? Bearing in mind what I'd learned in the afternoon – and he might have thought I knew it already – it made sense to want me out of the way as well as getting the cup back. But why had Shahin been so reluctant to go along with killing me? Was it because he wanted to dump me, bound hand and foot, before the Great King's throne – rather as a cat presents a wounded bird to its master? Or had I some other use? Shahin had never been one to let sex come before his wider interests.

And why was Eunapius suddenly out of fashion? If anything, I was more openly hated than ever. Questions, questions – so many questions.

33

'I will not *seek* the violent crown of martyrdom,' Theodore said mournfully. Antonia had got him into a chair between two columns and was looking about for help. 'Such things must never be sought. But if God, in His Infinite Mercy, calls me to stand witness to my faith, I shall be ready – yea, even though my belly be slit open and my intestines wound slowly out, I will never cry out but in joy.'

'How much has he drunk?' I whispered. I looked about the room. If I didn't shut the boy up soon, I'd be a laughing stock as well as hated.

'I could carry him out myself,' Antonia said. 'The problem is he keeps trying to kiss me every time I take hold of him.' She lowered her voice still further. 'Was that man with the painted face Eunapius of Pylae?' I nodded. She looked back, disgusted and oddly alarmed. 'When can we get out of here?'

'Spot of bother, dear boy?' Timothy asked, coming from behind one of the columns. He looked at Theodore, who now put his face into his hands and began rocking back and forth. 'Dried oysters in honey,' Timothy said with a laugh – 'that's what your boy needs. They'll bring him round in no time.' Losing interest in me, he put his flabby face close to Antonia. 'I really don't think I've had the pleasure of you yet, young man.' She fell back before the blast of his putrid breath. She looked at me and swallowed. I scowled back at her. This wasn't all her fault. But I'd tell her it was the moment we were alone.

'Stay here beside him,' I said coldly. 'I'll go and get some of the carrying slaves.' Timothy could be trusted not to rape her – not here, at least.

I turned, and found myself staring at Leander. He cleared his throat. Shining with sweat, his face was twisted into an obsequious leer. 'The Lord Alaric will surely agree with the most just observations of the Caesar Nicetas,' he opened with slimy respect. 'An empire that has no place for the Muses cannot be surprised when the Persians overrun its fairest provinces.'

I resisted the urge to kick him on both shins. Eunapius was beside him. While out of the room, he'd acquired another coat of paint for his face. I stopped and made myself smile at Leander. I could see that he'd shaved closely for his recital. But black stubble beneath his skin darkened the lower half of an already dark face. I spread my arms in a gesture of piety. 'We mustn't forget, my dear Leander, that now Heraclius is our ruler the Empire is under the special protection of Christ and the Virgin.'

That was a nice rebuke and it shut him up. Before I could hurry past him, though, I caught sight of one of the black lovelies who were never allowed to go far from Nicetas. Nipples erect, her body glistening with sweat, her mouth was open in a smile made wanton by the hashish she was chewing. I saw how her filed teeth glittered in the candlelight and watched greasy saliva run down her chin. She was a fine sight and I'd normally have regretted that this wasn't the kind of gathering where I could snap my fingers at her and be followed from the room. But I didn't have to wait for the smell of stale pus before my heart sank.

'We were discussing the magnificent achievement tonight of my poet Leander,' Nicetas said in a high and angry voice that brought a gradual end to all conversation in the room. With a loud bump, two more of his black eunuchs put his chair down a few yards from me. He opened his mouth to say more, but instead fell back and groaned as one of his monks hurried over and continued massaging holy oil into the more swollen of his feet.

I glanced left into Antonia's strained face. She was trying to get behind a column, but Theodore had caught hold of her left hand and was babbling about the punishments he'd brought on himself in this life and the next for his many sins. That he was too far gone to remember his Greek and had lapsed into Syriac was the only consolation I could presently find. As if herded like sheep, two hundred rubbishy Senators and various hangers-on were forming a wide semicircle about us. Even if Nicetas passed out from the agony of his monk's attentions, I'd never get through this lot without actual violence. There was nothing else for it. I wheeled about and made an ironic bow to Leander.

'I was much inspired,' I said, 'by your description of how the Lord Nicetas plunged without armour into the fray at the Battle of Antioch. His single combat with Shahrbaraz was perfectly Homeric. So too your opening account of the debate of the Saints in Heaven.' He grinned complacently and bowed to Nicetas, who was lost for the moment to everything but the manipulations of a foot that was looking the colour of an overripe fig. Someone in the crowd sneezed. Someone else laughed. 'But are you unaware of the conventions of hexameter poetry in Latin?' I added. Since he was a Greek of sorts, that was less a question than a provocation. I smiled and pressed on with explaining how the Roman poets had observed the rules of quantity in a language that may never have allowed it to dominate the ear, but had maintained a spoken rhythm by making accent and quantity coincide in the two last feet. It gave me the chance to insult him and every Senator in the room by quoting Vergil at length without interpreting its sonorities. Sooner or later, Nicetas would come out of his spasm of gasping moans and be glad of my kiss goodnight. He didn't like to hear Leander mocked – and tiredness and wine and the accumulated horror of the past two days were putting me into an irreverent mood.

I looked round again at Antonia. Still caught fast by Theodore, she was trying not to notice how Timothy was bouncing about her like a bubble of lard and making obscene gestures. By listening hard, and filtering out Leander's wooden praise for a poet he could understand no more than I could read the inscription on that cup, I managed to catch some of the whispered conversation Eunapius had begun with a Senator whose name I couldn't recall but whose face, sharp as a hatchet, was turned steadily in my direction. He'd set everything up, he was explaining. It would be a deciding moment no one could ignore. The nature of this moment I didn't follow. I looked about for Antonia. She was trying to keep

Theodore from falling off his chair. Timothy had now given up on gestures and retired behind one of the columns, where he seemed to be surreptitiously wanking under cover of his toga. Time, I thought, to gather me and mine together and make for the blessings of the night air. I turned towards Nicetas, ready to bring out a stream of fair words.

But Eunapius was finished with Lord Hatchet-Face. Standing between me and Nicetas, he stretched his arms wide for attention. 'My Lord Alaric,' he called in a voice that shook from some inner tension, 'it is the will of your betters that you should reopen the School of Rhetorical Studies. It must be reopened at once and Leander of Memphis appointed its Rector.' He wheeled round and bowed to Nicetas. He'd been expecting approval. He got a blank stare.

Ignoring Eunapius, I made a bow of my own to the mass of festering sores who'd been appointed to stand between us and a total Persian victory. 'My Lord Nicetas,' I said, speaking very smooth, 'If this is a suggestion from you, I must discuss its details with the Emperor when he returns from Cyzicus. So notable an exception to the Austerity Decree must be carefully prepared.' Blunt words, no doubt. What else to say, though? A private approach – not through sodding Eunapius – and I'd have had my seal, before the hour was out, on a snug little pension for Leander. I'd not have Eunapius puff himself up in public as the Voice of Nicetas. Made as it was, the request could only be a power game in which I was supposed to lose. I looked at Nicetas. The monk was doing things to his ankles that Chosroes himself might have admired. But his face remained a total blank.

Eunapius swallowed and stood forward. He looked again at Nicetas and then about him for moral support. 'You insult every man of taste in the Empire,' he croaked in a voice that said double or quits, 'when you sneer at the verses of our modern Callimachus.' He looked about once more. A few of the Senators were frowning. One was forcing his way to the back of the crowd.

I smiled at Eunapius. 'I think our poet has a mastery of the language that all must agree is remarkable,' I said in the maddening tone I'd used with Leander. 'I look forward to publication of tonight's performance. The novelty of his verses will be discussed wherever Greek is spoken – and perhaps beyond.' That got a snigger from someone lost in the crowd.

Eunapius twisted his face into a mask of outrage too extreme to fool anyone. Somebody else was making for the exit. 'Leander doesn't write his poetry in advance,' he shouted. 'It's all a work of the moment. You wouldn't appreciate that, of course' Plainly hoping for support, he looked again at Nicetas. Was the response a faint stirring of distaste?

I shrugged and took a step towards the thinnest part of the crowd. But it was now Leander's turn to make trouble. He bared his teeth in a smile that did his appearance no favours. 'Poetry that is written in advance, the Lord Nicetas agrees, has too much smell of the lamp,' he explained in the voice of one who speaks to an idiot child. 'I have always made it my custom not to write any of my verses. Much has thereby been lost and I can lament that my future reputation will not be all that it might have been. But the Lord Nicetas has provided me with a secretary to take my dictation. Tonight's poem will surely not be lost.'

I could say I'd learned something. I had an explanation for the repetitions and the unequal length of the books and the loose grammar, and particularly the lines that didn't scan even according to Leander's corrupt rules. If the resulting poetry had been any good, I might have been tempted to stay to discuss the merits of oral composition. *I might.*

I was given no choice. 'Isn't that how you barbarians do it?' Eunapius asked with yet another look at an increasingly displeased Nicetas. 'Aren't you from a race of illiterate savages? Do your people have poetry? Or do you simply howl and beat your chests when you rise above grunting at each other?' This jewel of repartee got a few muffled laughs. I noticed that the Lord Senator Hatchet-Face was now at the front of the crowd, his face impassive. Behind the crowd, Theodore cried out in terror, and I heard him fall off his chair. I bowed politely to Eunapius and didn't ask why my people should be denounced for a custom that he was praising in Leander. Talk about women's logic! Of course, there was more to this than women's logic.

'I bet you couldn't do better in *any* language!' Eunapius shouted. He struck an aggressive pose and laughed bitterly. 'Alaric, barbarian from the back of beyond,' he went on, 'I challenge you to improvise for us.' He stopped and cleared his throat. There was no spittoon in sight, and he was forced to swallow rather than spit. 'I challenge you to improvise on the excellencies of the poet Leander.' Someone in the crowd sniggered a repetition about howling and breast beating. Then, from near the front, a voice rang out in fair imitation of Leander's Egyptian accent:

Alaric, Alaric,
Only good for sucking dick!

That set off a ripple of embarrassed laughter. Without seeming to move, Lord Hatchet-Face melted backwards into the crowd. For some reason, the scared look went out of Leander's eyes. A fresh smirk on his face, he held up both hands to show no stain of ink on them.

'Poem, poem!' a few slurred voices began to chant. I fought off the urge to head-butt Eunapius in the face. 'Poem, poem!' the drunken crowd was chanting louder and faster. Smiling like a man who's just won a bet on his entire estate, Eunapius was clapping in time to the chant. Leander showed his hands again, this time to the whole crowd. He raised a cheer. I stared at Eunapius. This was the moment he'd been waiting for. Tough luck Nicetas was now looking thoroughly pissed off.

I waited for the chanting to die away. Less than this would have sent any of my ancestors berserk with a meat cleaver. Lucky for this lot I was His Magnificence the Lord Senator Alaric. 'My Lord Nicetas,' I said, bowing low, 'you will appreciate the hour is late, and that those who are with me have need of their beds.' I'd get me and mine out of this ghastly room. I'd send in an open and very beautiful letter of thanks the following morning.

But Nicetas was having none of that. He sat up in his chair and poked his monk away with his stick. 'You have been challenged to justify your contempt for my poet,' he snarled. 'I give you the freedom of speech to rise to that challenge.' He sat back and glared at Eunapius.

This wasn't going well. The only question was for whom? I could have insisted on a dignified exit. Or I could see what trouble there was to be made. Time for another gamble, I decided. I looked for a moment up at the circular candle racks. What metre? I wondered. Whatever I chose would need to fit the name Leander. It would have to be in Greek. I raised my arms for silence and walked about the edge of the crowd. I caught a look at myself in a silver dish someone had left on its side. The toga *did* suit me. Looking steadily at Eunapius, I recited:

> Leander writes not lest his hand
> Lack passion for his prostate gland,
> And so that not tonight shall he
> Be overcome by ecstasy.
> O wicked street boys, to deprive
> Our Poet of his daily swive –
> As if he'd meant their friend to kill,
> Or even much to use him ill.
> But threats or cash or plaintive cries
> Procured him nothing in their eyes,
> As, in some sewer, tightly held,
> His manhood and a knife to geld
> Those boys without a second thought
> In brief though final union brought.
> Now, when Leander dwells upon
> Those happy, happy days, long gone,
> When every cry of boyish fright
> For him was cause of fresh delight,
> No opportunity has he
> To recollect his ecstasy –
> Aside from reaching out his hand,
> Once more to stroke his prostate gland.

I finished and looked about a silent room. Half the audience had disappeared. The other half might have been at the wedding feast where Perseus pulled out Medusa's head and turned everyone to stone. The lead sliding off his face again, Eunapius was looking like a pig's bladder that has been overinflated and is ready to burst. Leander continued smiling and bobbing his head – but that would have been required from a man of his degree if I'd run over and stuffed shit up both his nostrils.

With a cry of rage or pain or both, Nicetas hauled himself to his feet. His stick wobbling as he tried to support his sickness-raddled bulk, he stretched out his free arm. 'Will no one respect my time of sickness?' he cried accusingly.

Eunapius was straight on to him. 'My Lord, My Lord,' he bleated, 'did you not hear the gross insult this savage . . .'

He was interrupted by a loud and slow handclap from the back of the room. 'Oh bravo, bravo, My Lord Alaric,' a voice called out in a shrill attempt at the feminine. 'We ladies fair dote on poetry. How sad one hears so little of it in our own degenerate age.'

34

Had I woken at this point and found myself still trussed up in Shahin's boat, I'd have told Antonia that I'd been having a bad dream. But I wasn't asleep. I'd gone too far with Nicetas, and only got away so far because, dressed in the most outrageous parody of aged womanhood anyone could imagine, Priscus had broken every part of the word and spirit of our agreement.

'What female dares invade this place of manly recreation?' Nicetas groaned in a deathly voice. He fell back into his chair and began a choking cough. The monk made another grab for his swollen foot. As Nicetas arched his back in pain, one of the chair legs gave way. Before his eunuchs could catch him, he'd fallen sideways on to the floor. He rolled about with a loud gnashing of teeth until his eunuchs could get him to his feet and support him on either side.

'Pray forgive me, Sir, if I'm out of place among so many persons of quality,' Priscus took up again in the same shrill travesty. 'But it's turning bitter outside and I felt I had to come in and see if either of my young gentlemen was in need of a shawl.' The front of the crowd parted, and Priscus tottered forward in his long, black robe and a black wig that, thankfully, hid those parts of his face not covered by a veil. He looked about and bowed to Nicetas, then headed for Theodore and Antonia. 'My, but you'll surely catch your death of cold if I don't get you both home to bed,' he crooned. Theodore gave a drunken burp and vomited where he lay. I waited for the smell of wine and stomach juices to drift in my direction. Antonia sat on the floor beside him. Holding one of his hands, she looked about to start crying.

I clenched and unclenched my fists. I blinked. I stepped forward and raised my arms for attention. 'My Lord Nicetas will surely forgive this break in our conversation,' I said, once more very smooth. 'And, since my son has been taken poorly, it is with the utmost sadness that I cannot bask longer in the glow of your hospitality.' Nicetas wasn't listening. Of a sudden, he looked past me. With a shout of anger, he reared forward and tried to point. One of the eunuchs lost his balance and the pair of them fell down, somehow pulling Leander with them.

This was my excuse for a getaway. As the crowd dissolved into loose groupings of artificially bright chatter, I tried to grab Priscus by the arm.

'Careful, dear boy,' he whispered. 'We wouldn't want that pretty toga spoiled, would we?' He lifted his right arm and the sleeve fell back to show a hand dark with blood. 'The streets of this city can be *so* unsafe at night for unaccompanied women,' he cried in a now soft falsetto. 'You will hardly credit the grossness with which I was several times addressed.' I stepped quickly out of splashing distance but continued with him towards the exit.

It was cool outside in the big courtyard. We made our way through the tangle of parked chairs and flaring torches. I stopped beside my own. 'Go inside with two men,' I said in Slavic. 'Theodore's passed out from drink. The girl's in danger of having her clothes pulled off.' Samo nodded. He looked blearily at Priscus and turned sober from the shock. 'I'll deal with him,' I said. Just go inside.' And things were bordering on the urgent. I'd looked back at Antonia before coming outside. Timothy was with her again. Panting like a dog, he may have been offering more advice on what to do with Theodore – that, or he'd been getting round to some other suggestion.

I stopped with Priscus near to a closed window. In the light that streamed through its many panes, I stared at him. 'What the hell are you doing here?' I demanded. I looked briefly at the window. 'That room is filled with your relatives and boyhood friends. Are you mad?'

'Sane as sane can be,' he said with a bob of his head. 'So unlike the silly boy I've just seen at his usual blundering best. Were you deliberately trying for an open break with Nicetas?' He dropped into his normal voice and put his head close to mine. 'Never mind this, however. I've heard about your adventure in the poor district this afternoon. I trust you weren't drawn into any communion with the Occult Powers. My own observations have led me to an absolute conviction that such communion brings dangers of a very real and concrete nature.' He flicked a night insect from his veil and smacked his lips. 'I say, though,' he continued, dropping the tone of dramatic urgency from his voice, 'wasn't that Timothy I saw beside your latest piece of fluff? He's piled it on horribly in the past few years. You'll not believe how pretty he was as a boy. I seduced him when he was eight and paid him by teaching the art of pulling the wings off flies.'

I clenched my fists. 'You have walked two miles through Constantinople, and dressed like something out of Menander, to tell me *this*?' I asked, trying not to shout. 'Fuck off home, Priscus. You've taken enough risk with all our lives.' I wouldn't even ask how and what he'd heard about my visit to the astrologers. That could wait.

Priscus took a deep breath and blew his veil outwards. 'Of course, I do have more to say, my dear – really important stuff that will put you in a much better mood with me. Have you ever wondered . . .?'

With a loud click, the window opened behind me. I stepped sideways to avoid being brained by it. Inside the room, Nicetas had been pulled back to his feet. Leaning unsteadily on the back of his broken chair, he was surrounded by his more determined hangers-on. 'I will give you Leander's *Lyric Hymn to the Virgin*,' he cried. 'Hear what beauties a *true* poet can achieve.' Eunapius threw himself to his knees and lifted his arms in a show of exaltation. Paying no attention, Nicetas wobbled forward on his stick to where Leander had given his performance. After a long, ragged breath, he recited:

Who aloft in the heavens rose
on fluttering waxy wings
and dared the cloudless realm
of Phoebus Apollo breach
sure for presumption
earned his mother's stony embrace.

Thee almighty protectress wise
by Heaven's decree to blaze
with sempiternal flame
so ending our darkness sent
equal the danger
so it seems of seeking to see.

O victorious all against
in battles unequalled those
by darkness granted sway
O Lady of might serene
Mother of Jesus
ever splendid Vision of Light!

Nicetas greeted the rapturous applause with a loud tapping of his stick. Everyone who hadn't already scarpered hurried over to join in the shouted acclamations. He collapsed into a new chair someone had brought forward. His monk would soon be at work again. I turned and looked into the darkness. Priscus was gone. In his place, Leander was fiddling with a lock of his greasy hair. 'It was an historic mark of My Lord's favour,' he slimed at me, no longer hiding his Egyptian accent, 'that these humble verses were taught to every staff officer to sing to the men before the Battle of Antioch.'

'Did they finish the song during or after the retreat?' I sneered. 'Oh, and didn't Icarus fall into the *sea*?'

Hands folded across his chest, Leander bowed silently. 'I have been sent, My Lord Alaric, to thank you for the return of something most valuable to the Lord Nicetas.'

I stopped looking about for Priscus. After waiting all evening for an approach of this sort, I'd been ready to dump all suspicion that he so much as knew about the cup. If Eunapius was up to something – that much was clear as day – I'd seen it confirmed that Nicetas couldn't conspire his way out of a chamber pot. Here now was Leander, bearing a request that no longer made sense, but that would need somehow to be fitted into a revived hypothesis.

Someone inside was starting up on a flute. Someone else joined in with a drum. At once, a regular padding of bare feet on marble indicated the black girls hadn't just been brought out for orna-ment. It was a bastard evening. I'd endured the whole recitation at a distance that almost exposed me to Leander's garlicky breath. I was now stuck with him again to miss the one compensating entertainment. The modern Callimachus waited for a break in the squealed, swaying rhythm that streamed from the open window. He leaned forward. 'Since I have often had the honour to be welcomed into My Lord's private quarters, I am able to confirm that she is a most headstrong girl. If she has caused you any trou-ble, I am authorised to apologise with the utmost sincerity.'

I had my back to the window. That meant I had a better view of Leander than he had of me. When I still said nothing, he smiled nervously. 'After she rejected the wholesome discipline of her father's household, she was sent to be instructed in the ways of humility by the nuns of Saint Tomalina in Trebizond. Even so, she escaped and returned to the scene of her old debaucheries in Constantinople. She was apprehended and brought home. Before she could be returned to the holy sisters, there to await an intro-duction to her future husband, she escaped again. That was the night before last. It was feared that she might be preparing a complete change of identity. My Lord wishes me to assure you that, now you have returned her, she will be more closely watched until she can be locked into the female quarters of some other house.'

A dozen yards to my right, I heard Theodore carried out. The change of air must have revived him. Still speaking Syriac, he called loudly on God to blind him, so he could look no more on the perfect beauty of Antony. He was cut off in mid-flow by a slap to his face. Samo grated at him in Latin to shut up if he didn't want a stick taken to his bare arse. The boy gave way to moaning sobs of 'Antony, Antony – how I love you, and how I sin!' Luckily, that too was in Syriac.

I nodded at Leander. There was an intellectual neatness in what he'd said. I no longer needed to revive an exploded hypothesis. And Theodore had given me time to ignore the chill spreading out from my chest. 'I am always the most devoted friend and servant of the Lord Nicetas,' I managed to say in a voice that didn't waver. 'I am also much in your debt for the goodness you have shown in bringing me news that the girl is now reunited with her loving father.'

Leander bowed again and smirked. Inside, there was a burst of applause, and the musicians turned to one of the slow dance tunes popular back then in the brothels of Syria. 'Does he *ever* go to bed?' I asked, allowing myself one flash of temper. Played out to its last variation, the dance tune could last all night.

Leander shook his head. 'The Lord Nicetas has been assured that, if he lies down to sleep, he will stop breathing,' he explained. 'It is his custom, therefore, to sit upright in chair through the night, sleeping and waking as the holy fathers who surround him direct.'

I controlled a sudden urge to burst out laughing. I bowed to Leander. As a poet of sorts, he was partly outside the usual hierarchies. 'Your conversation is always a delight,' I said, 'However, I feel obliged to take my leave of His Magnificence the Commander of the East.'

I stepped back from kissing Nicetas on the lips. 'You really are my dearest friend,' he replied without moving his lips. 'But, if it can't be the rectorship, Leander *must* have a job that will give him official status and a salary. You know that only you can seal that manner of appointment.'

I bowed low before the man who, in his cousin's absence, was supposed to be Regent. 'There was a time when the Treasury had a department of correspondence,' I said quietly. 'That was when Latin was still the official language and the clerks needed to be trained in the appropriate phraseologies. I could revive the post of director for Leander. The salary isn't much, but would give him the right to present birthday wishes to the Emperor. We could interpret that as the right to present birthday odes.'

Looking relieved, Nicetas signalled to his eunuchs. They got him from each side and pulled him to his feet. 'Let it be known,' he cried weakly, 'that our most beloved friend Alaric has opened poetic hostilities this night with Leander. At our next recital, Leander will make his reply.' He leaned on me in what might pass for an embrace. I smiled at Timothy and pretended not to notice the scared, apprehensive faces of those who hadn't already gone home. Nicetas sat heavily back in his chair and nodded at Leander, who went into a long and reverential bow in my direction. That got me more nervous looks. There were even angry murmurs when Nicetas stayed on his feet while I backed out of the room. One of the black girls who'd been playing with each other in the recital space broke into an exaggerated orgasm. I don't think anyone paid attention.

35

The wind had made another of its endless shifts of direction. Inside, with all the candles burning away like houses in a city taken by storm, it had continued sweltering till the end. Out here, in the quiet and increasingly unlit streets, I was glad of the cloak I'd put on over my toga. I was tired. Two days running, I'd been scared half out of my wits. I'd uncovered a web of treason the nature and extent of which remained unclear. Where was bloody Priscus? Why come out in that absurd disguise, only to vanish like a ghost?

Except I was tired, none of this mattered. Even before getting my people to check her story, I'd known Antonia was lying. I'd asked, only that afternoon, who her father was. Did it matter if her father turned out to be Nicetas? It did, of course. Anyone else I could have called straight into my office to present with a bill for unpaid taxes. Everyone owed something. No one was ever expected to pay unless he upset someone like me. I could have bought Antonia fair and square. Not so Nicetas. Save by the Emperor himself, he was untouchable. Whenever he wanted, he could have his daughter tied hand and foot and stuffed into a wagon rumbling east. I couldn't denounce him for treason. Beyond a hint from some scabby old fool who might already have been put out of the way by Simon, I had bugger all evidence of his complicity in anything. Heraclius wasn't Chosroes: especially against his own blood, he'd expect some grounds of probability. I could go after his creature Eunapius, but the Lord Commander of the East would only throw his hands in the air and plead ignorance. He'd be believed, because no one could doubt someone as thick as Nicetas was telling the truth.

But I could drop the whole line of thought. Heraclius was away. In his place, Nicetas was the supreme power. Antonia would be back scrubbing floors in Trebizond before that changed. And what of that? We'd met. We'd fucked. We'd argued. Theodore might be getting ready to offer up his soul in exchange for what he thought she was. I was His Magnificence Alaric – now of age. The girl dripped trouble from every pore. It was pure accident she'd kept me out of Simon's hands. Everything else about her was a complication. She'd now overreached herself – no doubt thinking her own father wouldn't recognise her got up as a man. Who was I to hurry to the rescue? If I tried, I was sure, I could put her and everything concerning her out of mind. Let silly Theodore sob his heart out when Antony didn't show for breakfast the next morning. If I never saw Antonia again, I was the Magnificent Alaric. I'd know how to keep a stiff upper lip.

There was a faint noise behind me. Priscus? No, not Priscus. However faint, he'd never have made a noise. 'Might our young lord be lost?' someone grated in a voice straight out of one of the lower poor districts. 'Aren't we a bit tipsy, to be out on our own so late and all?' Someone else added.

I turned and looked at the half dozen footpads. The closest of them had his cudgel already raised. Doubtless, there were a few knives tucked out of sight. I'd been passing the Central Milestone on my slow walk from Nicetas to the Triumphal Way. Slowly, I turned and went over to sit on the lowest step. 'Do you know who I am?' I asked.

'We might soon find out,' the man with the club said with a laugh. As I'd expected, sitting down had unnerved them. They stopped edging forward.

For once, I had no money with me. No chance of my usual dealings with the city trash. I flicked my cloak aside to show that I was armed. 'If you don't fuck off out of my sight,' I said mildly, 'I'll carve you up so fast, you won't have time to shit yourselves.' I'd left my favourite sword with Shahin. This one, though, had served me well that afternoon. When being got ready to leave Nicetas, I'd taken it from the doorman and held it up, so the lamplight could glitter on the many-folded steel of its blade. Bearing in mind the clothes I had on, I hoped I'd not have to use it tonight. One good look at me and the night vermin were slinking off in search of easier pickings.

I waited for the last footsteps to go out of range. I got up and arranged my clothes again. I turned and looked at the Milestone. It gave the name of and distance to every provincial capital in the Empire that the Great Constantine had ruled. London was near the top. So was York. One of the more recent Emperors had fixed a pompous inscription on its base that combined a Greek translation of Vergil with a quote from *Revelation*. It was a poor moon but looking at the inscription drew me to a graffito someone had chalked on another side of the monument. I thought at first it was about me. I didn't know whether to feel pleased or disappointed that it wasn't.

I heard another noise – this time a soft padding of feet coming towards the far side of the monument. I jumped noiselessly up the steps to the base of the inscribed column. Eight feet above ground, and sheltered between statues of Romulus and Augustus, I unsheathed my sword.

The padding of feet stopped. 'Where have you gone, Alaric?' Antonia quavered. 'I did see you, didn't I?' She hadn't lowered her voice. A few yards away, a scared night creature shuffled deeper into one of the flowerbeds.

I jumped down beside her. 'Run away from home again?' I jeered in Latin. 'If I didn't know him well enough already, I'd have to think ill of your father's control over his women.'

'Oh, Daddy's *easy* to avoid,' she laughed, going herself into perfectly fluent Latin. 'He said he'd beat me half to death, once he was done with Akimba. Silly idea! We used to be lovers, and she kept Daddy busy till I'd crept out of the room.'

Looking at her girly face under a hat that, in itself, might have screamed 'Rape me!' I wanted to hit her. Instead, I stamped my foot and put a scowl into my voice. 'You're mad if you think these streets are safe,' I said. What point, though, in nagging? From what Leander had told me, she must have known these streets by night as well as I did. The flash of anger gave way to tiredness. 'Where do you suppose you're going?' I asked.

'Home with you – where else?' she said.

I climbed the base of the Milestone again and sat on the uppermost step. I waited for her to join me. 'Listen, Antonia,' I said, 'you're a renegade nun and you may be the daughter of a traitor. There are limits to the sanctuary my house can give you. Other than that, you're a niece of the reigning Emperor. You may have noticed that, for all my fancy titles, I'm a barbarian immigrant. How long do you think it would take your uncle to remind us both of that?'

'But I love you, Alaric,' she said simply. 'I will never be parted from you.' She waited a moment. 'It's your turn now,' she prompted.

I sighed and looked at the moon. 'I knew it when I found you in the poor district,' I said, trying to keep my voice steady. 'I knew it, but didn't notice the fact for a while. It came on slowly and imperceptibly, like the passing of spring into summer. I was fully aware of it before we had sex. I wanted to tell you afterwards but didn't know how.' Since I'd already made a total fool of myself, I could see no benefit in holding back. But there was nothing left to hold back. I'd said it all, and with fewer words than I might scribble in the margin of a report. If I added that I loved her more than life itself, I'd only be inviting her to a suicide pact. I put my arm about her. It was a nice feeling.

'Alaric,' she said, now urgent, 'I said I came to see you yesterday on a whim. That's true but it was also because, after I'd untied myself the night before, I overheard Daddy saying what he planned to do to you when he became Emperor. I thought if he hated you so much, you must be worth seeing. So I cut my hair off when I was with someone who gave me shelter and got ready to bluff my way past your eunuchs. That was the whim.' She pressed herself close against me. 'Alaric, do you believe in fate?'

I didn't. But I was interested to hear more about her father's confession of treason. I said nothing. 'After the audience,' she took up again, 'I was getting ready to go away when I heard those men from Pontus complaining about Eunapius. They must have been twenty feet away in a dispersing crowd. But I heard them as clearly as you can hear me. Before I could realise what I was doing, I'd pushed my way through to them and taken their case. I didn't know what to do next. It was Simon who came up behind me and said which way you'd be going. I was sure he didn't recognise me. Everything after that you know. It was fate that brought us together. No one can ever tell me otherwise.'

I sat awhile in silence. I thought hard. 'Did your father really say he'd be Emperor?' I asked. I was probably clutching at air. But, if I could never marry an Emperor's niece, I might be able to beg for the daughter of a fallen traitor. In part, this would depend on whether her loathing of Nicetas was a settled or a brief embitterment.

'I told you he's a traitor,' she said. 'And I know exactly what I'm saying. I stood outside a door left ajar and heard Eunapius assure him it was all in the bag and he didn't need to lift a finger. That was the same Eunapius I met tonight.' I leaned forward into the moonlight. She caught the look on my face. 'The reason I told you yesterday I'd go with you to see Heraclius was so I could tell him the truth about Daddy. You don't know what he did to Mummy,' she ended.

I thought again. With anyone else but Nicetas, the facts she claimed would have jarred so much with what I'd seen for myself that I'd have to reject her claim. But it was easy to believe that Nicetas was half inclined to go along with a plot someone had brought him, and also willing to fit himself round the established order. One moment he'd be fantasising about tying me to the rack, another begging favours off me for his poet.

'Didn't you notice that Theodore is sweet on you?' I asked, changing the subject. I'd have to think this through. Nicetas wouldn't think to come knocking on my door for ages, if at all. In the meantime, Samo could outdo himself with keeping *Antony* as my guest.

She ignored the question. 'That wasn't a woman who interrupted things, was it?' she asked.

233

I stared ahead at the moonlit view I had of lower Constantinople. 'Does cross-dressing offend you?' I asked with a smile.

Antonia fell silent. 'Will you stop being angry with me if I tell you that I saw Simon again this evening?' she asked. 'I can prove everything I've told you.'

I took my arm away and looked at her. 'If you've wasted any more time than it's taken to tell me this,' I said sharply, 'I shall be very angry indeed. Will you share the details with me?'

She did share them and did it rather better than she had the previous day. Once into the courtyard of her father's palace, she'd heard men talking and taken shelter behind some roses. She'd heard Eunapius let out a cry of alarm and had looked out to see him with Simon. She'd been too wrapped up in keeping her scared breathing under control to overhear all that was said. But she had heard Simon announce a meeting for the eighth hour of this night.

I stared up at the moon. It was about an hour after midnight. Assuming Antonia had heard right about the eighth hour we had another hour to go – bearing in mind we were now a month beyond the spring equinox, it wouldn't be a very long hour.

'Any chance they discussed *where* this meeting was to be?' I asked.

She smiled uncertainly. 'They might have,' she said.

'Either they did or they didn't,' I said evenly. 'If not, we might as well go home and wait on events.'

She reached out and took my hand. 'If I tell you where the meeting will be,' she asked, 'will you promise to take me there?'

I got up and stepped down to the street. 'No,' I said with a firmness I should have used earlier in the day. This was why she'd waited so long before 'catching up' with me. I was in the shadow of the Milestone, so put the scowl into my voice. 'You will tell me what you know. I will then take you home before coming out again with Samo. You should know that this matter isn't a game. I suggest you should stop treating it as one.'

'If I tell you, you'll have to take me with you,' she said defiantly.

'I'll take you home!' I said. I had an hour at most to get wherever the meeting was to be. She knew Constantinople. Had she already made it impossible to get her to safety and get to the meeting? 'Look, Antonia, it's dangerous,' I said, now trying for a reasonable tone. 'If you insist on coming with me, you'll put me in danger as well as yourself. If there's fighting to be done, or running away, I need to move quickly. Did you learn nothing yesterday?'

She said nothing. Her face was in shadow. I could almost hear the time gurgling away through one of my expensive water clocks. I sighed. Boys want money, or freedom. Quite often, if you have looks or charm, girls want nothing at all. Women *always* make you choose. The choice Antonia was putting to me was outrageous. For all I knew, Eunapius and Simon would soon be making everything as plain as day and within a few hundred paces of where I now stood. All else aside, she might be throwing away her only chance of never setting foot again in that Trebizond nunnery.

I reached out with my right hand. 'We'll go home,' I said calmly. 'My Jews will be with me late tomorrow morning. They will tell me all I need to know.'

She took my hand and jumped down. She put her arms about me and kissed my cheek. I put my own arms about her and felt suddenly clumsy. 'Alaric,' she whispered, 'Simon said the meeting would be in one of the lecture halls in the Baths of Anthemius. I know a secret way in that the poor use now you've put all the prices up.'

36

Built in more prosperous and leisured days, the Baths of Anthemius still counted as a world in itself. Except I'd recently ordered it to be closed between sunset and dawn, you could spend your whole time in that vast complex and never see need to go outside. It had shops, restaurants, and a church, and a library and brothels. Once you'd paid your entrance money, there were free lectures on mathematics and history, and poetry recitals and performances of comic plays, and readings of such news as the government thought fit for public consumption. There was also the biggest heated pool in the known world and a gymnasium that, fitted out with the best nude statues taken from Olympia before the earthquake, doubled as an art gallery. Just providing marble for the vast central hall had left every former temple in Ephesus a shell of exposed and crumbling brick.

Now I'd taken the Empire's finances properly in hand though, the Baths were locked up and in darkness. Before noon the next day, the disused drainage tunnel Antonia had shown me would be bricked off and rendered at both ends. If they wanted a bath, the poor could stick to the cold pool outside. No wonder raising the entry charges hadn't so far reduced the number of times we had to change the hot water.

As we stepped into the central hall, I put a hand over Antonia's mouth. 'If you must speak, do it softly and into your clothing.' I said, covering my own mouth to avoid an echo. The tunnel had been completely dark and I'd had to trust her assurances that it was safe to pass along. Here, the windows in the dome far above let in enough light from the moon and stars to give bearings. There were four arched doorways, three of them leading to different areas of the sprawling complex. I looked hard at the bronze group of Hercules and Antaeus. If she'd heard right, the exit we needed was the one to which Antaeus was pointing with his right leg. 'Either lift your feet properly, or take your shoes off,' I breathed. I took Antonia by the hand and led her away from the worn limestone paths along which visitors were made to keep by day. Within our dark outer clothes, we'd show in this light as black on black against the porphyry cladding of the lower walls. We made our way towards the memorial Heraclius had set up to the unfortunate Emperor Maurice and his five murdered sons.

'Where are you going?' she whispered. She slowed and tried to pull me back. 'I said we had to go this way.'

I put a hand over her mouth again. 'So you think the plan is for us to go down that corridor,' I whispered as softly as I could, 'and knock on every door until Simon or Eunapius calls us in for light refreshments?' I stepped forward again, quickly passing across the entrance to the corridor. 'I don't want to hear from you again until I tell you it's safe to speak.' Of course, I'd been stupid to give in to the girl. I should have taken her home and waited for Baruch to report back in the morning. Even if not at first hand, he'd surely have found everything worth knowing. If there was something to be learned here, it couldn't be worth the risk.

But there was now the faintest sound of voices, and of a big door quietly opened and closed. And there was a flicker of light in the corridor leading in from the main entrance. My heart skipped a beat and everything in the surrounding gloom seemed to become sharper. No longer angry, nor scared, nor beset by guilt for letting her tag along – no longer even dog tired and longing for my bed – I pulled Antonia closer against the wall. 'Keep still,' I said, 'and try not to make any sound at all.'

Approaching along the wide access corridor, the voice of Shahin was unmistakable. 'Oh, but what splendid buildings you have in this great city of Constantinople,' he called out in Greek. 'I had quite forgotten how little we have in Ctesiphon to compare with these glories.' I pulled the hood closer over my face and looked across the two hundred yards that separated us. Two lamp-bearers were first into the hall. They separated and stood each side of the doorway, bowing as Shahin strode confidently past them. Perhaps half a dozen men filed in behind him – hard to tell exactly how many, given the light available, or the distance. Once inside the ring of columns that supported the arches that held the dome, he stopped and clapped his hands. He listened to the echo and clapped again. He moved towards the central statuary. He put his hand on one of the buttocks and, looking upward, recited:

> O Goddess sing what woe the discontent
> Of Thetis' son brought to the Greeks; what souls
> Of heroes down to Erebus it sent,
> Leaving their bodies unto dogs and fowls.

The laugh he brought out was the verbal equivalent of slapping himself on the back. And I had to admit he'd done a fine job on Homer. Leander could have taken lessons from Shahin with obvious profit. Even Nicetas might have heard the distinction between long and short syllables. 'But can't you bring in more lamps, Simon?' he barked. 'I'd love to see how high the ceiling is in here.' Simon's reply was an anxious groan. Shahin snorted, then laughed again. 'But I've no doubt I'll see this place again in daylight – this and many other places!' He stepped away from the bronze group and followed the lamp-bearers across the hall.

The procession passed by us not ten feet away. I'd been wondering if we'd be spotted from the lack of reflection where we stood against the polished walls. But Shahin, breathing hard, had stopped again, and was looking away from us at an oversize statue of Antinous. Simon hovered visibly between the nervous and depressed. Everyone else was muffled in his cloak.

'Is that you, Shahin?' Eunapius called from within the darkness of the corridor. 'Did you come alone?' He uncovered the lamp he was holding and took a heavy step forward.

'As nearly alone as a man can be when going about an enemy capital,' Shahin said with a contemptuous laugh. He straightened up from an inspection of the perfect thighs of Antinous – he'd always enjoyed rubbing himself off against mine. 'Are you so distrustful of your own slaves that Simon has to arrange meetings in public?'

'My Lord's palace may be watched,' Simon said, trying for an emollient tone.

Shahin sniffed loudly. 'Oh, let's get on with it,' he sighed. He stepped through the doorway and was followed by everyone else.

Antonia pressed herself against me. She put a cold and trembling hand on my arm. 'Will they really kill us if they find us?' she asked. I nearly jumped. I'd forgotten I wasn't alone. I suppressed the returning guilt and fear. I tried for a reassuring squeeze of her hand. It was the only answer I could give. Taking extra care not to scrape my feet on the floor, I continued moving towards the little access stairway.

Leaded roofs in the dark are treacherous things. There's a risk you won't notice until it's too late that you aren't standing on the level. I had to keep a tight hold on Antonia and make sure we both kept close by the line of glazed ceiling windows. Beyond this, it was easy enough to know which window we wanted. Ours was the only one in which every piece of glass shone bright. Ours was the one that was abruptly pushed open from below as we approached it, and secured with a two-inch gap. Hoping not to spoil my toga, I lay down flat about a foot away. In a kind of press-up that made no sound, I moved my face close to the gap. I pulled back as something with wings settled on my nose. I brushed it away and tried to get into the same comfortable position that I'd now lost. From out here, the lamps had seemed to fill the room with as much light as Nicetas had laid on for his recital. Looking in, I could see that the one lamp left burning sent out a pool of light that barely showed anything beyond the table on which it was set. I pushed my face closer and bobbed up and down and from side to side. I could dimly make out a blackboard on which someone had drawn and half-erased a demonstration from Apollonius. Except for the unattractively large feet joined to the ends of Shahin's short legs, there was nothing human to be seen.

No problem, however, with listening. I might as well have been inside the room. 'Greetings, Eunapius of Pylae,' Shahin said in a voice that mixed politeness with a dash of contempt. 'I generally like to see men before I deal with them. These are, to be sure, unusual circumstances. But I rejoice in finally making your acquaintance.'

Simon broke in with a reminder of how short the time was till dawn. 'We'll be out of here long before then,' came Shahin's easy reply. 'So long as your people keep the dock secured, my people are waiting out in the strait.' His feet moved forward and I heard a creaking of wood that reminded me of our times together in Ctesiphon, when he'd rock back in his chair and stretch out his arms. With a sudden bump, his chair was properly on the floor and his legs were pulled back. 'My dear Eunapius,' he said with a turn to the businesslike. 'I've heard much from Simon of your motivations and of what you are able to offer in return for our help. But let me ask you directly what it is that drives you and your associates to make an approach to the Empire's most deadly enemy. *Why have you turned traitor?*'

There was a long silence. But I finally heard someone get up and walk over to the door. It opened for a moment, then was pushed shut again. 'My Lord Shahin,' Eunapius began in an attempt at firmness, 'we do not regard ourselves as the traitors. We make this approach only as a last resort and in response to an Emperor who is himself subverting the Empire's most fundamental laws.' His voice trailed off and died. It was barely into this opening statement when it had lost all the unpleasant bounce of earlier in the evening. Eunapius coughed, cleared his throat and started again. 'We, the nobility of the Empire, are the true representatives of the Roman people. We are the living embodiment of their glory and guardians of their Constitution.' He stopped again. This time, when he started, he spoke quickly and made no effort at measured grandeur of utterance. Heraclius was taking his order's land away, he whined. By closing down, one at a time, every historic department in the state, Heraclius was abolishing every office of dignity and every subordinate office that should be

240

filled by the clients of the dignified. Heraclius was proposing to empty out the cities. Heraclius was raising the cultivators of the soil to an unnatural eminence and was even arming these men, and talking about raising an army from them that would be officered by men without birth and leisured education. Heraclius was listening to Jews and Armenians. Heraclius was giving inexplicable rights to merchants to arrange their own affairs and set their own prices. In short, Heraclius was turning the Empire upside down, and making it into a country as alien to its rightful governing class as the lost provinces of the West.

What Eunapius had brought out, in one tangled thread of rage and bitterness, was a fair summary of all that I'd already impressed on the Emperor, or was nudging him, a step at a time, to consider. With a bit of rearrangement and softening, I could easily have worked a transcript of all he said into a manifesto.

'So it's pretty young Alaric who's pissed your people off!' Shahin said in a voice of grave mockery that I doubted Eunapius was calm enough to notice. 'We had our own taste of his reforms last spring, when a mob of farmers stopped our advance into the Home Provinces. We certainly shan't forget the time he spent with us in Ctesiphon.' He sniffed and stretched again.

Eunapius stopped walking up and down the room. 'I'm told you had the piece of barbarian shit in your power all yesterday afternoon,' he did his best not to shout. 'Can I ask why you didn't kill him on the spot?'

Shahin gave way to openly mocking laughter. 'If I'd done that,' he sneered, 'can I suppose you and your friends would still be so keen to do business with me?'

The room was silent. At last, Simon struck up in his role as mediator. 'If you please, My Lords, I will outline the agreement that has been made. The best people in Constantinople will convene an extraordinary meeting of the Senate and declare Heraclius a public enemy. Those ministers who do not recognise the Senate's decree will be removed from office. The people will be promised the full return of their ancient privileges. The new Emperor will be Nicetas. The army will obey his order to arrest

Heraclius. He will then open frank and open negotiations with the Great King for a fair settlement of what all agree has been a long and exhausting war. This settlement will include an acknowledgement of those conquests of Imperial territory already made by Chosroes, and a granting of such other territories as may be requested. At the same time, the Lord General Shahrbaraz and his deputy Shahin will provide whatever armed support the new Emperor may require.

'Can I ask My Lords to confirm that this is an accurate overview of what has been agreed?'

'Absolutely!' Shahin said with what may have been a slapping of his thigh. 'I couldn't have said better myself. Peace and a renewal of friendly cooperation between the two Shining Eyes of the World. What more could any man want?'

I'd again forgotten that Antonia was beside me. 'What about Cappadocia and Syria?' she whispered. I dug my elbow in her side, and she was quiet again. So many silly questions – and hadn't this one just been answered? I may not have had much regard for their value but I was buggered if I'd let the Persians keep Syria and have Egypt handed over on a plate. Certainly not Cappadocia. That was undeniably ours, even on my map of a remodelled Empire.

'Then why are we waiting?' Eunapius asked in a low mutter. 'Heraclius has been out of the City a month. We were ready to make our move on Easter Monday. Delay has got Alaric sniffing round. Much longer, and support will drain away. I'm already having problems with some of the key people we need.'

'But, Eunapius,' Shahin said, still in jolly voice, 'have you forgotten a *certain object* that is much desired by the Great King? My orders are to do nothing until I have that in my own hands.'

'My Lord is aware that Alaric has possession of the Horn of Babylon,' Simon said. 'He beat us to it a few nights ago and we have not so far been able to take it from him. However, once Nicetas has control of the City, it will be a simple matter to break into his palace . . .'

I could almost hear Shahin wag his finger. 'Oh no, my dear but shifty Greeklings!' he cried. 'You produce my silver horn and my ships will sail into your Golden Horn. If you think this a harsh condition, please bear in mind what our experience of the Empire has been in the three centuries since the weakening began of its Latin element. I wouldn't trust you people to tell me it was dark outside.' He laughed coldly and pushed his chair forward. Now fully in view, he got up and pointed at the window. I got Antonia back just in time to keep her pale face out of view. 'I must have the Horn of Babylon,' he said. He sat down again and rocked on his chair. 'No Horn of Babylon, no Persian support.'

There was another long silence. It was broken by a muffled argument in the corridor outside. Below me, Shahin swore viciously in Persian and his legs disappeared. I heard the rasp of a drawn sword. 'Peace, My Lords, peace!' Simon cried, trying to keep alarm from wholly taking over his voice. I think it was he who pulled the door open. It was his voice that did now give way to alarm. 'What are you doing here?' he demanded. 'How did you find us?'

'I *am* the City Prefect!' Timothy answered in his plumiest, nastiest voice. 'It would be a sad dereliction of my duties if I weren't aware of your dastardly plot against the Empire.' He laughed and stepped through the door. 'Your men can take their hands off me,' he said with a turn to the menacing. 'They have already searched me.' He moved almost directly under my window. 'Ah, Cousin Shahin!' he boomed. 'I thought you'd be here. Delighted, of course, to see you again after so many years.'

37

After the slightest pause, Shahin spoke. 'My dearest Timothy,' he called, 'it is an absolute treat to see you again.' He giggled, and there was the firm smack of a kiss I was rather glad I didn't have to see.

'*Cousins?*' Eunapius asked. 'How can you be cousins?' I heard the scrape of a chair. Had Eunapius sat down in shock?

Timothy laughed. I heard the groan of a chair beneath his immense bulk. 'My dear Eunapius,' he said with pitying contempt, 'that question disproves the whole claim you keep making that you are one of us. Beneath the squabbles of our rulers, the governing classes of both empires are really one big happy family. We've been marrying each other since time out of mind. You really aren't one of us. Like our current Emperor, you're a man from the provinces. If we have so far allowed you and your associate to speak for us, I am here to tell Shahin that our patience is worn out. From now on, *I* will deal with the Persians. You will take my orders.' His voice brightened. 'Be in no doubt, Shahin, that I speak for the old nobility. Whatever Eunapius has told you is probably wishful thinking.'

'Would you care to elaborate on this?' Shahin asked, a scowl in his voice.

'Well,' said Timothy, 'I think we can rule out Nicetas as next Emperor. This little provincial here may have been telling you the same as he'd told us – that the Emperor's cousin is in the plot. From what I saw of his behaviour this evening, he's as ignorant of things as young Alaric was until yesterday. And Alaric, I have reason to believe, is a couple of days at most from rumbling us all. We never wanted Nicetas. We've now decided that we'll not lift a finger to make him Emperor.

'But it's all arranged!' Eunapius cried, horror in his voice. 'You can't go back on your word.'

Timothy cut straight in. 'Do correct me if I'm wrong, dear boy, but I was under the impression that Nicetas was to *lead* the revolution. You never told me he'd have to be dragged squealing from behind a curtain, like Claudius after Caligula got it in the neck.' He laughed. 'Do try to see reason. When you change emperors, it's a good idea to make a clean sweep. Now I mention Claudius, wasn't his first act to round up and kill everyone who'd been in the plot against his nephew? Don't suppose Nicetas will stay grateful longer than it takes to drape the Purple about his shoulders. Even if he doesn't have the heads off our shoulders, the armies may not obey him. Also, he'd never dare get rid of Sergius as Patriarch, or purge Alaric's men from the upper reaches of the Church.' He laughed again. 'These are general considerations, I know. But after tonight's display of underlying concord between him and Alaric, we're not having Nicetas.'

'So, who is to be next Emperor?' Shahin asked. 'We'll need someone to seal the peace agreement.'

'It may be an ambition that has come on late in life,' Timothy yawned, 'but I do have several emperors in my blood line. And there can be no doubt the nobility is with me, and that the bureaucracy would obey me. Oh, and I'll repeat that I *am* the City Prefect. That's a fine base from which to launch a revolution.'

'And you would still consent to our peace treaty?' Shahin asked.'

'I see no reason why not,' Timothy rumbled. 'You give us Alaric's head on a plate, and you can keep Syria with my blessings.'

Shahin leaned forward in his chair so I could see his bald patch. 'Then it's a pity you didn't catch our earlier conversation,' he said. 'We don't actually care who is Emperor. But the deal we offer is the same. You give us the Horn of Babylon and we'll fall in with whatever you decide among yourselves. Until you give us that, you're all on your own.'

There was yet another silence. Then Timothy spoke. 'I believe Eunapius did mention a certain object of ritual importance to

Cousin Chosroes,' he said grandly. 'I have still to know, however, what exactly it is. Can you enlighten us, Shahin?'

'No,' was the answer. 'I don't ask questions of Shahrbaraz, nor of the Great King. I can simply repeat my orders. You'll get nothing from us until you put the Horn of Babylon into my hands. At the moment, Alaric has it. Have you any idea of how to get it from him?'

'I have an idea,' Simon broke in, plainly and comically desperate to pull the conversation back in order. Timothy grunted very loudly. Simon ignored him. 'The barbarian boy's taken up with a girl who seems to have turned his wits. I spoke briefly with her yesterday morning. She's from Trebizond.' He paused to let the significance of that trickle into every mind. 'She must have relatives there. Perhaps we can use that when the Persians move in.'

Shahin laughed. 'Oh, I saw that for myself yesterday. The poor boy is utterly smitten. I couldn't resist having a little fun over it. If you can find a use for that, good luck to you. However, must I repeat that we shan't move against the Black Sea cities until we have the Horn of Babylon? That's all that matters to us. You give me the Horn of Babylon and I'll make anyone of your choice Emperor.' He got up. 'Now, much as I've enjoyed my first visit to Constantinople since the outbreak of war, I am alarmed that Timothy knew I'd be here. If he could find out, Alaric might. You obviously have much to discuss among yourselves and it isn't for me to involve myself in that conversation.' He moved towards the door. 'Please don't feel obliged to stand on ceremony. I can find my own way out.'

Shahin went out, leaving the room in the longest silence yet. I was aware once more of Antonia beside me. Simon had spoken as if he didn't know who she was. Yet it had been my impression that he did know. Was he trying to be more in this than a middle man? Worth thinking about when I had the time. For the moment, I turned my attention to the continuing silence below. It was broken by a quiet laugh from Timothy. 'Now you've gone and done it,' Eunapius cried bitterly. 'You've muddled everything.'

'On the contrary,' Timothy said with evident pleasure, 'I've saved my people the trouble of hearing more of your lies. This

Horn of Babylon, I now learn, is not some incidental token of good faith. It is the only thing that Shahin actually wants. I therefore propose to leave aside the matter of who is to replace Heraclius. Our present task is to prise the Horn of Babylon from Alaric's grasp.'

'It has magic powers,' Eunapius said quickly. 'Whoever knows how to use those powers can make himself master of all things. Isn't that so, Simon?'

'My Lord,' Simon came straight back, a nervous tone in his voice, 'the Persians believe any number of things at variance with the teachings of Holy Mother Church . . .'

'Shut up unless you're spoken to,' Timothy snarled. 'What's this about *magic powers*, Eunapius?' Even someone brighter than Eunapius would have had trouble evading the brief but effective interrogation that followed. It ended in more silence. Timothy broke this with one of his long and appreciative burps. 'Well, this being the case,' he said thoughtfully, 'why are we giving the thing to the bloody Persians?' he burped again. 'Magic powers?' he asked again, now wonderingly. 'That might explain why Shahin took the risk of coming ashore. Magic powers, eh?' He paused for thought, then: 'Very well,' he said, now brisk, 'I say we keep Shahin dangling, just in case we need Plan B. The new Plan A, though, is that we put all effort into getting this Horn of Babylon for ourselves – and before that bastard savage works its powers out for himself.'

He stopped and grunted his way through various workings of his mind. 'Now we've seen that Nicetas isn't committed,' he began again, 'getting my people to act is out of the question. Without Nicetas to back me, I can't arrest another member of the Imperial Council. I suppose we could have another go at waylaying the little shit as he goes unguarded about his business. Or, since we've tried that now more than once, there is the girl. I believe I saw her this evening. She's a pretty enough creature, and I could well understand how he was almost squirting into his leggings every time he looked at her. Perhaps Eunapius could use his own connections in Trebizond to see what pressure may be imposed from that direction.' His voice brightened. 'Yes, we'll get the Horn of Babylon, and then we'll see if it can make me Emperor – and then what sort of Emperor!' He laughed, and there was another alarming creak of his chair.

'You *can't* be Emperor!' Eunapius said, aghast. 'It has to be Nicetas. Without him to take over at once, Heraclius can't be arrested in Cyzicus.'

'If you must reopen the matter,' Timothy snapped, 'I can and *will* be Emperor. There's nothing more to be said.'

'There's a great deal more to be said,' Eunapius replied. 'Everyone knows your brother was deprived of his governorship for heresy. The Church would never stand for you.'

'Do I hear right, that Nicetas has offered you his daughter in marriage?' Timothy asked with a sudden sneer. 'I wouldn't take his word on anything. Everyone knows how he just "forgets" promises. Otherwise, don't count on staying alive long enough to step into his purple boots once he is Emperor.' He went into a long and wheezing laugh. I glanced quickly into Antonia's face. It had the dead look a fine lady is trained to put on for a chariot race in the Circus. All else aside, why was Simon keeping her identity to himself?

'Just stick with me, Eunapius,' Timothy said with a return to easy humour. 'How about the Lord Treasurership – and Alaric's palace, of course?' Eunapius said nothing. 'Oh, but let's call on the Will of God,' Timothy sighed. His chair creaked again. 'I've one of Alaric's new coins here. The reverse, for some reason, has a motto in Latin.' He read slowly and with a misplaced accent: "*Deus Adiuta Romanis.*" I'm told it means: "May God Help the Romans." Heads, and you can have Nicetas, and Shahin too. Tails, and it means God wants me.'

There was yet another silence in the room, this time ended by the ring of silver on marble. 'Fucking thing bounced,' Timothy snapped. 'The result doesn't count.'

Another silence. This time, it was Eunapius who spoke. 'That was a cheat,' he shouted. 'I saw you move your hand. If we must do this, let's do it fairly.'

'My Lords,' Simon broke in, 'I do suggest . . .'

'. . . that you shut up in the presence of your betters!' Timothy said quickly. 'I'll do the toss again.' He moved directly beneath me and flicked the coin upwards. I watched it come closer, glittering as it turned over and over in the lamplight. This time, it stuck against one of the glass panes and bounced into the upper gatherings of my toga. I pulled myself back and went through my clothing. I found the coin too late to throw it back down.

'Can we talk about Alaric?' Simon asked despairingly.

Neither Eunapius nor Timothy was listening. 'Get that table over here,' Timothy ordered. 'We'll climb up together and see what God has decided.' There was a loud scraping of wood and another cut-off protest from Simon.

I jumped to my feet. The plan of escape I'd worked out involved continuing along the roof to the far end of the corridor. From here, we could climb down into a little area used for holding deliveries of wood for the furnaces. There was a little door I could unbolt that led into a side street. Unless Timothy's weight was too much for the table, we'd never get out of sight in time. I took Antonia by the arm and hurried her back the way we'd come. We were barely on to the stairs down to the main hall when, with a smashing of glass, the window flew fully open and Timothy was braying how God had indeed helped the Romans.

'I'm not marrying that creature!' she whispered fiercely. 'I'd rather die.'

'Shut up!' I hissed. I took hold of Antonia by the shoulders and pushed her against the curving wall of the stairway. 'So long as no one realises I was watching,' I said, 'it's a stalemate. The Greeks daren't move without Shahin. He won't help without my silver cup. All we need to do is get away unobserved. Now, keep quiet, and let me go first.'

'But you've got to stop Daddy,' she breathed. 'You don't understand how he hates you.'

I stood up straight. 'Arresting Nicetas while he's Regent – and with an unknown part of the administration on his side – isn't something I fancy trying,' I said firmly. 'I'll write to Heraclius in the morning. He can hurry back with the small army he took with him. In the meantime, we carry on as normal.' I listened for any sound of approaching footsteps along the roof. There were none. No one would follow us down this way. Timothy had found his coin. He and Eunapius might well argue over its answers till dawn. Shahin and his men should be halfway back to whatever dock he was using. I thought of what I had to do. It was a two-day journey by fast courier to Cyzicus. I suppressed the urge to go there myself. That would only alert everyone. I'd have Simon and half the city guard after me. And what of Antonia? What of Theodore and Maximin and all my other people? No – it had to be business as usual.

We crept down the stairs. There were a couple of lamps burning there, but the main hall should be empty. Our luck ought to hold.

It didn't. I poked my head briefly round the corner and, in a parodic echo of the previous day, found myself looking into Shahin's face.

His eyes widened for a moment in the gloom. He blinked and then smiled. 'Hello, Alaric,' he cried softly in Greek. He steadied himself against the statue of Antinous. 'I never doubted you were listening overhead. But I was beginning to fear you'd found a less obvious way out of here.'

I shoved Antonia backward and stepped into the hall. 'Were you fellating that statue?' I asked with mock outrage.

He shrugged and grinned. 'From the shine on that perfectly formed member,' he sniggered, 'I'm hardly the first. Such admirable men, these Greeks of the olden days, don't you think?' He kissed one of the thighs and stood reluctantly back.

I thought of going for my sword. That would never do. I could cut my way past Shahin, and take out the two men who were still squatting on their haunches beside the bronze of Hercules. But the noise would send Timothy and Eunapius into a foaming panic that was the last thing I wanted. Shahin gave a friendly smile and spread his arms. 'I think I can guess yours,' he said, 'but I do have my own reasons for avoiding any public fuss. Any chance of a quick word in private?'

38

Shahin turned from his inspection of the book racks. 'Not much of a library,' he sniffed. 'Most of this stuff is barely fit for heating the baths.' I was by the door. His two men had followed him up the wide staircase to this upper level and were looking impassively in at me. I smiled at them and shut the door in their faces.

Again with his back to me, Shahin pulled another book from its leather case and unrolled it a few turns. 'So this is the latest fashion in poetry?' he asked accusingly. He dropped one of the spines and allowed the book to unroll completely. 'These modern Greeks are sadly decayed, don't you think? Perhaps Chosroes is right that the time is come for a new language to dominate the East.' He sniggered and went back to his inspection. 'But look at this metaphor. It doesn't even scan.'

I walked across the room and, keeping just out of reach, bent down to look at the opening sheet of the book. Shahin tipped the lamp forward so I could read the neat rows of text. 'It's not so very bad,' I said. 'You should have been where I was earlier tonight.' I straightened up. 'But I don't think your main interest here is literary criticism. Can I take it that you'd like to bypass those losers downstairs and deal directly with the possessor of the Horn of Babylon?'

He sniggered again. 'It has its convenient side,' he said, now in Persian, 'that you overheard everything. So, yes – let's talk about the Horn of Babylon. I do wish I'd known, when we had that yummy dinner onboard my ship yesterday, that you had it. We could have saved much time – and avoided so many embarrassments.' He dropped the other spine of the book and perched himself on one of the reading tables. 'How can I persuade you to give it to me? I don't imagine money will tempt you. I daren't make *you* Emperor: you'd find a competent general, and ease his path straight to Ctesiphon with gold and diplomacy. So what price has pretty young Alaric in mind?'

'You could try guessing,' I answered. I moved the lamp to another table, where Shahin's rhythmical swinging of legs wouldn't tip it over. I pulled over a chair and sat down a couple of yards from him. If I could arrest him, I'd kill the plot stone dead. But he was easily a match for me with his sword – that was one exercise he'd never neglected. And there were his men to keep in mind. At best, he'd get away. At worst, the noise would bounce Timothy and Eunapius into a revolution that might succeed.

Shahin watched my face. He smiled knowingly. 'You can't keep the silver cup,' he said. 'You can't give it to Heraclius. But you've probably worked that out for yourself. As for those idiots we left snapping at each other, you can't make a deal with them. Since old Priscus croaked his last, Timothy has taken over as shitbag in chief. He'd have a knife in your back before he could draw breath from saying "Many thanks, dear boy." So why not bring it to me while I wait at the docks? You can come with me to Shahrbaraz. Bring the girl too. You'll be surprised how merciful and forgiving Chosroes can be to those who give him what he wants.'

'That would be a side to the Great King's character I haven't yet seen,' I said. 'How about telling me why the cup is so important?'

He giggled again. 'Since the cup goes where you go for the moment,' he said, 'let's talk about you.' He straightened his face. 'Look, Alaric, my orders include an express instruction to keep you from harm, so far as I can, and to beg you to come back to Ctesiphon. Chosroes promises a total safe conduct and will swear any oath to that effect.'

'I've seen how your boss keeps his promises,' I said. Far down in the main hall, I heard a noise. It was followed by one of Timothy's rumbling laughs. Either they'd finally settled on the next Emperor, or they were sick of arguing. I walked across to the door and listened. I turned back to Shahin. 'Supposing I refuse to do business with you?' I asked.

'You'd be a fool, Alaric,' he said. 'You owe fuck all to Heraclius. Everyone else in this Empire is praying for your death. Come back with me to Ctesiphon. The Jews will always put in a kind word for you. Our own Christians are at war with the Empire over theological trifles – and they appreciate your efforts at securing a toleration within the Empire of their heresies. All Chosroes wants is to put some ideas to you. I know he still likes you.'

I walked to the far end of the room. I put my hand on a solid rack that had once contained a full set of Livy. The brass plate on one of the square openings still gave the name and title of the work. Some of the slots, I'd found on an earlier visit, were now filled with trashy novels in Greek. The others were used for a guessing game with dice. I turned and stared back at Shahin. The moon had shifted and he sat within a shaft of its dim light.

'I'll grant that Heraclius may not be pleased to know I've learned his secret,' I said. 'However, I've always been able to bring him round. I don't feel so sure about the Great King. And why should I trust *you*?'

'That's a chance you'll have to take, my beautiful darling,' he chuckled. He got up and went over to the door. He pulled it open and possibly a dozen of his big Syrians filed in. 'Now that we're alone, I think I can risk a little noise. Take the boy alive,' he ordered in Syriac. 'I want him unhurt.'

Shahin and his men were thirty feet away. I was beside one of the bigger windows. Though glazed, its lead framework was perished. Beyond this, I knew, was a ten-foot drop to a tiled roof. 'Oh, Shahin,' I said, 'you can't be serious about taking me. It'll soon be dawn. If you expect to march me all the way home to get that cup, you'll be making your way back through the City in broad daylight.'

His men were coming forward in loose formation. Shahin kept behind them. 'That isn't my plan at all, my pretty,' he called soothingly. 'I'm assuming the attraction between you and that girl is mutual. You're coming with me – though perhaps to better quarters than we managed last night. If the girl brings the cup tomorrow, I won't kill her. If she doesn't, you must appreciate that you're almost as big a trophy to carry back as the cup itself.' He bowed satirically and touched his forehead. He dropped his voice to a bureaucratic snarl. 'I don't want a mark on him,' he reminded his men.

The big window was a foot behind me. I could have chosen better rooms for a getaway when Shahin called for his parley. I didn't fancy a second tiled roof in one day – not in a toga, not in the dark. But the library had been safely distant from the tunnel where I could hope Antonia had made her own escape.

Of course, I'd wasted my time. Even as I weighed the benefits of pulling the window open, or jumping straight through it, you can guess who sidled into the room. I say sidled – with that over-done creeping across the floor, Antonia would have been booed off any stage where she was playing in a chorus of conspirators. Luckily, everyone else was now making too much noise to notice her. The first Shahin knew of her was when she got behind him.

'Move an inch,' she cried in a poor approximation of the manly, 'and I'll saw your head off.' She pulled him backwards and tight-ened her grip. I saw the dull sheen of steel in the moonlight.

Shahin opened his mouth and laughed. 'What splendid taste you have in women, Alaric,' he cried in Persian. 'So many the chances I passed up at our last meeting.' Letting out a squeak that was probably meant to be a growl, Antonia pressed the blade harder still against his throat. 'Shall I order my men to put down their swords?' he jeered. 'Or shall I just shit myself with terror?' As he finished, he produced what may have been his best ever artifi-cial fart. A moment later, he went limp. Surprised, or trying for a better angle, Antonia relaxed her pressure. That was the end of her hostage-taking. I couldn't see what Shahin did with his left arm. But I did hear the thud of her knife against one of the bookracks. He twisted round and knocked her to the floor. With a cry of triumph, he was waving his men forward again. 'Change of plan, Alaric!' he sniggered. 'Go for that window, and you'll never see her again.'

But I'd already given up on the window. Sword in hand, I punched his closest heavy aside, and dodged past another, and was level with Shahin before he could draw breath again. I gave up the chance of killing him. Instead, I snatched Antonia into my free hand and threw her towards the door. 'Get out!' I said urgently. I turned back to deal with Shahin. But he'd got himself behind one of the tables and was calling out a stream of orders in Syriac. I reached for the lamp and threw it at the men. It went out at once and crashed uselessly against a wall, but gave me time to dart past them after Antonia.

Out on the big landing, I paused to get my bearings. The best way out was down the stairs. The soft patter of feet on marble, though, ruled that out. If we turned sharp left, there was another room with an open balcony. We could barricade ourselves in there till Shahin ran out of time. I reached out for Antonia. She wasn't where I'd expected her to be, but cried out from behind me. I turned in time to get one of the dim shadows with the flat of my sword. I heard his head strike loud on one of the marble balustrades. Before I could reach out again, someone else grabbed hold of my cloak. It was now all a blur about me of darting shadows. I stepped backwards and raised my sword. Antonia cried out again and I think she wriggled free. Because I lunged in her direction, most of the blow from behind landed on my shoulder. Even so, I staggered and lost my footing on the topmost step. I grabbed at nothingness, but thought I'd catch my balance. I didn't quite. The best I could manage as I fell backwards was to twist so that I rolled down the first flight of steps. Dazed and winded, I pushed myself to a kneeling position against one of the balustrades and patted round for my sword.

'Someone, get a light!' Shahin roared. 'Find him. I want him alive.'

Antonia was suddenly beside me. 'Get up,' she moaned, pulling at my clothes. 'I don't think they can see us.' I rubbed my head and looked about. Far above in the library, someone had struck a light. Someone else was feeling his way down the stairs. The moment we ran for it, we'd be seen. But it was that or be found anyway. Still feeling for my sword, my hand touched on the face of the man who'd broken my fall. I didn't recall the impact, but hoped he was alive – that, or that I hadn't made him bleed. Just as much as Shahin, I needed no signs of violence left behind in the baths.

Antonia pulled harder. 'We must go,' she moaned, her voice hovering between desperation and tears. I gave up on my sword. Holding hands with Antonia, I stumbled down into the main hall and let her take me towards the door that led down to the furnace rooms. I pulled it open and looked back into the hall. Leaning over the balcony, pointing and calling out, Shahin was surrounded by men carrying makeshift torches of papyrus. A few yards behind me, two dark figures had stopped chasing and, swords in hand, were now creeping forward.

I slammed the door in their faces and didn't wait to feel if there was a bolt I could draw. We fell down more steps into the complete darkness of the drainage tunnel. Expecting at any moment to hear the creak of wood on rusty hinges and a shouting of many voices, I kept hold of Antonia and rushed along the tunnel. We crashed once into a wall where it curved. I think I stumbled twice on the uneven floor. But there was no sound of a chase behind us. In a silence broken only by the crunch and echo of our own footsteps, we ran the length of the tunnel and came out into the comparative brightness of the moonshine that lit up the rubbish-filled depression hiding the tunnel's entrance.

In silence, we walked together in the shadow of the immense warehouses that lined every street in this part of the City. It would need supreme bad luck to bump into Shahin or any of his people out here. I had no sword and Antonia's knife was somewhere on the library floor. Even so close to the dawn, there was some risk of thieves or of drunken youths of quality out for one last thrill.

In safety, though, we came once more to the Central Milestone. The sky behind the Great Church was already bright. Before long, the public slaves would be out to clean the streets. With them would come the working lower orders about their business. I turned in the direction of the Triumphal Way.

'We did it!' Antonia said flatly. 'We got away.'

'We got away again,' I corrected her. I thought of a brief lecture on the folly of getting involved in men's work. But, in the growing light of day, I stared down at the sorry thing my toga had become. You could now soak it in urine for a month and the stains wouldn't come out. As for the long rip from the waist down . . .

Antonia caught the look on my face and went into quiet though helpless laughter. It was impossible not to join in. Hand in hand, shaking with a mirth no observer could have explained, we made our way round the big fountain Constantine had set in a square laid out to commemorate the religious concord he thought had followed the outcome of the Council of Nicaea.

What a fathead he'd been! Still, he'd given his name to the City. That could make anyone's name immortal.

39

I stretched out lazily for my wine cup. Making sure not to spill any on the silken sheets, I sipped with exaggerated delicacy. 'You will marry me?' I asked, trying not to sound as eager as I felt.

Antonia wriggled free of me and sat up. Since dawn, we'd coupled and slept, and coupled again and again, and slept. It was hours since I'd told Samo to go away and tell anyone who asked that I was still indisposed. Long before then, I'd barely noticed how the sun had reached its blazing zenith and the rumble of traffic far below my sleeping quarters had died away. But the long ecstasy was over. Bruised and bitten, sore from the unobserved drying up of every fluid supplied by nature for the normal satisfaction of lust, I kicked the bedclothes away and wiggled my toes.

Antonia frowned. 'And this is something you'll still want tomorrow and the day after tomorrow?' she asked. 'You'll still want it after I've helped you bring down Daddy? Love isn't the same as fucking.' She stopped a sharp intake of breath. 'I learned that the hard way when I was thirteen,' she ended with a slight tremor.

I put my arm about her. I swallowed and looked at her. 'If it means taking the first ship out of here to Italy, and then to the realms of barbarism where the name of Heraclius is barely a name, we shall be married,' I said.

She played with one of her nipples. 'I don't think I'd like to leave Constantinople,' she said, now with a smile. 'But I appreciate the sentiment.' She sat up and stretched. 'Do you think Uncle will be here by next week?'

I pulled her to me, and kissed her. 'He'll have my letter by Friday,' I said. 'Give him a day for getting over the shock, and then another two for asking advice of everyone down to the latrine slaves – we can expect him a week after that.'

'He'll have to kill Daddy, of course,' she said firmly. Hers had been the Imperial Family just under five years. Some of its members hadn't needed long at all to forget the normal bonds of affection. I looked into her eyes and did my best not to see their ruthless flash.

'Heraclius doesn't kill his own,' I said with a slight emphasis. 'So long as we can make out the charges in private, he'll have your father shut away. He can be the Fortified Monastery's first guest of quality since the rebuilding.'

She sat up again. If my own energies were fast recovering, she now had other things on her mind. 'Too close,' she said. 'You must get him sent to Trebizond. The place is so dreary, you can beg for him to be spared blinding.' Apparently as the mood took us, we'd been moving back and forth between Greek and Latin. But I could now see the key to her own usage. Except with Heraclius, it was a while since I'd used Latin other than as a means of concealment from nearby Greeks, or to communicate with my own Western domestics. As a language of power, it had a strange and even creepy sound on Antonia's lips.

'Don't you think we're running ahead of ourselves?' I asked. I couldn't say what sort of wife I'd thought I might find. It would be someone, I hadn't doubted, more willing than this to stay out of sight and not ask too many questions. I looked at her again. Never mind, I told myself. Marriage always came down to the luck of the draw. Assuming Heraclius didn't stuff me away beside Nicetas in the Fortified Monastery, I might easily have done worse. I lay back with my hands cupped under my head. I stared happily down the length of my body. I wiggled my toes again. Yes, things might have gone worse than they had. Though they hadn't yet reached their conclusion, I could see my way to a conclusion. It was a matter of keeping me and mine safe till Heraclius put in an appearance.

Antonia put a hand on my chest. 'I think I've worked out most things for myself,' she said, now less tigerish. 'However, I'd like to see the Horn of Babylon. Assuming that gross animal Eunapius was telling the truth, isn't this what brought us together?'

I looked across the room at the late afternoon sunlight that streamed through all the windows. Soon, we'd have to get up. I'd call for baths to be brought in and filled for us. I'd call for women's clothing for Antonia to put on and take her down to the library, where Theodore would be seeking comfort in the sermons of John Chrysostom, or possibly in the Revelation of Saint John – he preferred its vengeful tone to any of the Gospels. One of the many secrets this building contained could and should be fully disclosed. After that, there would be lawyers to summon and announcements to be drafted, though left unpublished until the day when we could get Heraclius to say the right word. And there was an Empire to save as well – not to mention the continuing business of its financial and other governance to be transacted. I stared up at the ceiling. Could I really get away with the alternative suggestion of more sex? I decided not.

'It's nothing much to see,' I began. 'But it is connected with Heraclius and your father . . .'

Behind me, on my right, someone rattled the handle of my innermost door. 'Are you in here, Father?' Theodore cried uncertainly. 'Antony hasn't been seen all day. I'm really worried about him.' I put a hand up for silence. How had he got through the other doors? The answer to that was a rattling of keys and the soft click of a lock pushed open.

It was too late to pull the blankets over us. All I could do was smile stupidly back as the boy came into the room and looked at us. He fell to his knees. His mouth opened and closed. I hoped he'd cover his eyes to blot out the vision of total sin he'd stumbled upon. 'Antony!' he croaked despairingly. I jumped out of bed and hurried over to the door. How the buggery had he laid hands on the master keys? I'd take my fists to Samo if he'd drunk himself blotto again and let the boy steal them from his belt. I closed the bedroom door and walked slowly back to Theodore. Antonia had got a sheet about her body. I looked round for something to put on. There was nothing within reach.

I sat on the floor beside him. I put a hand on his shoulder. He didn't shrink back, but continued staring at Antonia. She pulled the sheet closer and moved to sit on the edge of the bed. 'Listen, Theodore,' I said softly. 'I was hoping to break this to you in a less – ah – shocking manner.' I didn't think he was listening, but went on even so. 'There were reasons for this deception. These reasons are now passed. But I do most humbly apologise for not having taken you into my confidence.'

He wasn't listening and I could be glad of that. 'It is my own fault,' the boy said calmly. He looked into my face. 'I have committed the ultimate sin in my heart, and this is the beginning of my punishment. Blessed be the Name of the Lord.'

I'd seen him in this mood only once before. That was when he'd eaten too many honeyed figs. I'd only stopped things from ending badly by sending Martin into his room to take back the scourge I'd neglected to throw away on taking possession of the palace. Martin had prayed with the boy for the better part of Christmas Day and slowly brought him to his senses. But Martin was on Lesbos and the visions of lust Theodore had welcomed into his mind, and their brutal disabusing, weren't in the same class as an attack of indigestion. If I'd had anyone to send out of the room, I'd have called for Father Macarius. He was a disgusting, smelly creature, whose only worthwhile feature was his ability to keep out of my sight. If there was anyone, though, who could stop the gathering descent into lunacy I was watching, it had to be the chaplain.

But Antonia was on her feet. 'Alaric,' she said in a voice that wasn't to be resisted, 'please leave the room.' I shook my head and nodded towards Theodore. She came closer. 'Go and see if the baths are ready,' she added, not turning in my direction. 'There are things we need to discuss alone.'

For the first time, I was looking at the cup in daylight. Rather, I was pretending to look at it. Whatever the light, whatever my interest, there was nothing more to be learned from an inscription in an unknown and probably dead language and a picture as crude in its own way as anything I'd seen in Egypt.

'What did you tell him?' I asked without looking up.

261

Antonia closed the office door and came over to my desk. She sat down opposite me. 'I told him the truth,' she said. 'Because I am the only one who can possibly be blamed for what has happened, it was my duty to tell him the complete truth. You'll agree that was the least he deserved.'

I nodded. I put the cup down and turned to Antonia. The maids had done her proud in yellow silk. There could be no doubt of her sex. 'Did he cry much?' I asked. She nodded. That may have been a good sign, I thought. Tears had always so far meant that Theodore was getting over his cause of grief.

'He told me he was going to pray in the chapel,' she said. 'He believes it was a temptation from the Devil but that God intervened to save him.' I stared again at the cup. It was grossly ugly. If I chose not to give to Heraclius, the world of art wouldn't suffer a jot if I sent it off for minting into more of my new coins. So Theodore was blaming the powers of darkness. A night in the dark with one of my dancing boys would have done him more good. But I was now at least sharing the blame.

Antonia changed the subject. 'So this is it?' she asked, nodding at the cup. 'This is the Horn of Babylon that Daddy wants so he can give it to Shahin?'

'Yes,' I said briskly. Antonia had brought Theodore back to what few senses he had. I was glad of that, but didn't wish to dwell on the force of personality this had taken. The cup was much easier to discuss. 'I've been wondering if the wording is some elaborate modern code. Apart from recent cleaning, though, it's unquestionably ancient.' I put it down before her. 'I've cleaned it again,' I explained. 'It had none of the usual signs of poison. It's quite safe to touch.'

She frowned and sat back. 'Do you *really* think that,' she asked. She ignored the impatient face I pulled. 'I heard what Eunapius explained last night. Don't forget too that I was there when your eunuchs set hands on it. Neither was killed by poison. Perhaps they temporarily drained its power. Perhaps it likes you. But can't you at least see how evil it looks?'

Time to show who was the master, I decided. 'Antonia,' I said, 'this is a piece of metal shaped by men whose bodies had crumbled to dust before the Jews built Jerusalem. Whatever harm it can do is purely in the mind of anyone who believes in it.'

'Oh, believe what you will,' she said quickly. 'But lock it away. You mustn't let Daddy or the Persians take it from you.' We could agree on that. I lifted the cup and saw how it glittered in the sunlight. When enough people share them, imaginary terrors become real. We couldn't have this carried into battle against us. Our armies were demoralised as it was. I went back to my earlier thoughts of mint value. Assuming five pounds of reasonably pure metal, the cup would make about four hundred of the new coins. That would put an end to all this nonsense. The cash would certainly come in handy. I wiped off my fingerprints with a napkin and put the thing back into its box. I put the lid on roughly where it had been levered away by the Master of the Timings. But that gave the whole thing a tatty appearance. I took the lid off again and dropped it into one of the trays on my desk.

I changed the subject. 'You did know that your father had promised you to Eunapius?' I asked. She thought, then nodded. That explained the risk she'd run in getting me to take her along to the recital. She wanted a look at her intended one. If he'd been younger or less nauseous to look at, would she have sided so decisively with me? I put the thought aside. Unlike her father, Antonia knew when to keep her options open and when to stand by her choices.

She was looking at the cup again. On its bed of silk padding, it was beginning to remind me of a body in an unsealed coffin. I picked up the box and locked it away in the secret cupboard. I glanced out of the window. It would be a late dinner. 'Get Theodore from the chapel,' I said. 'He'll take you to the dining room. I'll join you there with a full explanation of the past few days. Before then, there are one or two matters that need my attention.' The excuse I gave for this was a look at the five baskets of documents the clerks had dumped beside my desk.

40

Hands behind my back, I stared down at Priscus. 'You swore blind you wouldn't shit on me again,' I shouted. I dropped my voice. We were a long way from the inhabited areas of the palace and the walls were thick, but I brought my voice under control. 'I was a fool to believe you.'

Priscus twisted again on his filthy mattress and laughed into his pillow. 'But Alaric, my dearest young stunner,' he croaked, half triumphant, half desperate not to give way to open, mocking laughter, 'it was a harmless deception – and do try to see how well it's turning out. I watched you earlier in loving mood with your intended. Just think what joys I've brought into your life, even if they were unintended.'

Not moving, I hardened my face. 'I could have been killed a dozen times over,' I said. I realised too late how pompous I must be looking. I shut my eyes and let out a long breath. 'You could have let me in on your plot,' I said. Too late again, I realised how feeble that sounded.

He rolled over on his back. 'Don't be silly, Alaric!' he laughed. 'I knew you could deal with poor Shahin. You hardly stayed on his ship long enough to digest your dinner. As for last night, I did intend warning you but I decided at the last moment to trust in your unfailing luck. The girl overheard enough. No need for Uncle Priscus to join in the fun. And you did have the cup on your side.'

Breathing heavily, I glowered at the grinning skeleton before me. 'I see you now admit to knowing all about the cup,' I said darkly. 'So let's try for a little frankness. You heard about the Eunapius conspiracy on one of your night walks through the City. Instead of bringing word of it to me, you went and stole the cup.

264

You stuffed it inside the main gate, then let word get back to Simon that I had it. I suppose I should thank you for getting word to Shahin to come and save me from Simon.'

Priscus sat up and reached for a mirror. He rubbed at the lines on his face. 'You must believe me for once,' he said with an earnest turn, 'that I do have your welfare in mind. Can we speak frankly about the cup? It really is what everyone says it is. It's not supposed to do anything nasty for seven days. But you have been touching it with your bare hands. No one outside the initiated has ever done that before. God knows what you've set in motion.'

I fished about in a pile of clothes for the baggy tunic he wore when there was no chance he'd leave the palace. How could he make these rooms so untidy? No – how could he make them so *dirty*? I had five trusted slaves dancing attendance on him. Doubtless, he liked to keep these attic quarters in much the same state as the whole palace had been when I first moved in. But he might have had some regard for the poor bloody slaves I'd given him. I checked myself. Talk about regard . . .

He staggered to his feet and took the tunic from my outstretched hand. 'Will your face go any redder if I continue talking about the supernatural?' he asked with a turn to the serious. I said nothing. 'You will have it your way, Alaric,' he sighed. 'Be a love, then, and tell me if you can see a bottle of green fluid. Until you can find us a new compounder, I plan to be more economical than I've become.' Turning, he nearly kicked over a full chamber pot.

I sat down on the one chair that wasn't heaped with soiled undergarments. 'It was you who killed the man I found in the side street,' I said. 'And, since you knew what he was looking for, why did you treat that intruder so cruelly?'

He shrugged and pulled the seal off a small ceramic wine vat. He looked at the dark fluid. He took a swig from it and smacked his lips. 'This is good stuff,' he said. 'I hope you can find more of it.' He passed it to me. It *was* good wine. And I'd been privately blaming Samo for depleting my stock of it. 'The man in the street had been trying to kill me and was able to tell me something useful before he died. The man I put under your bed was your freedman.

He had certain duties to you that a few gold coins didn't abolish. You'll be a proper fool if you weep for him.'

He held out his hand for me to give the wine back. 'Yes, I *did* set things up. As with all good conspiracies, some things I carefully planned, others I left to chance. I got wind of Shahin's dealing with Eunapius and, through him, with Nicetas. At first, I thought I'd only caught Nicetas in the little web I spun. I would eventually have brought him to you without much fuss. It was when I saw how Timothy and all the others were getting sucked in that I set properly to work. I had to use you to bring things on from treasonable talk to treasonable action. But it's done, and my advice is to hurry off to Cyzicus with the neatest discovery of a plot even I can remember. I may not be able to share your glory when Heraclius comes back breathing fire. But I'll revel in your description of the trials.'

'You did all this to get even,' I pressed on. 'These were the men who gloried in your fall. Stuffing them was to be the "final achievement" you've been wittering about for years. I don't know how you did it without showing yourself but I'll never believe Timothy would turn spontaneously to treason. It's all a massive work of entrapment.' I took another mouthful of wine and gave Priscus the rest to finish. I began to see his side of things. I began to see my own as it might appear to a reasonable man. So what if Priscus had found some way of acting out of sight as an agent of provocation? He deserved his revenge. And I'd now have a clear run with Heraclius. There'd be no more obstructions in the Imperial Council. There'd be no more Timothy, dripping poison in every ear he approached. Eunapius no longer counted. Nicetas would be lucky if he only got a room in the Fortified Monastery.

'All's well that ends well, dear boy,' Priscus said with another smack of his lips. 'I don't need to spell out every step of my twisting way, nor every benefit that will flow from it. Just rejoice that we've won. Yes, rejoice – simply rejoice. *And get rid of that fucking cup*. It's done everything it was supposed to. Reseal the box and give it to Heraclius when you see him in Cyzicus. He's a miserable sod anyway. He'd only notice the improvement in his public fortunes.'

I helped Priscus pull the tunic over his head. I watched him fiddle with the cord that held it about his waist. At last, he got his fingers working and tied it in a loose bow. 'What will you do with Theodore?' he asked. 'Don't answer me back if I say you've been a crap adoptive father. Something like this was waiting to happen.'

I stood up. 'I've decided to withdraw my objection to his studying at the monastic school in Chalcedon,' I said stiffly. 'I'll arrange for him to go across to the Asiatic shore the moment it's safe for anyone to leave the palace.'

'A wise choice,' he tittered. 'He'd be wasted in any other occupation. Besides, you wouldn't want him to hang around and spoil your new and happy life. The next time I pray, I'll make sure to ask that she doesn't start looking like her father when she grows old.'

I picked my way over to the window and drew up the blind. The sun had already vanished behind one of the higher neighbouring buildings. I frowned. What hours he kept were his business but, when I was in a better temper, I'd ask Priscus if it wasn't time for a change of name and particularly of address. By all accounts, the small property I'd recently acquired in Crete was just the place for a man's retirement from active life. Sun, sand, sea, anonymity – and as much papyrus as anyone could need for his long-delayed memoirs. Now he'd done everything he wanted with his life, what more could Priscus need?

Though long after darkness had fallen, dinner was better than I deserved it to be. 'I wish you both every possible happiness,' Theodore had said twice. He was a rotten liar, both on principle and from inexperience. He'd kissed Antonia and called her Mother, and the three of us had drunk together from the same cup. Otherwise, I'd filled up what might otherwise have been long silences with a coherent and reasonably full account of all that had happened since Monday. No mention of Priscus, to be sure. No more than I absolutely needed about the cup, either.

'The Emperor should be back within the next ten days,' I'd ended. 'Until then, we are all of us still in danger. I have already

267

instructed my own revenue officials to stop and search every ship within a fifty mile radius of Constantinople, and to stop and search every person entering or leaving the City. I will order greater vigilance tomorrow morning. This will reduce the possibility of contact between Shahin and the conspirators. Speaking of the conspirators, I don't think, after what happened at last night's recital, they will attempt a revolution. They can no longer be certain that Nicetas would accept the Purple if it were offered. No one but a fool would put Timothy forward as Emperor. The only way out of the equilibrium that currently exists is for the conspirators to lay hands on the Horn of Babylon. There might be a direct assault on our gates by a mob of the poor. However, beneath its elegant façade, this palace is effectively a fortress. Properly defended, it could hold out against a regular army. That leaves subterfuge. None of us must go out into the City. None but my usual clerks will be allowed to enter, and they will be searched on entry and kept to the public areas.

'We are like a man swimming under water to avoid a barricade,' I'd ended with a smile. 'We can see the final length. So long as we keep our nerve and avoid useless movements, the air we've taken in should carry us forward to safety. But none of us must leave these walls. If either of you see anyone or anything out of the ordinary, you must bring it at once to my attention.

'Do you understand?'

So the dinner had ended.

Afterwards, I went up alone to the palace roof. The street lighting still at full burn, Constantinople was a cheerful sight. I stood for a long time looking west, to where the blackness started beyond the land walls. Beyond that grim and battle-scarred line, the Empire shaded imperceptibly into the world of barbarism. Bearing in mind all that had happened in the past three centuries, Constantine's choice of the new Imperial City had been inspired. His establishment of the Christian Faith may or may not have been a mistake. His hope that it would open an age of peace and external security had been falsified by events. But you couldn't fault his choice of Byzantium. The New Rome had now survived the Old by two centuries. So long as that held itself together, the barbarians could dash themselves against its walls as that fly had against the oiled parchment. We'd hold off the Avars and the Slavs and all the others until better days came and we could restore the Danube frontier.

If I turned and walked across the roof, I'd be able to look out across the equal darkness of the sea. Somewhere out on that was Shahin, waiting his chance. How to chase the Persians off was a matter no one discussed except in vague generalities. Chased off they would be, however. If no one else could, I'd see to that. I'd lead no charge in any victorious battle. But I knew how to see to it that, in the long slogging match this war had become, it would be the Persians whose strength gave out first. Whether or not we found ourselves a decent general, Chosroes would be the first to run out of money, and his whole rickety empire would promptly implode. We'd do it with sound money and balanced finances, and a population that looked to the Empire as the least bad alternative in a world of generally shitty choices.

All this we could do so long as Constantinople itself held fast. And it would hold fast, so long as I held this palace. We were about to see if the confidence Priscus had always shown in his grandfather's lavish spending on brick and iron was justified.

41

'Thank the Senator Eunapius for his most helpful suggestion,' I said. 'However, the purity of the new coins has been announced in public and more than half the first issue has been minted. Remind him of the Emperor's speech to the Senate on how the Empire has long benefited from a stable medium of gold exchange, and of how the time is come to let the common people enjoy the benefits of a stable medium of silver.' I paused and, putting up a hand for shade, opened my eyes. 'There's no need to show me the finished letter. But do send a copy to the Lord Nicetas. Instruct the messenger to read all of it. Tell him to read it louder if His Lordship appears to fall asleep.'

The clerk finished scratching on the soft wax and bowed. Trying not to leave a stain on it, I picked up the sheet of very expensive parchment that Eunapius had covered with his idiot suggestions. Sending out the coins with a copper core, I ask you! But why bother writing at all? Had the plot finally crumbled? If so, did those behind it think I knew nothing and that they could go back to troublemaking as usual? Or was I supposed to think everything was normal? I looked harder at the neat writing. What I'd assumed, when it was read out, was a long grammatical mistake turned out to be a kind of elegiac couplet. I'd taken it for granted Eunapius was still working for Nicetas. Was this evidence he was working *with* Nicetas?

Hard to say. I tossed the unrolled sheet at the nearest clerk. It was an official communication and would have to go in the archives. A shame, this. Gone at with a sponge dipped in vinegar, it could have been made almost as good as new.

I sat up and stared at my legs. Might they be turning red in the sun? Glaucus had insisted on a proper tan – 'Real men don't hide from the sun,' he'd said the previous morning. 'They rejoice in bodies the colour of polished wood.' The men he'd had in mind, I hadn't dared answer, weren't northern settlers born in Kent. Was I now overdoing it? I wondered. I noticed the clerks were all staring at me with close attention. I stretched both arms and yawned. Too many questions for this heat. I pointed at another of the clerks. This was one who looked as if he was in urgent need of a piss. Best to see what he'd brought over from the Treasury.

Antonia came into the garden, Eboric prancing beside her with a sunshade. 'Alaric, I need to speak with you,' she said in Latin. Annoyed, I got up and watched the clerks part for her to come forward. Though, as agreed, she was wearing men's clothes, you'd need to be blind to overlook her actual sex. From their deferential bowing, the clerks knew rather more about her than that. Our upper bodies stretched forward and met in a kiss that avoided any contamination of her clothes by the oil and sweat that ran down my body. Someone began wiping my back with a towel. Wincing, I took it from him and wiped my face. That was hurting as well.

I clapped my hands for attention. 'Gentlemen,' I said, 'you are all excused for one quarter hour of the sundial.' I moved to a stone bench and took the cover off a jug of cooled fruit juice. It was only Saturday. Just two entire days had passed since making our commitment. It felt like a year. It also felt as if we were meeting for the first time.

But I'd show I was still master in my own house. 'You could have worn something baggier on your chest,' I said once we were alone.

She smiled and shrugged. 'I've had a letter from Daddy,' she said. 'It's all out in the open.' She waved a large sheet of papyrus under my nose. The few lines of writing it carried looked like the production of an angry child. 'He wants me home at once.' She smiled again and stood back. 'As for clothing, shouldn't you put some on?' Before I could reach forward to take it, she dropped the sheet on the ground and wiped it underfoot.

'I trust you haven't sent him an answer?' I said carefully. I took the face she pulled as a negative. 'Then, if you haven't made too obvious a footprint on it, I'll send it back with a polite query.' I bent down to recover the message. The skin on my upper back seemed very tight. I focused on the message. This wasn't the first time I'd seen her father's own handwriting. Never mind the large scrawl, nor the evident and possibly not unreasonable fury – his spelling would have disgraced a tradesman.

Antonia took the message from between my forefinger and thumb. 'Theodore had another bad dream last night,' she said.

I looked away. 'Theodore's always having bad dreams,' I said. 'Was this one about hellfire? Or was it the one he often has, about being molested by giant bugs and then buried alive in rose petals?'

She lowered her voice. 'It was the man with golden wings again,' she said. She noticed that Eboric was listening and went into Greek. 'Talking of hellfire, you do know the colour you've gone?'

Trying to look unconcerned, I sat back a few inches into the shade of a potted olive tree. 'I've shown you the icon of Saint Michael he keeps in the chapel,' I said firmly. 'That has golden wings and a sword and a horrid look on its face. That's the origin of his dreams.'

'And a beard of many curls?' she asked, 'And speaking a language that sounds like Syriac, but isn't?'

'So he's been dreaming about the cup,' I allowed with a careless wave of my arm. It was bright red from the wrist upwards. 'Perhaps I was dreaming about it last night. I'm surprised you weren't. Thanks to that cup, we're all stuck here like passengers on a ship. Dreams are the least of our worries.'

'And Maximin?' she asked impatiently. 'He hasn't seen the cup, but kept his nurse awake half the night, crying out from terrors he couldn't describe.'

'If the poor child couldn't describe his terrors, why assume they were about my silver cup?' I asked in my most reasonable voice. 'You didn't have a long career as a petitioning agent. But you can't have forgotten that you don't go to someone with a problem unless you also have a solution. So why not come out with it, and say what you'd have me do?'

She stuck her lower lip out. I already knew that meant trouble. 'Theodore believes you should throw it into the sea and let Father Macarius purify every room in the palace,' she said.

'Then Theodore's a fool,' I said, now impatient, 'and you're a fool if you believe him. The cup stays where it is until Heraclius gets back.'

I'd been right about the trouble. 'Theodore believes the palace is haunted by the ghost of its previous owner,' she announced. 'He's often been woken at night by the echo of footsteps and heard voices in rooms that he can't locate.' I frowned. Theodore had got rather fast over the loss of *Antony*. His regard for his new 'mother' wasn't wholly to my taste. But Antonia wasn't finished. '*I've* heard strange footsteps,' she said. 'And why did Samo stop me yesterday from going along a corridor into one of the unoccupied areas? What are you hiding from me?'

I stood up. 'Rats,' I said quickly – 'it's the rats. And there's poison all over the floors in those rooms. It wouldn't do to go walking in them with bare feet.' I smiled feebly. I was already trembling from a slight fever that shouted 'sunburn!' Perhaps I should put some clothes on.

I took Antonia's arm and led her in the direction of the swimming pool. It would still be in shadow and I felt the need of a plunge into its icy depths. I still had time before the clerks returned. I'd ask for the sake of it but knew Antonia wouldn't join me.

She stopped beside the entrance to the gymnasium. 'I looked in on you this morning,' she said in Latin. 'Do you really need the big Slavic boy? Can't the old man wrestle with you?'

'I find it useful to reinforce what I've learned,' I said cautiously, 'by instructing others. Rado is a most enthusiastic student.'

She sniffed and stepped back to look at me. 'I don't think you'll be rolling in sand for the next few days,' she said, the hint of a gloat in her voice.

She looked round. 'Come, Eboric,' she said, all imperial of a sudden. 'It's time I showed you how to cut roses so they don't wilt within a day.' With a tiny bow to me, he padded after her, a look of happy eagerness on his face.

★　　★　　★

As hath unto us been oldenly divulged by Homer of glorious repute . . ., reason reinforced by readings of Holy Writ . . ., the charms of correct diction set fire to in the breasts of all them what was correctly inteached . . .

I let my eyes skim over the three sheets of sewn parchment contained in the scroll. Because of its bearer, there could be no doubt this time who'd been showing off to his secretaries. 'What's the message?' I asked.

Leander stared down at the tiled floor. 'My Lord Nicetas instructs me to demand safe return of his daughter, Antonia,' he said. 'He specifies that she is to be released at once, so that medical assistance can be procured in the event that her belly is already filled with yellow-headed trash.' He looked up. 'My Lord will be aware that these are not my own words,' he said, biting his lip.

I kept my face still and forbidding. 'Tell Nicetas,' I replied, 'that I don't know what he's talking about. Any other message?'

Leander shuffled nervously. 'I am further instructed to say that, if you are disinclined to hand the girl over, you may keep her on condition that you send back with me an object that does not require any name or description.'

I let the scroll close on itself and leaned back in my chair. Such a pity none of this was in writing. 'Tell Nicetas again,' I said, 'that I don't know what he's talking about.'

'Then my final instructions,' Leander whispered, 'are that you should attend on My Lord Nicetas to explain yourself in person.'

I smiled coldly. 'Can't do that,' I said. 'Following two sudden deaths, I've been advised to put my entire household into quarantine.' I looked over at the water clock. 'The quarantine will start the moment you're out in the street. If he pleases, your master can check this with the Prefect's local deputy.' I got up. 'I'm sure Nicetas wouldn't want to see me while I might be dripping contagion from every pore,' I added helpfully. 'He's already a martyr to those legs of his.' I led the way to the door of my office. I pulled it open and waved into the gloom of the corridor. 'Now, you can't wish to stay longer than you must in a house of sickness. Please allow my steward to lead you back to the main gate.'

Leander stopped beside the statue of Polyphemus. I thought he was about to ask about his salary. Instead: 'Please give my regards to the Lady Antonia,' he said with a scared look at the headless victim. 'But tell her that the Lord Nicetas is really angry. There's nothing I can do this time to calm him down.'

Once he was gone, Antonia came out from behind the screen. 'I was hoping Daddy would keep up *some* show of decency,' she said.

I overlooked the hurt tone in her voice. 'And I was hoping the letter I sent yesterday would keep him quiet a few days longer,' I said. It was only Sunday. There were days and days to go before the earliest time when Heraclius might return. We'd have to see how long I could keep the quarantine excuse going.

I opened the door and stepped out on to the balcony. Church services were over, and the Triumphal Way was crowded again. After the heat and silence of my office, it was good to stand looking into the breeze. I went closer to the stone balustrade and waited for Leander to come into sight. After wondering if I'd missed him, I saw him pass into the middle of the street and scurry across to the cover of the far colonnade. Another moment, and Simon stepped into the sunlight. He was followed by an agitated poet and some of the usual big men. Ignoring the shouts of various carrying slaves, they stood talking together in the middle of the street. Simon looked up suddenly. Our eyes met. He shaded his eyes to get a better look at me. I waited till he must be able to see me again, then smiled and gave a little bow. He continued looking at me. A man bumped into him, and was grabbed and pushed into the dust by one of the heavies. Still looking up at me, Simon didn't seem to notice. He was still there when I decided I'd had enough.

I stepped back, wincing from the sunburn as I bumped into Antonia. 'Best not show yourself,' I said. 'Everyone knows you're in here. But we can play by the rules a little longer.'

'What will happen next?' she asked. I stepped back inside. I'd put on a very light silk tunic. Even in this, however, any movement was enough to remind me I had no skin on my shoulders. 'Do you suppose he'll lay a formal complaint with the Prefect?'

'That would be the next step,' I said. 'The Prefect will then send his bailiffs over to demand your surrender. Of course, I won't let them in. But we'll have a counter narrative to our own to beat down when the Emperor gets back. It can be said that we're scandalously shacked up together, and are justifying the breach of your father's authority with a pack of lies about treason. Let's hope Nicetas is as indecisive in this matter as in everything else. He can't be sure how little evidence we have.'

There was a knock at the door. Theodore came in. After a loving glance at Antonia, he turned to me. 'Samo has crushed a finger,' he said, 'but begs to inform you that he's shut off the external water supply.' He opened and closed his mouth, possibly wondering what question he could ask.

'Give him my thanks and sympathies,' I said. I looked at the boy. No harm in explaining things to him. 'We are to regard ourselves, until further notice, as under siege,' I said. 'Our own cisterns are full enough to last a month of normal use. We don't want to risk contamination from outside.'

He leaned against the wall. 'You mean poison?' he asked with a scared look at both of us.

'Yes, poison,' I said – 'poison or some other pollution.' I smiled and brightened my voice. 'However, since we're under siege, there will be a break from my normal duties. That means I can spend more time with you in the library on your Latin and History. We'll start work again on Tacitus after lunch.' A resigned look on his face, he bowed.

I thought of the nice opium ointment I'd borrowed off Priscus. Would it be too great a loss of dignity, I wondered, if I asked Antonia to apply some to my back?

42

Thus, having, in a reign of three years, nine months, and twenty-eight days, lived as a tyrant, Caligula discovered, by sharp experience, that he was not, after all, a god.

Theodore let the aged papyrus roll close on itself. He rubbed his eyes and sat back from the hunched position in which he liked to read. 'The sentence structure is *very* complex,' he said apologetically.

I looked about the main room in the library. So many books I'd gathered about me, all looking neatly back at me from their appointed spaces in the book racks. So many dear friends. So many guides. I cleared my throat. 'Good Latin,' I explained once more, 'is far more complex than good Greek. I think also it's always been more removed from the spoken language. But if you can put Tacitus so well into Greek, I don't think you'll have trouble with any of the recent authors.' I thought of the theological section in one of the smaller rooms. It was a while since I'd been required to dip into those muddy pools. Their chief problem, though, in either language was callous inhumanity or a prolix reasoning from absurd premises. The illiteracies of the Latin writers were mostly their importing of words and constructions from Greek. None of this should trouble Theodore.

I watched the boy take the scroll in both hands and wind it back to the beginning. He replaced it in the leather sleeve and took it over to the right space. I'd written a year before to the Emperor's man in Rome, directing him to make a thorough search of the libraries that remained there. He hadn't been able to complete my set of Tacitus. There were still five gaps in the space I'd set aside for all thirty books.

I waited for Theodore to come back to the table. I smiled. 'Because we presently have the time,' I said, 'I'd like to you translate the whole of Plutarch's Life of the Elder Pliny into Latin.' His face dropped. 'If possible, I'd like to see your draft before dinner tomorrow.'

He started forward at the noise by what may have been a block of paving stone crashed against the main gate. 'Should we not go and see how big the crowd in the street has grown?' he asked.

I shook my head. 'I don't propose to take notice of that until Samo comes and tells me it has filled the side streets.' His face turning paler by the moment, Theodore bowed and went off to his writing desk in the theology room. When he was out of the room, I got up from my chair and went over to a big lectern close by the window. Books in the modern style have their uses. Portability isn't one of them. My complete Herodotus needed two men to lift it and it could only be read while standing up. Of course, I was in no mood for Herodotus or anyone else. But I could see the shadow Theodore was casting from the other side of the open door. It wouldn't do to be seen scoffing another opium pill so soon after the last.

Aware of the response I'd get, I pulled the blind fully up. 'Don't be a bastard, Alaric, Priscus whined from under his blankets. 'You know how the daylight hurts my eyes.'

'Then you should try getting up in the morning, like everyone else,' I replied. He groaned loudly and the bed shook from his continual twisting. I paid no attention. If I wanted to see out of the window, I'd need to stand on something. I walked across to the nearest chair. I'd been with him when these clothes were brought in, washed and neatly pressed and folded. Instead of wearing them, he'd used them as a hiding place for uneaten food. I lifted one of the cloaks of fine wool I'd given him as a New Year present and only just avoided being splashed with the stinking slime in one of my best silver dishes. Carefully, I lifted all the clothes as a single unit. The babble of chanting and angry shouts that drifted through the window went straight out of mind.

'Where did you get all these new silver coins?' I asked. The sealed pouch had been slit open, and I had to bend down to retrieve the loose coins I'd disturbed.

Priscus lifted one of the blankets and looked out briefly. 'Oh, don't worry about that,' he said vaguely. 'I took them from a bandit I killed and was keeping them for a rainy day.' Another lie! There were only a few hundred of these yet in circulation. He must have been dipping into one of the sealed cash boxes stored under lock and key in the cellars. I controlled myself and finished stuffing coins through the gap in the leather. There was one missing from its compartment. I looked about but the floor was too cluttered to justify the effort of a search. A thought drifted through my head. I'd leave that for the moment, however. It required too much elaboration. I carried the now empty chair to the window. Though on the top floor, the quarters I'd given Priscus had their only window set back from the street. I had to squeeze my shoulders through and block most of the light that came in before I could see anything below.

Now out of bed, Priscus stood behind me. 'Impressive size by the sound of it,' he allowed, 'but still no sign of positive direction.' I heard him pull the stopper from another jar of my best wine. 'We faced down a bigger mob when my grandfather had this place. Word had gone round again that he was eating human flesh. We had fifty thousand of these animals screaming their lungs out till the authorities finally decided to do their job. I don't think we'll have much trouble from the mob now assembled to call for your head on a spike.' From the gulping noise that followed, he was draining half the jar in one go.

As I scrabbled forward another few inches, a loud roar went up from every direction. It went on and on, growing louder. It only died away to become a huge and grunted chorus of 'Kill! Kill' Kill' Kill!' Maybe Priscus was right about numbers. To be sure, the fall of population since the old days had diminished the size of any potential mob. But there must be thousands and thousands down there. It was a nuisance I couldn't see them. I'd hoped I could avoid showing myself on one of the balconies. I slid back till my feet made contact again with the chair.

279

Priscus took this as a sign of alarm. 'I've told you many times, Alaric,' he laughed, 'this place was built with trouble in mind. Haven't you ever noticed the curve in all the outer walls, or the handy murder holes above every gateway? I think I heard the portcullis let down before each gate. The iron trelliswork on them is four inches by four. Though you may not appreciate their military value, think of them as saving on the expense of repairs to the bronze sheeting on the gates.' He drank again. I heard his shuffling step across the floor and the renewed squeaking of his bed. 'The only weakness is the front balconies. Make sure the guards you put there stay sober. I did think of having them bricked up when I took over. But you do need some air in this place.'

I stood down from the chair. 'Do you fancy coming up to the roof with me?' I asked. Not for the first time, his prejudice against the daylight was an affectation that got on my nerves.

Under the blankets, he curled himself into a ball. 'You are joking, my dear!' he giggled. 'If you want to look down from there and shit yourself with fright, don't expect me as your witness. Now, do pull that blind down again and leave me to get some sleep.'

I leaned both elbows on the front parapet. I stood away. Walking backwards up the tiled roof, I got my body more or less horizontal. I couldn't see the front steps or the ten feet or so beyond them. But I could see how, for a hundred yards or so both ways, the Triumphal Way was packed with the noisy, swarming bodies of the poor. I tried to settle my nerves by calculating the size of the crowd. Priscus had sneered that it might have reached ten thousand – as if that were itself just a mild expression of the people's disapproval. It looked to me closer to fifty, or even a hundred, thousand. The rest of the City must be deserted.

No one seemed to be looking in my direction. I slithered down again and put my hands on the top level of bricks in the wall and pulled back and forth. No movement. I pulled myself forward and, ignoring the pressure on my sunburn, kept my upper body straight. This gave a better view of things. Because I could see more of it, the crowd seemed much larger. Now its rightmost extremity was in sight, I could see how it was still being joined by newcomers. Right at the back, I could see a couple of closed and unmarked carrying chairs. Most of the crowd wore the dark clothing of the very poor. Here and there, though, were individuals or groups dressed in white. One of these robes was topped by a splash of red hair that could only belong to one of the senior managers in the Food Control Office. 'A favourite has no friends' was a saying I'd often had cause to repeat to myself. To be fair, I hadn't gone out of my way, in the previous few years, to win friends in the administration or among the people at large.

But my attention was pulled back to the main area before my palace. Big men of the usual type were pushing and threatening to clear two spaces within the crowd about fifty feet apart. In these spaces, high stepladders were being set up.

I stretched forward still more to see what more was happening. With a slight jolt, the wall moved outwards a little. Scared, I threw myself back and knocked all my breath out on the tiles. I shut my eyes, trying not to remember the terrors of that roof in the poor district. I slid down on to the bubbled lead. I looked at the parapet wall. There was a horizontal crack halfway up its rendering. I pushed gently against it. No more movement. All else forgotten, I looked up at the lovely blue of the afternoon sky. It didn't matter how rich I'd made myself: the money I spent on maintenance alone for this palace would have made me the richest man in Rome. That took my mind off the sudden death I may just have avoided. I looked again at the wall. Beyond it, all was now silent.

I picked up the chair I'd brought up with me and carried it along to another part of the wall. Making sure this time not to lean forward, I stood on the chair and looked down. Both ladders were occupied. At the top of each stood a man dressed in white. Their heads looked swollen far beyond any normal variation. I blinked and looked harder. Up here, the sunshine was still pitilessly bright. Far below, it was dappled by increasingly long shadows. One of the men was in shadow, the other half in shadow. Before I could focus properly, though, I had my answer. The man nearest me let out a loud and inarticulate buzzing. He reached up and tapped at his head. Leaning forward so he didn't lose balance, he put up his other hand and pushed at his face. They were wearing the masks actors used in the Circus when they had to stand away from the permanent amplifying walls.

'Will you now share my own judgement, Alexius?' one of those bastard seditionaries cried in a voice that boomed and echoed about the confined space. He took both hands from the rail at the top of his ladder and stretched them cautiously in the direction of my palace. The movement pushed his amplifying mask out of its correct position against his face, and what he said next was a muffled shout. Buggery things to use, these masks. Worn properly, they could project a voice to the back rows in the Circus. You could sometimes hear the voices if you looked out from the top windows in the Great Church. But it was a matter of getting exactly the right distance between a wearer's face and the mask's inner wall. I think that's one reason why, even without masks, actors don't look round by turning their necks, but twist their whole upper bodies – it's the long training, you see, to keep a mask in the right place.

Alexius was having better luck. Then again, the natural sound of his own voice indicated some prior training. A failed actor, perhaps? 'Oh, my oldest and dearest friend, Constans,' he cried with perfect clarity, 'I freely admit that I was too indulgent in my opinion of the young barbarian. I never supposed he would go so far as to abduct the pure and beauteous daughter of our most beloved Commander of the East.'

That, and the resulting shouts of anger from the crowd, gave Constans time to put his mask right. 'I freely pardon you,' he said, no longer needing to raise his voice above the conversational. 'How could a man of your inborn goodness imagine the depths of infamy to which Alaric the Degraded has finally sunk? Indeed, *who* could imagine that the sweet and virginal daughter of the Lord Nicetas could be snatched, even by the Persians, from her monastery, and be carried off to shriek and twist in such lascivious embraces?' He stopped for breath, then: 'Oh, but I can shut my eyes and see her now. I see her penetrated again and again by the stinking meat that swings between those barbarian thighs. I see a tongue that is filthy from lies and blasphemies, thrust into secret places that the very angels in Heaven do not permit themselves to see.'

His mask went out of position again and his voice trailed off into more buzzing. 'Daddy always did have a theatrical touch,' Antonia said behind me. I turned and stepped down beside her. She was back in men's clothing, a short sword strapped about her waist. Sword in hand, Rado stood beside her, looking fierce and protective.

'Is everyone armed downstairs?' I asked in a voice that was just too high to be commanding. Looking more relaxed than I was feeling, she nodded. I waited for another roar of anger to gather force and die away. 'It's about the worst choice your father could have made,' I said, trying to match her lack of concern. 'In his place, I'd have used my powers as Regent to deprive Alaric the Degraded of his offices. I'd then have sent the Prefect with a unit of the city guard to demand entry. Better still, I'd have made a better try at negotiating. Instead, we have an apparently spontaneous riot in the making that may easily run out of control. Whether or not this hails Nicetas as Emperor, it won't break in here, and I imagine every property owner in the City is cursing his name.'

As if he'd read my thoughts, Alexius was back in action. 'Why does the Lord Nicetas not take action against this enemy of God and man?' he asked in a rising tone of question. 'Why does he not declare Alaric a traitor and an outlaw? Why is it for us, the Roman People, to cry aloud for justice.'

'You surely forget, Alexius,' Constans replied, 'that Nicetas has no power to remove from office those appointed by the Emperor. Whom an emperor has appointed only an emperor can remove.' That was an odd view of the law but it got a predictable if ragged cry of 'Nicetas to the Purple! Down with Heraclius!' I got on the chair again and looked over the wall. Someone at the bottom of his ladder was waving frantically up at Constans. He'd gone beyond his brief. Not caring how he wobbled, he raised his arms for silence. 'The very furniture in that palace is of gold and silver,' he improvised. 'Every room is stuffed with silk and other precious fabrics. The slaves Alaric has about him are of surpassing beauty and all are gagging for the touch of our clean-limbed Romans. Everything within those walls has been taken from our mouths and the mouths of our children. Why do we wait outside this house of *our* treasures?'

That got everyone off the subject of who should be Emperor. I watched the great, enraged mass of the poor surge forward. Every gate was protected by its portcullis. The beating of many wooden clubs against the bronze sheeting of the normal gates was loud but ineffectual. The gap about his ladder closed up, Alexius swayed and wobbled. He slid to the ground just in time for his ladder to go over and be swallowed in the swirling crowd. I didn't need to walk round to see what was happening against the other walls of the palace. The noise alone told me we were under attack on every side.

'All is in order up here,' I said to Rado. 'I appoint you commander of everyone not guarding the balconies. Form them into a mobile force, ready to give support wherever needed.' He puffed his chest out and gave a lovely smile. Antonia nodded her agreement, and he hurried from the roof.

She watched him go. 'I'm not marrying you for them,' she said, leaning close to me. 'But I was wrong about your slaves. I do like them a lot. I'm surprised Daddy wasn't murdered by his long ago.'

I thought of the look on Rado's face. 'They like you as well,' I said. I was glad at once there was too much noise for me to be heard. I was jealous of poor Theodore. I was jealous of my slaves. If I wasn't careful – and if I survived – I'd turn into a proper bastard.

I think I was heard. Antonia smiled. 'Unlike Eboric, I'd not call Rado talkative,' she said. 'But I know he worships you. Never mind going to bed with you – he'd cut off his right hand if you asked.'

I thought. I felt a surge of pity, then of tenderness that ended in guilt. 'I'll never ask for that,' I said firmly. 'But it may be time for promotions within the household. Let's see how the boy does with his mobile force.'

Antonia was looking at my stained tunic. She looked away and walked back to the exit from the roof. She waited for the noise to go into one of its rhythmical low points. 'I heard all that talk of fucking and sucking,' she said. 'Will you be appalled if I say that my secret places hunger for the meat between your thighs?' In the clothes she'd put on, she did look decidedly lush. 'I promise not to scratch your sunburn,' she added.

'Don't worry about that,' I said thickly. 'Do keep the sword on as well.'

Together, we went down into the dark interior of the building. The roar of the crowd faded as we reached the bottom of the staircase from the roof. It was replaced by the endless crash and its echoes of the assault on the main gate.

43

Not caring if she was naked, Antonia leaned over the balcony and spat at the smashed bodies of the men I'd sent to their deaths. It was hard to recognise the demure being I'd rescued from the poor district in the Jezebel soaking up the groans of the crowd. I bent and finished pulling the grappling hook free of the baluster. I'd not throw it on the heads far below – that would only get it reused. I placed it carefully on a rush mat. Even if not dropped on it, iron can do horrid things to marble. I stood up and, to a gathering roar of disapproval, put my arm about Antonia and tried to lead her away from the edge. 'I don't think it's wise to show yourself in this manner,' I shouted in her ear.

'Wave the knife at them,' I saw her lips describe. 'Show how you killed a whole stinking rope of them.' She turned her radiant and almost orgasmic face downwards again. She stretched forward over the balcony. I don't think she noticed the arrow that missed us but split on contact with the stonework barely a couple of feet to our left. The mob was drifting back to its favourite chant of 'Kill! Kill! Kill! Kill!' The dozen bodies had already been taken up and were being passed overhead to the far side of the Triumphal Way. Men were reaching up to dip napkins in the blood. Monks danced about with upraised arms. The dead aside, everyone down there was having a decidedly good time. The sudden roar of triumphant hatred was evidence of that. It drowned out the chanting. It even covered the renewed battering of long poles on the gates.

Someone poked me hesitantly in the small of my back. I turned. It was young Eboric. His normal duties were to look pretty and attend on my various wishes. This afternoon the front of his tunic was covered in a splash of fresh blood – not his, though, I could be

sure from the pleased look on his face. 'Pardon for the disturbance, Sir,' he piped into my ear. 'But Samo begs to inform you
that he's cut two ropes they managed to get on the office balcony.'
Fascinated, he stood beside Antonia to look over the balustrade.
The crowd was still emptying its lungs up at us and jumping about
as if someone had poured itching powder down every single back.
He remembered himself and turned back to me. 'He says I can tell
you that I cut the throat of a man who managed to climb over,' his
lips described in Lombardic. 'Samo threw him over the edge. He
left red mist in the air even after he'd burst open on the paving
stones.'

'Very good,' I said, patting the boy on the shoulder. I glanced at
him again. It may have been the mood I was in, but Eboric was
looking decidedly fanciable. I embraced him and felt a thrill of
renewed lust that was checked only by a pursing of Antonia's lips
– and by another arrow: this one still went wide, but embedded
itself in one of the wooden beams. I got them both inside and
pulled the glazed door partly closed. I looked down at my chest. I
was thickly smeared with blood from Eboric's tunic and this had
now imprinted itself over the boy's lower face. 'Any casualties on
our side?' I asked in Latin. Eboric shook his head. One of the older
slaves had been bruised by a slingshot ball while urinating triumphantly over the balcony. Otherwise, all the dead and injured were
on the other side – heavily on the other side, he added to an
approving look from Antonia.

I dabbed at the blood with a dry sponge. I had more luck getting
the blood off my knife. 'Have we used any of the molten lead yet?'
Again, Eboric shook his head. More good news – it would need a
mountain of scaffolding to get that off the upper walls. 'Then it's
the balconies we need to watch – oh, and we need to keep them
from starting another fire against the portcullis by the lesser gate.' I
slid my knife into its sheath and tossed it on to the bed, and let the
boy set to work on me with a piece of the silk sheet that I'd somehow ripped apart in the long climax of my coupling with Antonia.

The archers had finished taking up residence atop one of the
victory columns and were now shooting volley after volley of

arrows at every opening in the upper front wall. Mostly, they were still firing wide. But one of the arrows smashed through the glazed door and whizzed by so close, I felt its displacement of air against my nose. It buried itself noiselessly in the upper bed hangings. If only it wasn't madness to close the balcony shutters. I took Antonia to one of the far walls. Unless I was a complete duffer in the military arts, nothing could reach us here. I stood beside her and stared at a large plan of the building. 'There's an escape tunnel from the lowest level of the cellars,' I said in Latin. I pointed at a line of coded text on the plan. 'If they do break in, I want you to take Theodore and Maximin, and all the female slaves and those under age, and make a run for it. I believe the tunnel comes out into the Great Sewer. Get yourselves to the Kontoskalion Harbour and bribe yourselves on to the first ship towards Cyzicus. The rest of us will hold the ground floor, one room at a time.'

Antonia shook her head. 'Don't be silly, Alaric!' she laughed. 'Any palace this age that had a flaw in its defences would have been burned long ago.' She walked back to the middle of the room and let Eboric help pick her clothes up from the floor. 'I don't know about you, but that was the fuck of a lifetime with those bearded faces climbing over the ledge.'

That wasn't quite how I'd have described it – not, at least, after one of the bastards had nearly skewered me from behind. But I joined her and began untangling my leggings from my inner robe. We were just about decent when Theodore staggered in. Eyes screwed shut, hands over his ears, he danced close to the balcony in full sight of the archers. 'Has God truly abandoned us?' he sobbed. He opened his eyes. Suddenly thoughtful, he looked at the torn and crumpled bedclothes.

Outside, the crowd was settling into one of its silences. Dinner time? When there's so little real chance of plunder, the poor don't riot for free. I hurried over and peeped round the corner of the balcony. I was right about the food. Handcarts were being pulled into a big space made against the colonnade. Also, the seditionaries were back. In their speaking masks again, it was hard to see which was which. I wasn't kept long in suspense.

288

'I think, dear Alexius, I may have been unjust to the barbarian,' Constans opened after much buzzing and tapping. 'It must now be plain to the meanest understanding that the girl is no more than a bitch on heat. It may even be worth asking who seduced whom.' He stopped and waited for an unenthusiastic laugh to ripple through a crowd that was, for the moment, more given over to being fed than stirred to action.

'Surely the Lord Nicetas is doubly betrayed,' Alexius replied, unable to keep his voice free of uncertainty. 'To have his dearest friend shack up with a daughter who's had enough cock inside her to reach beyond the topmost rung of this ladder is too much for mortal flesh to bear. Overcome by grief, our gallant Commander of the East has retired to the private quarters of his palace. I am told he looks to the Roman People to secure the justice that a corrupt administration of the law has denied him.'

His voice trailed suddenly off into a kind of muffled burp. The crowd was otherwise engaged and Alexius looked to the men standing at the foot of his ladder for guidance. One of them shrugged and called up something that I didn't catch. I leaned against the wall. 'Corrupt administration of the law,' he'd said. Did this mean the conspiracy had fallen apart? That was what the evidence suggested. If Timothy was sitting on his hands in the Prefecture, that gave Nicetas a choice between waiting for Heraclius to come back and gambling everything on the mob. Or, since he'd apparently returned to his usual dithering, Eunapius and Simon were trying one last push to save their necks.

I looked at Eboric. He'd recovered the arrow from the bed hangings and was testing its point against his thumb. 'Go down and see what Cook is preparing for dinner,' I said. 'Tell her we'll have it in the garden at dusk.' He bowed and darted out of sight. I looked at Theodore. He'd fallen to his knees and had his arms raised in prayer. 'I thought I'd given you a Latin exercise to complete,' I said coldly. 'Please go back to the library.' I raised my hand to stop him. I'd specified dinner outside to avoid the reverberant echoes of the pounding on the gates. I didn't want Theodore wailing like someone on the rack when I finally got myself into the library to oversee the transfer of the most precious volumes to one of the cellars. 'Correction – go and sit in the garden. The sun is no longer strong enough to burn you.' I stepped quickly across the killing zone. One of the archers had been waiting, and I saw the blur of his arrow about a foot in front of me. It went straight through the wood of what may have been an original painting from ancient times and buried itself in the plaster of the wall. I tried to look carefree, though the picture had been ruinously expensive. 'The Lady Antonia and I will spend the time before dinner inspecting the defences.'

I couldn't fault Samo's intention. Our spirits had needed raising. If only I hadn't been the only one at the dinner table who could follow his rendition of tribal war songs recalled from his youth. If only also he hadn't insisted on dancing boys with swords and a harp accompaniment that had kept us at table till some time after the last fading of the day . . .

Priscus and I were on the roof. He looked down over the sea of torches. 'It needs more than possession to make siege engines dangerous,' he said. I pointed in the dim light of the moon at the crack I'd opened on the parapet wall. He grunted and let it take his weight regardless, as he kicked his chair closer against it. 'If your surmise is right about the defection of everyone who matters, those things are hardly more useful than continued banging on the gates.'

An icy feeling in my stomach, I pointed down at the tallest of the wooden towers. 'You can get a ladder from that to any of the balconies,' I said. I looked again at the bright carpet of the torches. A ten-foot gap was opening and closing as some kind of procession I couldn't see moved slowly though the glare towards a point on the far side of the road.

Priscus followed my pointed finger. He snorted. 'My poor civiliany Alaric, even scaling a ladder takes more skill than this lot can assemble. What your people need to do is wait for a ladder to be clogged up with shouting fools, then push it out and to the side with a pole. Did I ever tell you about how I beat off the next to biggest night attack at the siege of Hadruma?' He seemed about to drift off into one of his internal reveries. He stopped himself. 'There's a lesson for you in all this,' he said with a low chuckle. 'I left you this place with a first-rate armoury for defence. If you hadn't let the bow strings perish, you could have seen these engines off with a hail of burning arrows. So much money spent on keeping everything clean and in its place – so little on the real fundamentals!'

A barely broken voice drifted upwards from the far side of the Triumphal Way: 'The diameter in inches of the cord bundle must be equal to eleven-tenths the cube root of one hundred times the weight in pounds of the ball,' it read haltingly. 'Please don't ask me, though, what it means.' Something was snarled back in a much lower voice. More voices broke out in an argument I couldn't hear.

Priscus laughed again, and stretched his arms forward to crack his knuckles. 'So, they've found themselves a catapult!' he sneered. 'I'd like to see them get it loaded, let alone aimed and fired. It's a six-month course to be an artillery officer, I'll have you know. The extraction of cube roots – especially where the number itself isn't an exact cube . . .'

I'm sure I was meant to find comfort in the outlining of a method that required you to imagine petals dropping off a flower, and must have taken twice as long as doing the calculation properly. But the bare mention of catapults had completed the freezing of my insides. 'What would you do about the archers out there?' I asked, changing the subject.

'Oh, just hang leather curtains on the outside of all the balconies,' he said easily. 'The last time I needed them, they were in one of the boiler house lockers. There are special brackets already set into the external ornamentations. Get them rigged up before morning, and the archers can shoot away till their thumbs drop off for all the effect they'll have.'

He blew his nose between forefinger and thumb. I watched him wipe his hand on what had been a fresh tunic. 'Now, my boy, where was I with my demonstration?'

Somewhere out in the darkness, there was a sudden sharp click-ing. This was followed by a whizz overhead that grew fainter till it ended in a distant impact against something solid.

'Well I never!' said Priscus. This time, he sniffed hard and swal-lowed his snot. 'Beginner's luck, of course. You'll find that angle of approach is sure sign they haven't unlocked the counterweight lever. If they want to rain death on the Egyptian Quarter, who are we to complain?'

He'd barely finished to draw breath, when the whizz of a second stone ball through the air ended in a crash that knocked the pair of us against the roof tiles. I lay for a moment, wonder-ing if I'd been seriously injured. Absorbed in myself, hardly noticing how I slid down on to the lead, I didn't hear the landing of the ball once it had splintered and bounced back from its place of impact. But I opened my eyes to a noise of desperate and terrified shrieking and another of those rising groans of horror from the crowd.

Priscus was already on his feet and was pushing at the wall. 'Come on, my lovely!' he crooned, going into a rhythm of pushing and relaxing, pushing and relaxing. 'Come on, my fucking lovely!' I was still sitting up and rubbing the back of my head when, with a dull scraping of brick against brick, the wall gave and he jumped backwards. The stone ball must have hit us just below the parapet. I guessed its parts had landed somewhere in the middle of the Triumphal Way. The brick mass of the wall would have landed almost directly below. The new and louder screaming must be those who'd pressed themselves close to the palace wall for safety and had more or less survived the arrival on their heads of a half ton of brickwork.

I paid no attention to Priscus, who was jumping up and down in silence, his arms raised to heaven. I got on my hands and knees and looked over the jagged edge of the roof. I was in time to hear a slither of detached facing blocks from the wall. There were fewer torches on the ground. Those remaining darted about like alarmed ants. I was aware of a low and general moaning, and of calls for help from those of the injured who could speak.

'I don't think they'll be trying that again,' Priscus crowed beside me – 'at least, not in the dark.' He went back to his victory dance, only stopping when he trod on his cloak and had to sit down abruptly to avoid pitching himself into the darkness. I looked over the edge again. The torchbearers had congregated directly below. By much squinting and telling myself to set aside the glare, I could just see the frenzied work of recovering the dead and living.

Priscus cleared his throat. 'You did secure all the hidden ways in and out?' he asked, sounding nervous for the first time.

I continued looking down. 'Unless there's another approach you haven't told me about,' I answered, 'the only way still open is into the Great Sewer – and I've placed a couple of boys there to listen for movement.' I scrambled back from the edge and stood carefully up. 'I don't know about you, but I'm more worried about that bloody catapult. Has the former Commander of the East any suggestions?'

There was now a flare of torches a dozen yards along the roof. 'Are you safe, Master?' Rado cried urgently. 'We've been looking everywhere for you.' I looked round. Priscus had vanished into the darkness. I looked down at my tunic. In the approaching light, I could see a dark patch that had to be dirt. I brushed the worst of it away and stepped forward.

'There will be no other attack tonight,' I said firmly. 'We remain on full alert, nevertheless.' I hurried forward. I didn't like standing so close to a sheer drop. Equally, the faintest shuffling of bare feet over tiles had told me that Priscus was lurking only a few feet above me, and most of the men and boys clambering towards me weren't in the know.

Heart sinking into the pit of a stomach that was itself twitching, I thought of what had to be done. 'Rado,' I said in what wasn't quite a commanding voice, 'I need to speak with you in private.'

44

'Can I do you a favour, dearie?' I paid no attention to the elderly whore. 'I do special rates, you know, for men of the cloth.' She reached forward to touch my hood.

I stopped myself from flinching back. 'Piss off, you foul creature of the night!' I grated in a Syrian accent. When that didn't work, I shoved her hard in the chest and stepped over her drink-sodden body.

Stuck inside my palace, I'd been dithering between two views of what was happening. Either the whole lower-class population of the City was laying siege to me, or there had been a general collapse of order. The truth, I'd found, was somewhere in the middle. We'd emerged half-smothered from the Great Sewer into the usual dark and silence of the night. All the brothels around Salvation Square were closed and in darkness. The only sound as we passed by the Leiriope Park was of the watchman, snoring in his box. Throughout the whole south-eastern quadrant of the City, everything seemed entirely in order.

Here, outside the Circus, though, you could see the evidence of a more than local disturbance. It was here that the owners of the wine shops mostly didn't live above their premises and these had been looted. No one in sight to stop them, men were reeling from fired buildings with jars of drink or other property in their hands. The narrowest part of the street was blocked by what may have been a crowd of hundreds, brought together for the sale or purchase of stolen property. The voice of the auctioneer was almost lost in the clamour of shouting and threats. But it was brisk bidding for a load of spices and silk that must have come from one of the less solid warehouses beside the docks.

I looked about for Rado. He was five yards behind me and still kicking the old whore. I hurried back for him. 'Leave her alone,' I hissed in Slavic. 'You'll draw attention to us if you kill her. And *do* stop swaggering. You're supposed to be a bloody monk!' He stopped at once and stood to attention. Glaucus was right – his days were over as a dancing boy. He'd seen to that with his efforts in the gymnasium. But, now he was swathed in black, I no longer saw him as he'd been brought to me the year before. He was getting tall as well as broad.

Ahead of us, the street was blocked by two drunks, going at each other with sharpened roof tiles. The cheering crowd they'd gathered completed the blockage. I took Rado by the arm and led him to a recessed doorway. 'Listen, boy,' I asked, 'why do you suppose I brought you with me tonight?'

'To be your bodyguard, Master,' he replied, standing straighter.

'And how do you think I want you to behave?' I asked again. 'As a man of your tribe? Or as a city tough? If I wanted the latter, I could hire the winner of those two fools over there.' I could almost feel my rebuke sinking into the boy's spirit. I waited a moment, then – 'What is your heart's desire?' I asked.

'To earn my freedom,' he said, fighting a sudden tremor in his voice. 'I'm not clever with writing and things like that. Perhaps all I can do is become a soldier.' He stopped again and controlled himself. 'I want to be like you, Master.'

It was a more focused answer than I'd expected. But I squeezed his hand. 'Then be what you are,' I said, 'not what you think I'd like you to be.' Not answering, he turned away from me.

The fight was ended almost as quickly as it had begun and I took the opportunity to step forward into the wavering light of the torches. Staying in character, I made sure to walk round the still body of the loser. I found myself looking at a table on which some-one had spread a few dozen singed papyrus books. '*Come on, Alaric, move on,*' I told myself as if I'd been giving another order to Rado. You can be sure it was a worthless order. I picked up the tattiest and perhaps the oldest of the books, and carried it over to where a fresh torch had been lit. It can never hurt, where books are concerned, just to have a look. With a skip of my heart, I found that I was holding the *Twelve Letters of Carneades on the Pragmatic Acceptance of Knowledge*. I'd thought his works were long since lost. The only full outline I had of scepticism was a plodding work by an Athenian doctor. I unlaced the book and unrolled it to the first page of text.

'Lovely stuff, don't you think, Father?' I pretended not to hear the owner of the stall, and continued squinting at the faint script. This would be hard to make out in any light. As it was, only the central column of text was legible. I read this a second time, now committing it, clause by clause, to memory: *If, then, it cannot be proven, in the sense required by the philosophers, that there is an external world, it does not seem necessarily to follow that we must reject the existence of this world. So far as we believe that there are external objects, and that these influence our mental state, it strikes me as reasonable, O Cleomenes, to say that, while always suspending final judgement, we may pragmatically, on applying certain common sense tests ...*

The stallholder raised his voice and put his face closer. 'I'm told they're all strictly orthodox, Father. They came from a good home, and would grace any sacred library.' I nodded and rolled the book to the protocol sheet. It was too stained to read in the light available. The script and general appearance, though, said it might be five hundred years old. Mobs never go for public libraries unless there's a monk to urge them on. Most likely, one of the houses of the great had been sacked. What might have begun with a nod and a wink from Nicetas had turned into an uprising against everyone with decent clothes on his back. It took immediate pressure off my own walls. At the same time, had it left Nicetas with any choice but revolution against his cousin? Heraclius wouldn't be pleased to come home to a burned and looted capital.

'How much for all of them?' I whispered, forgetting my Syrian accent. It was an unwise question. The answer would have tested the morals of anyone but an illiterate saint. Mine failed before the stallholder could finish naming his price. You should never not buy a book. I fished deep inside my robe and pulled out a handful of clipped silver. 'Take everything first thing in the morning to the shop of Baruch, the Jewish banker,' I said, speaking low. I paid no attention to the man's funny look. 'Tell him to give you this much again. Talk to anyone about our business,' I added, 'and you'll be garrotted in the central garden of the University.' While the stall-holder turned away to count the silver in the torchlight, I grabbed Rado by the sleeve and pulled him deep into the jostling crowd.

Even for a pair of monks – monks, at that, with some vicious metalware concealed about their persons, the covered passageway was an unwise choice of route on an evening like this. It would have to be a few more of those packed streets and then a walk along the ascending street where the City Prefect had his offices.

The Prefecture buildings were locked up and in darkness. This much I'd been ready to expect. If he was still up and going about his duties, Timothy would be in his own palace, five blocks away from mine. Keeping in the shadows, we hurried upwards in the direction of the Central Milestone. We passed side streets where at least one attack had been made, but where the occupants were looking to their common defence. The bodies lying in the gutters or swinging from the brackets where torches should normally have been, were warning enough against more predatory attacks in this district. Once or twice, someone stepped out in front of us. But why stop anyone like us? 'God bless you, Fathers – have a care on a night like this,' was the most we got.

The general call of bed, and the known risk of injury, had thinned the numbers outside my palace. As on the night I'd got back from my first brush with Shahin, the siege was little more than dark bodies stretched out beside dying bonfires. I looked out from the darkness of the colonnade. In the faint glimmer of moonlight, it wasn't possible to see the extent of structural damage caused by the catapult ball. But I knew the price of marble facing slabs. Three patches of these had come away. I could be sure every one of these had broken where it landed.

'There are three guards, Master,' Rado whispered in my ear. 'Do you want me to lead them away? Or shall we kill them?'

297

'Guards' was rather a grand word for the scruffy thugs who were taking their ease about five yards away. But there may have been more of them – the catapult itself was blocked from view unless we stepped out into the moonlight. Even three wouldn't be so easy to take out at once and without noise. I moved deeper into shadow and waited for the boy to follow.

'Stay here, but keep an eye on me,' I said with slow emphasis. 'Only come if I call you.' I patted him on the shoulder before he could protest. 'When did your people ever waste their lives on a frontal assault?' I asked. 'Now, wait for me to call you or wait until your own sense tells you otherwise.'

I walked thirty paces back the way we'd come and broke cover a long way from the catapult. Looking neither right not left, and skirting several pools of congealing blood and any place on the pavement where the assembled dregs hadn't yet fallen asleep, I made myself walk slowly across the wide expanse of the Triumphal Way. I stopped before my main gate and stared at the effects of the bonfires that had been lit there. The iron portcullis was bent in slightly, but should still go smoothly up into its housing. The gate itself was scratched and dented, but could be put right in half a morning. The cracked and smoke-stained marble would need specialised care. So too the chipped stairs. Sixty feet above me, two men were speaking in the rough Latin that barbarians of different races use when speaking together. If they leaned over the office balcony and saw me, they might choose to forget the orders I'd given for reactive force only. But I'd done enough to set up my excuse. I turned and made my way back towards the colonnade.

I slowed to a shuffle as I passed by one of the siege towers and the catapult came in sight. I'd believe Priscus that the siege towers were useless. And, unless it could be got repeatedly up and down the front steps, the battering ram was more likely to injure its users than open any gates. It was the catapult that mattered. I blinked a few times and tried to focus harder in the gloom. For once, I could see, I'd been right and Priscus wrong about something military. This was one of the iron machines we'd lately set up on the land walls. Given the right setting of the angle bars and the right degree of torsion, it could throw a fifty-pound ball to hit a point somewhat lower than any of the balconies. A few dozen of these hitting on one point would bring down at least part of the front wall. Properly handled, a smaller catapult than this could knock through stone like a mason's hammer. It could turn brick to clouds of choking dust. It could shoot a chain of iron balls at ground level and slice advancing men in half. Even after his army had run away, five of these had almost won the Battle of Antioch for Nicetas. Sad for us they'd fallen into Persian hands. I could laugh and poke my tongue out at anything else. This darkly glittering monster couldn't be left in place.

I stopped where I could get a proper look at things and lifted my arms in prayer. The most obvious weak point in the catapult was its bowstring – I call it a bowstring, though it wasn't far off an inch of plaited silk strands. Cut through this and you'd need special machinery to pull the torsion springs back far enough for a replacement to be fitted. This was assuming a replacement could be found. A raking blow with my sword and we could go back to toughing things out till Heraclius chose to grace his capital with his renewed presence.

Now I could be sure there were only three of them, the guards weren't a problem. The real problem was fleshing out the plan I'd thought over between coughing fits in the Great Sewer. I needed an unhurried go at the bowstring and a safe escape afterwards. How to get that? I glanced under the colonnade. I only saw him because I was looking; but Rado, still as a cat before a mouse hole, was looking back at me. He was expecting something clever.

A voice called out nervously on my left: 'Has he decided *anything* yet?'

Leander of Memphis stood with his back to the main source of light. But I could almost hear the cold sweat on his face. 'I was nearly killed when the night attack went wrong,' he added, coming forward another step. He lowered his voice. 'Of course, I'm not scared to die in the service of My Lord.' He struck a pose and tried for one of his poetic growls. 'But it's the lower people, you see – many of them have said they won't be coming back tomorrow.'

45

I stared at Leander. Was this a nuisance? Or was it one of those strokes of luck so great and so bizarre that it's hard to know what use to make of it. I bowed slightly, wondering how best I could play for time. 'The Lord Nicetas instructs you to continue about your duties,' I said in my best Syrian accent. It was just the sort of answer you could expect from Nicetas in an emergency. I watched Leander's shoulders sag and racked my brains for what to do with him. Enticing him under the colonnade for a quick blow on the head seemed the easiest option but might be a waste of a good opportunity. 'He wishes to be told, however, why the catapult has not been tried again. Treason has been committed in removing it from the walls. It was not carried here to stand as an ornament.'

'Oh, but nothing can be done till morning!' Leander groaned. 'Didn't His Lordship get my last message?' I shook my head. No cause for suspicion here. He knew Nicetas. He dropped the question. He hopped lightly across the last few yards that separated us. 'The man with the instruction book got frightened when people said they'd hang him,' he explained. 'He went home ages ago but said he'd try to understand all the hard sums in his book in time for a morning attack.'

I thought quickly. The plan I'd had in mind was dead. Time to make up another. 'Let me see the catapult,' I said, putting a note of involuntary interest into my voice. Leander stepped back and bowed.

I'd known one of the guards was listening to us. He'd been watching me from the moment I stepped out of the shadows. 'You just keep away from that thing,' he warned us. 'You heard the orders.'

Leander took his hat off so he could give a haughty toss of his head. 'My good man,' he said, 'your orders come from a youthful clerk, who takes his orders from me. And *I* represent the Lord Nicetas. Your new orders are to stand aside and allow your betters to go about their business.'

'Well, don't you go messing about with that thing,' the guard said flatly. 'It's done enough harm already.' He waved at the other two guards. 'Come on. I don't fancy being anywhere near if those two jokers let that thing off again.'

I watched the three men shamble towards one of the more distant bonfires. For the first time in two years, I was beginning to see some merit in the New Callimachus. Kissing him was out of the question. But I'd make a point of not killing him unless I really needed to.

Leander climbed up and balanced unsteadily on the catapult's wooden stock. He pointed at one of the bow arms. 'It's really just a big bow,' he said learnedly. 'But, when you're shooting arrows, it's the bow itself that gives the tension. This is much cleverer. Can you see how its arms are buried in those elaborate twistings? They look like elongated balls of wool, but are many rods of coiled bronze.' I said nothing but moved closer to the silken cord. The guards were far off, and had their backs to us. Leander's most likely response when I pulled my sword out would be to shit himself. I wondered again how much noise the torsion springs would make when they snapped back into place. Thanks to Leander, it probably didn't matter.

He noticed where I was looking, and laughed. He climbed down again beside me. 'Yes, Father, it *is* a gigantic bowstring. You put your stone ball in the special pouch woven into its centre. Now, you don't pull the string back by hand. Instead, you attach it to the hook in this block of wood. This thick rope here pulls the block back. You wind the rope back by turning that big wheel thing.' He pointed again at the torsion springs. 'When the bowstring is wound fully back, the wooden arms come back as well, and they pull the bronze twistings back.' He laughed. 'You can't imagine how powerful those twistings are. Four powerful men can't move one of them even an inch. Winding them back needs two men with wooden levers to pull on the big wheel. When the tension is released, they spring back too fast for the eye to see.'

He paused for breath and struck another pose, this time, pushing his fingers between the strands of the nearest torsion spring. 'I tell you, Father – and I tell you as a man filled with ancient learning, who helped interpret its instruction book into the common Greek of our own age – this is the *ultimate power in the universe!*'

'My son,' I said, nearly forgetting to sound foreign, 'are you not overlooking the power of Him who stands above all earthly powers?'

I was expecting a long whine of piety and a convenient upward glance. Instead, with a sudden lapse into glumness, he sat down on the stock. 'But is there no one to talk His Lordship into a diplomatic solution?' he asked. 'Has he forgotten it's his own daughter who may be destroyed if the power of this thing is fully unleashed?' He covered his eyes. 'I've known her since she was just a little girl. Nicetas can't be serious about giving her up to the mob.'

Eyes still covered, he fell into a fit of horrified sobbing. It was long enough for me to check what I'd briefly felt when stroking the bowstring. Yes – the silk strands were cut at least three-quarters through each side of the central pouch. This wasn't anything you might expect from clumsy use. Someone had cut it from underneath. Gently, I pushed a fingernail into one of the notches. Perhaps three-quarters through was an understatement. I'd already seen that the torsion springs were set to maximum stretch. Pull it back as far as the first trigger mechanism and the string would certainly fail. Tensed as it presently was, it might go at any moment. I pulled my hand back from the string and stepped away from the machine. Leander was right about the torsion springs. They were enormously powerful. If the bowstring snapped, they'd send its two lengths whipping about like flexible razors. I'd heard of one battlefield accident where an operator's head had been sliced off.

'So the assault is to be at dawn?' I asked.

Leander looked up and spread his hands. 'I was hoping you would tell me that,' he said. He covered his eyes again and uttered an almost poetic groan. 'If we don't get proper orders soon, even those who bother coming back will only stay for breakfast. I don't want this thing to be used again. But what are we all to do if the revolution goes out like a lamp exhausted of its oil?' He put his hands down. 'Oh, Antonia,' he sighed, 'if only, for the first time in your life, you'd done as you were told. You'd soon have got used to Eunapius!'

I stepped further away from the catapult. In his genuine despair, Leander was rocking back and forward on it. I could almost fancy I was looking at the remaining strands as they snapped, one at a time. No point in asking who'd set things up for a catastrophic failure. I turned and stared at the looming mass of my palace. When I got back inside, I'd call him names for keeping another of its hidden doorways to himself. I'd pointedly not ask how he'd got past the guards. There could be no spoiling his present fun, however. He must be somewhere up on the roof, hugging himself and breathing self-endearments, as he beheld what an utter fool I'd been made to feel. All the way here, I'd been turning over what to say to Antonia when I got back. 'Wake up, dearest,' I'd been thinking to call. 'Don't worry about the catapult. I've just slipped out and disabled it.' Nonchalance on one side, astonishment on the other – a nice long fuck to keep us happy till dawn, and then a clear view of baffled rage, or even death or dismemberment, brought on by the ever-resourceful as well as beautiful young Alaric. Oh, I'd have Priscus for this!

But it wouldn't be a wasted journey through the night, I suddenly told myself. I looked again at Leander. 'Two men travelling together are surely better than one at a time like this,' I said. 'Why not come back with me, my son? You could speak the message of peace and diplomacy directly to the Lord Nicetas. Will he not still be awake? Does he not hang on your every word?'

'He did tell me to stay put and wait for instructions,' came the hesitant reply. Leander looked about at what little there was to see in the gloom of the Triumphal Way. 'And the important men about him won't like anything that sounds like a compromise. But I can't say I like it out here all alone. Some of these people have rough ways.' He brightened. 'And, if you don't like the idea of going back alone, I suppose I could come with you as protection. A man of the church shouldn't be expected to risk himself alone in these streets. You never know what might happen on a night like this.'

'Indeed, my son,' I said. Unmoving in the darkness, Rado hadn't enough Greek to follow the discussion. I'd have to trust him to guess what I was about and play along.

I didn't fancy stepping any closer to the catapult. Leander had stopped rocking back and forth on it, but was now kicking his heels against the stock. I stretched out my arm. 'Come with me, my son,' I said. 'All that can be done in this place you have done well.' I waited for the faint look of doubt to vanish from his face. There was a five-foot space behind the statue of Cicero. Any vagrants sleeping there could be sent packing with a few coppers.

I shuffled into a more comfortable spot on the ledge and leaned back against the chilly bronze. 'I won't tell you again,' I said. 'If you don't keep your voice down, my friend will have no choice but to cut your throat.'

The light here was just good enough for me to see Leander run his fingers again through his hair. 'But you're mad,' he said, now in soft panic. He'd tried that argument already, without effect. He cast round for another. 'How do you know I won't betray you the moment we're in the palace?'

Good point – though also easily answered. 'The young man with the hood still over his face knows who you are and what you look like. All you know about him is that he's rather big and has a talent for holding a knife to your throat. Aside from him, my household is filled with slaves and freedmen I've always treated well and who have more than a certain regard for me. This, I hope you'll agree, makes for an imbalance of power you should keep continually in mind. If anything happens to me, you'll be dead meat the moment you show yourself in public.'

I put a smile into my voice. 'Now, let me go over again what I've told you. This time, if you don't keep begging for mercy, you might understand it.' I waited for him to finish slobbering more wine from his flask. Scaring him was easy – and there would be more of that to come. But I really needed him at least minimally on side.

'The City mob doesn't count,' I said, starting over. 'Your boss can't be Emperor. The Army wouldn't hear of it. He won't carry the respectable classes after a night like this. Unless someone brings him round before it's too late, he'll be nursing two blinded eyes in the Fortified Monastery, and his poet will get all the blame for sending him as mad as everyone thinks he must be. That means *you*, Leander. Even if Heraclius is tender to his cousin, he'll think nothing of having you racked to death, or torn apart by hyenas in the Circus. We are talking about high treason, after all.'

I waited for him to stop farting. I'd applied the stick. Time, now he was on the verge of moral collapse, to show the carrot. 'Leander, there is, in one of my filing boxes, a sealed patent granting you a position in the bureaucracy. It's worth forty seven *solidi* a year. You can rent a small house on that and keep two slaves. I've added a variation that gives you this by right, not at will. Once published, only an emperor will be able to cancel the appointment.' I waited for this to sink in. 'Is it your highest ambition to spend the rest of his life spraying flattery at Nicetas? He's not exactly an ideal patron.'

Leander put both hands on his belly and leaned forward. I thought he was about to vomit. Instead, he was crying. 'How do I know you'll keep your word?' he sobbed.

Another easy one to answer. 'I have a reputation for honesty and fair dealing,' I said. I stood up and moved away from Leander. He was deep in shadow but had the best sight of me a waxing moon allowed. 'This is a reputation that brings many advantages. Why should I risk it on doing you over? Oh, I may, now and again, wriggle out of big promises. But I can always find a convincing excuse for that. And it's against a deep background of promises to people like you that I *never* break.' I waited for the logic of my case to seep into his mind. 'So, I put it to you, Leander: I'm your best chance of staying alive and of making it to a security that few poets achieve. *Will you get me in front of Nicetas?*'

He kept his head almost between his knees. But I could tell from the way he breathed that Alaric the Golden-Tongued – Alaric, who could make the worse appear the better reason: Alaric, who was presently telling the truth – had made the necessary conquest. Search me what I was to tell Nicetas when, like Cleopatra from her carpet, I appeared before him. But neither of the main alternatives to talking sense into the fool was greatly to my convenience. Now he was my prospective father-in-law, watching him dragged off to the Fortified Monastery had lost all its old charm. And, if one of them had just been put out of action, there were over a hundred other catapults that could be unbolted from the city walls.

I reached out to Leander. 'Put your hand in mine,' I said softly. 'Get me to Nicetas. I'll do the rest. Do this for yourself – and for Antonia.'

Something metallic scraped against the street side of the statue. This was followed by a light patter of feet. I pushed Rado back. 'No, stay here with the little Greek,' I murmured. Sword in hand, I darted out of cover.

The street was empty – rather, it had been almost empty. In the moment before it disappeared, though, I'd seen enough of the flutter of dark cloth against the darker shadow of the far colonnade.

I took a deep breath. I shut off the approach of a rage darker than the shadow of the colonnade. 'I won't ask you to explain yourself,' I said in Latin. 'But you can come out of hiding.' How she'd made it this far in life might be used as a minor proof of God's existence.

46

Though it was well past the midnight hour, the square in which Nicetas had his palace was brightly lit. Two huge torches burned above the main entrance. Armed men stood beneath, stopping and mostly turning back the flow of visitors. Right in the middle of the square, a gang of drunken proles was raucously hailing Nicetas as the new Emperor. As yet, no one took notice of them. Leander hurried us past the line of well-dressed supplicants and seemed about to avoid the guards altogether.

Not quite. 'Here, mate, where do you think you're going?' The guard stepped backwards through the gateway and leaned his right arm against the wall. He drummed the fingers of his left hand on his breastplate.

It was Leander's turn to step backwards. He pressed shaking hands against his thighs and tried for an easy smile. 'I am Court Poet to His Magnificence the Commander of the East,' he squeaked. 'If you send for your superior officer, he will readily confirm that I am not to be delayed as I go about my Master's business.'

The guard's answer was to hawk and spit, his gob just missing Leander's feet. He turned his attention to me. 'Big for a monk, aren't we?' he asked. He stood on tiptoe and peered suspiciously into what I hoped was the darkness within my hood. One hand raised to pull at the hood and he'd have been dead before he hit the ground. I'd have been halfway to the Central Milestone, with Antonia pulled along behind me, before the other guards could check that he was dead.

I kept my arms folded inside the long sleeves of my robe. 'I am Father Gregory,' I said in my Syrian accent. 'The Lordship's poet has brought us through all the danger of the streets on a mission of great importance.' I bowed respectfully, shuffling forward an inch to finish the work of concealing Antonia.

Still looking closely at me, the guard took his arm from against the wall. It might have been a friendly action. Just as likely, it allowed him all the quicker to go for his sword. 'Where are you from?' he asked in Syriac. 'The Lord Nicetas has his own spiritual advisers in residence. Why does anyone need more than that?'

He was lighter than most Syrians and his Greek was completely idiomatic. He'd taken me by surprise. But I bowed again. 'From Edessa, my son,' I answered in his own language. I'd been there more than once. I could describe its sights well enough for anyone who wasn't a native. It was where I'd learned my Syriac. I tightened my grip on the short sword I was pressing with my right hand against my left forearm. 'We were asked to send holy oil from the lamp that burns before the relics of Saint Aerumenus the Merciful.'

The guard looked at the satchel I had about my neck. Someone behind me coughed loudly. Someone else began a jingling of coins in his hand that could have only one meaning. He looked at me again. 'You can go in,' he said, now back in Greek. 'Captain Silenus is at the top of the main staircase. Make your way straight to him. Don't go near the private quarters. We've had orders to kill on sight.'

'My own quarters are this way,' Antonia whispered. She pointed at a door that, flush against the wall, was the same colour as the wall. She stood before it and was about to rap against it with her knuckles. 'Daddy has a eunuch on guard there at all times,' she explained.

Leander got in before me. 'Please, My Lady,' he begged, 'don't tell *anyone*. Aren't we in enough danger?'

She pulled her hood back and frowned. 'You always were a wet blanket, Leander,' she snapped. 'Why don't you just go off to bed?' Though still barely above a whisper, her voice was loud enough to set up a sibilant echo in the big hall.

'You can put that fucking hood back on,' I snarled in Latin. I'd shown a most remarkable restraint in not stripping her naked before the statue of Cicero and slapping her arse till she cried – not, I might add, that she would have cried. Not having any obvious alternative in mind, I'd let her change clothes with Rado, and given him a direct order to wait for us near the secret entrance to the Great Sewer. He'd nearly boiled over with anger at the order, and I'd been sorry to see him go. I'd then let her tag along on an adventure that I was too proud to explain had no specific purpose. But I'd not stand by and let her queen it over the palace eunuchs. Even if, in my present mood, it was only so I could knock her about afterwards, I wanted the two of us to stay alive.

'I was only going to . . .' She fell silent before I could step on one of her feet. Drifting from one of the state rooms it had been Antonia's idea to avoid was the unmistakable whine of Eunapius in rattled mood.

His voice was overlain by one of Timothy's contemptuous laughs. Eunapius waited for this to finish. 'So why didn't *you* try persuading him?' he asked with a show of defiance.

'Never mind drinking, dear boy,' Timothy said in a whisper that carried all the way to us. 'You won't get a horse to water if you can't first flog it to its feet. I'm going home, to think what to do next.' He stopped a few inches short of coming through the door. I could see the shadow of his bulk cast by the bright mass of candles within the room. 'Whatever I do, Eunapius, will not involve you. Take it as friendly advice or as a threat. But, when I have made such arrangements as I must, I shall not be grateful for the efforts you made to entice me and my friends into this dangerous apology for a plot.' He turned and continued into the hall where, for want of anywhere to hide, the three of us were trying to look inconspicuous.

'Ah, Leander!' Timothy cried, spreading his arms in satirical good humour. 'Barely one moment ago, the Lord Nicetas was lamenting your absence – and here you now are!' He twisted his face into a polite smile. 'Was the catapult attack a disaster, or only an embarrassing failure?'

'Forty people died, My Lord – mostly in the panic,' said Leander. 'However, I am assured another try will be made in the morning.' He looked at me from the corner of his eyes. 'I was told the Lord Alaric would be pulled dead or alive from the rubble of his stinking lair.'

'Dead would be some consolation for all the trouble he's caused us!' Timothy snorted. 'His capacity for staying alive has disordered every plan in sight.' He walked over to a big mirror that was hung against the marbled walls. He arranged his wig and pulled at his baggy features. He looked at me and sniffed appreciatively. I'd managed, in the Great Sewer, to avoid treading in the yard thickness of its various deposits. Without the ventilation of the outside breeze, though, its miasma was spreading about me again like an invisible fog. 'I don't care what anyone says,' he muttered to his own reflection. 'The Intelligence Bureau *must* have got wind of this plot. Now it's plain there will be no change of Emperor, it's a matter of hours before the agents come off the fence.' He turned away from the mirror. 'I'm out of this plot and glad of it,' he said with loud finality. He made for what I supposed would be one of the side entrances. Stopping this side of a big doorway, he turned and looked back at us. 'Eunapius,' he called softly, 'I'll make myself plain to you. The next time we meet must be in an interrogation cell without a shorthand clerk. I can't have you denouncing me to Heraclius. Your good friend Simon has a ship ready in one of the coastal harbours. Why don't you just sail off in it and throw yourself on Shahin's mercy? One way or the other, you're taking the whole blame for this when Heraclius gets back. You might as well give yourself some chance of staying alive. Yes, go and see Shahin. The Persians can be most hospitable – even to those who have only tried to do them a service.' He laughed grimly and continued into the next big room.

Eunapius dropped into a padded chair beside the mirror. 'Oh Jesus, what am I to do?' he called in soft despair. 'I'm a dead man after tonight.' He buried his face in his hands. 'He's right about the Intelligence Bureau. I'll be arrested at dawn.' Antonia turned her hooded face in my direction. I shook my head. When you don't know where to go next, best stand still. Eunapius sat upright. With most of his face powder transferred to his hands, he looked much older, and the twitching of his jaw muscles was fully evident. He stared at Leander. 'You do know that the young shit got a message to Heraclius before we sealed him in that fortress he took from old Priscus?' he asked bitterly. Leander bowed silently. Safe inside my hood, I smiled. Anyone with an ounce of intelligence would have set pickets at all the city gates. I'd been worrying about that for days. Any moment, I'd been expecting to see the messenger's head sent over one of the balconies by a slingshot. Well, the idiots had let him go. By now, even Heraclius would have finished with dithering. He would be assembling every regiment within a three-day march from the City. He'd be preparing letters of instruction and reassurance for the provincial authorities. In the next few days, he'd turn up outside the walls. No one would slam the gates in his face for the sake of Nicetas. Because I'd discovered the plot, I could probably insist on due process for the plotters. That would allow me to watch the executions with an easy mind. Also, a month of trials could be made to produce a wider benefit.

How did Eunapius know any of this? From Nicetas, I could have no doubt. Perhaps a stern message had already arrived from Cyzicus. You didn't need that to set Nicetas into one of his fits of total immobility – but it might have helped.

Suddenly, Eunapius jumped to his feet. 'Leander,' he said urgently, 'Nicetas listens to you. He respects your – your genius.' He took hold of Leander's arm. '*You* speak to him. You were there. You've seen the catapult. We just need a morning bombardment and Nicetas can be Emperor. It's the barbarian who's in our way. Without him, everyone will gather round Nicetas. But he's got to give the order for attack. You've *got* to speak to him!'

There was a sound of boots coming down stairs. 'What's all this fucking noise?' someone asked in a vaguely military voice. 'Doesn't no one go to bed in this place?' That was a nuisance. I'd been speculating on the benefits to be had from pulling Eunapius into a darkish corner for a few pointed questions, followed by a visit to Nicetas. The dark head looking over the balustrade told me to

311

keep my mouth shut. Good advice! I was winning. It might be for the best simply to go home and wait.

Eunapius hurried past me into full sight of the bleary guard. 'His Magnificence has asked us to wait outside a while,' he said with a stab at firmness. 'You may return to your place of supervisory inspection.' With a laughed obscenity and a scraping of feet, the guard tramped off out of sight and hearing.

Eunapius turned back to Leander. 'Come on,' he said. He moved towards the room filled with candles. 'We can grab him before he falls asleep in his chair. We'll have him all to ourselves.' He took Leander's hand in his and stepped through the doorway. Since he hadn't told us otherwise, I followed. I didn't look round but had no doubt Antonia was close behind me.

On entering the palace, we'd skirted the areas I knew from my own visits. But, passing through empty, though vast and brilliantly lighted rooms, I could sense we were making our way towards the recital room. Sure enough, we reached the far end of a gallery filled with more art than I'd thought had survived from ancient times, to hear a muffled sound of drums and flutes on the other side of the door.

Uncertain again, Eunapius stopped. 'Try to look confident,' he whispered to Leander. For the first time, he turned to me. 'He was complaining about his legs when we left him. There's water and bandages in the usual place.'

47

Upright in his chair, Nicetas opened his eyes. He focused on the three of us and reached for his walking stick. 'I sent you away, Eunapius,' he said wearily. 'I said you had failed me and that I wouldn't receive you again. Why are you back so soon?'

Antonia moved two paces to the left. She might have done this to let Nicetas see there were four of us. It also served, though, to block my view of one of the best dildo dances I'd seen outside a brothel. Stark naked, her father's black girls weren't at all put out by the lateness of the hour, or by their master's lack of attention. I allowed myself one final look at the glistening, upturned breasts of the girl nearest to me, and turned my head back to the overdressed invalid for whom they'd been kept out of bed.

Eunapius poked Leander in the back. 'Come on!' he hissed, not moving his lips. The poet stepped forward and bowed with his arms stretched out. 'I bring news of our preparations for the final assault,' he began in a voice loaded with dramatic potential.

Nicetas paid him no attention. 'There is a letter from my Imperial cousin,' he said, still weary. He gripped harder on his stick and pointed me towards a silver side table. I bowed and walked slowly across the room. Formal communications from the Emperor were written in gold on a purple background. This was a personal note. The parchment sheet was folded in three and it wouldn't do for me to be seen looking at it. One glance at Nicetas was enough to guess the generality of its contents. Never cheerful, he now radiated dejection. I carried the letter back and presented it with a low bow. Nicetas didn't move. 'I have been dismissed as Regent,' he said after a long silence. 'The Patriarch is appointed in my place and Alaric in his place till he gets back from Nicaea.

Alaric has full authority to take such steps for the security of the Empire as he may think just and expedient.'

Behind me, I heard Eunapius fall to the floor. I suppressed my own desire to throw off this smelly outer robe and join the girls in a performance of the high step. With shaking hands, I put the letter on a spare footstool and cancelled the nap I'd had in mind for when I got home. The morning would be spent more productively getting Theodore to help write out six dozen arrest warrants and a terrifying proclamation. I'd drifted in with no idea what actions I could take to justify this entire digression from the work of buggering the catapult. But just standing about and looking nondescript had done enough for me so far.

Nicetas lifted his stick again and prodded me in the stomach. 'Must I suffer all night without the ministrations of Holy Mother Church?' he asked peevishly. Eunapius had said the bandages and water were in 'the usual place.' Search me where that might be. But Nicetas prodded me again and pointed a wavering finger at a polished chest beside the window. I bowed and went over to it. No bandages inside, unless I was supposed to tear up the cotton towels folded in a neat heap. I'd seen enough of Nicetas, though, to know the use of the other things I found. I gave the bowl and water jug to Antonia. The other things I carried back myself.

Leander started again in a voice too loud to shake. 'The foul and bestial barbarian trembles behind his shattered walls. The renewed bombardment at dawn will cast down those walls as if they surrounded the city of Jericho. Then the Roman People will stream through the breach and find him wherever he takes cover. Was it not Sophocles who said that every barbarian excretes in his moment of death from every orifice?'

It was actually Callisthenes – but never mind that. While the poet's voice rose to a squawk of enthusiasm, I set about my own work. My stomach had been turned any number of times by the sight, and the smell, of those inflamed legs. I'd never had cause to touch them. I undid the lower bandages and kept myself from puking by thoughts of my proclamation. I knelt back and allowed

Antonia to do the washing. Trying to recall how I'd seen it done, I poured oil into a silver bowl and mixed in a double handful of something dark that had the consistency of roughly ground charcoal. I rubbed some of this between both hands, before starting work on the ankles.

With a long gasp of pain, Nicetas got me a sharp blow of his stick on my upper back. 'Not so hard!' he cried. 'I'm not yet in Hell! The sacred earth from Sinai calls for only the lightest touch.' He fell back again and groaned. I felt him scrabble for something. The crackle of parchment told me he was reading his cousin's letter again.

Behind me, the door opened. 'I thought you'd still be awake!' Timothy said in his official voice. The door closed with a soft click, and there was the sound of leather soles on marble. Nicetas struggled to sit up again. With desperate urgency, he pushed the letter into my face. I turned to Antonia. But she was kneeling too far away to take it. He poked the letter inside my hood. I twisted my face this way and that, till the folded sheet was against the back of my neck. Assuming it said what I'd been told, it might come in handy once I was out of here. There was no certainty Heraclius had bothered writing to Sergius or me directly.

'I said I'd give you till noon,' Timothy said. 'Bearing all things in mind, I'm having the mob cleared away as soon as there's enough light for my men.'

'So why have you come to tell me of your betrayal?' Nicetas whined.

Timothy laughed. 'Not out of politeness, you can be sure! What I want from you, my jumped up little provincial, is the names of your ringleaders among the mob. If you have any trace of common sense, you'll agree on the value of having every last one of them hanging from the city walls. Even with Heraclius running the Intelligence Bureau, there are some kinds of evidence you don't leave lying about. When our Lord and Master gets back, we need the past day to look as much as possible like a spontaneous collapse of order. The only alternative is for you to carry the whole blame.'

Nicetas hit me again with his stick. 'But keeping order is your job,' he whined. 'You can't shuffle the responsibility for that on to me. It was you who let the mob gather outside Alaric's palace.'

Timothy laughed again, now with an unpleasantness that reminded me of Priscus. 'Oh, I've got a signed note from silly Eunapius here, telling me to stand everyone down. I may get the sack for taking this as a direct order from you. But I'm presently only interested in keeping the head on my shoulders.' I heard Eunapius scramble to his knees and begin a sobbing excuse – a piss-poor excuse, I'll tell you it was: that sort of instruction he should have gone off to deliver in person.

Nicetas suddenly drew his legs back. 'What are you doing?' he asked me. In answer, I held up one of the maggots I'd been picking off his raw, ulcerated flesh. 'You must *never* do that!' he cried in horror. 'Let them feast on what God has given them.' There was no answer to that. I stared silently down at the heap of squashed bodies. Nicetas dragged his legs further under the chair. He poked me sharply in the chest. 'Who are you?' he asked angrily. 'I don't remember seeing you before.' In Latin, he let out a brief apology to God. He looked at me again. He raised his stick as if to hit me across my face. He checked himself, but opened his mouth and drew a long and ragged breath. I hadn't seen any guards on my way in. But who could say how many there were outside the main door to the room? Timothy was here. He'd surely have come with a file of prefecture guards to keep him safe.

But it was Leander to the rescue. 'I can feel the Muse about to come upon me!' he cried in what was supposed to be a thrilling descent. He clapped his hands together. The soft and wailing music that had never so far let up came to an abrupt end. I heard the rustle of clothing and the soft patter of his feet as he wheeled about in his poetic manner. Then:

> O golden youth, this day
>   By seven and thirty summers blessed,
> That only joyful thoughts we pray
>   Shall animate thy breast.

Who cares for Alexander?
  Pelopidas who knows?
Than thee a manlier commander
  Who shall dare propose?

This day, O splendid, golden youth,
  By seven and thirty summers blessed,
Those who love thee know in truth
  Of all days is the happiest.

Leander fell silent in a completely silent room. I watched Antonia's shoulders tremble in one of her quiet laughing fits. Unfair, I thought – this had been one of his better productions. No one else moved. Nicetas was first to speak. 'Bravo, my Poet!' he cried. 'Though my birthday is still four months away, was ever such a gift made by a poet to his patron?' Timothy cleared his throat. But Nicetas wasn't finished. 'Leander, I say as a man famed for both learning and taste, that no poet, ancient or modern, has approached you in genius of inspiration or elegance of style.' He reached once more for his stick, but this time missed it. With a sigh, he waited for it to stop its loud rolling across the floor. With another sigh, he pulled his left leg forward, then his right. 'If only, my dearest friend, you would work miracles other than with words. Our heads sit so weakly on our shoulders.'

For the moment at least, Nicetas had forgotten about me. I could have grovelled at the man's feet till he got sick of us all. I could then have crept off with Antonia back to my palace to wait on events. But the idea I'd been turning over was now complete. I finished washing my hands and stood up. I pulled at the main tie of my robe and let it fall to the ground. 'Since you've asked for a miracle,' I said, stepping free of the grubby cloth, 'how about this one?' I bowed to Nicetas. I bowed to Timothy. I bent down and fished for the Emperor's letter. I picked it up and glanced at the childish hand. Nicetas had got this one right. A few words, followed by the impression of a signet ring on beeswax, had made me, until His Holiness could make it across the straits, supreme ruler of the Roman Universe.

More silence. Then, with a squeal of fright, Eunapius was on his feet and making for the door. Antonia got there first. He dodged the punch she threw at him. He wasn't so lucky when she got out a lead cosh. She landed a blow to the side of his head and stood back to watch him thresh about. 'Hello, Daddy!' she said, pulling her hood down. 'We've come to ask for your blessing.' She came over and took my hand in hers. 'Poor Mummy would have envied me rotten, I'm sure you'll agree.'

Never vocal at the best of times, Nicetas had the look on his face of a man who's just taken an arrow in the chest and isn't sure yet if it merely hurts or will finish him off. It was Timothy who broke the silence. He snapped his fingers at Leander. 'I want two chairs over here,' he said. He looked at Antonia. 'Make it three. And put another against that door.' As he sat down carefully, the music started again. Slow and undulating, the girls formed a new line with their dildoes. Together, we made the four points of an irregular rectangle. Leander stood behind Nicetas with bowed head. Eunapius had crawled away from the door. A miserable and unmoving heap, he was in sight and in convenient distance for killing.

'What's in that letter?' Timothy asked. I unfolded it and held it up to read. He sniffed. 'I haven't seen what you sent the booby. But, since you haven't tried arresting me, dear boy, I might as well ask what deal you have in mind. At this stage in proceedings, you'll find me refreshingly open to a deal.'

I smiled coldly. He'd learned much from Priscus, even down to the intonations of his voice. I'd always known he was a snake posing as a buffoon. Time to see if he was clever enough to recognise his own true interest. 'At dawn,' I said, 'you clear the street outside my palace. I accept your claim that you were ordered not to intervene. I believe Nicetas when he says he was held prisoner in his own palace and orders were issued in his name. Such other dirt as I may have on you and your friends will disappear.' I looked at Eunapius. The logic was inescapable. When something goes wrong, someone must be blamed. When the right people can't be blamed, someone else must be. But Eunapius couldn't be allowed to stand trial – not before Heraclius, not in public. All I had to do was kill a man in cold blood and I could have my heart's desire. I passed over the detail. 'Nicetas will, of course, accept me as his son-in-law and use every possible endeavour to persuade the Emperor not to withhold his own consent.'

'Strikes me as a very fair deal,' said Timothy with a smack of his lips. 'Everyone wins.' He looked at Nicetas, who still hadn't moved. 'Shall we take that as a "yes"? Or would you prefer to die in the fighting to liberate this palace?'

As one, we all looked at Nicetas. His expression still hadn't changed. Just when I was beginning to think he'd had a seizure, he leaned back in his chair. 'What would you do if you were me?' he whispered to Leander.

'If I were you, My Lord,' came the instant reply, 'I'd get off my lazy, fat arse and kiss my son-in-law.'

We turned to watch the complex and unending gyrations of the dildo dance. All, that is, except poor Eunapius.

48

I looked up at the sky again. At last, dark blue had turned to light and was now turning a chilly grey. For some while we'd been able to hear the crowd that was reassembling far below and to see the rush lights a few of its more thoughtful members had brought along. Looking down, I could see the dim shapes scurrying about in the Triumphal Way. Some of them were in clusters and were carrying what I could only guess were the dead in their winding sheets. There weren't enough for another rendition of 'Kill! Kill!' But the monks were already in place and I could hear them praying for the dead in their ferocious nasal whines.

'Do you think you can trust him?' Antonia asked.

I smiled to myself. 'If I trusted him,' I said, 'I'd be down there beside him.' Making sure not to lean on the undamaged stretch of the parapet where we were all gathered, I stood on tiptoe on my chair and bent forward. In the improved light, I could see more of the catapult. Someone was sitting on it beside the torsion springs and seemed to be reading from a scroll to someone else, who was hurrying about with what may have been small projectiles. Not the best sign of good faith, I told myself. But, we'd see who got killed if anyone tried to fire the thing.

The light was improving moment by moment. Standing just outside the colonnade, there was Timothy's unmistakeable bulk and possibly Leander beside him. I stretched as far forward as I could without putting any weight on the stuccoed brick. The compact and still masses of what could only be the city guard were reassuring. They blocked movement each way along the Triumphal Way. We'd agreed that the mob would be allowed to gather within limits. Anyone else would be turned back. Once the signal was given, both wings of the guard would press forward and let people out a few at a time. Doing this, they'd nab everyone they could identify from the list Eunapius had finally supplied.

A big hand took hold of my belt and pulled me back a few inches. 'Can't have you falling over,' Samo said in Latin. Antonia laughed nervously. Best not to argue. I turned back to looking at what was happening below. In their usual place, the ladders were being set up. I couldn't see the seditionaries. But Alexius was somewhere close by, getting his mask right with a recitation of one of the prayers for Easter.

With a final look at the sky, I jumped down from the chair and smiled at the senior men of the household. 'Gentlemen,' I said, also in Latin, 'let me go through the arrangements one more time.' A boy, who seemed to have turned decidedly pretty since my last sight of him, poked a wine cup at me. I gave him a very warm smile and sipped at the contents. As I'd ordered, it was laced with what I hoped was a strong stimulant. Priscus hadn't been in his quarters when I got back, so I'd sniffed at each small bottle in his collection till I found something that smelled just right. I hoped it was. After a sleepless night, I wanted to keep awake – not have to keep telling myself that the troll and witches and dead relatives dancing about me weren't actually there. I sipped again and felt my nose begin to itch. A couple of the bigger slaves were taller than me. I got back on the chair, and looked at the small and silent crowd. I looked harder in the fading gloom. I frowned. 'Where is Theodore?' I asked.

'He was praying in the chapel,' a boy called out from the back of the crowd. I frowned again. I'd seen candles burning away in the chapel before we took our hit from the catapult. Could the fathead have been in there all night? It wouldn't be the first time in the past week. I sighed. Why couldn't he pray in the daylight like everyone else? Wasn't that supposed to be God's first gift to the world? It was certainly free – unlike wax candles. But I composed myself. So long as Timothy continued to see his own best interest and was able to re-impose order on the streets, this was all set up to be a glorious day. I looked at Antonia. She set off another of those warm feelings inside me. Or perhaps it was the stimulant. I could feel I'd picked right among those unmarked bottles.

I cleared my throat and looked in the direction of the boy who'd spoken. 'Go and tell Theodore that I want him up here at once,' I said. 'Tell him it's an order.' While the boy took a short cut across the roof tiles, I cleared my throat again and began with the main business. 'In a few moments, Samo will go down to the room above the main gate. There, he will await the shouted signal from young Eboric.' I glowered at the little blond stunner. 'Eboric will watch for the agreed signal outside. At its first appearance, he *must* run from my office, downstairs to the entrance hall. Samo will then pull the lever that raises the portcullis.' I put on a look of grim mastery. '*Do you both understand?*' Samo sniffed nonchalantly. Eboric smiled sweetly. I focused on Samo. Though barely able to get up to the roof without a wheezing attack, he had great static strength. Apart from me, he was the only man in the building able to set in movement the geared monster that would pull up a ton and a half of iron as if it were another gross of candles for Theodore. He looked almost sober. I'd have to trust him. I nodded to him and he began slouching off towards the exit from the roof. He stopped short of the open hatch to hear out the rest of what I had to say.

'Once the portcullis is up,' I went on, 'we'll hear the first reading of my proclamation. Among much else, this will order the crowd to disperse. After that, and while much of the crowd is still present, the City Prefect will walk alone to the foot of the steps and wait for the gate to swing open.' I paused to settle a nervous tremor I could feel making its way into my voice. 'The gate is already secured by a single bolt. I will open it myself and walk out alone to embrace the Prefect. It will be all the evidence the assembled witnesses need to show the restoration of concord among the higher classes of the City.' I paused again. I looked at faces that had turned surly. I waited for someone to finish interpreting my words for those slaves whose working language wasn't Latin. 'Some risk is unavoidable,' I said firmly. 'Of course, you will remain in arms behind the gate, ready to give such help as may be required. And I will remind you that, until further notice, the public areas of the palace will be closed to everyone you don't know by name or face.'

Panting slightly, the boy messenger was back. 'Begging pardon, My Lord,' he trilled, 'but Master Theodore won't leave the chapel. He says the Devil is abroad in the palace, and that he must finish praying for all our souls.'

Bloody idiot! I thought. But I had only myself to blame. I should never have indulged his taste for theology. Those ghastly books had turned his mind. 'Then let him stay with his icons,' I said heavily. 'He has neither civil nor military function in this morning's proceedings.' Yes, let him stay down there babbling to his ever-more disordered imagination. His sour face would only damp our own spirits.

'I'll go and get him,' Antonia broke in. 'I'll tell him it's his duty to behold the triumph of good over evil. That should bring him up here.' I nodded, hoping she wouldn't be too long. This was, after all, as much her triumph as mine. I stood down from the chair and watched her pass through the little crowd. No one could have called Antonia sweet by nature. Neither was she stupid. She'd seen her father's household management and she'd seen mine. I knew the slaves had all been wondering what sort of wife I'd finally bring home. Now, as she went out of sight, every face turned back in my direction showed something between liking and adoration.

And now the sun was up. Spreading jagged shadows over the roof tiles, it heralded the beginning of our triumph. It was Monday again – another petitioning day. Today's petitioners, plus those stood over from the previous week, would make a backlog to add to all the others. Before making my way back from Nicetas to the Great Sewer, I'd pulled one of my chief clerks out of bed. Sooner or later this day, my people would turn up with a wagonload of official business. Dealing with all my routine work and going through everything Nicetas had allowed to pile up – and sorting out and covering up matters as agreed with Timothy – would need more than a few drops of stimulant.

But we'd won. I stared right at the tall victory column. There were no archers positioned on its viewing platform. Perhaps I should have been less cautious and put myself and the rest of the audience on one of the balconies. I watched and waited. Moment by moment rising higher, the sun broke suddenly into the Triumphal Way. Its first shaft of light struck the gilded pinnacle of the monument. It was the agreed signal to start proceedings. Timothy bounced lightly over to the catapult and raised his arms for attention. Everyone round him looked across the road to my main gate.

The gilded pinnacle was gleaming like a beacon. Still waiting, I willed the sound of our own response. It came just as I was thinking to hurry downstairs to see what was causing the delay. With a dull roar and much clanking of gears and iron, the portcullis went up. Timothy gave his orders. Men raced off in both directions and disappeared under cover of the colonnade. The seditionaries in their masks came from somewhere that had been out of my sight and climbed slowly up their ladders.

'My dearest friend, Alexius,' Constans opened with much buzzing, following by a complete loss of sound. He reached up with his free hand and nudged his mask into place. 'O Alexius, such news have I been given to relay to the brave and formidable Roman People who are gathered here about us.' Carefully balancing himself, he reached down to his belt and produced a standard sheet of papyrus. He turned his head to stare at the front wall of my palace – I supposed the recess of its gateway and the bronze gate were to act as an additional reflector – and raised his voice.

'In the name of Heraclius, Caesar, Augustus, Faithful in Christ, to the Senate and People of Rome,' he boomed. 'Let all who are present hear and obey the wishes of the Ruler of the Universe, ordained by God.' So, to increasingly depressed incredulity, he read out my instructions to the City. It was a long text, bulked out with formulaic utterances designed more to impress than enlighten, and with repetitions of the main points that you must have in anything intended for reading out to the common people. The sun was already on the marble of the victory column when Constans finished. He'd been heard in silence. The silence continued after he'd finished.

324

It was broken by Alexius: 'I think, dearest Constans, that we speak as one when I say that we have never wished anything for His Magnificence the Lord Senator Alaric but the greatest and most unending continuation of good fortune. Moreover, the Lord Nicetas is himself blessed when he blesses . . .'

Alexius had been waving his arms about to show how he was warming to his theme. A sudden scraping sound from far beneath where I stood had him clutching the top of his ladder. Ignoring the remains of my sunburn, and the possibility of another break in the wall, I leaned forward as far as I could. I managed to catch sight of Timothy's sideways scuttle.

Rado saved me the trouble of speaking. 'Someone's opened the main gate, Master,' he cried.

With the reading of the proclamation, the crowd had parted like the Red Sea, leaving a wide space between the front steps of my palace and the colonnade on the other side of the Triumphal Way. Both wings of the crowd now edged further back and I saw some of the men in better clothing turn and push their way out of it.

Oh, fuck me – it was Theodore! 'Behold the Horn of Babylon!' he called out in his highest and most demented voice. 'Behold and fear the earthly symbol of all satanic power!' Before I could draw back and dash for the stairs, he came in sight. Dressed in a white gown too long for him, a withered olive wreath on his head, he stumbled forward, holding up the box, within which the silver cup glittered in the reflected light of the sun.

'Go from this place, my people, lest you too be accursed – lest your souls too be lost to the powers of darkness.'

Still unseen, Antonia's voice rang out: 'Come back, you bloody fool. Can't you see, you're spoiling everything?' She rushed forward into sight. She stepped on to the long trail of Theodore's robe and put her arms about him. They went down together.

With a long roar of terror and rage, both sides of the crowd streamed forward. They came together again, and Antonia and Theodore were lost within its joining.

49

Sitting here in Canterbury, I can tell you the route I must have taken. I'd have hurried along the central well of the roof to the doorway and the stairs down. These led to an unlit corridor lined with closed doors, each of which gave access to its own labyrinth of attic rooms. From here, it was more stairs – not the grand staircases, with side ramps for carrying chairs, for the use of persons of quality, but dozens of narrow flights, designed to get slaves up and down with the least delay. From the bottom of the flight painted red, it was another long corridor, past the domestic administration of the palace, to a heavy door, wooden on my side, sheathed with bronze on the side of the entrance hall.

I can describe the likely journey from the roof. But I can't remember taking it. The first I do recall is hacking the raised arm off one of the intruders who'd seen his chance of loot once through the wide open main gate. His screams added to the general pandemonium of noise and fighting all about me. It looked – and smelled – as if a whole army of the rotting, reanimated dead had streamed in through the gate. And more were trying to get in. The gate was blocked by them. Though pushed from behind, those in front were held back for the moment by Samo. Just inside the gate, he was bawling war songs and laying madly about with his broadsword. There were already bodies and body parts piling up at his feet.

Eyes blazing, bloody sword in hand, Rado crashed into me. 'We can't get to her, Master,' he shouted. He pointed at the blocked gate, then turned to slash at someone who was trying to pull the gilt scroll from one of the statues. I tried to shake some sense into my drugged mind. How had Rado and everyone else got down here so fast? I was sure I'd left him behind on the roof. I gripped hard on my sword and prepared to charge at the gate and cut my way through.

From behind me, there was a sudden scream of many voices. I turned to see the kitchen women and maidservants stream into the hall. All of them armed, all of them probably thinking of their dead menfolk from when they were taken as slaves, they hurled themselves into battle with the Greek intruders. It was less a battle than a slaughter. With them advancing down the hall like a phalanx of harpies, there was no chance the palace would be taken by storm.

I stabbed someone in the guts when he ran at me. I got some-one else in the bladder. I jumped on to a statue plinth that I think had been kept vacant for Priscus when he died, and slapped the blade of my sword three times against a bronze torch bracket. 'All able-bodied men in formation behind me,' I shouted in the comparative silence that followed. 'We're going outside!' I stepped down and waved my sword threateningly at those in the gateway who were still turned in my direction.

I gave a quick inspection to my little army. You'd never have thought they were slaves – no, not even the epicene youth who spent much of his time shrilling over mixtures of depilation wax. Every one of us a marauding barbarian again, we raised our swords and let out the battle roars of our various races.

I heard a discordantly high voice among the shouting. I looked for and pointed at Eboric. 'Not you!' I barked. 'You're far too young.' Rado gave him a rough push away from the group. He sat down cross-legged beside a man I'd seen him kill and began to cry.

I took a step forward. 'Kill only if you have to,' I remembered to shout as we picked up speed. Of course, I'd heard similar exhorta-tions from the Church, when handing over heretics to the civil authorities. Mine had exactly the same effect on the blood-frenzied mob that followed me against the wall of trapped and terrified humanity. We hit with something like the impact of a drunkard deflowering a virgin.

*   *   *

327

Trying not to slip in the blood I was shedding, I forced my way to the foot of the steps. I looked about for the last place I'd seen Antonia and pushed on alone into the crowd. I pushed and punched and kicked and prodded. I could guess that the city guard was pressing forward from both directions. Everyone intent on loot was already inside the palace. Those I was now pushing through were, for the most part, more frightened than hostile. A gap opened before me. I don't know if it closed behind.

'Antonia!' I bellowed in a voice as terrifying as my strong right arm. 'Antonia, where are you?' I felt a sudden pricking against my right side and turned in time to rake my attacker across his throat. Spraying blood, he fell back against a monk, whose arms were raised in terror and in prayer. Clutched at by the dying man, the monk went down, and his warning cries to those stepping on him were lost among the general clamour. Swept sideways by a collective shudder within the crowd, I tried and failed to reach out to him. I saw him get to his knees and go down again. My heart beat still faster and black spots came in front of my eyes. I tried to work out where I'd last seen Antonia tangled up with Theodore. It must have been somewhere now behind me. But I could no longer turn. As if held in the arms of a dancing giant, I was moving further and further away from where I wanted to be.

The crowd thinned out as I came in sight of the catapult. I stumbled forward. 'Where is she?' I shouted at its scared operator. He opened his mouth to scream and tripped forward over the tightened bowstring. I had enough sense to throw myself forward as it finally snapped. I heard its high singing tone a few feet overhead and its return, and the dull thud of wooden arms into the dense crowd of fools who'd thought there was safety beside those stretched torsion springs. Ignoring the shrieks of the injured and dying, I scrambled back to my feet and killed a man who might simply have tripped over me. I killed another man who came at me with a length of wood. I killed yet another who was standing in my way. Like a man who cuts his way through brambles, I pushed forward to where I was sure I'd heard a woman screaming. I must have passed through the oncoming city guard, but have no recollection of doing so.

It was Simon who was driving the wagon. He looked round at my bawled challenge. Laughing like a madman, he turned back to raise his whip. I lifted my sword and darted forward. One of his men squealed something and scrambled backward in the wagon. Laughing as madly as Simon, the other man lifted something dark and very large and swung it over the tail of the wagon. Once again, I can't remember the exact sequence of events. Thrown at me like that, the dead Treasury clerk should not only have thrown me backwards, but also dashed my brains out on the paving stones. Instead, I somehow landed on top of the squelching body and was back on my feet almost at once. I had to unhook my sword from where it had gone into the chest cavity. But I was soon racing forward again and wondering how I could best jump on to its tail. Though the rest of her was out of sight behind a crate, I'd seen Antonia's legs kicking away like a hanged man.

I ignored the hail of correspondence scrolls and leather satchels thrown out at me. I ignored how, bouncing up and down with joy, the man who'd heaved the body at me now reached out, showing the wooden box and the cup within it. 'Stop, or I'll have you flayed alive!' I roared. I was running continually faster to keep up with the quickening pace of the horses. But I was just a few feet away from leaping on to the tail of the wagon, sword in hand to hack at anyone who tried to stop me. Simon looked round again. He shouted an order in Syriac and box and cup were pulled out of sight. Straight after, both men set hands on the big crate and pitched that at me.

I had to throw myself sharp right to get out of its way. The crate bounced once past me on the hard paving stones, and again. On its third landing, it burst, sending papyrus sheets in every direction. I looked against my will at the slithering, disarranging heap of Treasury correspondence. I was far from the screaming mob outside my palace and, my breathing aside and the pounding of my heart, the main sound on a completely empty Triumphal Way was Simon's continued and maniacal laughter as he plied the whip and the horses picked up more speed.

Now the crate was gone, I could see everything. 'Don't follow us, dear boy!' Timothy called back at me. He clutched Antonia harder against his vast front, a knife at her throat. 'Stay where you are – that is, if you don't want me to saw the little tart's head off her shoulders.' He laughed theatrically and was joined by a chorus of laughs and obscenities in Greek and Syriac.

My heart was pounding now like a brothel drum. I couldn't move. But I put what little strength I could find into my voice. 'You can't get away with this,' I shouted.

'I can and will, my fine young savage,' Timothy called happily across the increasing distance between us. He put his knee into Antonia's back so she reared up again and screamed. 'Lady Fate has slipped me a better deal than you had in mind. If you ever want to see her again in one piece, the whore is our passport out of the City.' He watched me raise my sword and take a step forward. 'I've warned you,' he shouted with another pull at Antonia. 'Don't follow us.'

The wagon was thirty yards away and still picking up speed. It was moving almost as fast as I could run. Another few moments and it would vanish behind the Belisarius Memorial. Someone plucked at my sleeve. I pulled away and spun round, sword raised to strike.

Leander fell down and clutched at my ankles. 'My Lord,' he babbled, 'please, My Lord, don't kill me.' I turned back to see what I could of the wagon. It had now gone out of sight. Faint sounds of rejoicing drifted back. They merged in with the continuing riot and probable slaughter far behind me. My domestics weren't up to producing that volume of noise. The city guard must have weighed into the chaos. When in doubt, massacre had ever been their maxim. My legs gave way and I sat heavily in the middle of the road. The sun still slanted from the east, leaving tall shadows all about and a faint chill in the air. It couldn't have been a quarter of a summer's hour from when I was looking complacently down from my roof, to the completion of a horror that hadn't yet impressed itself fully on my mind. I fought off the urge to bury my face in my hands and looked stupidly round. The Treasury clerks who must have been following me along the road, had caught up. Some of them were lamenting over the murdered body of their colleague. Others were hard at work, gathering up scrolls and loose sheets for heaping up before the statue of Cicero.

I looked up at Leander. One sight of his twitching face, and I pulled myself together. 'Can you tell me where they've gone?' I asked. Covered in blood, a man ran past me. Another, who seemed to have limped his way out of the massacre, fell against the colonnade. He slid down, leaving bloody trails from his hands on the marble, and was still. I got Leander's attention by raking my sword on the paving stones. 'Where have they gone?' I asked in a voice that I couldn't stop from trailing off in despair.

'I overheard someone say there was a Persian ship in the Kontoskalion Harbour,' he answered after as great an effort as my own to keep his voice steady. 'How can there be Persian ships *anywhere*. Are they besieging us?'

I silenced him with an impatient wave. I thought. The Kontoskalion was the smallest of the harbours facing south. It opened on to the juncture of the straits and the Propontis. It made sense that Shahin had put in there. It was naturally sheltered and needed no bar to protect it – or to be shut against outgoing vessels. Driving his stolen wagon, Simon would need to turn off long before the Central Milestone and go past the law courts, down a bumpy incline. From there, it would be a quick ride through a road that bisected another poor district. He and his could be onboard with Shahin before I could get there with help. Even starting now, I'd have to run to get there in time.

I got up slowly and leaned for support on Leander. I put all active thoughts of Antonia firmly out of mind. Giving way to horror and despair wouldn't make me run any faster. I pointed back along the road. 'Go and tell any captain of the guard you can find where I've gone,' I said. I shook my head at his scared face. 'I want as many armed men down there as can be spared.' I pushed him in the chest. 'Go!' I shouted. I controlled my voice. 'Explain yourself to anyone in uniform,' I added. 'He won't hurt you.'

I sheathed my sword. Behind the ceremonial façade of the Saint Evagrius Monastery, there was a stepped alley leading down to the ruins of an old bathing complex. From here, I'd have to keep the sun as my guide through the courtyards of a poor district I'd never yet entered.

I lost my bet on our relative speeds. Knocking two of my own harbour officials out of the way, I ran along the docks and then to the end of the stone jetty. 'Stop that ship!' I shouted at no one in particular. I looked at Shahin. From across ten yards of water, he stared placidly back.

'Accept, my beautiful Alaric, that you've lost on this occasion,' he called out in Persian. 'Now, here's the best deal you'll get. So long as no one follows us, the girl stays alive. Once I no longer need her, you get her back alive. Can I say fairer than that?' He clapped his hands. Naked, a rope once more about her neck, Antonia was forced out on deck. She opened her mouth to cry out to me but a rag was stuffed between her teeth. Shahin ordered his men to pull her back inside. He leaned forward over the rail of the departing ship. 'Do as I say and you will see her alive again.' Unable to do otherwise, I fell to my knees and stretched out my arms to the departing ship. Shahin laughed and slapped both hands on the rail. 'And remember,' he jeered, 'we Persians *always* keep our promises – did not the Great King tell you that himself?' He put up a hand to cover his mouth. 'Go home, Alaric, and count off the days till your bright reunion by impaling the Greekling conspirators against your Lord and Master Heraclius. I'm sure you have a complete list of them.'

He took out a napkin and waved it in mock farewell. Timothy came out of the deck cabin and, waving, stood beside him. They spoke to each other and rocked back and forth with laughter. The oars splashed more insistently on the silvery waters and I watched the ship move slowly out of the unguarded harbour. Out in the open sea, its sail came down with a gentle crash. Still kneeling, arms still outstretched, I watched until it vanished in to the disc of the still-rising sun.

'I've orders from the Prefect to arrest you, Sir,' someone said behind me.

Not getting up, I twisted round. Swords at the ready, the two harbour guards were stood well away from me. I closed my eyes in a supreme effort of will not to fall apart. I pointed at the other men streaming through the harbour gate. 'If you speak with the city guard,' I said with a composure that startled me, 'you'll discover the true state of affairs.' I closed my eyes again. 'This being the case, I want the Harbour Master here at his earliest opportunity.'

'You fucking bastard!' old Simeon shouted in my face. 'Was this what you were planning all along?' He waved at the dense thicket of the dead who covered the Triumphal Way. Sobbing quietly, relatives and friends of the fallen searched and poked among the bodies. They disturbed the usual million flies that had emerged from nowhere and kept back the hungry dogs. But amid the wreckage of so much life, normality was already returning to Constantinople. Not looking about, scented cloths pressed to their faces, men hurried past the dead about their business.

As calm as any man can be who's bruised all over and covered in dried blood, I stepped away from Simeon. He'd lost a shoe in the panic and was still clutching a placard that said 'Death to the Pension-Stealing, Yellow-Haired Bastard Alaric!' Other than that, he'd come rather well through the massacre. Perhaps there were some too old and useless even for the city guard to think it worth killing. Avoiding the main patches of setting blood, I walked over to the catapult. I'd heard it go, but paid no attention to its effects. Tucked away somewhere in my head, there was a formula that would tell me how many thousand pounds of force the torsion springs had given each six-foot arm of the catapult. No need for calculations, however. Swarming with more of those bastard flies, the dead lay about like heaps of smashed and twisted statuary – statuary mixed in with the waste from a butcher's market.

Simeon tugged at my sleeve. 'My youngest boy is in there,' he cried in an old man's voice that no longer accused anyone of anything. 'I can't pull him out.' He sat down in the mess and wept.

Drained of energy, I sat down beside him and thought what to say. My drug had long since worn off. The weariness now hit me with the force of that dead Treasury clerk. I put a hand on his shoulder. 'Listen, Simeon,' I said, 'go home and wait. I'll publish an amnesty towards the end of today. Until then, your placard will only get you into trouble. Go home and come out again this evening. The dead will all be laid out in the Prefecture building. You can collect your son from there.' I noticed we were sitting a couple of feet from one of the ladders the seditionaries had been using. Its pine rungs were splashed with blood. 'I'm sorry for your loss,' I said quietly.

'It's the Master!' someone shouted behind me. I got slowly to my feet and turned. It was Rado, leading a half dozen of my armed slaves. I could guess they'd gone off to look for me before Leander could get back with the news of where I was. Covered in blood and dust, they steadied themselves and gave the universal barbarian salute of sorrowful triumph.

It was Samo who got to me first. He'd looked out of the palace at the noise. Now, a body under each arm, he lumbered towards me. Eboric danced beside him, a severed head in his hands. 'Master!' Samo cried – 'Master, we can't find her anywhere!' I fell into his outstretched arms. At last, I felt some shred of comfort. It broke through the iron grip I'd taken on myself and I found myself crying and crying as if I'd never stop.

50

'Don't blame me, Alaric,' Priscus said indignantly. 'I was out all night – *and* in your service. I disabled the catapult for you. I covered you all the way to your meeting with Nicetas and watched you come out arm in arm with Cousin Timothy. You didn't notice but I killed five men last night – *five* men, mind you, and every one of them out to get you. When am I supposed to have found time for dressing up and scaring silly Theodore completely out of his wits?'

Anyone else would have had a point. Not Priscus, though. I continued staring at him across my office desk. High on something else from his box of potions, I'd sealed every arrest warrant and given every order needed to retake control of the City. Now, as the sun was losing its power, Priscus was out of bed and ready for the argument I'd so far tried to keep out of mind.

I scraped my chair back and gave him the look of a man invested with absolute power. 'If Theodore tells me he saw a demon in the chapel, or an angel, or Jesus Christ himself, we can agree he was deluded. However, he's claiming he saw a figure dressed in black, who told him where the secret cupboard was, and how to get it open, and then to take its contents out of the palace. I'll grant that everything else that happened was beyond even your control and that you knew nothing about my deal with Timothy. But, unless you can tell me who *did* appear to the boy, you'll pardon me for blaming you.'

Priscus shook his head sadly. 'It was meant to be, Alaric,' he said. 'Didn't I tell you about the powers of the cup? It's no accident it went out of your possession just as the seven days were coming to an end. You really should think yourself lucky. Shame about the girl, though, I'll freely admit.'

I stood up, disordering a stack of draft proclamations for the next day. 'You can stop wittering about that fucking cup,' I snarled. I walked quickly over to another stack of papyrus and reached under it. I never had put the box properly together. The prised off side had remained separate throughout the past few days. Now, I held it up for inspection. 'I was wondering why a box otherwise so elegant was only painted to look like ebony.' I pushed it close to Priscus. 'Look what I found underneath when I scraped the paint off.'

He took it and tried to read the writing in the advancing gloom. It was very small and covered both sides of the slat. 'It's letters and numbers and fractions,' he said defensively. He brightened a little. 'Astrological incantations,' he added. 'They must have been put there when Heraclius ordered a box for the cup. You know what he's like.'

I raised a hand to silence him. 'Look again, dear Priscus,' I said. This latest drug was one of his happier discoveries. It abolished tiredness and had left me with a clear and even moderately serene mind. Priscus could see nothing, so I took the slat away from him and carried it across to the window and squinted at what I'd been able to reveal of the underlying script. You can ask why I hadn't thought of this earlier. The scraped underside of the box must have shown something, had I only turned my attention away from what it contained. Knowing what really mattered would have simplified everything. Too late for that, however. I thought of the bleak sentence in Thucydides: 'When error is irreparable, repentance is useless.'

Unmoving in his chair, Priscus looked down at the floor. I stood over him. 'The names of towns and places are given in a substitution cipher,' I took up again. 'I'm sure you can break it in your head. The coordinates are given in plain text, and refer to a map that may be indicated, though not drawn, on another part of the box. The numbers after that ought to be clear to someone of your experience.' I stopped and pointed at random. 'So what do you suppose this means: "Hilltop fort"; such and such coordinates; "two hundred and thirty"? Or look at this: "Cordyle" – a city, you

336

may be aware, on the far south-eastern coast of the Black Sea – no coordinates needed or given; "three hundred". Could the whole box possibly contain a listing of the location and numbers of every military unit engaged in defending the Home Provinces from invasion? Don't ask me why Heraclius chose to have his cup surrounded by a listing that every officer in the Persian army would give his right hand to see. But he did. And ten sides of that listing are currently on a Persian ship sailing east. I don't doubt the cup itself means something to our Lord and Master – I might guess it was meant to give protection to the named forces he wanted to enclose it. The cup may have some meaning to Chosroes. But do you really think a man like Shahin would risk himself in our home waters – and inside the City – for a lump of silver?

'If it was you whispering in Theodore's ear, how does it feel to be the man who may have done for Shahrbaraz what Ariadne's ball of string did for Theseus? With that listing in their hands, they can pick off every defensive position in the Home Provinces. Or they can bypass them and, within three months, be looking across the straits at the City walls. You don't need me to tell you how fast an offensive army can move – or how slowly defence plans can be changed and communicated in an orderly fashion. Would you say, Priscus, we were very fucked, or only fucked? Are you still proud of yourself, O former Commander of the East?'

There was a knock on the door. I stepped away from Priscus so he could hurry behind his usual screen. It was Samo – drunker than usual and more glowering – together with the Deputy Head of the Intelligence Bureau and one of his junior subordinates. The Deputy Head gave me a perfunctory bow, before sliming his way towards the chair that Priscus had just vacated. He was a large man and plainly looking forward to a rest after the long climb to my office. I continued standing.

I picked up a sheet of papyrus and spent long enough reading it for the man to begin fidgeting. The subordinate stared impassively at a painting of Demosthenes. I decided on the tone to adopt and put the sheet face down on my desk. 'In the past few days,' I began coldly to the Deputy Head, 'three facts have come to my attention. The first is a conspiracy, led by the City Prefect and involving several dozen members of the Senate, against Our Lord the Emperor. The second is the unopposed presence within the City of the admiral appointed by the Great King to defend the coastal regions of his Syrian conquests. The third is your own total inaction in the face of these connected threats to the security of the Empire. A fourth, and possibly more serious, fact is your apparent failure to maintain our espionage links in Ctesiphon and the alienated provinces. Have you anything to say in your own defence?'

What he made was a piss-poor defence. Leave aside the misprision of treason charge he deserved – anyone in his office with an ounce of competence would already have known that Nicetas was in the clear. I'd stood over him all through lunch, dictating the terms of our continuing deal. Blaming him was as useless as blaming one of the victory columns. A better defence would have involved full disclosure of what information the Bureau had gathered. It could have at least supplemented my own sources.

I put up a hand for silence. 'You are convicted out of your own mouth,' I said with calm menace. 'I could order your execution on the spot as an accessory to treason. Instead, I find you guilty only of gross negligence. I dismiss you from your position and cancel your pension. I exile you to Ragusa on the Adriatic coast. There, if the barbarians do not take the city and kill or enslave you, I appoint you to the lowest grade in the tax inspectorate. You may rejoice in your continued possession of life and in the employment of your talents in a position to which they may be better suited.'

And that was the end of a man who'd been getting on my tits for two years. I glared him into silence and turned to his subordinate. 'You, John of Salerno,' I said in his native Latin, 'are now Deputy Head of the Intelligence Bureau.' To add to the drama and the show of absolute power, I picked up his sealed notice of appointment and handed it to him. 'I have been made aware of your abilities and your zeal, and have no doubt you will justify your unprecedented advancement through five grades.' His answer was to fall to his knees and kiss my ring. An Italian among Greeks, a closet devotee of the Old Faith, promoted wildly out of turn, and by another outsider whose fall would put an end to his own career – yes, I could reasonably trust John of Salerno to remember who'd put the olive paste on his bread. I'd missed those daily reports from the Bureau. I'd now made sure not to be without them again.

I turned back to the disgraced Deputy Head. 'Don't blubber about the Emperor,' I said with chilly contempt. 'For all practical purposes, I currently *am* the Emperor. There is no appeal from what I have decided. Be grateful I've booked you a place on the dispatch galley to Syracuse that leaves tomorrow morning. If you aren't on it, your replacement will take such action as he may think appropriate.'

There was nothing else to be said. I waved both men out of my presence and walked over to the window. I looked down to the Triumphal Way. Now the last daylight had faded, it was again a sea of torches – this time, though, the torches of those whose job it was to scrub and sweep for as long as it took to remove all trace of the recent disorders. As promised, the bodies were all laid out for identification and collection in the Prefecture. With named exceptions, my amnesty was in place and no further enquiries would be made of what the dead had been doing outside my palace. I was no Creon by nature. My policy was to avoid any chance of a modern Antigone. Heraclius would come home to a City cleaned up and at peace.

I closed the office door and went back to my desk. 'If you don't mind an old man's judgement,' Priscus called uncertainly from behind his screen, 'that was a masterful stroke. You've put yourself straight back on top of the pecking order.' I said nothing. He shuffled over to his chair and poured himself a cup of wine. 'It wasn't just the fucking, was it?' he asked with a sudden firming of tone. 'Nor was it the chance of getting into the Imperial Family. Does the girl really mean something to you?'

I looked at Demosthenes and waited for the pain that had broken through the drugs and the wall of self-control to crawl away again. It was for dark little Greeks, swarming in streets built by their ancestors, to wail and rend their garments when faced with disorders of the spirit. For Alaric of Britain – no, for *Aelric of England* – it should always be a stiff upper lip. 'She is to be my wife,' I said once I was sure my voice wouldn't tremble.

Priscus drank his wine. 'You have set a trail on Shahin?' he asked quietly.

I shook my head. 'Everything that could keep up with his ship is with the rest of the fleet in Cyzicus.' I reached for another heap of documents and pulled out a listing of the forces available. 'Heraclius has left the City undefended by sea. We haven't even enough city guards to spare for sending a dozen fast riders to alert the coastal cities.'

'She is a member of the Imperial Family,' Priscus reminded me. 'It's an ancient rule between us and the Persians that members of each ruling family are treated well. Who was that Emperor who was captured by the Persians three hundred and odd years ago? I'm told he was treated very well.'

'It was Valerian,' I answered automatically. 'According to one account I read, King Shapur had molten gold poured down his throat. Another account I read in Ctesiphon says he was flayed alive, and his skin was stuffed with straw and set up as an ornament in the Great King's bedroom.'

There was a long silence. One of the lamps was running low on oil and I watched the shadow of my own wine cup flicker against the wall. Priscus gave a long sigh. 'The box is important,' he said. 'But we're talking about contingency on contingency here. The Persians have always been crap when it comes to gathering intelligence. You may be assuming too much about Shahin's knowledge. Otherwise, you have to assume the Persian General Staff will believe the box isn't a clever trap. Beyond that, Chosroes will need to be persuaded to call off his planned invasion of Egypt – *and* that his armies can march through the Home Provinces, *and* that they can get across the straits, *and* that an absolutely impregnable city, just purged of treason, will then tamely open its gates. Before any of that, you've just got yourself into a position where you control everything that Heraclius hears. The box and its cup disappeared ten days ago from those who, for whatever reason, had it in their possession. That's all he needs to be told.

'Must you let a silly thing like love mess everything up?'

I didn't answer. Instead, I stood up and walked to the linen map of the Empire still spread out on the office floor. I pointed at the Black Sea coast. 'Shahin is cautious,' I said. 'He won't put in anywhere west of Trebizond. But his ship has a draught shallow enough to put in almost anywhere. He doesn't need an actual port. The other question is which route will he take towards the zone of Persian conquest?'

Priscus was staring up at the gilded plaster on the ceiling. 'You'll never catch up with him,' he said flatly. 'Even starting tomorrow – and even knowing his route – you'll be days behind him. You'll be days behind him by ship, that is, if he's going no further than Trebizond. As for that whole region, once you're out of the coastal plain – why, you'll be lost in no time. You'll find no reliable guides even in Trebizond, I can tell you. Unless you can come up with your own version of Ariadne's ball of string, you might as well give up on any thought of going after Shahin.' He looked steadily at me. 'My advice is to stay here. Make yourself absolutely irreplace-able to Heraclius, and wait on events. I do assure you, the Persians won't kill the girl. She's far too valuable.'

There was another knock on the door. Priscus had no time to get himself out of sight again. But it was Samo alone this time. He dropped a folded and sealed sheet of parchment in my hand, before reeling back through the door.

I broke the seal and read. 'Sergius arrived in the City just before dark,' I said. 'He begs me to attend on him and tell him what to do.' My regency was officially over. I'd have to skip another night's rest if I wanted to lay down the right course of action to His Holiness the Patriarch. But every important decision I'd taken already. Sergius would change nothing.

I went over to the door and opened it. 'You may never have thought you'd hear this from me, Priscus, 'but I have urgent need of skills in which no man living may be your equal.'

341

51

His nerve mostly recovered, Eunapius tried to smile at me across the table. 'I'm not talking to you, Alaric,' he said. 'Whatever I have to say is for the Emperor alone. Are you going to kill me? Are you going to put me on a rack? I hardly think so. You're simply not the sort for that.'

I'd taken yet another dose of stimulant. I ignored the shadows that always darted about the cellar just out of my sight, and stared at Leander. Looking scared and miserable, his face was turned down at a sheet of papyrus on which he'd so far written a date and time and our three names. I shut my eyes and rubbed the marks of strain from my face. I sat up and reached into a satchel for another sheet of papyrus, this one covered in untidy handwriting that continued beneath the seal.

'Eunapius,' I began again, 'I have in my hand a sworn denunciation from Nicetas. This and much else prove your treason beyond reasonable doubt. Heraclius will not question the written testimony of his own cousin. The longer you refuse me information that is urgently needed for the safety of the Empire, the greater will be your eventual punishment. Now, let me repeat myself – where is Shahin going with the Horn of Babylon? Where will his ship put in? And where has he agreed to meet his army of escort?'

Eunapius hawked and spat. His gob missed me and landed on one of Leander's sleeves. 'Piss off, you puffed up ball of barbarian shit!' he laughed. 'Everyone knows you're holding me and I claim the rights of my class. The moment Sergius sets foot in the City, your regency lapses. I demand safe delivery to the Patriarch and then my right of audience with the Emperor. Once he's heard what I have to tell him, your day will be over for good.'

342

I leaned forward across the table. 'I've given you every chance to answer my questions,' I said. 'I've even offered you a conditional immunity from prosecution. What I will give you now is your last chance. *Will you answer my questions?*'

'Piss off!' he said again. He looked in my face and his nerve began to drain away. 'I don't know where they've gone,' he whined. 'Shahin never told me anything. You need to question Nicetas.' He pointed at Leander. 'Why don't you ask *him*? He knows more than I do.'

I sighed and stood up. This was going in circles. Given time, I could have broken through both outright defiance and claims of ignorance. But there was no time. 'Then you give me no choice, Eunapius,' I said in sorrowful tone. I went over to an iron door. 'Will you relent?' No answer. I rapped gently against the door. I watched it grate slowly inwards and turned to see its effect on Eunapius.

He looked, blinked, and opened his mouth to scream. He tried to get up but was pushed back into his chair by Samo. 'You're dead!' he sobbed. He put his hands up to cover his eyes. 'Everyone knows you're dead!'

Lamp in hand, dressed in his favourite black, Priscus stepped out and flashed me a happy smile. 'In a manner of speaking, I *am* dead,' he answered. 'Be assured, though, I've never felt better.' He looked at Samo and spoke Latin. 'Bring him through,' he said. 'Keep tight hold of his shoulders. People often try to bash their heads in at times like this and we can't have that – can we, now?' He chuckled and held the lamp against a face that he'd painted all over with white lead.

The stairs led to a room below what I'd always taken to be the lowest level of cellars in my palace. For this reason, it was still as filthy as everything else had been when I took over from Priscus. For this reason also, it was still fitted out with the instruments of his favourite recreation.

'Don't worry that pretty young head of yours, Alaric,' he said in Latin. 'Torture is hardly ever for its own sake. I don't think we'll need any *physical* nastiness here.' He went back into Greek and waved at Leander. 'Hold the lamp closer to the traitor's face,' he cried grimly. 'Let everyone see the infamy stamped upon it.'

Priscus sat in a chair padded with cushions the damp had long since rotted. He took a long sip of wine. 'Eunapius,' he asked in his friendly voice, 'do you remember that time when Phocas the Tyrant was Emperor and I marched into your father's house with a dozen of my Black Officers?' Eunapius sagged forward, but was held tight in Samo's massive arms. Priscus smiled and took another long sip. He tapped his forehead and smiled. 'But how could you forget that day?' he asked. 'It was you who denounced your father for not cleaning a graffito promptly enough from the outer wall of his palace. It was all very embarrassing. I was drugged out of my head and arrived under the impression that your brother was the man I wanted. Anyway, do you remember what I did to young Stephen once I had him tied down naked on his bed? Do you remember how he squealed like a dying pig and how your mother fell dead from the horror of what I did? You should do. After all, you got back five-sevenths of the estate when Phocas confiscated it, and didn't have to share it with an inconveniently elder brother.

'Now, would you like me to do to you what I did to poor Stephen? Or shall we be civilised men of the world? Look at that nice clean sheet of papyrus our poet has brought down with him. One way or another, we all know, it will soon be covered with every answer that young Alaric wants. Shall I pour you a cup of this lovely red wine? It might help the distressing hoarseness that I shan't blame your voice for having acquired?'

Eunapius let out a loud fart before shitting himself. The cold air took on a smell of inward bodily decay. 'Don't let him touch me, Alaric!' he shouted. He twisted to get free of Samo and managed half a step in my direction. 'I'll tell you everything.'

'That's the spirit!' Priscus cried. At his little desk, Leander controlled his hands sufficiently to lift a pen.

Eunapius ran his tongue over dry lips. 'Before I say anything, though,' be babbled, 'I want Alaric to swear that I'll walk out of here alive and that I shan't be harmed in any way. I'll tell you where Shahin's taken the girl. I'll tell you what he's planning with the magic cup. But I want Alaric's spoken promise in front of you all.'

Priscus frowned and got slowly up from his chair. He went across to a filthy curtain and pulled it down to show an old cartwheel fixed to the wall. He nodded to Samo, who dragged Eunapius round to see it. 'Silly young Alaric is no longer in charge of this interrogation,' he said in a voice I well recalled from his days of glory. 'You had your chance. We're now following *my* rules.'

Priscus sat down again. He sipped delicately at his wine. 'Did you ever watch a man broken on the wheel?' he asked. 'I don't suppose you've had that pleasure. Even old Phocas had limits to what he'd let me do in public. But I've seen it done quite often by the Avars when they want to make an example of one of their prisoners. It's ever so cheap and simple, you see. Even barbarians can't mess it up.' He got up, wine cup still in his hand. He walked slowly over to the wheel. 'See these straps here?' he asked. 'The purpose is to spread you naked on the wheel, arms and legs apart. Once you're in place, that drunken ox of a freedman will take up the hammer that you should be able to see just beside the wheel. He'll start by smashing your ankles – one or two blows on the bones of greatest sensitivity. If that doesn't loosen your tongue, he'll move to your wrists, and then your knees and elbows. Your hips and shoulders will be the final horror.

'And, Eunapius, don't suppose it will be other than horrible. Forget burning alive, or hooked gloves, or even the bite of a starved hyena. Breaking on the wheel produces the most staggering and continuous pain. And you might last for days down here in the darkness. So long as the barbarian doesn't break the skin, your limbs will swell up like inflated bladders and you'll keep enough blood elsewhere to stay alive. I remember one time – it was during the great siege of Mantella, you know – when the Avars somehow laid hands on my commanding officer. Using a screen of women and children to put our archers off, they broke him a hundred yards outside the city wall.' Priscus paused for dramatic effect. He drank more wine.

'In no time at all, I saw a battle-hardened veteran turned into a sort of huge screaming puppet writhing in rivulets of blood – a puppet with four tentacles, like a sea monster, of raw, slimy and shapeless flesh mixed up with splinters of smashed bones. He was luckier than you'll be: he lost enough blood to die before the afternoon was out.' He stopped again for wine and burst into helpless giggles.

He controlled himself. 'Don't force me to do that to you,' Priscus urged. 'Why not make it easy for yourself and answer dearest Alaric's questions. He won't let me hurt you after that.'

The threat was enough. Between screams of terror and more farting, out rolled the details of Shahin's plan. In the brief intervals of silence, I heard the steady scratching of Leander's reed pen on papyrus. Before the confession was over, he'd filled one sheet and was halfway down another.

'Anything more to add?' Priscus asked after it was over.

'Don't hurt me – please!' Eunapius sobbed.

Priscus laughed. 'I promised our fastidious young Light from the West that I'd lay hands on you only when all else had failed. You must appreciate, however, that your last chance of really civilised treatment vanished when he called me in. You told me yourself that I was dead. We can't have anyone around to disabuse the world of that belief – can we, now?' He got up again, a lead cosh in his hand. One blow to the right temple and Eunapius sagged dead in Samo's arms. He dropped to the floor and lay with his eyes still glittering in the lamplight.

Priscus turned in my direction. 'I know I've often disgusted you, dear boy,' he said with a smirk that cracked the lead on his face. 'But how was that for interrogation?' He bowed and put his cosh away.

I shrugged. 'He could have avoided this,' I said evenly. Treading carefully to avoid the patches of damp filth, I went and looked down at the body. I turned to Samo. 'Have it dumped in one of the flower beds down the road,' I said. 'Complain to the Prefecture tomorrow about the unfinished work of collection.' Samo grinned and nodded. He took the cup of wine Priscus had poured for him. They shook hands and stood together to admire their work.

I sniffed at a scented napkin and told myself again that all this could have been avoided. It was true. But you have to see things as they really are. I hadn't laid a finger on Eunapius. Even so, I'd killed him in cold blood. Had the end justified the means?

'He was telling the truth?' I asked.

Priscus laughed. 'I expected better from you than that, dear boy,' he said. He poured more wine for himself and gave the jug to Samo to finish. He sat once more in his crumbling chair. 'He told us everything that could have been learned by making a window into his soul. Whether this accords with the true state of affairs depends on whether Shahin took him fully into his confidence – and, of course, on what Shahin himself was told.'

He finished his wine and reached inside his cloak for one of his powders. I waited for him to come back to order. 'Alaric,' he started in a less patronising voice, 'I know your view of torture is that it's a game between two demented beasts – between one who enjoys inflicting pain and another who'll say anything to stop the pain. But it's far more sophisticated than that. Unless he's thick, a torturer soon gets a nose for the truth. You should think about that the next time you plague Heraclius with your ideas of abolishing the rack.'

He sniffed, then blew his nose. He stared at the remains of the powder he'd put up his nose. 'Yes, dearest Alaric, what Eunapius told us was the truth to the best of his knowledge. It's up to you to find if he was told the truth, or if the plans have been changed in the light of circumstances.

'But do accept, my dear, it's useless knowledge. Though you've learned it's the Larydia Pass they're headed for, you still can't outrun Shahin. I repeat that you'll only get lost in the mountains trying. And, if you do catch up with him, how do you expect to surprise him with the three dozen armed men he's got with him? Give up on it, my dearest. Take my word for it about Antonia and come upstairs. We can start thinking of your report to Heraclius.'

I said nothing. He frowned. 'Then you're throwing away another fine opportunity,' he sighed. 'I thought you'd learned something from that brave but lunatic mission to Ctesiphon. It

347

was only Nicetas then who wormed his way between you and the Emperor. This time, you may not be so lucky.' His voice turned cold and thoughtful. 'But we have unfinished business, don't you agree?' He turned a predatory stare on Leander. 'Dead men don't walk. If they do, none must see them.' He repeated himself in Latin for Samo's benefit. They laughed softly together.

I didn't look round, but I heard Leander fall to his knees on the cellar floor.

I stopped by the statue of Cicero and breathed in the fresh night air. Leander caught up with me. 'You didn't need to take me home, My Lord,' he wheezed. Knowing my face was in the shadow of the moon, I smiled. His hands fluttered close by my sleeve. He thought better of catching hold. 'Would My Lord like me to return to Egypt?' he asked. 'I could leave tomorrow. I could take ship to Cyprus and pick up another ship from there. I wouldn't stop in Alexandria. I'd go to Antinoopolis. I'd – I'd . . .' He trailed off into scared silence. I could hear the continual questioning in his voice. The Lord Alaric had saved him from Priscus and the wheel. Had that been simply to save the trouble of ridding the palace of two corpses? How safe was he out here in the street, with me in arms beside him?

I took a deep breath. The wreckage of the dawn had mostly been cleared away. Old Simeon might, at this moment, be in the Prefecture, raising hands in prayer over his dead son. These few hundred yards along the Triumphal Way, though, and I could almost tell myself nothing awful had happened.

I reached inside my night cloak. 'Here is your patent, Leander,' I said gently. 'Present it during the day to the Treasury Chief Clerk. After that, you need to go on the first day of every quarter to the Payment Office. There, you'll collect thirty *solidi*, or their equivalent in silver if gold is in short supply.'

He cleared his throat to speak. I put my hand on his shoulder. 'I told you I keep promises,' I said. 'I only reserve the right to vary them upwards. Now, I'll not go in with you. Nicetas might be awake in his chair and I don't fancy another meeting with him.'

I didn't look left, though I thought I'd seen a shadow flitting about in the darkness. I raised my voice. 'I don't think I need remind you of the need to keep your mouth shut for the rest of your life. But I will advise you never to go out again at night.'

'What have you done with the boy Theodore?' he asked with a sudden change of subject.

I smiled again. 'The last time I looked in on him, he was praying in the chapel,' I said. I thought of our only conversation that day. 'Beat me – kill me – burn me alive,' he'd wailed, slapping more salt into the open wounds left by the trampling of the crowd. I'd sent him away with frigid kindness. Perhaps I should have thrashed him with the scourge he'd made for himself. After all, the worst punishments are often those you heap on yourself.

I took a step forward. 'I'm leaving the City at noon tomorrow,' I said. 'I may be gone some time. Please make sure to report everything said and done by Nicetas to John of Ragusa. You'll find his office in the building that sits above the entrance to the spice market. Don't be put off when, on your first visit, you're told he doesn't exist.'

52

Rado leaned forward on his horse. 'Is your arse hurting again, Master?' he asked. I pretended not to hear him. Instead, I took advantage of the stop to look again at the dreary expanse of hills and ridges and mountains and valleys that surrounded us on every side. He waited until it was plain I'd not reply. 'You shouldn't hold the reins so tight, Master,' he added.

I put aside the groans of agony now coming from every muscle between my toes and my jaw. 'You're a free man, Rado,' I said. 'It's no longer appropriate to call me "Master". You may call me "My Lord" or use my personal name, as the preference takes you.' I tried to sound cheerful. 'You might even call me "Father".'

Not answering, he gave his horse the slightest flick of his unspurred ankle and moved forward as if the two of them were a single being. He stopped at the edge of the ravine. He looked down several thousand feet into a bank of white mist. If this was the one we'd been skirting most of the afternoon, there was a meandering stream beyond the mist. In the spring, it would be swollen to a surging torrent.

I gave up on the pretence that this was other than a stop for my benefit and climbed stiffly down from the saddle. My horse was probably more relieved than I was. He didn't collapse into a heap of unconsolable helplessness. Rado looked politely ahead. 'The pass we want is between those two mountains over there,' he said. I followed his pointed finger to a blur that may have been twenty miles away or may have been a hundred – if I knew how high we were above sea level, I'd be able to calculate the distance to the horizon. Without numbers to put through the formula, I might as well have been blind. Rado pointed again and drew a path in the air. How he could see two mountains there, or know what sort of pass ran between them, were questions I chose not to ask.

My own silence continued till it bordered on the embarrassing. 'There really are no mountains in England?' he asked once more.

'Just hills,' I repeated. Could I get away with implying that I'd spent my own barbarian childhood riding up and down them? I still hadn't said that the hills of Kent were nothing like these wild crags that, except for the peaks looming far above them, I'd have called mountains. For the first time ever, I thought nostalgically of hills covered in bouncy turf, and valleys dense with oak and birch and chestnut. I shifted my sore bottom a few inches to a patch of what counted here for grass. 'Mine is a rather settled race,' I said in the best careless tone I could manage – 'farmers mostly. Before then, we invaded by sea.'

He nodded. It was an answer that recovered me some status. Unlike him, I'd not spent the whole wild dash from the Senatorial Dock to Trebizond rolling about my cabin in a pool of sick. Oh, I'd been His Magnificence the Lord Senator until Rado had chosen these scrawny horses in preference to the much finer beasts on offer. And I'd kept up much of the pretence right till the moment he'd seen a path invisible to me, and taken us off the lovely road that led inland *via* Pylae. Twelve days later, and a boy who'd never quite learned to dance for me in Constantinople was maturing, almost as I watched him, into something not always likeable but always admirable. Old Glaucus had complained about his narrow focus in the gymnasium. I could see now that this wasn't a fault: it was Rado. I'd told him we needed to move fast. And fast, therefore, we'd moved. Every time I showed I was getting used to the pace he'd set on horseback, the pace would be increased. We had, in twelve days, covered a distance on my map I'd never have thought possible. The steadily increasing speed Rado had maintained was remarkable – so, too, his granite certainty, from moment to moment, of exactly where we were. It didn't seem to matter that he'd grown up a thousand miles to the west, and was as new to these mountains as I was. If my backside was hurting more than at any time since I'd taken my first steps in Latin, who was I to complain?

Water flask in hand, Rado slid down beside me. I let him straighten and massage my legs as if I'd been Nicetas in one of his more helpless moods. 'It's a bit like where I was a boy,' he said wistfully. He looked round at the edge of the ravine. 'My father's people sweep down from mountains like these to burn or levy tribute on the Greek cities.' He laughed. 'I remember how we once took on a whole column of the Emperor's soldiers, when they marched out from Thebes to force us back to the Danube. We threw big rocks down at them till they were all dead. I don't think they even saw us!' He laughed again, now fiercely. Leaving me to drink from the flask, he got up lightly and perched again on the edge of the ravine. If there was room for a bug to crawl between the front of his boot and the edge, I'd have been surprised.

'Am *I* a Greek now?' he asked uncertainly, not looking round.

I took advantage of being unobserved to loosen the collar of my quilted jacket. So high up, the wind was icy. A few moments out of it, and though dipping now towards the western horizon, the sun was hotter than on the coastal plain. I could already feel the sweat running down my chest. Avoiding the sun, I looked up into the astonishing purple of the sky. That alone was enough to set my nose twitching. I looked back at the stony ground. We were thousands of feet above sea level. But the smoothness of the smaller stones put me in mind of the pebbles on Dover beach. That, in turn, put me in mind of Xenophanes and his claim of endless vistas of time preceding the emergence of man. Could it be that thousands – indeed, tens of thousands – of years before, this had been a seabed? How violent must have been whatever earthquakes had brought about the present order of things? And everyone was fighting over a cup that was young by comparison!

Rado hadn't yet looked round for his answer but I was aware of how long since he'd asked his question. 'Yes, you are now a Roman Citizen,' I said. Everything else was beyond me but I could still sound authoritative on the Law of Persons. 'The normal rule is that no slave freed before he is thirty can become a citizen. Instead, he recovers the nationality of his previous condition. In your case, however, and that of all the other underage slaves I freed, this rule was set aside on my declaration that you had saved my life. In the formal sense, you are no longer a barbarian. I suppose we should be speaking to each other in Latin rather than Slavic. Unless you plan to settle in Africa or Italy, you should also learn some Greek.'

The legal niceties went over his head. Or perhaps they didn't matter. 'Samo told me too I'm now your son,' he said. 'But my father was put to death when we got taken in the western mountains.'

How to answer that one? Every time you want something fast, you can trust lawyers to take a complex law – rendered more complex by some 'clarifying' decree that Heraclius *might* or might *not* have published – and make a total balls-up of it. The other manumissions could go through the normal process. Even after backdating the special cases to the day of my Regency, though, I'd been assured adoption was the only way of cutting through the complexities. An hour after registration, you can be sure, the lawyers had dropped in again, carrying enough papyrus rolls to fill a latrine trench, and begged my pardon for getting it wrong. By then, the number of my sons had expanded irrevocably from two to five – none of them mine other than in the sense prescribed by law.

Thoughts of children actually sired by me brought on another stab of the ache deep within that dwarfed the pain of riding. I closed my eyes and focused on that until it went away. Nothing good came of dwelling on things beyond my knowledge and control. I'd made my plans and I'd carry them through grimly, not flinching though I went to my death. I smiled at the back of Rado's neck. 'It's a formality required by Greek tribal custom,' I explained. 'It makes our own relationship somewhat irregular. But you'd soon have been fully grown in any event.'

I was saved the trouble of further explanation by a rattling of hooves on loose stones. Without any other warning, my other new 'sons' emerged from what I'd taken for a sheer drop. From the pleased looks they flashed us, they'd been competing again at who could ride fastest without any noise. It was easy to guess that Slavs could move about this sort of terrain like a cat over roof tiles.

That's why I'd brought Rado. If I weren't so aware of my own failings, I'd have been pleased to be shown again that Lombards were the same.

Jealous, I kicked out at the dead goat Eboric threw at my feet. 'Where did you get that?' I asked sharply in Latin.

'It fell off a rock and died, Master,' he said with a winning smile. His brother was already dismounted and going at it with a knife. I dropped the pretence of envy posing as anger. Eboric was getting prettier by the day. His brother wasn't less than easy on the eye. Besides, it would be nice to have something for dinner that didn't give the four of us a bellyache.

I told myself not to feel – or, failing that, not to show – any pain, and got unsteadily to my feet. I walked over to my horse and took out the big map I'd brought from Constantinople. Rado brushed some dust from a flattish rock and waited for me to unfold the linen sheet. 'If you're right,' I said in Slavic, 'we must be here.' I jabbed my finger at one of the stylised blobs that signified a mountain. 'The village from where the boys stole the goat is probably this one.' I pointed again. There was no certainty in either claim. The map had been another rush job – superimposing my own drafting office coordinates on a military map was bound to multiply any initial errors. Rado stared intently at what I was sure meant very little to him. He made a casual remark in Latin and looked quickly round to make sure the boys were watching his show of equality with the Great Lord Alaric. Purely for my own benefit, I traced a depressingly long route from where we might have been to another blob. 'The Larydia Pass will be over here,' I continued. 'All this being so, the question is whether we've outrun them.'

'I think we have, Master,' Rado said, still in Latin. 'You tell me the Persian's legs are too short for him to ride a horse properly. If the Lord Prefect is with them, he can't ride at all. That means they would have to come down the secondary road.' He looked at me for support and ran his finger along a blue line. Either he was learning to understand the map or he'd got lucky. I nodded. 'From the distance you told me the road covers, we must be three days ahead of them – perhaps more.' I nodded again. The agreed plan was to intercept Shahin and his people as they moved through the narrow pass that Rado believed was the only one they would dare attempt. It joined at what the map said was a suspiciously exact right angle with a much wider pass that would, with a few detours, bring a small escort of honour directly from the zone of Persian occupation. They'd be worn out from their own dash southward. They'd be in no kind of formation. Carrying Timothy, and travelling over broken and nearly impassable ground, would soak up much of the effort that, on the road, would go into providing an armed escort. They'd be more focused on their triumphant meeting with the Great King's representatives. The four of us stood no chance against an armed band hurrying along a level road but the night smash and grab I had in mind was just conceivable in the pass. Or so it had seemed in Constantinople.

Eboric came and stood on the other side of the stone. He looked in awe at the broad linen square. 'The streams show the valleys are descending the further inland we go,' he said shyly. He ignored Rado's look of outrage. 'We've surely outrun them. But they might not be so far behind us.'

I folded the map away. Rado could give the boy the kicking he'd earned while I was pretending to sleep. For the moment, I'd learned everything I wanted. I looked once more at the surrounding desolation. The mountain peaks were capped white with unthawed snow, their lower reaches green with scrubby trees. The valleys were hidden in mist or lost in the impenetrable shadows of late afternoon. Twelve days of fast and nearly continuous movement lay between us and the sea. Except the map told me otherwise, the mountain chain might stretch another hundred or even a thousand days to the south. I felt a returning attack of the horrors. Had Antonia refused to cooperate? Had she tried to escape? Had Shahin been his usual lying bastard self, and tossed her body overboard the moment his ship was safely out in the straits? Would I be left with nothing, when I finally caught up with him, but the cold satisfaction of tying his severed head to the mane of my horse?

I looked at Eboric's brother. He was fast with his knife. 'It won't be dark for a while,' I said in Latin, so everyone could understand.

'I think we should hold off from dinner till we've found somewhere to rest for the night.'

Rado got in first with his reply. 'But, My Lord, we can't get to the next safe hilltop till long after dark. It's best to camp here. If we start before dawn, we can be within a day of the Larydia Pass by late afternoon.'

The two boys nodded in unison. I looked south-east at what seemed to be one mountain among many. Between us and that lay a jumble of other high and low places, some glittering bright in the late sun, others in total darkness. I could have told myself I was mad to trust three barbarians who'd never been here in their lives. Instead, I remembered something Priscus had once said about how every military art rested on the ability to look once at any terrain and see it as a series of points in three dimensions. 'Either you've got that, dear boy, or you haven't,' he'd said dismissively. 'You just go back to finding the money to pay for the fighting – and making sure that what we're fighting for is actually worth defending.'

I gave in. 'Then we'll keep the fire out of sight,' I said. Three heads nodded politely. I sat down. 'I'll take the long midnight watch.'

53

I dreamed that I was in a room filled with dazzling light. Except the light came from no particular direction, it was like the time when I was lost in the Egyptian desert. All about me, lines of poetry had been turned to balls of coloured light and revolved slowly in paths determined by their patterns of long and short syllables. It was very beautiful to watch and reminded me of something in my early childhood.

At home and in bed, the dream could have gone on all night and given me something to think about in spare moments during the day. Here, it never effaced the fact that I was lying, cold and stiff, on top of a hill so windswept that the few bushes able to take root spread out over the ground, never more than six inches tall. Without needing to open my eyes and look at the moon, I could feel it would soon be my turn to get up and take my turn with the watch. For the moment, I lay still. The wind was up again. Its gentle and continuous moaning was something I now only noticed at times like this. I'd soon learned to accept it as a welcome blotting out of the distant and far more sinister howling of the wolves. In the summer months, I knew, there was safer prey for them than armed men huddled about a fire. Try believing that, however, when you've childhood experience of the creatures, and when you're one of the huddled men. They were up and about, I could be sure. If I listened hard enough, I'd hear them. The wind was up, but not yet enough.

I began to drift back towards the room filled with light. The dream hadn't entirely faded, but coloured balls that had been resolving themselves, one after the other, into lines of text glowed brighter and brighter again. Then it was all gone and I was awake. 'If you won't let me come too,' Eboric whispered in his sulky tone, 'I'll wake him up and tell him.'

I think Rado poked him hard in the chest. He let out an obscenity in his own language I hadn't yet heard. 'And if it's nothing?' he asked, returning to Latin. 'If it's nothing, you'll get him up for no reason? Stay here and look after things. If he does wake, tell him I'll be back in time for my watch.'

I threw the blanket aside and sat up into a blast of chilly air. 'What have you heard?' I asked.

Rado wiped an angry snarl from his face and got up. 'I don't know, My Lord,' he said evasively. 'It may be something I've felt more than heard. It may be a trick of the wind.' He stepped towards me and reached down for my blanket.

'He said he heard horses, Master,' Eboric said quickly. He twisted sideways to avoid being kicked into the embers of the fire. 'I'm sure I heard a harness jingle.'

Shahin, running far ahead of any conjectured time, and far from his only sensible route? Not likely. A local traveller about his business? I looked at Eboric's childish pout. I looked at the dark shadow that was Rado's face. 'Where did you hear them?' I asked. I walked with Rado to the ravine edge and followed his pointed finger down to the left. The moon was heading towards its midnight zenith. If with deceptive clarity, I could see for miles in every direction. Looking down, I stared into total darkness. I put aside the mournful sound of the wind. The wolves had run out of anything more to say to each other, or were out of hearing. I held my breath and listened hard.

It was only the briefest snatch but you don't mistake armed men on horseback. I turned and looked into the unearthly glow on Rado's now tense and excited face. 'Can you tell how far away?' I asked.

He went to the edge and leaned over. 'Not far below us,' he said after a long pause. 'There's three of them and I think they've come out with padded harness.'

Eboric and his brother were already at work on their bootlaces. I raised a hand for attention. 'The pair of you stay here,' I said, quiet yet firm. I waited for their looks of disappointment to fade to sullenness 'You need to keep an eye on the horses,' I explained. 'Be prepared to get them ready for an immediate retreat.'

Rado looked for the right words. Not finding them in Latin, he went into Slavic. 'You should stay here, Master,' he said. 'I might be faster on my own.'

I frowned. 'Whatever's down there,' I said, 'I need to see for myself.'

After so long of having to treat me like a mounted invalid, Rado could be forgiven for believing I'd been denatured by seven years of prosperity in the Empire. On two legs, I could be still as much the predatory barbarian as he was. To be sure, we had no hills in England like these. But there were animals to be hunted, and travelling strangers to be robbed; and I had grown up surrounded by mile-wide expanses of shingle. It was hard to say which of us was more silent and more unseen, as we hurried down the steep incline. We reached its bottom about a mile from where we'd left the boys in charge of the horses. Dark caps pulled on tight to cover our hair, we crouched together behind a large boulder and waited.

We heard the muffled jingle of harness long before the three riders came in sight. They moved slowly, picking their way over the loose stones. From the first, I thought the horses were bigger than anything normally seen in the mountains. One look at how the moonlight glittered on their helmets and the hairs stood up on the back of my neck.

'Persian regular army,' I breathed into Rado's ear. He stiffened beside me, the same thought probably going through his mind. I watched them come closer. There could be no doubt what they were. I could see their helmets and the fish-scale armour under their cloaks. I could see the outline of their leggings and boots. Still moving slowly, now and again letting the horses cool their hooves in the little stream, it was an officer in front and two men behind.

'Night foragers?' Rado whispered uncertainly.

'I don't see what else they could be,' I said. 'Though, if it's at least a two-day ride to the Larydia Pass, and still more to the big pass, what are they doing *here*?' I thought of my map. That might easily be wrong. But Rado and the boys knew where they were. The details might be less sharp in their minds than they claimed in front of me but that couldn't put us two days south-west of where they said we were.

I strained to hear the low conversation. From right to left, they were passing by not twenty feet away, and all I needed was for the officer to speak up a little or turn in our direction. I thought at first they'd pass completely out of hearing. But there was a sudden noise of more horses approaching from our left and the men sat up straight.

Rado leaned closer. 'How big were you told the escort would be?' he asked. I pressed my head against his for silence. said the new arrivals were about a dozen men on horses similar to our own. So far as I could tell, they had no armour. The hairs on the back of my neck were beginning to stand up.

The officer rode forward a few paces and raised his voice. 'Have you found anything yet?' he asked.

'Nothing to scare whatever old woman issued your orders,' the man in charge of the larger band jeered in the rough Persian of a highlander. He leaned to the right and spat. 'But we found a real old woman. She told us she saw two blond boys on horseback stealing a goat.'

'Obviously not locals,' the officer grunted. 'They may indicate nothing but I'll report back.'

The highlander spat again. 'Good riders, she said – too good for escaped slaves. But too young, I got the impression, to be western federates.'

'You made sure to kill her afterwards?' the officer asked anxiously. 'You know the orders.'

The highlander laughed unpleasantly. 'We killed the whole fucking village. Shame we had to leave all their food behind.'

'Good,' the officer said. 'Nothing must be left to chance.' He stopped and looked sharply right. Someone or something had started a light shower of stones down the far wall of this minor pass. He clutched harder on his reins and got out his sword. He began a babbled charm to ward off evil. Even before I saw his sword's dull glitter, the highlander and his men were dashing on horseback up an incline steeper and rockier than the one Rado and I had come down. Together, they reached a point about fifty yards up, before stopping for a quiet laugh. The highlander was first back to the officer, what may have been a rabbit skewered on his long sword.

'Very good,' the officer said with a recovery of dignity. He put his sword away. 'Don't bust a gut over it but if you find either of the blond boys, try to take them alive. And remember the order not to split up.'

Eboric and his brother had the horses already loaded when we got back. Now, they were fighting tears of disgrace as they covered the fire with a mass of tiny stones. This wasn't the time for flogging their arses raw. Nor would I punish them. 'It was just bad luck,' I'd said after telling all three what I'd heard. 'And it may not even be that,' I'd added. 'After all, we have learned something.'

I was right. We *had* learned something. If only I could be sure what it was. I put wilder conjectures aside and turned to Rado. 'The questions are piling up,' I said, wondering how to express them without sounding panicky. I looked at the pebbles he'd arranged on the flat rock. The moon was past its zenith and each stone and heap of stones cast a shadow. 'It's no surprise the escort should be made up of Persian regulars. But why night scouting parties, and why so far out? And who's being chased by them?' I fell silent. I'd thought at first they were after me. That would suggest Shahin had already met the escort and he was guessing I'd not be far behind. But the ruling out of blond hair had been too emphatic. Also, if they were just looking for me, why the murder of anyone who'd seen them?

I reached forward to touch one of the double lines of pebbles at the top left extremity of Rado's map. 'Are you absolutely sure this is the only pass that Shahin can use?' I asked in Slavic – I'd more chance of a frank answer if no one else could understand.

He nodded. 'I've been looking for days at the shape of the mountains,' he answered in Latin. 'Never mind your painted map – we've seen nowhere else they could use. As for the escort, there's no other pass that makes sense.' The two boys nodded vigorously.

I could have interrupted here to ask how they knew anything about the location of the passes, let alone their width. But I'd chosen them for the skills they'd learned before they were taken. I'd seen no reason so far to doubt I'd chosen right. If Rado's confidence weren't enough, the boys had been scampering all over the place. While he'd been keeping me from falling off my own horse, they had been over every inch of the ground ten miles either side of our journey and ten miles ahead. I nodded grimly and waited.

'The escort might be lost,' he continued with a frown. 'But those rough men on horseback are like my people. They *can't* get lost – not enough to be this far off course.'

We could stand here debating all night and still not get anywhere. I looked at the mounds of little stones and wondered which one represented our hill. 'If, shall we say, a dozen of your people were hunting us,' I asked, 'what would they do?'

Rado pointed at a different mound and turned matter of fact. 'Given a few dozen of us, we'd keep a watch on these paths – here and here – and we'd send lines of horsemen over each of these hills. There'd be boys with dogs going before them. You'd need to be a mountain fox to escape that kind of dragnet.' He began moving pieces of gravel about in a way that set my heart sinking faster than the moon. 'Just a dozen, though – and without orders for an all-out search – and we'd scout round till morning in the most obvious places. After that, we'd keep to the highest points and look down to see if anyone was moving.'

I moved to look at the shadowed pattern of stones from another angle and tried to superimpose on it my own compound map. I pointed to the intersection of the passes and traced a line to our hill. 'We can take a risk once we're out of this immediate area,' I said. 'Until then, we'll see how far we can get by night. We can sleep once the sun is up.' Rado nodded.

I was about to issue another of my 'instructions,' when Eboric's brother came and plucked at my cloak. 'There's a line of horsemen coming up from the north,' he whispered. 'You can't hear them. But, if you look hard enough, you can see the moving shadows.'

362

54

We spent the remaining hours of darkness jumping at our own shadows. Once or twice, we heard men calling to each other at a great distance. But, once Rado had guided us over a seemingly impossible ridge, we moved steadily forward, now entering one of the more sheltered upland areas. Here we passed over expanses of scrubby grass that soaked up the sound of hooves. There were even little copses of trees to hide us if required.

Then, as the sky gradually turned blue and the sun began moving down the highest mountain behind us, Eboric's brother hurried back to us.

'Smell of burning ahead,' he reported.

I'd already noticed. 'Was it round here that you stole the goat?' I asked. He nodded. Rado and I looked at each other. He tickled the right ear of his horse and moved silently forward. I gave my own horse the slightest touch of spur and held on to avoid being thrown.

We were going uphill again and we got off to lead the horses once we'd reached the line of stunted trees that hid from us the remains of the smoking village.

'Well, someone had to carry all the food away,' I said. I sat on the remains of a stone wall and tried not to look at the three children who'd been butchered a few yards from my outstretched feet. The smallest had been dashed, head first, against a rock. The grass was patchy with dried blood and gobbets of brain. The problem with war, I've always insisted, is that it substitutes too much chance for the game of skill that is diplomacy. The truth is I've never liked the random killing that war involves. Within reason, soldiers on the field of battle are fair game. It's the non-combatants I feel sorry for. By the look of things, these villagers had been caught as they sat down to their evening meal. They'd all been killed without mercy. Some of them had tried to fight back. Some had been tortured. It had made no difference. They were all dead now.

Rado pulled a woman's dress down to make her body respectable. 'You did say, Master, that the highlanders weren't able to carry the food away.' He sat beside me and watched the boys as they went about filling buckets from the village stream. My people had run out of people to kill and rape and things to burn a century before I was born. Regardless of the wider questions of right and justice, I'd grown up in a world of small farming communities and it was natural to pity these unfortunates. Rado and the boys came from bandit races. They'd been too young to join in the killing before they were taken. At the same time, they'd been fed and brought up on the proceeds of collective murder. Pity must have been as alien to them as it was natural to me. The boys were less put out by the horrors we'd stumbled across than I'd been by that body outside my palace. They were much more interested in getting water for the horses and in seeking out anything edible that hadn't been carried away.

To be fair, Rado was on the edge of disapproval. Our first sight of death had been something so fiendish, and so plainly inspired by joy in suffering, that he'd let his horse rear sideways. He looked at the dead face of one of the children. 'They could have used these people to carry the food for them,' he said. He clenched his fists and looked up at the sky.

I sat in gloomy thoughts until the sound of buzzing flies became a cause of depression in itself. 'We know there's more than one village in these parts,' I said. 'Or someone else might have come along afterwards for the foraging.' I stared at the jumble of animal prints and cart grooves that led to the south. A distancing tactic I'd often found useful was to see death as evidence of something else. 'It must have been a big party to justify so big a foraging operation and so far off its probable course. How big do you suppose Shahin's escort might be?'

Rado continued looking at the open eyes. 'It's not an escort but an army,' he said quietly.

'A big army too,' I agreed after a long internal sigh. 'And you know we'll need to see it for ourselves.' I was holding my linen map. I spread it on the grass before us. I've said our agreed plan was to head straight for the Larydia Pass, and hurry along it, so we could creep down behind Shahin from his right. I drew a finger along the big pass without a name. Looking there would take us at least a day off course. 'Tell me, Rado – how long would it take one or both of the boys to get a message to Trebizond?'

He looked away from the map and stared fixedly at the burnt shell of what had been a little church. I made my own calculations. The fleet should by now have arrived at Trebizond. It should be carrying whatever forces Heraclius had been able to draw away from the defence of Thrace. Even without the Great Augustus in charge, it would take an age to get everyone this far south. If what we could see about us, however, was general between here and the big pass without a name, it was much more than an escort Shahin was hurrying to meet.

'Eboric is the youngest and lightest,' Rado said after his long silence. 'Alone, he could be back on the main road within five days. With money and a sealed permit from you to use the posts, he could be in Trebizond two days after that.'

Seven days back to Trebizond! I'd guessed their grudging praise every evening had been clever jollying along. I'd thought, even so, I was doing better than that.

Rado looked me in the face. 'And the Lady Antonia?' he asked slowly.

I looked back at him. I could have given him a curt instruction to help get the horses under cover. He'd have obeyed and not raised this matter again. But, young as I was, I'd already freed slaves by the hundred and kept many close by me afterwards. Rado had come to a moment I'd seen again and again, and only regretted when I didn't see it. It was as if I were watching the last taint of slavery fade from his spirit. It was time to start treating him as a man.

'If you are serious about joining the army,' I said, 'I will get you started as a junior staff officer – once, that is, you've learned to read and write and to understand Greek. The hardest thing you'll then learn isn't obedience to orders. You've had enough experience of that and, much as you hated it sometimes, it was always fundamentally easy. So long as you take it seriously, authority is harder. It dumps on you an endless series of decisions that affect the lives of others. Many of these decisions involve setting aside personal considerations.

'You know well enough I'm not soldierly material. But I do help govern this Empire. We came out here on a personal rescue mission that involved ending a possible threat to the Empire's security.' I waved at another of the bodies and at another that had already been pulled about by some scavenging beast. 'You can imagine as well as I can what may be coming through that pass. I don't know if we have the forces to drive it back. But our duty is to do our personal best. You asked yesterday if you had become a Greek. The plainest answer is that we are both Greeks – by circumstances and the law of nations, if not by birth. These are our people and there are tens of thousands more along that army's line of march.'

I paused and waited for all that I hadn't said to go through his mind. I put my hand on his shoulder. 'The boys came along as scouts, not as fighting men. The fighting was always to be done by us. We'll get to Antonia and we'll carve up the fuckers who lifted her out of Constantinople. But the plan has to be changed. We need to see what's in the big pass. We'll cross the pass in its wake and hurry forward to Shahin across the long side of the triangle. There's a risk we'll miss the interception but that's a risk Antonia would take if our positions were reversed. It's a risk you'd have to take if you were in my position. Life is often rather shitty. You don't make it better by going for the soft option.'

I stood up. 'Let's get inside the barn. We'll rest till noon. You and I will take turns with keeping watch.'

I walked across the litter of bodies and smashed possessions to where the two boys were throwing water at each other. I turned and called back to Rado in Slavic: 'You will never call me or any other man "Master" again. You do know that, don't you?' He nodded.

I was right about the foraging. Our journey so far had taken us through regions too bleak to be populated. These uplands had enough covering of soil to support much grazing and even a few hardy crops. Or they would, had there been either people or animals left to share the work. Foraging inside enemy territory is never gentle. Even if you forget about the rape and the random killing, it means stripping people of all means of support – usually not excepting their bloodstock or seed corn. You feed an army by starving everyone else within reach. But whoever was in charge here seemed to have commanded a general extermination. Again and again, we passed by burned villages with not a single survivor. Sometimes, the dead were fresh enough to be advertised only by the clouds of flies generated to feast on their blood. More often, they were announced, and in full sick-making horror, by sudden shifts of the breeze.

There were no survivors to look at us as we passed. Everywhere was picked too clean for the Persians to bother with patrols. But for the flies and all the other beasts of carrion, we were as alone as if we'd still been in the honest wilderness of the mountains. An entire subdivision of a province that paid reasonably large taxes lay about us in desolation. And it was worse than desolation. Village after village – even the few monasteries in our path – had been made into museums of human beastliness. There came a point at which even the boys left off their chattering. If only, after hitting that low point in the journey, we'd been able to justify leaving a path that took us through every place of former habitation.

On the second afternoon of this nightmarish progress, Rado tried for a conversation above the instrumental. He'd stopped to wait for me to look in a shattered church – I needed a village name to reconnect me with the map. 'Samo told me,' he said when I rejoined him, 'that you'd commanded everyone in the Empire to be armed.'

I looked away from a circle of impaled children. The boys among them had all been castrated. I could see their tiny genitals gathered into a heap of solidified slime. 'Only where the new land law has been brought into effect,' I answered. 'Though right on the frontier, southern Pontus remains effectively on the old system.' Would he understand the politics of local obstruction? He might, but with more explanation than I felt able to give. 'Forbidding arms and military combinations to the people,' I added, 'was the policy of rulers in more settled times, who thought it the best way to guarantee the peace. All it does in the end, though, is to disarm victims.'

I looked at the sky and tried to clear my head. The hazy cloud I'd seen coming on all day was thickening into heavy banks of grey. The sun still shone to my left but would soon be blotted out.

Rado watched me. 'It won't rain till evening,' he said. I could be glad of that. Mountain storms aren't for riding through and I was longing for better shelter than another scorched charnel house.

I thought again of politics in the Imperial Council. 'Since you can't be expected to know the answer,' I said, 'I won't ask it as a question. Instead, I'll say that, of all the provinces or districts within provinces where the land law has been brought fully into effect, not one has fallen to the Persians. In every case, professional armies have been driven back by irregular units filled with men no different from these.'

Rado reached out to guide my horse round a hole in the ground I hadn't seen. 'So you do want to make the Greeks more like us.' He said. 'Is that why everyone hates you?'

I laughed bitterly. It saved me the embarrassment of yet more thanks. 'Talking of "us",' I asked, 'do you imagine anyone will ever take our land away from us? Any foreign invader with sense in his head takes one look at armed men and tries his luck elsewhere.'

They also keep the bastard rulers under control, I might have added but I'd seen something shining up at me from the ground. 'It's a mailed glove,' Rado said, following my glance. I didn't answer. 'It was probably left behind by whoever needed a bare hand for carving up those boys.'

Still, I said nothing. No longer bumping my way through those mountains, I slid off the horse with a semblance of grace and reached down for the mass of silvered chain mail. I walked stiffly over to a felled tree and sat down for a proper look. I raised my voice. 'I may have some bad news,' I said with a ghastly smile. I reached inside the glove and plucked at its lining of yellow silk. The Royal Guard was never sent into battle. This wasn't some fixed law of the Persians. It was simply that the Royal Guard's sole function was to protect the Great King, and no Great King in over a century had left Ctesiphon except to run away from his own people, or to shift himself to one of his summer palaces.

You could take the whole flash of light inside my head and work it into a syllogism: This glove is part of the Royal Guard's parade uniform; the Royal Guard never leaves the Great King's side; therefore, what we're headed towards is the biggest invasion force since Xerxes, and Chosroes is at its head. I put this in looser terms to Rado and the boys. I also accepted that one swallow didn't make a spring – the glove *might* have been a present, or a trophy, or a talisman. But I no longer had any reasonable doubt of the truth. Why else kill everyone in sight, unless it was to keep the invasion under wraps till fifty or a hundred thousand men could burst out of the passes and make for the coastal cities? And I could imagine how Chosroes had enjoyed giving the order. Policy aside, he really was the sort of man who made wicked old Phocas the Lamb of God by comparison.

We rode on in silence. Insensibly, the fertile uplands were giving way again to harsh wilderness. The smell of death had gone from our nostrils. The horses were calmer. The boys were cheering up. More and more, Rado was intervening to keep me moving in his appointed course.

All at once, we came to the peak of the hill we'd been climbing. Before us, the land fell away to another endless expanse of bare hills and shadowed valleys.

I got off my horse again, and stood as close as I dared to the edge. In silence, I pointed south. I didn't need to get out my map or to guess where the big pass might be. There, ten or twenty miles away, was all the proof I could have needed of what I already knew. The dust cloud thrown up by the advancing army put me in mind of a city on fire.

Rado spoke first. 'I've never seen anything like this,' he whispered. 'It's a whole people on the move.' I nodded. I'd never seen the like either. Though I'd read about it, and often sat with Priscus in his talkative moods about the past, I'd always thought it was one of the conceits bad poets like Leander use when they can't make anything sensible scan.

I stood away from the edge and sat down. I smiled at Eboric. 'Be a love,' I said, 'and get my writing case from your saddlebag. You'll be carrying an oral message back to Trebizond. But it's time to get your pass in order for the postal stations along the road.'

Even as I spoke, a long peal of thunder drifted across the valley.

55

I poked my head cautiously forward and looked once more down to the bottom of a pass that had no name I ever heard. I call it a pass, though the word may put you in mind of a gentle dip between two mountains. A better word might be canyon. It might have begun, countless thousands of years before, as a river which, in its spring flooding, had insensibly worn its way several hundred feet down. More likely, it was a split in the world's outer skin – a product of the forces that had raised the hills and mountains in the first place.

Whatever the geographic truth, the long straggling column filling the pass was as I'd imagined it. No, it was worse. After little flurries on and off all night, the skies had finally opened with the dawn. By the time we were able to peer down to the bottom of the wide pass, we could have been forgiven for thinking it was a defeated army creeping along before us from right to left. Without visible beginning or end, often knee-deep in water, the vast invasion force might have had trouble keeping up with a garden slug as it hurried out of the sun.

Rado pointed at a long covered wagon pulled by eight white oxen. 'Is the Great King in that?' he asked.

'Nowhere big enough or grand enough for Chosroes,' I answered. 'Besides, he'll be at least half a mile away at the front of the column – fresh ground to look at, sweeter smells for his nose, and so on.' I fell silent and leaned a few inches forward. Most likely, the wagon was to carry the less important secretariat officials, or some part of a cousin's household. Its wheels had long since come off. In their place were fitted improvised runners that would have done better on snow. All that stopped it from scraping and bumping and turning over into the grey and littered water was its speed of progress. I leaned forward still further. Yes – it was for someone's dancing girls. They'd been kicked out to trudge behind it in their bedraggled finery. Slaves struggled behind them, carrying ruined musical instruments and bundles of soaking clothes. Behind these came drivers of animals for someone's kitchen. Still further behind, I could see another big cart. Covered with purple canvas, surrounded by monks – probably of the Nestorian heresy, probably singing in Persian – it was anyone's guess what this carried. I'd missed any sign of the fighting men. They would have been bunched about Chosroes.

It was a nuisance having to watch this lot go by. I had no doubt Chosroes himself was down there. Almost certainly, so was Shahrbaraz. Somewhere out of sight was the cream of the Persian armies. They were all shuffling along – without weapons, without armour, wholly out of formation. Except for the colour of their faces, you'd have been pushed to tell the difference between the Royal Guard and the dregs of the south-eastern levies. Even with Nicetas in charge, you could send a few thousand of our own men into action and the greatest war our world had known since Alexander's conquests would be over in time for dinner. And here I was, reduced to watching the chance of this drift by in the rain. We couldn't even start a landslide – not that this would do any good: as said, Chosroes and the people who mattered were already out of sight.

I pulled myself back and clambered with Rado down the rocky outcrop. The boys were already down and waiting. Glancing right and left along the path for sight of yet another patrol, we made for the clumps of bushes where we'd left the horses. From the state of the ground, I could guess the patrols had been more active when the Great King himself was passing by. Though still about, they were no longer much of a worry. It helped that, if no longer driving, the rain had settled into one of those continuous drizzles that soak almost without declaring their presence. Most of the Persian scouts up here, I knew from experience, would be huddled under their makeshift shelters.

We led our horses over the four hundred yards of broken ground that led to the forking of the mountain streams. I'd opened the matter to discussion the day before. The boys had the same right to be heard in this as Rado and I. All that had come out of this was who should be the one to leave us. I'd settled that by a disguised testing of whose Greek was less basic. Nothing was left in doubt. We'd had a day to get used to what was inevitable. It was as if we were walking to an execution.

I smiled nervously at Eboric's brother. 'You will get rid of the package if you think you're about to be stopped?' I asked again.

Already mounted, he took his cap off and swept wet hair away from his eyes. 'No one will see me go,' he said calmly. 'No one will ever catch me.' He glanced at the sealed package in his hands. 'The biggest danger is that I'll be hanged as a thief when I show this to the Greeks.'

I relaxed slightly. He wouldn't be able to read the tiny script that covered both sides of the parchment sheet. But it confirmed in outline everything he could describe in his own words, and gave him plenary authority to command whatever assistance he felt he might need. 'Show that to any of the postal officials and you'll be hero of the hour,' I said. 'Use your common sense with the gold.'

There were other things I wanted to say. But none of them amounted to more than an excuse for delay. The light was good. The rain was manageable. The Persians weren't about. It was time to go. The boy leaned forward for me to embrace him. Eboric and Rado patted him gruffly on the back and shared a joke with him – incomprehensible even in Latin – about picking mushrooms on a mountain top.

The boy set off and let his horse carry him slowly to the first stage in the long climb. He turned and looked back at us. 'I won't fail you, Alaric,' he called back softly. 'But I want you to know that we're doing this for you, not a bunch of shitbag cowardly Greeks. You just get the Lady Antonia and don't stop running away from this lot till you've joined me in Trebizond.' With that, he wheeled round and, with a jump forward that reminded me of a ball shot from a catapult, was almost immediately lost to sight.

'He won't be stopped,' Eboric said with easy certainty. 'The Greeks only caught us when we came back for our mother's body.' He pushed his chest out. 'We were only boys then,' he added. I nodded and continued looking at the last place his brother had been visible. There were great banks of mist rolling down from the mountains. If they reached the pass – especially before nightfall – we could look forward to a still slower and more chaotic progress of the army. That was what we needed. Leaving aside the general considerations, we had to get through that struggling mass of humanity to continue our journey to the right interception point. A touch of mist would do us no harm.

I wondered again just how many men Shahin had with him. I'd told Rado the boys hadn't come along to help in the fighting. But, if we couldn't creep in by night and do our business, what use would the two of us be? Whatever use all four of us might have been, there were now just the three of us. The whole journey here, I'd been racking my brains for any better plan than I'd made up in Constantinople. Nothing so far had occurred to me.

Rado swore suddenly in Slavic. 'Patrol in sight down below, and I think they've seen us,' he said in Latin. I looked round. Three men in uniform were leading a horse over an expanse of jagged stones. I'd taken it for granted no horses could be got across that. So, it seemed, had Rado and the boys. By tacit agreement, we'd gone round it ourselves. I nearly felt cheerful at the thought of their joint failure. But, from the direction they were taking, I found it hard to believe the men had seen us. Even before the mist arrived, the rain had softened everything to a gentle blur. How visible were we – unmoving and against a background of colours that blended with our clothing? The three men looked more interested in taking a short cut than in flushing out possible spies.

Oh, but one of the men had now seen us. Pointing and waving his arms, he was jabbering to the others in the shrill argumentative whine usual among the Persian lower classes. The other two stopped and looked in our direction. If we looked back and didn't move, they might move on. But they'd finished their deliberations and were coming in our direction. We could make a dash for it. They were a quarter of a mile away and the horse wasn't bred for mountain work. There was no chance they'd catch us. But they might then raise an alarm that would force us into another detour – and how many more of these could we afford?

'Let's see how well we've rehearsed,' I said. I put up a hand to check that the turban we'd made from one of the blankets was still in place. The appearance of ochre that Eboric had made on my face with a burnt twig had probably turned to black rivulets, running down cheeks whitened with cornmeal. Not that it mattered how sordid I looked – that was the desired effect. The men had found their way to smoother ground and were coming rapidly closer. I waited till the man in front had stopped and mounted the horse. It was time for action. I waved my arms theatrically and pushed Rado to the ground.

'What are you doing out of the pass?' the mounted man asked in a voice that was plainly intended to sound both gruff and haughty, but that managed neither. It was low-grade provincial. It even had a tinge of Syriac – he was dark enough for south-east of the Euphrates. He looked thoughtfully at our horses. 'I asked you a question,' he said, raising his voice.

I stopped pretending to thrash Rado and made a perfunctory bow. 'Greetings, O Master of all creation,' I said in a Persian that sounded both greasy and heavily Armenian. 'Will you honour me by taking your ease with one of my brothers?'

The mounted man shifted on his saddle and looked at his two companions. His uniform aside, there was no sign of the martial virtues in him. The companions were about as low as you can get once you hit the dregs of an army. Not even a morning of driving rain had washed all the dirt from their faces. The weeping scabs about their lips were hideous things to behold. Their shapeless, stunted bodies made the wretches who'd rioted outside my palace robust by comparison. They clutched at each other, whispering and giggling, now looking at Eboric, now pointing at me. Their conference over, they plucked at the mounted man till he bent down and listened to their urging. 'We'll be late,' he whispered down at them. 'Orders are orders and it'll be flaying alive if we don't get there in time.'

There was more whispering. The nastier of the companions pointed at the three of us, his tongue darting from side to side of his revolting mouth. The mounted man looked at me again. His face twisted into a crooked smile. 'If you really are a pimp,' he said, 'you won't get much custom up here.' He waved for support at the rocky waste that lay all about. 'Why aren't you down in the pass with everyone else?'

'We come all the way from the great city of Tibion,' I whined, twisting my face to make the coating of burnt twig run in nastier rivulets. 'Yet who will buy my boys? Surely, we should have offered ourselves to the Greeks, for all the fortune I shall make among you worshippers of the female parts.' I clapped my hands. After a shrill curse in Armenian, I kicked Eboric between his shoulder blades. He got slowly up and began an insultingly feeble rendition of one of his bathhouse dances. There wasn't much he could do about his pretty face. But the slow, plodding movements in wet clothing might not have raised interest in a profligate high on *hashish*.

That, however, is what the companions showed various signs of being. Giggling and rolling his eyes, one of them sat on a low stone and began rubbing at his crotch. The other turned his attention back to the mounted man. There was more whispering and pointing. But the mounted man shook his head. He leaned forward. 'How did you know we were coming?' he demanded. 'How could word go round, as far away as Armenia, of an invasion we still haven't been officially told about?' He sat upright again. 'Did you see any Greeks on your way through the mountains? If you did, you'd better tell me. I'm on my way to the Great King himself,' he finished with a toss of his head.

I stretched open hands towards him and simpered like a eunuch. 'Would I be here had I found Emperor's gold to be earned?' I asked in return. My sword was out of sight. But I had a knife up my left sleeve that I could probably get straight in his throat. Still on the ground, Rado was no longer pretending to whimper but was looking steadily at the larger of the two footmen. We could take them out, I was sure. We should do it sooner rather than later – for how long would it be just the three of them? Ideally, though, we needed that man off his horse.

The mounted man sat back, his mouth turned down in disgust too severe to be genuine. He looked again at Eboric, who'd made sure to fail in his hopping pirouette and was struggling to get up again. He turned to the companion who wasn't rubbing himself off and who now whispered harder from behind both hands. They spoke back and forth, with much sniggering and nudging at each other and endless gloating looks at the three of us. I knew what was coming but made sure to continue looking scared and uncertain.

I was right. The mounted man finished his whispered conversation. They had time, I'd heard him agree. Biting his lip, he stared at me. 'How much?' he asked.

I spread my arms wide and smiled in a manner that suggested my teeth weren't up to viewing in daylight. 'For you, My Lord, three silver *dirhams* – five if you want the boy to take off his clothing.'

The mounted man looked into my face. 'I don't care for boys,' he said. 'I want *you!*' Both companions burst into a high whining snigger. They ended with more fluttering of tongues.

All very flattering, I suppose – though my flesh crawled at the thought of touching any of them. That poor diving boy in Constantinople might not have had worse teeth than this lot – and his face hadn't been covered in sores that glistened red in the continuing drizzle. But I broadened my smile. I bowed and touched my forehead. 'If it is hips or lips My Lord is desiring,' I smarmed, 'I shall not be found wanting. But I can also divert, if My Lord so commands, with the masculine office.' I flexed my hips and tried to look wanton through burnt twig and a seventeen-day growth of stubble.

'Lips only,' he breathed in an ecstasy of lust long unsatisfied. He checked himself and looked once more at the horses. 'I'll pay you by letting you go.' He pointed at a large boulder. 'Take your clothes off,' he groaned. 'Do it to me naked.' He closed his eyes and shuddered. He opened them again and looked at Eboric. 'I want to watch the boy piss on you afterwards.' He pointed at Rado. 'Kill him if he moves,' he said to his companions.

One of the footmen got his sword out and poked Rado in the chest. He made a cry of inarticulate triumph and got his free hand under his leather breastplate to scratch one of his nipples. Rado played along, dropping on all fours and starting a terrified plea in Slavic. Looking both suspicious and lustful for his own turn with me, the other companion squatted on his haunches and clutched hard on his spear. Their leader was too far gone to do other than retire out of sight and wait for me. With more sniggering, and clutching of weapons, these two watched me undress. Don't ask how a man with my physique managed to look submissive out of his clothes. No doubt, the rain helped. I'd been wet through all day. Now, I was cold as well.

56

You can be sure I didn't stay submissive. The foul-smelling pig was no sooner lying beneath me, gasping and running his hands up and down the muscles on my back, when I snapped his neck, and Eboric sat on his legs to stop them from kicking any stones loose. I didn't even have to kiss those putrid lips. By the time I looked out, shivering in the rain, Rado was casually sitting on a rock with his feet raised in the air. One of the footmen was curled in a ball and dead. The other was choking his last with my steel knife in his throat.

'Good lad!' I said, slapping Rado on the back. He really had been wasted as a dancing boy. Eboric too. I kissed him on the cheek. What better sons could any man desire? I looked down the incline. There was no one coming. Rado shook his head and smiled happily. I stretched my arms and looked up at the sky. Now I was used to the cold, I felt deliciously sensual in the rain.

But I pulled myself back to the matter in hand. 'We'd better get rid of the bodies,' I said. I thought about the boulder. My own kill was already there. We could dump the other two on top. I thought again. I looked at Eboric. 'If you can strip them, we'll cover the bodies with stones.' He nodded eagerly and vanished behind the boulder. The wolves would have them out soon enough. By then, though, there'd be no one about to make a fuss. Just in case, we'd hide the clothes separately.

I sat on a stone and reached for my trousers. I noticed an ingrowing hair on my right thigh and picked at it. Rado put his legs down and turned his head slightly. I'd heard it already. 'I shouldn't worry about the noise,' I said.

'What does it mean?' he asked. The dying man had stopped twitching. He reached forward and recovered my knife.

'Do keep the knife,' I said. 'You've earned it.' He perked up at once. It was a lovely object. He'd been admiring the thing since Trebizond. He cleaned it on the dead man's jacket and balanced it in his hand. More of the faint but massive roaring drifted up from the pass. 'Singing eunuchs,' I explained. 'The Great King keeps a choir of a thousand. If memory serves me right, that's one of the audience anthems they're practising.' I stretched both legs out and wiggled my toes. I suddenly realised that Rado had been copying me. I smiled. 'Eunuchs have a tendency of melancholia that needs to be carefully managed,' I explained further. It was one explanation – one among several. A gust of wind caught my upper back. I put my trousers down and reached for my undershirt. Everything was soaked through. I twisted the linen until water splashed over my knees.

I glanced at the dead man. 'It would have been useful to question him,' I said.

Rado stood up. 'Why?' he asked sharply. He twisted in the direction of the singing eunuchs. 'What is there to learn?' He looked at me, suspicion on his face.

Eboric came from behind the boulder. He turned the dead man's leggings inside out and held them up for inspection. 'He lost a lot of mess in these,' he said.

'It's often the case when you break a neck,' I said. 'I believe it's the same with garrotting.' I looked at my own stiffy. I got up and stretched again. Eboric smiled expectantly but I shook my head. This wasn't the time or the place. Besides, I was thinking very hard. Rado had said seven days, going direct, from here to Trebizond. How long would it take a fast horseman – not able to make use of the postal stations – along the road from wherever Shahin had put in on the Black Sea coast to here? I could suppose a few days longer than we'd taken. Then again, Shahin had set out a day earlier than we had and must have landed a couple of days ahead of us. A direct messenger could do it. But why do it? There was no reason to suppose Shahin had known about the invasion. Why send anyone ahead, only to make contact with a small escort that might easily be missed? Why risk even one man who might be better employed on protecting Shahin and his precious cargo? Correction – why do without a man who might be better employed keeping Shahin's skin intact?

I noticed that Rado was still staring at me. 'Why not give the crotch a rinse in that little puddle there?' I asked Eboric. 'And let's have a look at his other clothes.'

You do get used, after a while, to wearing someone else's dirty clothes – even when you've just caused him to die in them – though it never gets easier once you've known better. The dead man had been smaller than me in every dimension. But Persian uniforms were made to be a baggy fit. So long as I didn't try for any sudden or ambitious movement, this would do.

I looked at my reflection in the puddle. There was nothing I could do about my face, but the head covering under the helmet sorted the problem of my hair. I straightened up. The dead man's horse would be a bigger problem. There was a look in its eyes that suggested a certain dislike.

Even if you can tolerate them individually, massed choirs of eunuchs are an acquired taste. Eunuchs obviously think other-wise. And, looking down at the beardless, radiant faces, who could blame them? So far as I could tell, all real movement along the pass had come to a stop. The occasional splashing forward through two foot of increasingly sewery rainwater was best explained as a closing up of gaps.

Rado pointed at a spot point about a hundred yards forward. 'That will be the best exit,' he said into my ear. I looked at the sheer opposite wall of the pass. I'd already seen how the gentle inclines on this side gave way on the other to much steeper, rougher places. My map showed the tapering gap between the passes as a standard blob of colour. To get from one pass to the other, though, would mean going over a smallish mountain.

The eunuchs suddenly turned their faces to the sky and buried the sound of their voices in a long clashing of cymbals and little bells. Alone among the grey multitudes brought to a halt along the pass, they had contrived at least to look happy.

I noticed Rado was looking at me. I smiled and shuffled forward on my chest, pretending to look for a less uncomfortable leaning position in my Persian clothes. 'What are you planning, My Lord?' he asked in a low, implacable voice.

I pretended not to understand him 'Getting into the pass will mean going back a few hundred yards,' I said. 'It's then a matter of forcing a way through a dense and mostly ill-tempered mass of humanity. Best avoid the eunuchs – they won't shift for anyone. Their baggage carriers will be much easier.'

Rado slapped his hand impatiently against a stone. 'And you'll be coming with us?' he demanded.

I took a deep breath and pulled myself away from the edge. Two weeks with Rado really had been like watching a butterfly emerge from its chrysalis. He hadn't understood those dead Persians, but he knew me well enough. 'I want to see what's happening,' I said, carefully choosing my words. 'I know the King of Persia, and I can tell when he's planning to show himself to the people. We need to know what course the army is taking and anything else that Chosroes cares to reveal.'

Rado was silent a moment. Then – 'But you can see him from the other side of the pass,' he said. 'We're sending word to Trebizond. What more is there to do? We came for the Lady Antonia. We'll soon be running out of time.' There was a sound of alarm, and of horror, in his voice that indicated he wasn't only thinking of Antonia.

I slithered down and looked at the horse I'd inherited. It was proving an unbalanced liability. If I went down into the pass, the first thing I'd do there was to be parted from it. I waited for Rado to come and sit beside me. 'I've sworn fealty to the Emperor,' I said. 'I'm one of the rulers of the Greek Empire. I won't go into detail again but these duties override all others.' I ignored Rado's cry of anger, and hurried on. 'Be at the highest point across the pass at dawn tomorrow. I'll meet you there. If I'm not there, press on with Eboric to intercept Shahin. You've been reverting by the day to mountain raiders. I'm little more than surplus baggage. Shahin won't be expecting trouble. Creep in by night, if you can

– and only if you can – and snatch Antonia. Explain everything to Antonia. She'll understand.'

I stood up and reached for the horse. It whinnied suddenly and reared away from me. The sooner I could get rid of it, the happier I'd be – happier and safer. I still hadn't tried mounting it. Nor would I. Rado soothed it down. Walking slowly, I led the way along the narrow path to where Eboric was hiding with the horses in a sort of cave with an open roof. On our left, the eunuchs were deep into a song that celebrated the many virtues of Chosroes. You could hear the Great King's fingermarks all over it – hardly surprising he had to write his own praises if you bear in mind how many court poets he'd murdered over the years. You couldn't call it bad exactly. No one could deny that Chosroes had better taste than Nicetas and more technical skill in Persian than Leander had in Greek. But the overall effect was still absurd and it must only have been fears of the impaling stake that kept the eunuchs from being pelted with filth by everyone who had to listen to them.

As we approached the hiding place, the path turned sharply away from the pass and the sound of the choir no longer blotted out all other noises. I could hear the universal patter of rain and the gurgling of the many little streams in which it was collecting. I could hear Eboric's whispered complaint that he was hungry and Rado's sharp reply that the last remains of the goat couldn't be scoffed till evening. 'Get the horses ready,' he said in a softer tone. 'We're moving out.'

We were back on the main path when a Persian voice called from behind me: 'What the fuck have you been playing at?' I turned and saw a dismounted officer making his way towards me. There was no doubt he'd been speaking to me. I gave my best effort at a Persian salute and stood to attention.

I'd still been dithering. Rado and Eboric together might have been able to tip the scale in the balance of fears and uncertainties. There's nothing like having your mind made up for you. 'Carry on past me,' I said to Rado in Latin. 'Remember what I said.' Eboric's mouth fell open with shock and I worried for a moment that he'd insist on a futile gesture. But Rado kept him moving.

Another few moments and they were both leading the horses round a big rock that had bushes growing from it.

Water squelching from his open boots, the officer hurried across the last few yards that separated us and poked me in the chest. 'What do you think you've been doing half the sodding afternoon?' he asked in the tone you put on for an idiot child. He poked me again, before lapsing into a manner more anxious than angry. 'If we aren't there soon, we'll be lucky to get off with a flogging.'

'I think my horse is a bit lame,' I said in an Armenian accent so strong, the officer had to listen hard to me. I stumbled through a few set phrases in Persian, ending with a look of blank stupidity.

'Oh, for an army filled with natives!' the officer cried. But I'd explained my appearance and enough of my absence from whatever I was supposed to have been doing. With an impatient snort, he waited for me to get the horse turned round and to follow him over to the file of other dismounted horsemen. One of these gave me a funny look. But the officer was almost shaking with impatience and we set off as fast as we could lead the horses. We passed by the eunuchs again and the steep incline Rado had chosen for our departure from the pass. We picked our way steadily past the stationary mass below us on the right.

57

Even at fifty yards, I could see that Chosroes was out of sorts with the world. His throne had been set up on a broad and reasonably flat rock that overlooked the pass. In the harsh sunlight of these mountains, he would have been a glorious sight. His throne was of white marble. He was dressed in his favourite yellow. The idea was plainly to have had Shahrbaraz and his other generals standing behind him, and behind them a few dozen priests of their fire-worshipping faith. The thousands upon thousands in the pass could have looked up to behold their Lord and Master arrayed in all His Majesty.

Of course, the rain had spoiled everything. The tall hats of the priests had collapsed over their faces and robes that should have flowed clung in a less than flattering manner to their bodies. Chosroes was more or less dry under his canopy. But this was only kept from sagging inward and leaking over the royal head by regular poking with a rod, so that water splashed on the silvered armour of the Royal Guard. The Great King and latest alleged posterity of Cyrus slumped on his throne. As ever, the old fraud Urvaksha was huddled on the ground before him. His hat too had fallen down his face. But you couldn't mistake the golden collar about his scrawny neck, or the golden chain which led from the collar to the Royal Hand. Nasty creature, I'd always thought him. Though blind, he'd sized me up soon enough and thought the same of me. Luckily, Chosroes had broken with his general custom and paid no attention to the gibbered warnings of betrayal. A shame the poison he'd accidentally eaten on my behalf hadn't finished him off.

The Persian officer slammed his fist against my leather breast-plate. 'Move yourself, fuckwit!' he groaned. 'Must I tell you *everything*? Where were you this morning, when Shahrbaraz spoke to the army?' Looking vacant, I let my mouth sag open. The officer swore again. He looked quickly about and leaned closer. 'You don't have security clearance,' he whispered, leaving a gap between each word. 'If you don't want to be thrown head first over the edge, give me your sword. You can have it back afterwards.' With another slap of his hand on leather, he pushed me towards the back of the disorganised and shivering mob of guards. 'Go on, then – just get over there. Stand at the back and try not to look like a moron. Leave the horse for the grooms.'

I shuffled across to stand in place. I counted a dozen Royal Guards. These still had their weapons and stood in formation close beside the Great King. The rest of us, it was clear, were there to fill up the numbers. It was a bit of a come down from public appearances in Ctesiphon, where Chosroes wouldn't have thought to show himself without the whole of the Royal Guard. How many had he brought with him? I wondered. The plain answer was that he must have brought all of them. The question, then, was where they were. Guarding the harem, perhaps? I had one answer as we were pushed and nagged by a couple of eunuchs into a more regular formation. Each of the Royal Guards was given his own sunshade bearer. The rest of us were left to get even wetter. Silvered armour doesn't come cheap. When you're already spent out on a gigantic invasion, a bit of rust on iron underlay becomes a serious concern.

One of the senior eunuchs now set about arranging us in detail. Speaking a Persian so rarified even the natives didn't understand all of it, he poked and prodded with a cane until we bore some resemblance to a guard of honour. 'Taller men at the front,' he shrilled quietly at me and then at a hulking beast whose beard was so dense it made his face look like the back of his head. I gave up the pretence of not understanding and let myself be pushed into a standing place one away from the front, and perhaps fifteen men along from Chosroes on my left.

So long as the bearded one next to me didn't breathe too hard, I could hear snatches of the conversation with the Grand Chamberlain. 'If it isn't in the iced compartment,' Chosroes said in the silky drawl that, once heard, no one ever forgot, 'it must have been stolen.' He snatched up an ivory scratching stick and pushed it inside the front of his robe. Grunting like an ape that's being fed, he rubbed it back and forth. He finished and took it out. He leaned forward to sniff the teeth. Displeased with the smell, he tossed it aside. 'Why is no one looking for it?' he asked.

The Chamberlain darted forward to pick up the scratching stick. 'If I might suggest, Your Majesty,' he wheedled, 'somebody, somewhere in the baggage train must have a replacement. I can send out a demand once the review is finished.'

I couldn't see him but Shahrbaraz now spoke. 'Everything's ready, Your Majesty,' he said gruffly. 'If we don't start soon, the rain will get worse again.' It wasn't the hushed, deferential tone most would use to a borderline lunatic vested with absolute and arbitrary power. Then again, whether or not he was actually mad, Chosroes wasn't stupid. If the only military leader of any talent thrown up on either side by eleven years of war didn't choose to address the Great King in a deferential squeak, he'd not have a bowstring tied round his neck.

Chosroes held up a hand for attention. 'My dear friend, Shahrbaraz,' he cried sternly, 'when Xerxes sat on a throne such as this at Abydos, it hadn't been pissing down all day. He could see his entire fleet and army in one glance. If that mist comes any closer, the best I'll be able to do is smell the assembled swine who call themselves my army.'

The reply was something I didn't catch. Nor could I hear what Chosroes said after that. But the polite laughter from the Chamberlain and the other eunuchs told me it wasn't relevant. Chosroes raised his hand again. 'Enough, enough!' he said. 'Be seated beside me, O greatest of my generals. The army has been brought together and must see us together and at one in all our deliberations.' He wriggled upright on his throne. Eunuchs ran forward to catch the loose cushions before they could hit the ground. 'Where is my fucking melon?' he suddenly spat. 'I've been fancying it since breakfast.' He took his scratching stick from Shahrbaraz and set about his calves.

Urvaksha looked up from muttering over his tangled strings. He turned conveniently sightless eyes in my direction. 'The knots tell me one of the serving boys ate it,' he cackled. 'The knots are never wrong – just let them be read by one who understands them. The knots are never wrong, I tell you!'

They hadn't served him well in the matter of the pickled goat's brain I'd let him pilfer from my dish. But Chosroes was leaning forward and slapping his thigh. 'Brilliant, Urvaksha!' he called out. 'Why is no one else willing to speak truth to power?' He tugged affectionately on the golden chain, catching his seer off guard and pulling him into a puddle. 'I will address the army on my feet,' he said, getting up and stepping forward to where he had his best view of the tired and perhaps nearly mutinous assembly in the pass. If only I could have got past the armed guards to give him one hard shove – if only one of the sodden eunuchs hurrying forward with the canopy had stumbled in the right direction – it wouldn't have been another missed chance of ending the war. But it was missed. As if he'd heard what I was thinking, he looked suspiciously round and stepped away from the edge.

'Time, I suppose, to weep,' he said in Greek. 'A hundred years from now, not one of these men will be alive.' He stopped for a low peal of thunder to roll down from the mountains. 'If I have any say in the matter,' he tittered into his sleeve, 'a hundred years will be more than pushing it. Ten is too many for this assembly of human trash.' He turned to Shahrbaraz. 'I'm ready to face my loving people,' he said in Persian.'

Somewhere behind me, a gigantic gong rang out, louder than the renewed thunder that accompanied it. I couldn't see into the pass from where I was standing but there was a ragged blare of trumpets from down there. After a long silence, the eunuchs struck up in unison:

Dārom andarz-ē az dānāgān
Az guft-ī pēšēnīgān
Ō šmāh bē wizārom
Pad rāstīh andar gēhān
Agar ēn az man padīrēd
Bavēd sūd-ī dō gēhān

Their voices and the bell-ringing accompaniment died away to reveal more thunder. This was blotted out again by a roar of cheering from below. While this continued, Chosroes mounted a small platform that had been carried forward. How the canopy bearers kept him dry was a tribute to the education of his court eunuchs. The rain was coming on harder and beat against us in great, heavy sheets. But Chosroes had now put on his biggest crown and, his unwetted beard poking forward, he raised both arms to take in the adulation of his army. He spun round and round, the heavy silk of his robe spreading out to make him look like a cone. The priests stood up and bowed. The Royal Guardsmen roared and beat their swords on their shields. We, the military rubbish, let out an inarticulate cheer. Far above, the clouds lit up in a dim flash. This time, the thunder rolled on and on. Depending how wet you were, you could take this as a further nuisance or as a dramatic accompaniment. Chosroes was able – and, I suppose, required – to take it as the latter. He raised his arms and walked quickly up and down his platform.

The cheering reached its end. Chosroes stood at the front of the platform and looked steadily at a depression in the far wall of the pass.

'Men of Persia,' he began, 'I have allowed you into my presence so that I may share with you the plans I have been revolving in my mind.' Whoever was in charge of the acoustics had messed up badly. His voice sounded weak at twenty yards. Through rain and thunder, how much of what he was saying could be heard down below was hard to say. The Persians never had been much good at the technical side of things. But this was a failing that, in itself, might tell something about the planning behind the invasion.

389

Chosroes stroked his beard in a manner that must be striking terror into his acoustics adviser and raised his voice to an undignified shout. 'There are those, men of Persia, who say that we are weak. They say that our crops blacken in the fields, and that our men sicken and die of the sweating pestilence. They say that our victories are a product of Greek failure – that the Greeks are badly led and that they have too many other frontiers to guard.

'But I tell you, men of Persia, that we are strong. We are the children of destiny. We are the ones whose glory shall be remembered at the end of time.' I was right about the acoustics. There'd be no free places on his impaling stakes once this was over, and once he'd laid eyes on whoever had told him to speak towards the far wall of the pass. He stopped for applause. Because he had stopped he got the applause, but it was more polite than frenzied. Everyone round him, to be sure, cheered himself hoarse. It was the wise thing to do. I think it took every mind off a sky that had turned the colour of lead.

Chosroes gave another glare over his shoulder and raised his voice to a scream. 'When my royal ancestor, Xerxes, invaded Greece a thousand years ago, he made one fatal mistake. That was to leave the Greeks he had conquered with their lives. In every age of their history, the Greeks have been an irreverent, faithless race. Whether in philosophy or theology, they go out of their way to unsettle every mind. The Greeks cannot be conquered until they are silenced. They cannot be silenced until they are dead.'

He stopped to clear his throat and for the praise of those who could hear him. 'Oh, bravo, bravo,' we cried. 'Death to the Greeks. What have they ever done for us?' and so on and so forth. Down in the pass, the only noise was of raindrops on spread canvas. A couple of eunuchs hurried forward to place covered lamps about the Great King. They made it easier to see him, though the upward lighting did nothing to remove the impression that we were being addressed by the monster from a particularly lurid nightmare.

Chosroes turned and spoke directly to us in his normal voice. 'I have given orders for every Greek we encounter on our march to be put to the sword. We left not one living creature in the cities of

Pentopolis and Alanta. Every farmer, every shepherd on our march, has been hunted down and killed without mercy. That is the policy we will adopt as we press through the Home Provinces of the Greek Empire. Constantinople itself will be taken and it will be sacked till not one stone is left standing on another. We will kill its people. We will demolish its buildings. We will burn its libraries. When we have dealt with the great city of filth and corruption that sits upon the two waters, we will race forward and take Athens and then Rome. I will, on my return to Ctesiphon, give supplemental orders for the cleansing of Antioch and Jerusalem and every other Syrian city of the Greek pollution. It will be the same for Egypt, once it is returned to its ancient loyalty.

'And we will spread our message of cleansing wider yet. The lands and islands of the remotest West shall not be suffered to harbour one student of the accursed civilisation. It is my intention that no record shall be left to future ages of the Greek and Latin races. Their books and languages will be wiped from the face of the world.

'But let us return to present concerns. In every step of our progress to Constantinople, let our army wade knee-deep through the blood of slaughtered Greeks. None must be spared. Compassion for those we conquer is treason to me.'

He stopped, realising perhaps he was drifting away from the big themes. He turned back to face his army and took a deep breath. 'I, Chosroes the Mighty,' he bellowed, 'will take final revenge for the outrages heaped upon our nation by Alexander the barbarian.'

I doubt if it mattered whether the army could hear him. Probably everyone in the pass had heard of Alexander, though not of who he really was. As for Xerxes and his failed invasion, and all the other ancient Kings of Persia, perhaps one in a hundred down there had heard their names. I'd soon learned in Ctesiphon that Chosroes had Herodotus on the brain. Those Persians who didn't know any Greek had no history but childish chronicles with notions of dating that changed from one chapter to the next.

He'd finished – and there was no point in continuing. Down below, the eunuchs had started an impromptu medley of war ballads. There were limits to how those of us about him could express our delight at the Royal Eloquence and strategic wisdom. With a face as dark as the sky, the Great King walked from the platform. He didn't wait for the eunuchs to get their canopy over him.

'Chosroes,' I called out in a voice that was surprisingly calm. There are times when fear leaves you paralysed. Then there are times when you realise what you had always intended and what has to be done. 'Chosroes,' I called again, this time in Greek and using the Greek version of his name, 'can I have a moment with you?'

I'd called to him as he was going past about ten feet away. A couple of the Royal Guard had pulled their swords out and were moving swiftly across the rocky ground in my direction. Chosroes stopped and looked round. I took off my helmet and pulled at the black cloth that covered my hair. He gave me one of his blank and disconcerting scares. Then he smiled and hurried forward through the rain. He waved the armed men back into line.

'Alaric, my dear fellow!' he cried in Greek. 'I'd been wondering when you would show your face.' He took me by the hands. 'Come out of this awful rain. You'll catch your death of cold.'

58

I held the scroll in each hand, and unwound it to what I knew was a favourite passage. I put my mind into order and read:

Now that he had taken Athens, Xerxes sent a messenger back to the Persian capital, to announce his success. The next day, he called together all the Athenians who had deserted their nation and sworn fealty to him, and ordered them to make sacrifice on the Acropolis in the manner of their nation. It may be that the Great King had himself been ordered in a dream to make this concession. Or it may be that he was sorry to have burned the temple of Athene. Whatever the case, these renegade Athenians at once obeyed.

Chosroes interrupted: 'I don't think, dear Alaric, you are making a completely faithful translation of the text.' He pointed at one of the words on the page I had before me. 'The Athenians here are described as exiles, not as traitors. Also, there is no mention of fealty in the Greek of Herodotus.'

So far as you can when the man behind you has a sword to your throat, I shrugged. 'I can't argue with that,' I said. 'However, a literal translation into Persian might not make as much sense as you presently want. Where individual passages are concerned, some degree of paraphrase must be permitted.' Chosroes nodded and sat back. He looked about to see that everyone had noted his command of his mother's language. He smiled complacently and motioned me to continue:

I mention this circumstance because, on the Acropolis, there is a temple of Erechtheus, in which there is both an olive tree and a representation of the sea. These commemorate the ancient contest between Athene and Poseidon for mastery of Attica. Now, the Persians had burned this olive tree along with the temple. However, just one day after this, the renegade Athenians saw that the tree had miraculously put forth a new shoot about eighteen inches long.

Though not quite the Prodigal Son, I had few reasons to complain about my reception into the Great King's bosom. I was bathed and shaved and oiled, and arrayed in a clean and reasonably dry robe. I was sitting beside him, a smell of cooking drifting my way as often as one of the tent flaps was open. After a brief intermission, the rain was back and its rapid and continuous beating on the leather roof meant that I had to keep my voice loud as well as steady.

'There will be no olive shoots after *my* visit to Athens,' Chosroes said firmly. 'Such Mass as I may permit in the converted temple of Athene will be held in Syriac.' He looked about once more and laughed. 'But tell me, Alaric, you were in Athens some years ago. Does the sacred olive tree still grow there?'

'Justinian had it dug out eighty years ago,' I answered. 'Since the proscription of the Old Faith, no one had pruned it and it was undermining the foundations of a building he wanted for a monastery.'

'Did you hear that?' Chosroes asked the line of trembling boys for whom I'd been translating. 'Do you see why total extirpation is the only answer to the Greek menace?' He glowered and sat forward. 'But which of you will confess to sacrilege against my person?' he demanded in a voice that suddenly dripped menace. 'Who has eaten my melon?' One of the younger boys started to cry – not a good move when Chosroes was in this sort of mood. 'Silence!' he barked. He got up and pointed, his finger wavering now right, now left. 'Start at that end,' he said eventually. He sat down and reached for his scratching stick. Two of the guards stepped forward and seized the boy farthest on the right from us. They pulled him to the floor and ripped his shirt away. To screams that left me clutching the scroll so hard its papyrus split and crumbled, one of them slit his stomach open. Even as I told myself not to, I watched the boy's red and steaming entrails pulled out of his body and then at his shocked, uncomprehending eyes.

'Nothing in this one, Your Majesty,' the guard said, wiping his hands on a cloth. 'Shall I carry on with the others?' No longer screaming, the boy was letting out a shrill, rattling moan. His body flopped about in a dying rhythm.

'Chosroes turned the corners of his mouth down. 'In your own time,' he said. He looked at me. 'But Alaric, enough of Athens – tell my boys about the futile stand of Leonidas and his Spartans.' He got up and rummaged in a box. He came back with another large and battered scroll. I took this in hands that I forced not to tremble and unwound it to the relevant passage:

The Persians now attacked once more, and the Spartans, knowing that this would be their end, came out to fight in the wide area of the pass at Thermopylae. Driven on with whips by their officers, the Persians surged forward. Many fell into the sea and were killed. Many fell down on the ground and were trodden to death. Many more were killed by the Spartans, who knew they would soon be attacked from behind and fought on with the most reckless courage . . .

'Get on with it, Alaric!' The Great King urged. 'It is a most dramatic narrative. Don't deprive my boys of what awaits those who defy the majesty of a Persian King.' Perhaps the most awful scream I'd heard all year had brought me to a sudden stop in the reading. I took my eyes away from a splash of blood over my polished toenails, and forced myself back to seeking Persian equivalents for the Greek words in the column of text before me.

Giggling and talking gibberish to himself, Urvaksha had never stopped from playing with his tangle of knotted strings. Now, he bounced up and down, rattling his golden chain. 'The knots don't lie,' he cackled. 'The knots never lie.'

I waited for someone to bring a lamp closer to me, and went steadily through the last stand of the Three Hundred – the death of Leonidas, the fourfold repulse of the main Persian army, the culmination of a frantic slaughter that had held up the advance long enough for the Athenians to stop arguing with each other and get their naval counter-attack ready in the Bay of Salamis. Raising my voice above screams for mercy and of terror, I reached the closing stage of the battle:

At last, however, the Persians were able to attack from behind, and the surviving Spartans withdrew to a low mound at the entrance to the pass – that is, to where a stone lion is now placed in memory of King Leonidas. Here, they continued fighting against overwhelming odds. Those who still had them fought with knives. Those who had lost all their weapons fought on with hands and teeth. It was only by volley after volley of arrows that their resistance was ended and all were finally killed.

I think I was expected to continue into the next chapter. But one of the prettier boys suddenly broke free of the guards and ran forward and threw himself into a prostration. 'Please, Your Majesty,' he sobbed – 'please don't hurt me. I didn't mean any harm.'

Chosroes stopped scratching himself and got up. 'Come into my embrace, Babar,' he cried in a voice of soft affection. He took the boy and kissed his face. He squeezed his behind and pulled a face in my direction. 'You should have asked me, Babar,' he said. 'You should have said how you longed to share the sweet taste of my melon. How could I have denied you anything?' He kissed the boy again and stroked his oiled hair. With a spasm of rage, he pushed him into the arms of one of the guards. 'Take him away,' he screamed. 'Geld him. Blind him. Put him in a cage. I'll think of a punishment after dinner.' He kicked the boy backwards and stood over him. He looked at me again, his eyes shining mad. He controlled himself. 'No, don't take him away,' he said to the guards. 'Gag him and do it here. I want my friend Alaric to see the justice of a Great King.'

I'll pass over the ghastliness of all that happened next. If you've a taste for sick porn, you're approaching the end of the wrong memoir. It was eventually over. The unconscious boy was pulled out of our sight. The bodies of the dead and dying were dragged outside into the rain. The dozen boys who'd survived sat cross-legged on the ground. They sat in silence, their eyes turned down. Urvaksha was rattling his chain again and talking about his infallible knots.

'Is the lion memorial still there at Thermopylae?' Chosroes asked.

Cautiously, I shook my head. 'I believe it was taken apart and used to reinforce the pass a few hundred years ago,' I said.

'So what did they fight for?' he asked triumphantly. 'Where is Sparta now? Where even is Athens? If I hear right, it's a provincial town in the middle of nowhere. Why did they resist Xerxes? All he wanted was surrender.' He nodded to the man behind me. The sword came away from my throat and one of the eunuchs brought me a cup of wine. I avoided answering the question by sniffing at the cup.

Chosroes laughed. 'No poison for you, Alaric!' he said, pushing his face close to mine. 'No death for my young friend Alaric. Why, not even a sniff of the torments I resolved for you after your treacherous escape from Ctesiphon.' His face darkened for a moment. Then he was all grinning maniac again. 'Drink, my friend, and be happy.' He took the cup from me and lapped its contents with his tongue. 'Drink – it's perfectly safe.'

'The knots tell me he's a bigger snake than last time,' Urvaksha called up from the floor. 'They say you should kill him.' As if in agreement, the man with the sword poked me gently in the back. I sniffed and didn't look round.

Chosroes tugged hard on the old loon's chain, pulling him into a pool of blood. He laughed at the result. 'Don't listen to Urvaksha,' he said. 'Just because he was right about you last time doesn't mean we can't be friends – does it?'

I drank deeply. Even the best Persian wine tends to be disgusting – they mix it with honey to cover the sour taste of the grapes. This was no exception. But wine is wine when your nerves are in tatters. Chosroes took the cup from me with his own hands and looked about for the jug. 'Have you seen Shahin?' he asked, a slight tremor in his voice.

'I have met him,' I said slowly. 'We spoke several times in Constantinople. You might say I'm here because of the assurances he gave on your behalf.' I drank more wine and made a show of casting about for words. 'It took me longer to get away from the City than I'd have liked. Shahin had a good head start. Can I take it that I've beaten him to you?'

He pushed his face close again. He lurched back and went at himself with his scratching stick. A flash of reddened chest under the hair told me his skin condition had now spread up from his waist. His entire body might be a mass of rotting sores. By the look of things, not even heroic doses of opium could keep the irritation under control. Bad luck for him. Bad luck for anyone in his power. That meant me. Plans that had seemed sensible enough earlier in the day were beginning to crumble about the edges.

Chosroes finished with his scratching stick. He narrowed his eyes. 'I had a letter from Shahin the day before yesterday,' he said. I kept my face immobile and stifled a fart. 'He wrote it some while ago. All he told me there was that he'd soon be in possession of a most valuable object. Can you shed any light on his progress in this endeavour?' He looked at the yellow scabs on the teeth of his scratching stick.

I coughed politely for the sake of getting some moisture into the back of my throat. 'I believe he's travelling here, or to Ctesiphon, with the Horn of Babylon,' I said evenly. 'Unless he's a better liar than he used to be, he didn't know about the invasion, or that you'd be leading it.' I tried for the sort of smile a man gives who is trying for nonchalance and not quite getting there. It wasn't hard to manage. I stayed silent and counted slowly to ten. Like a lover who's put off the moment of climax far beyond any reasonable limit, Chosroes was beginning to shake. I got myself ready to confirm what he must have been asking himself again and again since I'd bearded him in the rain. I didn't dare allow myself to feel any the better for it.

'I'm here only because this was the easiest place to reach where I could claim asylum,' I said. I pretended not to see the slight sagging of tension in his body. I allowed myself a more confident smile. 'I never realised I'd be able to ask for it directly, or to remind you of Shahin's assurances.'

I stood away while the Grand Chamberlain himself cleaned the scabs away. Chosroes took no notice. His face took on an exultant smile. 'Is Heraclius still alive?' He whispered.

I shrugged. 'He wasn't in Constantinople when the revolution broke out,' I said. 'I did hear he'd been hanged by his own soldiers.

But I also heard that he was on a ship going west – possibly to Carthage, where he can still claim a bit of support.'

'So who is Emperor in Constantinople?' he asked.

I shrugged again. 'I didn't wait for the dust to settle,' I said. 'Shahin's people got the city guard to proclaim Nicetas, which I believe was part of the deal you sanctioned. However, Timothy, the City Prefect, was being proclaimed by the mob as I finally slipped out of the City. Assuming he had any real support, I'd say he was now Emperor. But I don't know more than that,' I ended. It was possible Chosroes was playing with me. He enjoyed these little games. Any moment now and Shahin might pop out from behind a curtain. How they'd laugh as I was dragged screaming from the tent. If I was lucky, I'd find myself sharing Babar's cage. Anything was possible. But not everything was likely.

Chosroes sat down and covered his look of relief by pretending to blow his nose. He was still watching me, though. I took another mouthful of wine. A good liar gets his way through relentless charm and a focus on what his hearer wants to be told. But I was in the absolute power of a man who was only alive because of his skill at seeing through ordinary liars. Babar's eyes and genitals had been arranged on a silver dish. I moved this to the far end of its table and put my cup down.

'It doesn't mean you've won the war, however,' I said. Chosroes looked up from his obvious reverie on that topic. 'As said, I got out while the dust was all still in the air. But I've no real doubt that Timothy is now Emperor. He's no fool. Once he's got his hands on the Intelligence Bureau reports, he'll scrape an army together from somewhere.'

'Spies?' Chosroes hissed. He jumped out of his chair and pushed his face very close – I could smell his foetid breath, and see the tiny dots his eyes were becoming from a dose of opium I hadn't seen him take. 'The Intelligence Bureau has no spies in Ctesiphon. I had the last of them crucified a year ago. I assembled this army without any consultation. I didn't tell even Shahrbaraz where it was going till the final orders had to be issued. The new Emperor will be told nothing by the Intelligence Bureau.' Gradually relaxing, he pulled back and laughed. 'You know, by the way, I flayed Roxana alive with my own hands? Her dying moans may have mimicked the sound of the orgasms you gave the slut.'

It was no more than I'd expected. No one likes an adulteress. But I still felt sorry for Roxana. I nodded and stared at my wine cup. Chosroes scowled something about the need for another purge. I'd done enough. More would be too much. I changed the subject. 'However, you did say that you were expecting me. Does this mean the Persians have now taken to the ways of espionage?'

A broad and wolfish grin spread slowly over the royal face. 'I could keep you in the dark, my dear,' he sniggered. 'But why should I keep from you one whose only word in the past two days has been your name?' He clapped his hands and pointed at one of the eunuchs. 'Go and get him,' he said coldly.

Two days? I thought. It couldn't be any of my people. Had Shahin sent a messenger after all? My innards turned to ice. I had my answer while finishing my wine. One of the flaps opened and a dark and very wet shape was pushed inside the tent. It looked round and saw me. With a howl of maddened rage, it rushed at me, only slipping at the last moment on the bloody silk of the carpet.

'Get thee behind me, Satan!' Theodore screamed in Syriac. He raked feebly in my direction with bony fingers from which all the nails had been pulled out. 'I know your secret!'

59

The rain had stopped. It was getting on for late afternoon but the sudden brightening of the sky put me in mind of morning. So too the sharpness of the chilly breeze. All about us, the interminable drumming of the rain was replaced by the gurgle of a thousand streams that would probably bring water gushing into the pass for days yet to come.

I stepped over the body of one of the gutted boys and stood at the edge of the tent's raised wooden platform. I knew Chosroes was behind me. 'Trying to count the uncountable?' he asked slimily in Greek. 'Or are we perhaps looking for an escape?'

I continued looking at the sodden crowd that stretched on and on, as far along the pass as I could see. Even without his coded squeals of hate, it was plain that Theodore must have been brought here by Priscus and had run away. For all I knew, Priscus might be lurking somewhere atop the bleak walls of the pass. He might be watching us. If so, I could be happy I wasn't alone. For the time being, it was enough to know that whatever sense Theodore had made under torture hadn't been enough to do for me. I was still in with a chance. I turned and smiled. 'No to both,' I said. 'And if my simple word isn't enough, why should I come here to spy when I no longer have a master?'

Chosroes stood beside me. We watched in silence as the base of his travelling night palace was unpacked and fitted together. The grovelling engineer had explained in Greek that ten-foot poles should keep it above the water – and should keep it safe from some other threat neither had thought to mention other than obliquely. The poles, I'd heard, shouldn't give way, so long as the upper floor was omitted from this evening's build. I've said the

Persians weren't that good at the technical aspects of life. Much as in the time of Xerxes, though, they had no shortage of Greek renegades to go some way to supplying their own defects. And the night palace was an impressive thing to watch taking shape. All wooden compartments and leather straps, it was already bearing its planned resemblance – if on a smaller scale – to the Summer Palace in Ctesiphon. Not for Chosroes to slum it in a tent like everyone else.

People were noticing that the Great King had chosen to show himself a second time in one day. Those closest by where we stood began pressing forward, raising their arms in prudent joy. He stretched out his arms in a pose that reminded me of nothing so much as a crucified Christ and held it for what seem a long time. 'The duties of leadership,' he sighed at last, dropping his arms. He kicked a piece of stray offal from the edge of the platform. It landed with a splash beside where another of the dead boys was lying face down. 'Since we don't have to keep up the pretences of your last stay at my court,' he began, 'I'll ask if you adopted the same democratic manner with Heraclius.'

'Not quite,' I said. 'Then again, an Emperor's not usually surrounded by men who have to check after every audience that their heads are still attached. The main problem is sycophants.' I smiled and looked him in the eye. 'Would you like me to fall down and slobber kisses on your slippers? Would it make you less inclined to do away with me? I'll be honest that I didn't come here out of any positive desire to see you again.'

Chosroes looked back at me. 'When the mad boy said you were sniffing about,' he said slowly, 'I did revive all the plans that went through my mind two years ago. That democratic manner, I can tell you, wouldn't long have survived the first nibble of my flesh-eating bugs.' He laughed. 'However, I had already put those plans aside. I grant you the asylum you still haven't begged in the manner prescribed by the eunuchs. You have certain verbal and literary skills that make it worth keeping you alive.' He fell silent. I think he expected me to ask what he meant. Instead, I worked it out for myself and felt my nerves begin to settle – Shahin hadn't lied: my next tour of Ctesiphon, if there had to be one, shouldn't involve a visit to the Shaft of Oblivion. I watched the small army of men hard at work on the night palace. I didn't like the look of those support poles. The palace, though, was turning out decidedly lavish.

Anyone else he'd have had sawn in half for this lack of attention. But Chosroes used the long silence for another go at his itching body. Reminding me of his own presence, my guard jabbed me softly in the back with the point of his sword. Once more, I ignored him.

'Nearly eleven hundred years after his death,' Chosroes opened anew, 'and every educated Greek knows about Xerxes. So many ages later and everyone knows who he was, what he looked like, and what he did and said. For all the incidental lies and exaggerations, Herodotus made him immortal. Do you not think the Great King who finishes the work that Xerxes began deserves his own Herodotus?'

A deathless record of his greatness – in my experience, it crosses the mind of every ruler who's been moderately successful. In the end, once others had seen to his victory, even Heraclius gave way and commissioned an epic from Leander. If I hadn't known him, I'd never have believed it could be for this that Chosroes had been so eager to lay hands on me again. But I did know him and had no trouble believing it was for this that the bastard hadn't got me screaming for death. I nodded wisely. 'But I thought you were planning to abolish the Greek language,' I reminded him.

'Don't test my patience, Alaric,' he snarled. He turned away and kept his face out of view while he tried to bring it back to a semblance of the human form. 'I got you translating Herodotus to see if your Persian was still as good as it always was.' I nodded again. 'The last native I commissioned to write up my conquest of Syria did a characteristically piss-poor job. It was all flowery descriptions and no structure. His nearest approach to directness of utterance came after I'd impaled him. I want someone who can write in Persian and think in Greek – someone who can trace the events of the present to causes in a remote past. I want another

Herodotus, with a more than a dash of Polybius. If you don't provoke me into finishing your life, I'm proposing to let you found a new school of Persian historiography.'

Urvaksha looked up from his interminable sorting of knotted strings. 'You speak the soft and fluting language of the enemy too well,' he whined. 'Your mother did you ill to teach it.'

Chosroes pulled hard on the golden chain. 'If you don't keep your fucking mouth shut,' he hissed in Persian, 'I'll have you flogged.' He glanced at me, then back at his cowering general adviser. 'You go too far in your boldness,' he said emphatically.

I sniffed at the implied warning. 'Your Majesty assumes, of course, that his own invasion will be more successful than that of Xerxes,' I said with a bow that hovered between the perfunctory and the insulting. I turned and looked at the rain-sodden multitudes – most of them up to their knees in water. 'I'm surprised this army's got as far as it has into Imperial territory.'

Chosroes lifted his head so that his beard jutted forward. 'With Shahrbaraz leading, we'll get to Constantinople in time for the August heat,' he growled.

I allowed myself a quiet laugh. 'You might get to Chalcedon,' I said. 'You then have six hundred yards of water to cross to the European shore – six hundred yards that Timothy or even Nicetas – will absolutely control. Then there's the city walls. Also, I don't think your extermination plan is likely to win hearts and minds inside the walls.'

From far along the pass, a low cheer rolled towards us. There was a patch of blue in the sky and a shaft of sunlight followed the cheering. Before it could reach us, the shaft was cut off. There was a long and universal groan. 'I'll confess, I'm not a military man,' I added. 'But you're leading what's already a dispirited rabble before it's met a stroke of opposition.'

Chosroes slitted his eyes and looked at me out of their corners. 'I do have a weapon of great power,' he suggested. He twisted round and looked fully at me. 'And, since I can see the thought in your mind, I'll tell you now I'm not talking about the Horn of Babylon. That might or might not get me inside the walls of the

404

City. But, Alaric, I have something else with me that is the stuff of dreams to all true devotees of the Christian Faith. That will certainly cause the gates to be opened.'

He stopped and tapped his forehead knowingly. The tiny gap in the cloud had closed over. It was turning colder and I felt another spot of rain on my face. Tugging Urvaksha as if he'd been a drunken dog, he led me back inside the tent. The eunuchs and remaining serving boys had done a fast job. The place no longer stank of blood and ruptured entrails. There was a wine jug in a bowl filled with crushed ice. A couple of pale boys stood ready with bags of rose petals to shower on the Great King. He waved them out of sight, and sat on his ivory chair.

I sat beside him and filled the wine cups. I ignored the guard who took his place behind me. Chosroes stood up and pointed. 'You, boy,' he called imperiously. 'Come out of hiding. I need you here to taste my wine. Taste the Lord Alaric's as well. If it makes you sick, you won't die soon enough to avoid the Great King's wrath.' He looked at the boy's pale, tear-stained face. He looked briefly at the parts of Babar arranged on the silver dish. It was too much for him. He sat back and roared with happy laughter.

I took up the third sheet of papyrus I'd now covered in my attempt at the Persian script:

Now, the deposition and blinding of his own father had caused great outrage among the Persians. At first, this was suppressed by a general and unrestrained terror, a secondary effect of which was the removal, by death or mutilation, of all who had served his father in senior positions.

In the second year of his reign, however, Chosroes found himself no longer able to keep the opposition from uniting. The first among many failures of the harvests in the southern and most fertile regions of his empire, combined with what appears to be the inevitable return of pestilence, diminished his support among the people. His refusal to command a war against the nomadic Saracens of the desert, who had raided almost to the walls of Seleucia, alienated the loyalty of the army.

On the very day when the price of food is said to have reached its highest level in Ctesiphon, a mob, directed by General Bahram, burst into the summer palace. As was his custom, the young King had given himself up to wine and every manner of debauchery. Even so, he escaped the massacre of his entire household by dressing in the rags of a common leper and making his way towards the Euphrates, where he claimed the protection of the Greek Emperor, Maurice . . .

I looked up from my text. Chosroes was still nodding and smiling. 'Is this what you *really* want?' I asked dubiously.

'Oh yes,' came the immediate answer. 'I want a philosophical history. That means telling the truth so far as it can be ascertained. And, since I'm well on the way to conquering the entire known world, I like what will be your dramatic contrast between the early and the mature years of my reign.' He took the sheet from which I'd been reading and squinted at the smudged mess I'd made of having to compose in a script that ran from right to left. 'I do particularly like the connection you make between food prices and Bahram's *coup*. Without spelling it out, you suggest a certain opportunism in his behaviour. Once we move beyond these sample chapters, I'll explain to you how, after the Greeks put me back on the throne, I had him locked away with his children until he ate them.'

He pushed the sheet back across the writing table at me, and arranged all seven into a neat pile. 'I'm so glad, Alaric, I haven't had you killed. You're the only man alive who can write history this objectively, and in Persian. Please keep it that way. I believe Shahin will be here within the next few days. If he doesn't corroborate your story at least in its essentials, I won't kill you – but I will make you watch the death of that Syrian boy you appear to have adopted.'

I pursed my lips and looked thoughtful. I could probably get over the loss of Theodore. But Shahin's arrival would bring Antonia into the Royal Clutches. The thought of that was enough to set my insides moving in odd rhythms. 'I wish you hadn't tortured him,' I said. 'I'm not sure his wits will ever entirely come back.'

406

Chosroes laughed. 'He had fuck all of those when he was brought in,' he said. 'He was talking to himself in a language no one could understand. He only spoke back in Syriac when one of his testicles was almost crushed – and that was to thank his jailor and ask to be roasted over a slow fire. You surround yourself with some very odd people.'

So Theodore hadn't talked yet. I could be glad of that much. I smiled weakly and reached for a clean sheet of papyrus. 'I believe you spent eighteen months in Constantinople,' I said. 'I'll need your help to compose the speech you made to the Emperor. There is a couplet by one of your old poets whose name I currently forget. But do you really plan to take the place apart?'

Chosroes looked round and dropped his voice. 'Of course, I don't,' he said in Greek. 'I said what I did to jolly the army along. You don't willingly destroy a city of such marvels. Its current population will be gradually eased out. But their lives will be spared. It's only the farmers I really want to kill – destroying the Greeks at the root, you see; no chance of olive shoots, and so on. For the rest, you will surely agree that the ruler of the world deserves to occupy no less than the capital of the world.'

'It makes sense,' I agreed.

He stood up and stretched. I'd been scribbling away for him for the remainder of the afternoon and the sky was turning dark outside. 'I don't like to be away from my palace at night,' he muttered. He snapped his fingers at the two guards who'd stood behind me all the time I was writing. 'Bring the Lord Alaric along. Don't lose him in the dark.'

60

If I hadn't known better, I'd have had to open my eyes wider in the gloom to check if they weren't being deceived. In the light of two double lamps, you might easily have thought you weren't looking at paintings on silk, and that a windowless room twelve foot by eight at best was in fact the vast hall of ceremonies of the summer palace in Ctesiphon.

But I did know better. I was standing in one among several wooden boxes heaped on a large wooden platform that was itself resting on about a hundred support poles. Third behind Chosroes and Urvaksha – and never allowed to forget the smirking armed creature close behind me – I'd crossed, on a causeway above the slowly ebbing waters from the storm, from the big tent to the base of the night palace.

Chosroes patted me on the back. 'Time, Alaric, to forget the cares of the day,' he said with slimy cheer. 'I always *so* enjoyed our little dinners in Ctesiphon.' Not answering, I went with him to the entrance and watched as the few serving men our weight limits had allowed pulled up the ladder. Below us, the whole immensity of the night palace was surrounded by a double circle of armed guards. Behind every fifth man in the innermost circle stood a slave with a flaring torch. The whole arrangement struck me as a fire hazard in itself. Otherwise, the palace must have been an obvious target for anyone above the pass able to shoot fire arrows. Any artillery would have knocked it to pieces before the ladder could be let down again.

A more pressing concern, though, was its general stability. Even in the gentle wind that moaned along the pass, the little silver bells above us were tinkling as if an irate master somewhere was calling for his slaves. One look at Shahrbaraz, and I could see that I wasn't alone in wondering if those ten-foot support poles had been such a good idea.

Either Chosroes didn't agree or he didn't care. With his own hands, he pulled the main door shut and drew its bolts. 'My chief general, of course,' he tittered, 'will go back to his military tent after dinner. But you, my dearest Alaric, will be locked into your own room, to sleep on your own silken mattresses. I would have given you a room in the tower – only the engineers became proper wet blankets towards the end of the day. Excepting my own, all the bedrooms are in a small block beyond the dining room.'

He waited for one of his serving boys to open the door to the dining room. Though not approaching his usual accommodation, this was respectably large. Indeed, at about a hundred feet by fifty, I think it amounted to most of the palace. It had no windows, but enough air came in through the gently grinding segments of the structure to keep the lamps flickering and us from choking to death in the smoke from the incense burners.

Chosroes walked briskly into the room. He stopped in the middle and turned round and round on the silk rugs that covered its wooden floor. 'Behold, Alaric, how civilisation is carried into the furthest wilderness,' he cried. He sat down on one of the nicer rugs and rocked happily back and forward. 'I'll let you watch the engineers dismantle this place in the morning. You can work a full description into your narrative of the invasion. The wall hangings, I must observe, are all cloth of gold.'

'He's a spy for Caesar!' Urvaksha spat. 'Everything you tell him will go straight to Constantinople. You're a fool to keep him alive.'

'If I might suggest, Your Majesty,' Shahrbaraz took up in his deep voice, 'the blond Westerner has betrayed you once already. Should you be so willing to trust him again? And so soon?'

Chosroes got up and watched the food tasters at work. 'You can hold your tongues, the pair of you,' he said in his silky, menacing voice. 'Each one of you is useful to me in his own way. That's all you need to consider.' He pointed one of the tasters at a lead pot of something that still bubbled over an oil burner. 'Once Shahin's confirmed his story, I'll ease his terms of confinement. Until then, he stays beside me and takes notes of all I say and order.'

Shahrbaraz bowed. 'It is as you command, O Great King,' he said with a nasty look in my direction. 'Shahin is, however, very late. None of the scouting parties we've sent ahead has seen him or his people. Until then, our only assurance that Heraclius has fallen is Alaric – a man whose lies delayed our conquest of Syria by a year. It is my duty to ask how we can know that he isn't here to encourage us into a trap?'

Chosroes pursed his lips, reminding me of a scorpion that can't decide whether or not to sting the frog that's carrying him across a pond. He smiled and turned his attention back to watching a man pat silently through the cushions on which we were to sit for dinner. He looked up suddenly at a slobbering sound in the corner. I followed his look. Hands tied behind him, Theodore was drifting out of the drugged sleep I'd procured for him, and trying to sit up. So far away, and in poor light, he gave an impression of recovering sanity. I willed him still to be off his head. I couldn't afford him to be worth torturing into any version of the truth.

'I know your secret, Alaric the Damned!' he called out in Syriac – a language neither of the Persians showed any sign of understanding. 'You have corrupted everything pure in the service of your Dark Lord. I renounce all bonds with you.' He trailed off into more of the nonsense language he'd spoken for most of his time in captivity. I managed a nervous smile in his direction. It couldn't be long before the Great King noticed the lack of affection in our relationship. It would have been for the best not to have him around – as ever, bloody Priscus had a lot to answer for: and what was *he* up to, I might ask? But it wasn't time for that question. I could sweat over it in bed. For the moment, I'd keep up the effort of concern for the idiotic boy's welfare.

'I'm not sure my son is hungry,' I said. 'But I do suggest another dose of opium to ease the pain. The last time I looked, his ballbag was swollen like a pomegranate. Yes – perhaps a few grains of opium, and on a heated spoon to quicken its effect.'

Chosroes flopped on to a mound of cushions and waved his vague assent. One of the eunuchs went over to a box and began fiddling with bottles. Chosroes reached out for a piece of unleavened bread. 'Come and join me, dear friends,' he commanded in a tone that indicated anything but generosity of heart. He watched Shahrbaraz stuff a piece of honeyed mutton into his mouth. He smiled. 'Tell me, General,' he asked, 'when can the army resume its march along the pass?'

Shahrbaraz swallowed too quickly and went into a coughing fit. 'Not for days!' he eventually managed to splutter. He drank from his water cup. 'Everything is soaked. Everyone is out of sorts. Getting the march under way again before we've got over the storm may bring on a mutiny – especially since we still haven't paid the bounties promised when we set out. I won't mention the state of the food supplies.' He stopped and narrowed his eyes. He turned a very grim stare on me. 'If that beast you haven't yet crucified is up to his usual tricks, I swear we're marching right into a trap. One sight of a Greek army with the state we're in, and my advice for the next five days at least will be immediate withdrawal along the pass. Reject that advice and you might as well keep a couple of good horses ready for a dash back to Ctesiphon.'

'Oh, Shahrbaraz, Shahrbaraz,' Chosroes laughed, 'are you really about to break all security in front of Alaric?' He turned to me. 'The good General here wants us to invade Egypt. Because we have Syria, it's easy for us to attack, and hard for the Greeks to defend. It's also rich enough to let us pay a few bills.' He turned back to Shahrbaraz. 'Well, unless you can show me your Greek army of resistance, we march for Constantinople.' He took a long drink and stared happily at the glittering cloth that hung down from the ceiling.

Shahrbaraz had already gone into another coughing fit. This time, I thought he'd burst a blood vessel on his forehead. I wondered if he was about to speak – as said, he was one of those people even Chosroes didn't dare murder. But a gust of wind now hit the palace at the wrong angle. With a long and alarming groan, it tilted enough to knock over a pot of earthworms in fish sauce. In silence, we watched it tip over on one of the rugs, and continue an irregular progress towards one of the cloth of gold hangings. Chosroes giggled and lolled back on his cushions. Shahrbaraz said nothing but attacked a dish of something that looked as if it had been squeezed from both ends of an overfed cat. I stuck a piece of bread into a dish of ground chickpeas and olive oil. Chosroes had never complained in the past about my disinclination to share his vile tastes in food. Anything richer than this at the moment and I'd only puke it up again.

In the extended silence of the dinner, I gave way and thought about Priscus. I could take it as read that Theodore wasn't up to finding his way outside the walls of the City by himself. He'd been brought along as general skivvy for Priscus. Even so, the two of them must have grown wings to get here so quickly. There was no chance Priscus could have known about the invasion. That meant he'd broken all his normal rules of life and come out to make sure I didn't mess things up. I should have been a little more open with him in Constantinople. Too late for regrets now – that was for sure. I thought of the best Persian for 'When error is irreparable, repentance is useless.' If all else failed, I could impress Chosroes with it – I could put it into his father's mouth when the execution-ers took out their bowstrings. Or perhaps not – it had too much smell in that context of a rhetorical excess. The Great King could be a harsh critic where historical writing was concerned. I repeated the sentence to myself in Latin and then in English and in every other language in which I was proficient. It kept me from reflect-ing too obviously on the square painted in red about the Royal eating place. So far as it could be, this room was an imitation of the summer palace.

Before I could figure out the best translation into English, Chosroes got up and clapped his hands. 'I've had enough to eat,' he announced. 'The dinner is over. I want everyone out of here except Alaric and one guard.' I couldn't say Shahrbaraz had even tried for jollity through the meal. I'd not miss his glowering presence.

★   ★   ★

You can be sure that, when he'd said alone with me, Chosroes hadn't meant that Urvaksha could unhook his collar and shimmy down the ladder with Shahrbaraz and the eunuchs and other flunkies – or that Theodore could be carried out like a sack of mildewed grain. It certainly didn't mean that my guard could go off duty for the night. With those exceptions, though, we were alone. The wind was rising, and the swaying and groaning of several tons of woodwork on its inadequate support was joined by the harsh beating of more rain against the walls.

Chosroes wheeled about again on his favourite rug. 'Alaric,' he whispered, 'I will grant you the boon of letting you ask me any question you please.' He tripped daintily across the floor and stood over me. I could go through the motions of getting my writing materials ready but I'd already seen that the eunuchs had left me with a heap of waxed tablets. Since I still wasn't to be trusted with anything that had a point on it, I might as well leave that part of the game aside.

'Ask, and you shall know,' he repeated. I got up and went for a chair for him to sit on. Staggering slightly as if from too much wine, I put it down so one of the faint red lines on the floor passed directly beneath it. The guard was watching me with eyes that didn't seem to blink. Though sitting down, his unsheathed sword rested on his knees. There was one cushion beside the general mass that hadn't been moved all evening. I could suppose the shock I had in mind would keep the guard in his place long enough for me to go for one of the curtains. Even with a sword, he'd not stand much of a chance against me.

I waited for Chosroes to sit down and made him a reasonably solemn bow. 'You spoke earlier, Great King,' I began, 'of something that is the stuff of dreams to all Christians, and that this would cause the gates of Constantinople to swing open for you. I take it, from the inflexions of your voice, that you were talking about the True Cross. Any chance of letting me see it in the morning?'

He looked back at me. Had I gone too far? No – he put a hand up to his mouth and giggled softly. 'You don't miss anything, do

413

you, Alaric?' he said. 'I probably should have you crucified as a spy. I might still do that, if Shahin confirms what everyone else believes – that you're a barefaced liar and are only here to divert me from the approach of a Greek army.' He looked about for his cup. I got up and carried it to him. I filled it from a jug and sat down close to the unmoved cushion. I had the guard behind me and could hear him settling back after my sudden movement.

Chosroes drank deeply. 'Getting into Jerusalem last year was hard enough,' he said. 'Getting into the Holy Sepulchre Church took three days of fighting. The oldest monks – even the bishops – took up swords and fought like the Spartans at Thermopylae. But Shahrbaraz got there in the end. With his own hands, he ripped the curtain aside and exposed what turned out to be a thirty-pound piece of shrivelled wood – thirty pounds of wood encased in two hundred pounds of gold studded with jewels of inestimable value. I'm glad he didn't burn it along with the church. My own Christian minority loved me beyond describing when I had it carried through the streets of Ctesiphon. I won't bore you with the accounts of the miracles worked by it as I rode before it. I don't imagine you believe it ever formed part of the cross of which the Jewish Carpenter was put to death.'

I got up again and bowed drunkenly. 'The story is that, when Constantine established the Faith, he let his mother demolish much of Jerusalem in search of relics. Apparently, she found all three crosses and was told in a dream which had been used on Christ and which on the two thieves. The Emperor then had the True Cross broken up, so fragments could be sent to every main church throughout the Empire. I'm told that if you were to reas-semble all the fragments they would make enough lumber to fill a ship. Not bad for something that one man was able to carry up to Golgotha. But I'm also told this is in itself another miracle.'

I put up both hands and burped gently into one of my sleeves. 'So you're planning to turn up outside Constantinople and show the True Cross to the people?' I asked. 'I suppose, if you handle things properly, that should open the gates for you. But what then?'

'Oh,' came the airy reply, 'I'll allow a three-day sack of the City. Anyone my people find will be fair game. But I won't allow the buildings to be harmed. I've got a Persian bishop with me who'll be the next Patriarch. Minus the gold, he can have the relic to put on show in the Great Church. I think I'll preside at the presentation. I once saw Maurice leading a ceremony there. It was most impressive. When I get up and speak, it can form the culmination of the first decade of your History. You'll need to instruct me on the differences between the Monophysite heresy and Imperial orthodoxy. They make bugger all sense to me.' He finished his wine and stuck his chin out again so his beard jutted forward.

I got unsteadily up. 'If Your Majesty will pardon me,' I slurred, 'I need to vomit.' I heard the guard snigger with polite contempt. All I had to do was stumble as I went by the cushion.

'Stop!' Theodore called in Syriac from the far end of the room. I looked at him. 'Stop, Alaric,' he said, now clutching despite his bound wrists at the wall hangings. He pulled himself to his knees and laughed bitterly. For the first time since he'd been found howling in the mountains, he switched into Greek. 'I know your secret,' he sneered. 'You've come here with Priscus to murder the Great King. But know ye not the words of Saint Paul:

Let every soul be subject unto the higher powers. For there is no power but of God: the powers that be are ordained of God. Whosoever therefore resisteth the power, resisteth the ordinance of God: and they that resist shall receive to themselves damnation.'

He fell down again in hysterical laughter.

Chosroes was on his feet and racing across the room. 'Priscus is dead!' he wailed. 'How can a man kill me when he's dead?' He reached Theodore and kicked him in the stomach. He turned him over and slapped his face. He kicked him in already ruined balls. He was wasting his time. For several years, I'd been aware of Theodore's belief in the purifying nature of pain. He really was now ready to receive the violet crown of martyrdom – he'd have gloried amid the flames. Chosroes stopped and turned in my direction. 'What are *you* up to, Alaric?' he asked. 'I welcomed you back. I trusted you. How were you planning to kill me?' The guard was on his feet, sword at the ready. His chain trailing behind, Urvaksha crawled in the vague direction of his master's voice.

'Kill him, O Great King!' he shrilled yet again. 'The knots never deceive. He came with murder in his heart. Kill him now!'

Chosroes looked at me. He looked at Theodore. He looked at the guard. From a sheath I'd already guessed was up his sleeve, he pulled out a steel blade of his own. He opened his mouth to speak, but was silent.

The silence was broken by a sudden pattering of hands on a drum. It came from behind a curtain on my right. Angry, the Great King turned to see who'd disobeyed his direct order to be left alone with me. The drumming settled down into a brisk and flowing rhythm that I well remembered, and the curtain was pulled aside.

Naked, covered all over in gold paint, Eboric stamped hard three times on the floor and raised lightly muscled arms in the opening moves of his orgasm dance.

61

I don't believe there was a man alive who could resist Eboric's charms. Even with a sword at my throat again, I could see that the boy was outdoing himself tonight. You can search me how he and Rado had got up here undiscovered. Ditto how they'd got themselves kitted out for the dance. But here they were and Chosroes was hurrying across to stop the guard from sawing my head off. 'We'll go on with our conversation after the end of what may be a *delightful* surprise,' he snarled. 'If it really is delightful and if you can prove any involvement at all in it, you may get a flash of my merciful side.' He sat down a few feet from me, and turned his attention back to the perfect unfolding of complexity.

I looked on, rigid with shock. Slowly, as the pattering of Rado's hands on the drum took on a firmer rhythm, I found myself able to think again. I'd taken a sudden and gigantic risk, and I'd got so close to solving every problem we faced. Right up to the last moment, the plan had unfolded as if someone had been directing things in a play. Now, for the second time in a month, that worthless shit Theodore had ruined everything. I should have listened to Priscus and left him to beg his bread in Athens. Failing that, I should have taken a proper look at him when he got to twelve, and dumped him in one of the more ascetic monasteries. By now, he could have been sticking skewers through his nipples and making everyone miserable with his visions of hellfire. If I ever got out alive of this latest catastrophe he'd arranged, I'd see to it that Theodore got a whole lifetime of moral suffering. I took a quick glance in his direction. Sure enough, he was on his knees again, peeping out from behind raised hands at the controlled indecency of Eboric's dance.

What I'd do if I ever got out alive! Looked at realistically, it was all up for me. I'd gambled and I'd lost. The question was should I make a deliberately futile gesture and get my throat cut? It would be an easier way out than Chosroes was doubtless considering. Or should I try insisting that the boys were strangers and that the plot was wholly mine and Theodore's? I didn't think he'd believe that – two Western barbarians whose working language was Latin: I might as well have claimed black was white. But it seemed wrong of me to take the easy way out and leave two boys who'd risked everything for my sake to carry the main punishment.

Rado was beating out a more complex rhythm and the dance was reaching its climax. Chosroes already had both hands inside his robe, and was fondling himself. He didn't risk penetrative sex nowadays, I knew – not since one of his wives had tried to do for him with a toxic pessary. But he might contain himself till he'd walked round and round Eboric, poking and fondling as the mood took him.

Slowly, now darting forward, now back, not seeming to notice who I was, Eboric came closer. I could feel a slight tremor in the sword still held against my throat and could hear a change in the guard's breathing. The boy raised his arms and lowered them, and the iron bracelets he had on each arm moved up and down the gold of his skin. He stretched out his arms in a gesture of endlessly wanton enticement.

Chosroes waved his own sword at me. 'Go and stand against that wall, Alaric,' he said evenly. 'Stretch out your arms as if you were already on a cross. Try not to move.' To the guard: 'Go and dance with the boy,' he said. 'Keep hold of the sword. Disembowel the boy if Alaric moves so much as an inch.' He looked at me and twisted his face into a snarling and triumphant smile. 'Your plot is discovered, Alaric,' he cried. 'Whatever you and these boys had planned won't happen now. When this dance is over, you're going down that ladder bound hand and foot. We'll see how much of your *democratic* manner is left this time tomorrow!' He lay back against a mound of cushions and pulled at his clothes until his scab-covered belly and crotch were exposed. He clenched both fists and arched his back. He looked again at me and let out a high giggle. 'You just stand there, Alaric, and watch me bring myself off without hands. I may see how well you can do it tomorrow – *without hands!*' He pointed at the guard. 'Dance with the boy, I command!' he giggled.

Drawn sword in hand, the guard lurched forward at Eboric and was left clutching at air. He spun round and tried again. Once more, Eboric shifted position almost without seeming to move. On his third attempt, the guard laid hold of the boy's left shoulder. He pulled him forward into a rough embrace. The drumbeat was rising to its fluttering climax. Chosroes steadied his voice. 'I've changed my mind,' he said. 'When I sit up, 'I want you to bring the boy forward and cut his throat. I want his blood splashing over me when I go off. Do you understand?'

Grunting over his throbbing stiffy, the power-crazed bastard had overreached himself. I could see this with the chilly calm that sometimes comes with despair. It was as if I'd stepped from the jostling crowds and the heat of the Triumphal Way into the entrance hall of my own palace. I knew what had to be done and I was free to act. Eboric was effectively dead. I was twelve feet away from Chosroes. I could break his neck before the guard could try to stop me, and before he could squirm to safety. So what if Chosroes ran me through first? I was only choosing a quick death over a slow one. More to the point, unless he got something vital, I'd have enough strength left in me to see to him. Eboric would be dead whatever happened. Rado would have the chance to make a run for it, or die fighting. What I'd had in mind earlier involved my own escape. Well, that was now out of the question. But I could still do the rest of the world a favour.

The guard held Eboric tighter and moved him slowly towards Chosroes, whose eyes flickered between me and the approaching treat. It was a matter of choosing the right moment. I needed to go for Chosroes when his normal reflexes were at their slowest. Carefully, I tensed every muscle. I watched for him to open his mouth to let out a groan of ecstasy.

Because I was too busy watching Chosroes, I missed the absolute precision of what Eboric did next. I saw from just inside my field of vision how he twisted round to face the guard and how he kissed him on the lips. I saw how he raised both arms aloft and flicked both iron bracelets to his wrists. I saw only in part how he smashed both bracelets at once against the guard's temples. I did clearly see the creature go down like something stunned in a pagan sacrifice. Still more clearly, I saw Eboric take up the dead man's sword and make a dash at Chosroes.

'No!' I shouted. I threw myself forward, grabbing the boy just in time. Even so, his oddly powerful momentum nearly carried the pair of us into the killing zone. I rolled on top of him and pulled him on top of me. We ended with the sword pressed between us. In all this, I'd barely heard the click of machinery as Chosroes tipped the hidden lever and then the deafening crash of his safety cage.

Every tyrant needs one, you see – and Chosroes had everything a tyrant needed. I'd never seen it in action in Ctesiphon. No one I'd spoken to ever mentioned it. Perhaps no one had seen it work and been left alive to warn of its existence. But I'd sat night after night with him, working out the function of the red square drawn on the floor and of the irregular contours in the coffered ceiling above where the Great King always sat when strangers were present, or those some turn of his frenzied imagination had given him cause to suspect of treason. I've said this room was a scaled-down copy of its counterpart back home. It was unthinkable its designers had left off the dual layer cage of bronze bars, eight foot by eight, that would in emergencies seal off the Great King from so much as a lucky bowshot. I'd now seen it do its work. Spikes on its underside had nailed it immovably to the floor. One of the projecting steel blades was barely an inch from my nose. Even after the reverberant crash was over, the whole of the raised palace continued pitching and swaying from the transfer of weight.

I let Eboric finish his orgasm dance. Then I lifted him, sobbing and twitching, out of harm's way. I sat up and took the sword. There was no one left to kill for the moment. But the guards down in the pass would need to be drunk not to have noticed the fall of the safety cage.

'You've failed again, Alaric!' came the snarling cry from behind the tight bronze strands of the cage. 'You'll never touch me now.'

There was a double lamp hanging from the ceiling behind the cage. By the light of this, I could see the bowed shape of Chosroes shuffling about.

I looked at Urvaksha. He hadn't been so lucky as his master. One of the fins had sliced him in half from right shoulder to left hip. The palace had settled into a slight tilt and I watched his dark blood run towards the far end of the room, where Theodore had gone still and quiet.

I turned away. 'Get dressed!' I ordered the boys. 'There's no time to lose.' I think a couple of the support poles now gave way together. It was like standing in the belly of a ship that's just hit something. I staggered to keep my balance. That isn't easily done when standing upright in relation to everything round you means you're off vertical by about twenty degrees. I gave up brandishing the sword and put it to use as a walking stick.

Rado brought forward one of the elaborate silk jackets in which they must have got past the guards. A dreamy smile on his face, Eboric stared at it. I kicked him in the chest. 'Come on,' I hissed. 'He'll get away and they'll burn us alive in this thing.'

I was wrong. I'd guessed that the security cage was only intended to ward off an immediate attack and there was a trap door to get Chosroes properly out of danger. But no one had allowed for the buckling of the segmented floor. I could hear Chosroes pulling and pushing frantically at an exit that might be jammed beyond hope. I saw him get up and caught the flash of his steel blade. He howled in the terror of being caught in a space that didn't let him stand upright. He rattled his sword against the bars. He went back to banging at the jammed trap door. He hadn't yet noticed that Urvaksha was dead. He would eventually care about that, I knew. Every tyrant needs his safety cage, or something like it. And every tyrant needs at least one certain friend. When he got free of what was now his prison, there would be blood on the moon in his wild grief for a seer whose predictions had only been an excuse for their friendship. But he was a prisoner and it suddenly appeared that whatever blood he finally shed wouldn't be ours.

421

I swallowed. I relaxed. I bent down and kissed Eboric on the face. 'I could never have asked for a better son,' I said gently. I helped him to his feet. I gave Rado a manly nod. 'But do get something on you. We need to be away from here.'

Even as I spoke, there was another sound of snapping wood and of groaning palace sections. I've never been in a shipwreck. But that must be what the sideways collapse of the far end of the room resembled – that and the shifted slope of where we stood to about forty-five degrees. One of the lamps had come off the wall and was already spreading a pool of burning oil across the floor. If the outside of the palace was sodden from the rain, its furnishings might, with luck, become a royal funeral pyre.

Eboric was still fumbling with his clothes. No time for niceties. I snatched the coat from him and threw it over his shoulder. 'We're getting out as we are,' I said calmly. 'Keep your mouth shut. If there's talking to be done, let me do it.'

Holding hands, the three of us slithered down the slope of the floor towards the collapsed far section. This had squashed an unknown number of the guards and I could hear maniacal shouting that took me back to the failed assault on my own palace in Constantinople. We slid down the silk rugs that still connected the two parts of the floor. I looked back once at the cage where Chosroes was now hurling himself about like a trapped wild animal.

'Don't leave me here, Alaric,' he pleaded. 'Don't let me burn. I'll be your friend again. I'll make you Emperor in Constantinople.' He raised his voice to a shrill scream. 'Get me out of here and I'll do whatever you want.' He raised his voice higher. 'Urvaksha – where are you, Urvaksha!'

Water was leaking upwards through the lower segments of the floor and the silk rugs squelched underfoot. Only one lamp down here had survived the collapse but it was enough to show us towards a sheared-off section of wall. Another few yards, and we could step out into the shouting, terrified crowd.

I heard Theodore behind me. 'Please, Father,' he begged in Syriac, 'take me with you.' I turned and saw him lying on his back, bound hands stretched out in supplication. No one could complain if I say that I gave him a kick of my own in the balls and hurried out alone into the darkness. Instead, I walked carefully back across a floor that seemed to have come to life beneath me and threw him across my shoulder.

The collapse we'd had so far wasn't the end of the destabilising effect of the fallen cage. There was another sound of snapping supports. This time, there was a crash that went on and on. I've said I was never in a shipwreck but many's the time I've seen a building catch fire and burn to the ground. This was like the final inward crash of floors. All that was missing was the explosion of sparks and the blast of intense heat.

I had my story ready for when I stepped out through the gap on the walls but no one paid the slightest attention. Dressed in the finery of a Persian noble, two naked boys beside me, another sobbing boy across my shoulder, I stepped right through a circle of men screaming orders at each other. We hurried across what remained of a wooden causeway. We nearly bumped into a party of armed men who were hurrying forward. I waved them aside and watched them step down into the water. I stopped by the dark wall of the pass and turned to look back at the stricken night palace. I'd been hoping it was on fire. All I saw was an irregular mass of darkness, framed by the lesser dark of the cloudy sky. I couldn't see anyone. But there was a rising babble of shouts that indicated someone would finally see a personal interest in going in to spring Chosroes from his trap. It was best not to be anywhere close when he was carried out into the cold air of the night, bellowing for vengeance.

'We tethered the horses in a sort of cave a hundred yards up on the left,' Rado whispered in my ear.

I nodded in the darkness. He couldn't have seen. I cleared my throat and laughed. 'Those weren't the orders I gave you,' was what I wanted to say. It would have been ironic and nonchalant, and fairly memorable, and worth quoting in the biographies. But I was beginning to tremble with delayed shock and I didn't trust my voice to sound as I wanted. I shifted Theodore to my other shoulder and patted Rado on the back. 'Good work, my son,' I said quietly in Slavic.

62

The rain had passed away and, although the clouds were still a leaden mass in the sky, it didn't seem likely to return. Happy in my riding clothes, I sat on a stone and watched Eboric scrub the last of the gold paint from his body under a cascade of water from a high outcrop of rocks. He was astonishingly pretty, I thought again. Little wonder Chosroes had been taken off guard. Adoption brings certain paternal duties that must be taken seriously. The avoidance of incest, on the other hand, is one of those technicalities to be observed only in public. Such a shame the circumstances of our getaway would keep my increasingly lustful hands off him for the foreseeable future.

I sighed and turned my attention to Rado. 'I have told you,' I said in an interval of the snarled questioning, 'that knocking him about won't get us anywhere.' Long before morning, Theodore had turned pious again and was crying out in Syriac for punishment. The savage beating that might actually have broken one of his ribs was no more than he was calling out for. Still, he deserved it, and it was improving Rado's mood from moment to moment. Who was I to interfere? But for this shitty little God-botherer, Chosroes would now be dead and the invasion would be over – and possibly the war as well. And we could be riding off to snatch Antonia at our leisure. Indeed, Shahin would probably hand her over in exchange for my promise of asylum. As it was, the whole upland plain behind us was crawling with mountain cavalry. It was only because the horses were worn out that we were having even this break from our desperate climb out of their reach.

I stood up and stretched. I walked over to where Theodore was trying to pull out one of his wobbly front teeth. I bent down to him. 'Listen,' I said in Syriac, 'I want you to tell me where you left Priscus. I need to speak with him.'

He opened his eyes. He burped and more bloody froth covered his mouth. 'Tell your disgusting catamite,' he whispered, 'that I've had a vision of him writhing in the lake of black fire. It is a sin to show parts that none should ever see but God. It is a sin to take pleasure in their filthy perfection.' He tried to spit at me, but knocked his head on a stone, and closed his eyes again.'

I stood up. 'No more beating,' I said firmly. 'You'll get nothing out of him when he's in this state of mind.' I pressed myself against a big rock and crept along till I could see the army of pursuit that had been set on us. They were all a very long way off.

'We need to sleep,' I said to Rado. 'Do you suppose we'll be safe here until it's dark again?' He nodded slowly. 'Good,' I said. 'Then I'll take the first watch.'

'You sleep first,' Eboric said behind me. 'Leave everything to us.' I frowned. 'Sleep, Alaric,' he said, now very firm. 'We'll wake you if anything happens. We need you rested for when there's more talking to be done.'

I sat up in the light of a rising moon. 'I said we'd take turns with the watch,' I croaked.

Eboric pushed a water canteen into my hand. 'There was no reason to wake you,' Rado said. He patted one of the horses and whispered something in its ear.

I got up stiffly and looked about. 'Where is Theodore?' I asked.

'He ran away just before the sun set,' Eboric answered.

I pursed my lips. 'If you've killed him, I'd like to be told the truth,' I said.

'Eboric's telling the truth,' Rado broke in. 'Theodore said he was hurting all over, so we untied him. While I was getting him some water, he pushed Eboric over and ran towards the grove of trees down there. He was singing a very queer song. He turned round once and shouted back that his master was calling him and that we'd all be punished for our crimes against him.'

425

I walked carefully to the beginning of the steep incline. The moon was past its brightest but I already knew which patch of deeper blackness was the grove. 'You could have gone after him,' I said to Rado. 'It's not a very big grove.' He and Eboric looked at each other. I sighed. No point in talking about duty. It was only words they couldn't read, in a language they barely understood, that made him their brother and me his father. As for me, I'd never felt comfortable with Theodore. We'd never shared real confidences or relied on each other. I'd never thought to fall asleep with him close by. I felt a small stab of pity for the boy. But he'd gone off of his own will. Let that be an end of the matter.

'Well, he won't be able to slow us down,' I admitted when I finally spoke. It was better than that. If the Persians caught him, they might take him back to Chosroes. That would mean some diminution in the search party for us.

I sat down beside Rado. I watched Eboric pull out some food they must have stolen in the pass. I looked up at the sky. Some time while I was asleep, the cloud cover had broken into harmless patches. Bright and unwinking, the stars looked down from the clear darkness between the patches. It would be a while before the wolves came out. Until then, the wind was setting up its familiar moan.

I took a sip of very sweet wine – the sort that's made for eunuchs. 'Do you remember how, when you first came to me,' I began, 'I said something about instruction in Greek?' They both nodded. 'What I then had in mind was enough Greek for boy slaves to make themselves useful. Now that your status is entirely changed, you must learn Greek properly. You must also learn to read and write.' I reached forward and stroked Eboric's cheek. 'None of these things is very hard once you put your mind to it. These modern Greeks are decayed far beyond the level of our own peoples and they can manage a basic literacy when money is there for schooling. You are both young gentlemen now of an exalted status. You mustn't do anything to let me down in Constantinople.'

Far behind us, on the wide plain, someone blew a trumpet. He was answered by a chorus of other trumpet sounds. 'Do you think they're being called back?' I asked.

'More like calling everyone together for a conference,' Rado answered. 'I've heard the Greek armies do this when they're hunting for slaves. I think they'll be up here before midnight.'

'Then we'd better move out,' I said. It would be no good if we were followed all the way to our interception of Shahin.

It was another sore-backside night. You don't get speed in the mountains by pushing horses into a gallop. Instead, you keep moving. Rado was taking us round the lower slopes of the mountain I'd seen on my map. I did suggest that going higher would shorten the journey. But that would take us through more of the scrubby wooded areas that both he and Eboric insisted were best avoided by night. Long before morning, they were agreed, we'd come to another of the upland plains. This should let us move quickly forward to a chain of hills and then to the middle point of the Larydia Pass. If they caught sight of us, there was no doubt the Persians would follow us all the way. The point was to keep out of sight while we kept moving. These Persians were the highlanders we'd seen three nights before. They were at least as good as Rado in the mountains. But he was sure we were ahead of them. So long as we weren't seen, there was a limit to how far they'd move from base. Eventually, they'd have to go back for further orders. I suspected they'd ask these of Shahrbaraz. I also suspected they were too valuable as scouts for even Chosroes to have them boiled in lead.

We reached the plain around the midnight hour. We'd spent what seemed an age pressing forward and mostly upwards, dark and jagged rocks all about us. Then as abruptly as if we were passing from one room to another, it was quickly downhill to another and more immense flatness. It went on seemingly forever. In daylight, it might be only twenty miles across. In the light óf an uncertain moon, it could have been the whole world laid out before us.

We quickened our pace along a path that ran reasonably straight to the north-east. We were passing by more little villages and larger settlements. All were in darkness. None seemed, though, to have been drawn into the tide of blood that Chosroes had decreed for the Greek inhabitants along his line of march. Either this side of the mountain was too far away for the tide of blood to have reached, or we'd finally come to a district where the new law was in force. It was probably both. Unlike those we'd passed by earlier, these settlements were all surrounded by earth walls.

Riding behind me, the boys were having another whispered conversation of jokes about nothing I could understand. Suddenly, they stopped moving. It took me a moment to bring my own horse under control. When I turned, they were a dozen yards behind me and listening hard.

Rado slid off his horse and put his ear to the ground. He looked up at me. 'They're after us!' he said. I got off my horse and led it back to where he was still crouching. I looked along the way we'd come. The path shone pale in the moonlight. I could see all the way to the looming blackness of the mountain we'd left far behind. I held my breath and listened. Nothing but the distant howling of wolves carried on the breeze.

Rado shook his head. 'I can hear them,' he said.

Eboric nodded. He pointed diagonally from where we'd come. 'They took the longer path round the mountain,' he said.

I held my breath again and looked and looked. I looked till spots danced in front of my eyes. Then, just as I was about to turn round and suggest their nerves were overexcited, I saw a very distant glitter. It was the briefest flash of something. I might have put it down to my own nerves or to some trick of the moonlight. But the boys were already taking the horses away from the bright glow of the path.

My heart was beating fast. 'Do you think they've seen us?' I asked.

'Hard to say,' Rado whispered. He looked up at the moon. 'To be sure, though, we'll be seen once the dawn is up.' He jumped back on his horse. 'We'll have to risk a canter along the side of the path. If they haven't seen us yet, they might give up. They are a *very* long way out from base.'

428

63

Once more the leadership passed openly to Rado. Without him in front, it was plain I'd have trouble controlling my speed. Away from the path much of the ground was low-grade turf. What wasn't spongy puddles was mostly flat stones or low clumps of bramble, invisible in the moonlight. Even at this speed, in the dark, there was a risk that one of the horses would stumble. I gave up on any appearance of controlling my horse and let it tag along behind Rado and Eboric. To our right, the path snaked forward into a distance without obvious end. Looking left, there was the darkness of woods. But they must have been miles away – miles across unknown ground.

Eboric fell back and was beside me. 'They're on to us,' he said with low urgency. 'Rado thinks the only option is to go back on the path and make a dash for it.'

I looked round and nearly shat myself. What had been the faintest and most ambiguous glitter was now the swift approach of a dozen riders. They were moving across the plain with long and easy strides, and weren't above a mile away. The moon was behind them but I could see its stray reflections on their helmets and mailed breastplates. They weren't coming straight at us, but were moving in a line that suggested they'd try to block our path. I looked behind. So far, it was just these pursuers. I grinned at the boy with an optimism I didn't feel. The only thing in our favour was that we had no weight of armour to hold us back when it came to the chase.

I think I've made it pretty clear that I was never an instinctual horseman. Killing, lying, scholarship, ruling – in all these and more, I've adorned three generations. The bond a rider has with his horse, though, wasn't something I had from birth, or ever managed to acquire. Give me a fast ship any day, if there's need to get about in a hurry. Even so, I kept up with the boys. I pushed my head down and pounded forward across the firm mud of the path. For a while, I was able to tell myself that we were travelling as fast as any Circus charioteer in full pelt. Surely we'd outrun the Persians.

But these were highland cavalry. They were men who'd done a better job of keeping their empire free of nomadic invaders than we had. If that weren't enough, they had a king whose displeasure was best avoided. They must have looked on us as I always have on anyone who's tried arguing theology or finance or anything else with me. They were effectively on their home ground. Doubtless, the boys could have outrun them. But that would have meant leaving me behind and I don't believe that crossed their minds. I didn't dare unbalance myself by twisting round to look. Instead, I could soon hear them. Closer and closer came the sound of many hooves and of jingling harness. Time, I decided, to face up to the inevitable. I had my sword handy in its saddle sheath. Armour or none, I had no doubt I could cut a few of the riders down.

'Rado, Eboric,' I panted, 'I command you to get out of here. Ride like the wind. I'll hold them off.'

I might as well have spoken in Persian. 'When I turn left, follow me!' Rado snapped. From any kind of distance, the hill had been imperceptible. But I felt the sudden lift as the horse turned upwards. It even seemed to move a little faster on the firm turf. The top of the hill was a long ridge. We turned right and continued on a narrow path. Uphill, their weight had told against the Persians and they'd fallen behind. The sound of their approach became fainter. For a while, I didn't hear it above my own ragged breaths. But this was a trick we couldn't play more than once. The ridge was leading gradually down and I could see no more hills. Rado had bought us a little more time. That was all.

Even on the descent, I could feel that my horse was running out of puff. The beasts Rado had chosen were bred for endurance, not sustained speed. He and Eboric were light enough, or had the riding skills, to keep going a long way yet. The Persians were heavier, but had grown up with skills I could barely imagine. For me, it was a matter of counting the yards before my horse simply stopped.

I looked about. We were still in open country. The moon was casting long shadows on every irregularity in the ground. But irregularities aren't the same as places of refuge. What we needed was a rope bridge across a ravine or a narrow path leading up through rocks. Out here in the moonlight, we were as visible, and would soon be as easily reached, as a louse crawling across white skin.

'I'm not going back!' I told myself. I couldn't go back – not to Chosroes in his likely mood. When my horse did stop – and that couldn't be long now – I'd get off and fight. I had a sword. I had a knife. I had size and weight and strength. If those didn't quite serve me, the most Great King Chosroes would see of Alaric was his severed head. I've never had time for the Stoics, with their endless talk of death as the quick way out of trouble. Instead, I'd go down fighting and, assuming such things exist, the shades of my barbarian ancestors could rejoice that I'd gone into the darkness sword in hand.

'Stop!' someone shouted in Greek. 'Stop or I'll kill you!' Thinking absolutely nothing, I looked up from the horse's mane. There were men running beside me. I was approaching a line of other men with spears pointing at me. A better rider on a bigger horse might have smashed his way through. But Rado himself was already surrounded. I saw him rear his horse up to trample anyone who came too close and I saw the glint of his short sword. But he was already stopped and more men were closing in on him. I couldn't see Eboric. Before I could get my one sword out, I felt the jab of a spear point in my side. 'Get off the horse,' someone said. 'Just get off. I want you on the ground – now!'

I sat up and made a grab at the spear. Its bearer hadn't expected that and I got it clean out of his hands. Holding it just below the metal point, I swung it about my head and managed to get the first man I saw on the shoulder. I threw it up in the air and grabbed it halfway along the shaft. Before I could use it properly as a weapon, two set of arms took me about the waist and pulled me from the horse. I fell heavily on the ground and lay there winded. My head was ringing and I could still feel the rhythm of the final gallop. I opened my eyes and was looking at two very young men. Both were pointing spears at my chest. I shut my eyes again and tried to think. I was a prisoner – that much was for certain. What I couldn't work out was how the Persians could have got footmen all this way and why they all appeared to be Greek.

One answer was the sudden and repeated whizz of arrows in the distance, followed by screams and babbled pleas in Persian. There was a terrified neighing of horses and shouted orders and laughter in more than one dialect of Greek.

I opened my eyes and focused on the nearest of the young men. He pushed his spear closer against my chest. His moonlit face looked as scared as I felt. I smiled and spread my arms wide on the ground. 'I am Alaric,' I said slowly and firmly. 'I am Lord Treasurer to the Emperor Heraclius. Please take me and my friends to your commanding officer.'

For a moment, he pushed his spear closer still against me. All he had to do was panic or stumble and I'd be done for. Then, a slightly older man put a hand on his shoulder. He spoke softly and the spear was taken away.

I smiled again. Arms still carefully outstretched, I sat up slowly. Rado was on his feet, arms raised, a spearman jabbing at him from either side. Held in a big man's arms, Eboric was struggling like a landed fish. I got unsteadily to my feet. 'No violence,' I called in Latin. 'These men are Greeks. 'We surrender,' I said in Greek. 'You can put your weapons down.' I glanced back along the ridge. A couple of hundred yards away, I could see dim figures darting about. They might have been finishing off any Persians who'd survived the arrows. Or they might have been bringing the horses under control. Our pursuers must have had their minds absolutely fixed on us. The interception seemed to have taken them as much by surprise as it had us.

I turned to the slightly older man. 'I don't know who you are or what you are doing here,' I said. 'But you have my thanks. Now, can I please speak with the man in charge?'

'Man in charge?' an amused voice said behind me. 'Why must it always be a *man* in charge? Women can do much more, I'll have you know, than shuffle between cooking pot and bed.'

A little earlier and I'd have jumped and looked dumbfounded. I was too worn out now, and too willing just to take things as they were. I turned and bowed to Antonia. Hard to tell in this light, but she looked rather less absurd here in men's clothing than she had in Constantinople. 'If only I had the authority,' I said with grave irony, 'I'd make you the new Commander of the East. Unlike your father ever did, you've just won a battle.'

We laughed and fell into each other's arms.

64

Holding hands, we lay together on the grass. Once more, the sky was the pitiless blue it has in the mountains. Now we'd finished with our lovers' reunion, we were talking and talking, and still there was more to be said.

'So, Shahin didn't kill Timothy?' I asked, cutting into a narrative that was nearly as disjointed as it was circular.

Antonia sat up and began picking at the few daisies within reach. 'Simon just about kept the peace,' she said. 'But every time he drank from the silver cup, or simply held it to his chest, Shahin seemed to go a little madder. By the time I killed that guard and ran away, he was seeing ghosts every night. The days were worse, of course – he was accusing everyone of wanting to stab him in the back to get the cup for himself. He'd sometimes scream so much, I thought he'd go into fits.'

She stopped and began threading the daisies into a chain. The easiest part of her story to follow was after she'd got away. That was a straight adventure. There was the braining of her guard with a large pebble, followed by a half-hearted chase by men terrified of the dark. After this, she'd wandered through the low hills beyond Mount Larydia, before staggering into a village and raising the local militia. She was lucky that she hadn't delayed her getaway – much longer and she'd have found herself in districts where the new law wasn't in force. As it was, she'd pulled rank on everyone and put herself at the head of a small army. The rest you can gather for yourself.

I blinked at the sun until I sneezed twice with great force and lay back happily on the warm grass. 'You don't know how far they've got along the Larydia Pass?' I asked.

Still pinching holes in the daisy stems, she shook her head. 'I wish you wouldn't do that silly thing with the sun,' she said. 'It makes your face look mad. Even Daddy laughs at you for it.' I frowned but said nothing. I waited for her to hold up the long chain and put it about her neck. 'We've been taking a short cut these past few days to try and head them off. Shahin has sixty armed men with him. I now have fifty. It's not enough for fighting but we can pick them off with arrows. We'll need to get a move on, though, before he can make contact with the big Persian army you saw.'

I sat up and kissed her. The daisy necklace suited her and I was reminded of how long we'd been apart. 'I haven't told you about the cup,' I began. 'It was only after you were taken that I discovered it was a gigantic fraud.' Antonia looked sharply back at me. 'It was always meant to fall into Shahin's hands,' I explained. 'Within reason, the harder we made his job, the less doubt there would be of its real value.' I stretched and gathered my thoughts. Best, I decided, to keep away from the details. Best too not to spell out that I'd come all this way for her alone. I knew I was only good at expressing passion when I wasn't telling the truth. 'The cup itself is worthless unless you believe in magic,' I went on. 'What matters is the alleged listing of military forces on the outside of its box.' I got up and went over to where my saddlebags had been emptied. I fished about for the side of the box Theodore had left behind. I carried it back.

'Don't worry about the code,' I explained. 'But every block of characters is the name of a place in the Home Provinces, with a number after it to show the number of men stationed there. It shows preparations for an in-depth defence. Anyone looking at these numbers ought normally to be put off more than a spot of border raiding. However, I *am* the Lord Treasurer – and rather a good Lord Treasurer. I know every taxable unit in the Empire.' I broke off and smiled. I thought again of the big map on my office floor – it should still be there as I'd left it. 'Half a dozen of the fortified towns claimed here are heaps of overgrown ruins. Several other places would need to have more defenders than inhabitants.

435

Taken generally, all the soldiers would need to be ghosts and their forts made from the morning mist. I've signed no orders to pay them or to maintain their defences. If the rest of the box is the same as this part of it, Shahin might as well be working for us. Timothy, by the way, *is* working for us.' I decided not to talk about a silver coin that he'd almost certainly got from Priscus. 'He's come along to make sure the story gets believed. It wouldn't be hard for me to think better of Timothy. But that takes nerve.' I laughed. 'In reality, the Home Provinces are without any regular forces at all. Everyone he hasn't committed to holding back the Slavs, Nicetas has shipped off to Egypt. I'm told they have no kit for desert fighting and half are already dead of some local plague.'

Eboric coughed politely and looked over the edge of the gentle dip in which we'd taken shelter. 'Rado's taken a full muster of forces,' he said.

I smiled at him and reached for my clothes. 'Time for work,' I said. I turned back suddenly and caught sight again of his face. A slight look of confusion there, I thought – perhaps too of jealousy. The bond between us could never be broken. He and Antonia had taken to each other from the start, and she'd welcomed him into the Imperial Family without so much as a raised eyebrow when told about the adoption. The bond could never be broken, but its nature was changed. Yes, so many changes, in so short a time – he'd need longer than he'd had to get used to them all.

Herself confused, Antonia had been thinking. She pulled at her daisy chain and crushed it in her hands. 'If the cup is a fraud,' she said slowly, 'what work is there left to do? Don't we just let Shahrbaraz scrape the paint off his parts of the box and wait for the Persians to withdraw?'

I shook my head. 'You haven't seen the size of the army he's leading,' I said. 'Whoever prepared that box was expecting it to be carried off to Ctesiphon, where it would be looked at and argued over by men with some freedom of choice. So much care and plotting – so much killing and risk of death – and all for nothing. It won't tip any balance now the invasion is under way. The army getting itself back in order on the other side of that mountain is big enough to roll over everything listed on the box – that and ten times more. Besides, you've got Chosroes nominally in charge – and he's got the True Cross with him. The box really is as worthless a defence now as the cup would have been.'

I stood up. 'We're no longer looking at a quick jump on Shahin. I'm afraid the new plan has to be a direct attack on that army before it can get out of the mountains. The militia you've commandeered is the Empire's only hope. If we fail, the road to Constantinople will be wide open.'

Antonia shut her eyes and thought. 'I'm pregnant,' she said with sudden annoyance. I looked at her and blinked. I sat down again beside her. 'I've missed two periods. A woman in one of the villages we passed by said I was surely with child.' More annoyed still, she threw away the remains of her daisy chain. 'How am I supposed to lead my men into battle?' she asked.

I waited till my voice was likely to be steady. 'I trust you'll not make any fuss when I send you off to Trebizond,' I said. 'Eboric will ride with you.'

No question of jealousy, or even confusion, for Rado. A command of Greek I'd assumed was too basic to bother with testing was easily good enough for taking charge of the militia. I found him pointing with a stick at one of his pebble diagrams. He was surrounded by about a dozen boys and very young men. Behind him, more young men were trying on the Persian armour.

He got up and saluted when he saw me approach. I suppressed a smile and saluted back. 'What news, General Rado?' I asked in Latin.'

'Fifty men and boys,' he said briskly. 'All of them able to ride in some degree. Not much discipline in the Greek sense – but practised irregulars, and all eager to give the Enemy a bloody nose.' He pointed at a boy with a blank face who was rocking from side to side on his haunches. About fifteen, he already had the wiry look of nearly everyone else up here, but, once you discounted the insane look on it, his face was still bordering on the pretty. 'He was brought in a short while ago. The Persians are raiding now on this

437

side of the pass, though for the moment only beyond the mountain. They rode into his village yesterday evening. It was the usual bloodbath. The boy got away because the priest shoved him under the altar and the church wasn't burned. The far side of the mountain's crawling with foraging parties. It's still safe this side because they can't carry food back over the mountain paths. Or they might decide to come across for the killing. It's hard to say.'

I'd called him 'General' with slight irony. He'd taken the promotion at face value and with good reason. In his easy authority among the other boys and men, he was beginning to remind me of Priscus at his best. I looked at the pebble map. 'We'll need more than fifty,' I said. Rado nodded. 'Unless you think otherwise, we'll need a couple of hundred men at least.' I sat down beside him. Though no one about us could have known any Latin, I dropped my voice. 'What little experience I have of these matters tells me that discipline is everything in a pitched battle. It's then that you're moving men about like pieces on a gaming board and you need every one of them to do as he's told. But all we're looking at is a sudden wild attack – rather like one of your own people's raids. It needs to look enough like a probing attack to scare Chosroes into listening to Shahrbaraz. Then we pull back and wait. Assuming we can find more men, how do you feel about that?'

Rado pursed his lips, almost managing not to look eager. 'So long as they aren't expecting us,' he said, 'and so long as we can go up another two or three hundred men, we'll be good for one very sharp attack.' He looked round. 'None of these people has seen real action. Once they've seen their brothers and friends killed beside them, it won't be so easy to manage a second attack.' He thought a little, then let his eagerness show fully. 'Have you seen some of them ride?' he asked. I shook my head. 'It's not bad for farmers. It's mostly sheep and goats they raise up here. They need to be mobile.' He stopped and looked again at his pebbles. 'Your own plan is based on the assumption of an attack on foot. If we can get a few hundred horsemen this good, though, I'd suggest a frontal attack over rocky ground. My father – I mean my *old* father – once led an attack like that on a Greek army. It worked. But he said these things have to work straightaway. If the enemy doesn't cave in, it's up to you to ride off like the wind.'

We both stood up. Shading my eyes, I looked into the sun. This was a big plain and the mountain was a long way off, across a landscape of grass and woods and more undulations than I'd seen the night before. The nearest village was five miles away. The messenger we'd sent wasn't back yet. What he told us would decide the matter. The earth walls I'd seen were encouraging, but not final proof. Was this a district where my law was in force and where the men had regular practice in arms? Or were the men here the same eunuchs with intact organs of increase who'd been slaughtered on the other side of the pass? If it was the eunuchs living here, we'd have no choice but to pull back to one of the armed districts. We could raise a decent force there and harry the Persians most cruelly. But there'd be no more chance of stopping them in their tracks. Over in the big pass, Shahrbaraz would still be pulling hairs out of his beard with the frustration of getting his army of soldiers and his armies of camp followers ready to start out in good order. Strike now, and we'd have a sitting target.

Even as I squinted into the sunlight, I had my answer. Their priest leading them, I saw another dozen men marching forward with spears pointing up. Their glitter in the noonday sun lifted my spirits for the first time since I'd left Antonia variously weeping and raging like Ariadne on Naxos.

I turned to one of the young men standing beside Rado. I remembered myself in time and spoke to Rado. 'Not everyone will be riding,' I said. 'How long to march a few hundred men to the big pass?'

Rado shrugged. 'My people never marched anywhere,' he said. 'Walking was for slaves and women. However, if we time the march so we can camp tonight in the mountain, we can keep out of sight tomorrow by skirting the far plain. That will get us in place for a dawn attack the day after next.'

'Sounds reasonable,' I said. 'But it all depends on how much influence Shahrbaraz may presently have with Chosroes. I suppose we'll soon have some indication.' I pointed to the stripped bodies of the Persians. 'Their non-return must by now have been noted. If the Grand General is still in charge, the whole army will stay put while he gets it ready for defence against a Greek army he's pretty sure is lurking in the mountains. If he's being countermanded by his raving lunatic of a master, there will be a search party for the missing ones and the army will be driven forward, ready or not.' I touched his arm. 'Which does my general prefer?'

Rado shut his eyes, as if thinking back to his days of national banditry. 'I'd rather have the Great King in charge,' he said. 'An army on the move is always a better target. If you'll pardon the comparison, that armed rabble we saw the other day is a bit like old Samo – attack him when he's leaning against a wall and he'll kill you; get him into a run down the road and he'll fall dead for you.' We both laughed.

There was a rider approaching. Rado was right about these people. He was coming up impressively fast. He stopped close by a heap of stones and jumped right off to run across the next few dozen yards to where Rado was sitting.

The young rider spoke rapidly in a Greek dialect with misplaced consonants. I had to interpret. Briefly put, he'd found Shahin and his jolly crew about twenty miles from the junction of the passes. They'd been joined by about a hundred men in uniform but there was no sign as yet of the main army.

'We can presume it's on the move,' I said. 'We'll see which of the three forces involved gets first to the junction of the passes.' Rado nodded. Almost absent-mindedly, he began tracing lines on the grass with his right boot.

65

The lunch we ate exhausted all the supplies Antonia's militiamen had brought from wherever she picked them up. But word had gone round every village of what was happening beyond the mountain. Every place we passed gave up its own tribute of food and clerical blessings and more armed men. By late afternoon, Rado had closed our numbers at just over three hundred, plus priests. There was no shortage of recruits, and all were on horseback. Rado put every one of them through a stiff test. Their horses were smaller than our own. The riders would have looked absurd if they hadn't also been small. But a lifetime of riding up mountains and over bare hills, and two years or so of practising in arms – and even Rado was clicking his toung with approval as he watched them dash this way and that in the formations he'd ordered.

'Come on, Alaric, I'll race you!' Antonia had called out as we approached another fortified village. My reply was a dignified harangue about her condition. In truth, I must have been the worst man on horseback in a hundred miles. Shahin, with his stunted legs, might have been less clumsy in the saddle than I was.

Three hundred we took for the fighting. Rado could have taken twice that number and more. But the unexpected number of volunteers only made him stiffen his test. Some earlier recruits he even sent back. We'd agreed there was a limit to the numbers we could effectively lead into battle. We also had to consider the need for a fallback defence if things went wrong.

Yes, leave out the priests, and we had three hundred men. Was I the only one of us to recognise the number's significance? Silly question.

By the time we reached the foothills of the mountain and late afternoon was turning fast to early evening, we might have been taken for an army of several thousand. The numbers we would lead round the mountain might be limited. Not so the numbers following behind to see us off. As we came to a place where I could stand on some rocks and make the speech I'd been turning over in my head, I knew that, even if the attack did go wrong, those murder squads Chosroes had unleashed wouldn't have it so easy here as on the other side of the big pass. Every man had his spear, every boy his bow and arrows. The very women were carry-ing arms.

I stood up and lifted my hands for silence. I waited for the tense babble of conversations to die away. I called Rado beside me. After a frigid stare in her direction, I allowed Antonia to come and sit at my feet. A speech in the Senate must be in the correct Greek of the ancients. You can be learnedly convoluted or as direct as Demosthenes. But the rule is to use a syntax and vocabulary, and even sometimes a regard for vowel quantities, that only those educated beyond a certain level can perfectly understand. If you find that the common people, when allowed in to watch the proceedings, are following what you say, you get some very sniffy looks from all the other persons of quality. It's pretty much the same in gatherings of bishops. Today, I was speaking to an audi-ence of illiterates. Most of them hadn't so much as seen the walls of a city, let alone been admitted to its more refined entertain-ments. I needed to inform, and I needed to inspire. No room, then, for allusions to Marathon and Thermopylae, or other things of no meaning to these people. At best, I might work in a reminder to how Samson routed the Philistine army with the jawbone of an ass. And, if possible, I'd leave even that out.

I took a deep breath in and out. I wiped sweaty hands on the seat of my trousers. I looked about for Eboric. I saw him near the front. I frowned at him for the gross disregard of orders in which he'd been Antonia's accomplice. He smiled sweetly back until I had no choice but to break into a smile of my own. I looked away and took another deep breath.

'People of the mountains!' I cried in my best and loudest speaking voice, 'you will have heard that a great and terrible army is approaching the land that you and your ancestors have known since time out of mind. I have seen this army with my own eyes. I have seen the King who leads it – a tyrant worse than Herod himself, who delights in blood and suffering. And I have seen the trail of death and utter devastation that the King and his army have already left on the far side of the big pass. Whatever you have heard, whatever you may imagine, is nothing compared with what I have seen.'

I stopped and waited for the scared murmur to die away. 'You can try running away. You can hide with some of your livestock in the far mountains. Perhaps the tide of blood will not follow you there. Perhaps it will finally recede, leaving you with your lives. But your homes will be burnt and your churches demolished. Your crops will be taken. Your livestock will be driven away. You may – perhaps – keep your lives. But you will return to nothing.

'You can run – or you can fight.' I stopped again and put a firm look on my face. 'Though it is so large that the earth may tremble at its approach, you have no cause to tremble at this army. It is filled with miserable slaves. They fight only because, if they turn and run, their own officers will punish them with death. They are demoralised by the weather. No serious thought has been put into feeding them. They are squeezed into a place where they cannot fight in their accustomed manner. There is a good chance that, few as we are, we can send them, falling over each other in their haste, all the way back to the Euphrates.'

I allowed myself a longer pause. No one was laughing at me. I'd go on to the end. 'I am Alaric, Lord Treasurer to the Emperor. I am the author of the law that has made you into the owners of your land. Because of me, you are beholden neither to landlords nor the tax gatherer. I have given you the right to arm yourselves and organise for your common defence. I have given you the right to turn yourselves, for the first time in a thousand years, from two-legged farm animals into men. I now call on you to defend what you have against those who would take it from you.'

I had thought of a final invitation for anyone who didn't fancy throwing himself under the stampeding elephant that was the Persian army to turn and go back home. The burst of enthusiastic cheering that followed what I'd just said cancelled the need for that. I looked over my little army of wiry men and grown-up boys, and told myself not to think how many of them I'd be leading to their deaths. This alone told me I wasn't the right leader. I glanced at Rado. He'd got the generality of what I was saying and had a look on his face of grim anticipation. This was what he'd been born to do. But for his capture, he'd by now be doing to us in the Thracian mountains what he was now about to do with us to the Persians. He'd put up with me in Constantinople – no, that was unjust: he was completely and unquestioningly mine. But I'd never again refer to his time as a dancing boy and sex companion. Long before he grew his first proper beard, the smell of horse leather would have soaked indelibly into him.

Antonia banged a fist on to one of my feet. 'Has everyone enough food to get us there and back?' she asked in her manly voice.

I glared down at her. 'This is the moment,' I said heavily, 'when Rado chooses five good riders to go off with you and Eboric to Trebizond.'

'Oh, shut up, Alaric!' she snapped. 'We aren't married yet and I *am* the Emperor's niece. Try coming the Big I Am with me and I'll make you look two inches tall.'

I tried to copy Rado's grim look – quite hard when you know your face is turning bright pink. 'If you think you're riding into battle with me,' I whispered, 'you've picked the wrong husband.'

'Then it's agreed that I'm coming with you as far as the battle,' she said. She got up and turned to the crowd, a small sword in her hand. She raised a loud cheer of her own.

Grimmer than Rado in their black robes and huge, scruffy beards, the priests were in a tight group at the front of the crowd. Once the most senior of these had preached his sermon on the evils of the Persian idolatry and the efficacy of the relic he'd brought along, and once they'd all raised their icons aloft to heaven, I'd give quiet instructions for Antonia to be sat on when it came to the fighting.

We made our camp at the halfway point round the mountain. On our right was a drop of several hundred feet, to our left a place sheltered enough to let a fairly thick grove of trees grow. The scouts we'd sent far ahead were uniformly reporting no enemy presence. Even so, we kept fires to a minimum and were ready to dart under cover at first sign of trouble.

Our only disturbance came about the midnight hour – long after everyone else, except the watch, had turned in. I was sitting up late with Rado in a makeshift tent. We were into our third cup of a sort of beer made with oats.

'It would be useful for Priscus to show himself,' I said in Slavic, answering his objection, 'because he has military experience and we have none. A certain forced courage and handiness with a sword doesn't make me into a general of any sort. As for you, with all respect, your only experience of battle against regular forces ended with your whole family dead and you standing unwashed in my office. And, until you can prove that you're the next Alexander, your age is somewhat against you.'

He looked happily at his feet – something else, I realised, he was copying from me. 'It's too late for second thoughts now,' he said. He put his cup down and played with the lamp. 'If you'd asked my honest opinion this morning, it would have been to load up four horses and get all four of us back to Constantinople. That Persian rubbish could then have carried on killing and burning everything in reach. If they ever made it to Constantinople, we'd have had plenty of time to find somewhere else to go. But you didn't think to ask my opinion. Now these people have fed us and hailed us as saviours, that's what we'll have to be. And isn't that what your duty – and, since you freed me, *mine* – requires?'

'Yes,' I said. 'That's our duty.' I drank deeper to steady my nerve. 'And duty is everything, whatever you feel about doing it. We may or may not be needed to save the Empire. But we have to try to save these people and others like them. What I'm wondering about is the practicalities. When all is said and done, we're not leading people like yours or mine into battle. These are untried amateurs.'

Rado laughed. 'Samo told me that untried amateurs like these saw off the Persians last year.'

'That was a raiding force, at the end of its supply line,' I said. 'Also, the numbers were more evenly matched.'

Rado laughed again. 'You said yourself that, if we hit them in the pass, their numbers won't count. Also, I don't think those animals we killed the other day were much above the common level. Our men are fighting for their homes. That means a lot. So long as we keep out of sight tomorrow, we'll take them by surprise and give them a bloody nose they won't ever forget.'

This was the moment when everyone woke up. It began as a commotion among the outlying watch. By the time we'd got our swords and were hurrying from the tent, it had turned into a noise, from many throats, of inarticulate horror. It sounded as if it would go on without end. It wasn't the Persians, we could be sure. But it was all they needed, if any were about, to tell them something was up.

'Shut up, the lot of you!' I shouted, sword in hand. I struck it three times against a rock. In the light of the torches that had now been lit, I looked at the hundred or so young men. I could guess they'd blundered into us and the knowledge that they weren't alone in the darkness had set them off. Sobbing or crying out with terror, shrinking from the sudden light, they cowered on the ground. One of them, I could see, had an arrow or a spear wound on his bare lower arm. Others looked as if they'd been knocked about.

'Put those torches out,' I ordered. 'One light only.' I turned to one of the priests. 'Try and shut them up,' I said. 'See if you can get any sense out of them.'

It was a nasty story, quickly told. As I'd suspected, the far plain was in a district without militias. Persian foragers had turned up at a cluster of five linked villages. Instead of the usual murder on site, they'd entertained themselves this time by gathering the whole population together and setting everyone off at a run towards our mountain. Those who'd refused to run, or couldn't, had been burned alive in their church. Of those who could run, those who fell behind were stabbed in the guts and left to bleed to death where they lay. The old went first and then the very young and the women, and then every man who couldn't keep up the pace set by laughing demons on horseback. Every tie of blood or affection was tested to snapping point. Those that didn't snap led to certain death. Those of the runners who survived, even for a little time, survived only as individuals – women who threw down their babies, men who cast their children aside, anyone strong enough and terrified enough to pull someone else out of the way and keep at the front of the terrified, gibbering crowd.

Of the five or six hundred who started on the run, I counted barely a hundred who'd made it far enough into the woods for the Persians to get bored and go off to pat each other on the back for a job well done. Of necessity, these survivors were the fittest and strongest, and those most terrified by the prospect of death into dropping every consideration of love or decency. Looking at the faces of these survivors in the light of a single torch, I saw fear – but I also saw the realisation of a shame in survival that would never fade this side of the grave.

'Give them food and drink,' I said. I turned to the priest. 'Give them what comfort you can.' I raised my voice. 'Let anyone who cares join us in the morning. We'll see how, even without training, men can fight when they have nothing left to lose.'

I paused outside my tent. Inside, Eboric had finally been pressed into giving a fuller description of my dealings with Chosroes than I'd so far given. He didn't know their full extent, and his lack of Persian blurred his narrative. But I listened to his low, trembling account of our banquet in the night palace as if I were hearing about somebody else. At the time, I'd been scared shitless and I'd been too busy trying to kill the Great King to reflect on things. After that had come the long strain of the escape and, after that, the reunion with Antonia and the preparations for the counter-offensive. Now, I sat down and put my head in both hands. It didn't help hearing the proud rise in Eboric's voice every time he found reason to explain how brave I'd been and how devoted to the safety of those I loved.

I looked up at the bright stars. I really wasn't another Leonidas. I was an English semi-bandit with a thick layer of civilian piled on top of that. Eboric was young and silly. I could expect him to see me as a hero. But Rado could see right through me. How he could have gone calmly back to his tent to sit playing with another of his pebble maps, was beyond me.

'Stiff upper lip,' I whispered in the darkness. 'Stiff upper lip.' Once more, I found myself speaking in English.

66

We shed our first blood about noon the following day. Our guides were leading us out of sight through some low hills, when we came on several dozen mounted and unmounted Persians. I won't say they were actually dripping with Greek blood. But they were close by a village we'd skirted, where every gust of smoke carried over on the breeze smelled of burning meat. The swagger of the foot-men and the squealing laughter of them all, told us enough of what they'd been about.

My own inclination was to wait and see if they'd noticed us – and, if they hadn't, simply to watch them go past. But Rado was already taking out his sword. 'Get them. Kill them. Strip them,' he rasped in his functional Greek. 'No prisoners. None to get away.' Before I could open my own mouth, he was galloping straight at them, every one of our horsemen close behind him.

It was brutal work, but complete and mostly silent. I cut down one of the horsemen as he tried to escape past me. It was an impressive kill, requiring me to dodge away from his own sword blow, and then skewer him through the side of his throat. Still sitting up and holding his reins, he was dead before I had my sword out of him. But I don't think anyone was watching. Mine had been the only horseman to survive the first rush of our assault. By the time I was beside Rado again, all attention was on the footmen.

'Gag them!' He commanded. 'Kill slow, but gag them.'

They did both, though with an emphasis on the slow killing. Icons held up to witness the torments, the priests who didn't join in darted about, exhorting the men to greater excesses. Rado looked on impassively as the banks of a stream now swollen to a

449

small river turned red with gore and was covered with parts cut from the bodies of the living. He raised his voice above the desperate, choking buzz of men who've had stones rammed into their mouths to keep them from screaming. 'This is how they fight their war against us,' he said. 'Will you complain if we fight back?'

I might have commented on his shift, in under a day, from speaking of Greeks in the third person to talk of 'us' and 'we'. Instead, I looked about for Antonia. She was holding hands with Eboric and watching as one of the captives had his eyes scooped out. 'The punishment is just,' I said flatly.

I was saved from the embarrassment of puking up my lunch by the arrival of one of our scouts. He rode straight in from the south and cried a happy greeting when he saw the blood his people were shedding. I looked carefully at the message scrawled by one of the priests on a piece of linen. I moved closer to Rado. 'Shahin's been lecturing Timothy and Simon in Greek about the arrangements,' I said in Slavic. 'There's to be a dawn meeting at the junction of the two passes. He'll present the cup to Chosroes. After a speech from Shahrbaraz, the army will be called to order and marched along the Larydia Pass.'

Rado smiled. 'Then we attack at dawn,' he said. 'They're plainly not expecting us. Even if we don't persuade them to turn back, we can make it look as if your cup and its box are worth fighting to recover.'

He fell silent and looked again at the stomach-turning slaughter beside the stream. As if reading my thoughts again, he put his hand on my arm. 'The punishment is just,' he reminded me. 'This isn't a war between mercenaries. When Greek swords are sheathed this time, there will be nothing left over for the slave markets.'

I nodded. This was what I should have seen when I first called him 'General' Rado. It was also clear demonstration to men who'd never seen violence on any collective scale that here was an enemy who could be beaten. And the weapons we'd taken would be useful, and the bigger horses. It would take far longer than we had to train our people to fight in armour. But we must have taken fifty swords.

I cleared my throat. 'When they're dead, we can dump them in those bushes,' I said.

It took a while before they were all dead. Afterwards, laughing and splashing each other in the stream, our men turned the waters back to a dull pink.

The rest of the day went well. No one who saw us lived to pass on the news of our approach. And many did see us. Some fought back – and we lost twelve men to death or serious injury. But our own losses only served to settle nerves and to shape us into a more cohesive force. Most of the Persians we came across, though, were too tired, or too drunk from beer or killing, to do more than throw down their loot and beg for a mercy that didn't come. Our initial recruits were running out of patience for slow torments. Not so the local survivors. They fought with little skill, but made up for this with a reckless ferocity that gave us ten of our twelve losses. After the fighting was over, they could have been taking lessons from Chosroes in the infliction of pain. They didn't even join in the retaking of the booty.

As the afternoon wore on, crude spears were entirely replaced by swords and shields and fighting axes. Our newest recruits now had their choice of horses, and many of the others were able to retire their own horses to carrying the supplies we'd seized. Though small, there was no doubt we were an army. Rado and I rode at its head. Behind us, as if that were their appointed place, rode Antonia with Eboric. Behind them were the priests, some holding their icons aloft, others carrying Persian battle clubs. Behind them, silent but for the occasional chanting of one of the more bloodthirsty Psalms, rode the men.

In England, I'd often joined with bandits. In the Empire, I'd seen regulars in action. I hadn't imagined anything in the way of what I saw unfolding from one encounter to another. No one could mistake our men for other than irregulars. But they were irregulars made into ruthless and effective killers by a combined passion to defend what was theirs, and revenge for what they'd lost, and now by a swelling religious mania. Any feeling I'd had, that I was leading men to a meaningless death, was at least temporarily washed away in the cataracts they opened of Persian blood.

Antonia summarised things as the sun began to sink lower in the sky. 'Why did you spend so much money for Daddy,' she asked, 'on hiring barbarian mercenaries? It can't be just because he's a shit leader that every army you gave him ran away at once. Is arming the people part of your plan to beat the Persians?'

'Yes,' I lied. The truth was that I'd been pushing the militia idea for local defence, and because I'd never got over a barbarian's disgust at the thought of an unarmed people. One day of this and I'd have been mad not to arrive at the idea of a whole army – offensive as well as defensive – made up of armed farmers.

Or perhaps I wasn't lying. I couldn't say how often I'd been through Herodotus, or how much I despised the standard commentaries on him. It wasn't because, in some blurry sense, the ancients had been more noble than us, or because the matchless eloquence that inspired them hadn't required years of hard study and forgetting of their own language before they could understand it. They'd sunk their differences and come together to fight like cornered rats against the Persians because, each and every man of them, they'd had something to lose greater than their own lives. What I'd enabled probably had been in my plan from the start. I just hadn't dared put it in one of my memoranda to the Emperor.

We'd spoken in Latin. Rado now broke in. 'Give us ten thousand more like these,' he said, 'and we'd burn Ctesiphon to the ground in two years.'

I smiled. 'It might take a little longer than two years, though,' I said. Being me, I also thought of the money we'd save.

The previous night, camped on the mountain path, had been one of nervous apprehension. This evening, in a hollow above the Larydia Pass, we might already have been a victorious army. I had to deliver a long speech, filled with warnings and descriptions of what we'd soon be facing, before I could bring everyone back to sobriety. I was helped by the closeness of the main enemy. Since late afternoon, I'd been taking messages from our scouts about its approach. Still in no apparent order, it was gigantic enough to have got my clerical spies writing in words and tone lifted straight out of Revelation. Now, with rising force, the wind blew from the east. Seven or eight miles weren't enough to dissipate the clatter of drums and cymbals, or the shriller sounds of the thousand eunuchs in full voice.

Before the darkness fell entirely, I set off with Rado for some reconnaissance of our own. We led our horses into the pass and walked with them over moderately smooth ground. The moon was past its best and a return to patchy cloud gave us a poorer view of the coming day's fighting ground than I'd have liked. Bearing in mind my ability to commit whole books to memory on one reading, and a generally powerful memory, I've always been surprised, where not ashamed, of my vagueness over the details of topography. But, for all his public deference, I was there to accompany Rado, not the other way round. He took me on a slow zigzag along the pass, stopping every now and again to pay special attention to some feature of the ground, or to dwell on the slope of some downward approach.

The junction of the two passes covered about the same area, and was about as smooth, as the Circus in Constantinople. The remains of several stone buildings and the bigger parts of a crude statue suggested how important the junction had been in very ancient times. A brief flash of moonlight from behind the clouds showed deep notches over the statue base. I had little doubt this was a kind of writing and no doubt that I'd not be able to read any of it.

'This is where we'll hit them,' Rado whispered. I turned from looking at the statue. It *was* covered in writing, and this was broadly similar to the scripts I'd seen in the ruins of Babylon. This was a natural place to put on a show and I was sure this had to be the place where Shahin would present the Horn of Babylon, together with its supposedly more precious container, to Chosroes. All the chief Persians who'd come along with the Great King could behold and wonder. It was in this broad space that what sounded a slow and chaotic approach could be mustered into a regular march towards the coastal plain.

'We can hide ourselves a half mile behind Shahin,' Rado added. 'We can ride forward in silence. When I give the signal, we can pull together into the formation we've practised and sweep forward. If it all goes right, we'll hit them like a mailed fist into a eunuch's belly. We can kill a few hundred of them before pulling back. When their own cavalry try to follow, the archers above can let fly. If there is no pursuit, they can move forward and rain death in places we can't reach. After we've pulled back, we regroup and attack again elsewhere. That's how my people do it. It will have to do. Whether it's enough . . .' He broke off and shrugged.

The noise of music from the big pass became louder and more continuous, and was joined by a long burst of cheering. I looked about me. I could forget the size and smoothness of where I was. What suddenly seemed more important was the height and steepness of the rocky walls surrounding it and the frequently rocky ground of the Larydia Pass. Once we'd shown ourselves, it would be a matter of conquer or be crushed.

We'd seen enough of things down here. All that now remained was to take ourselves along the upper ridge. We needed to see what cover there was for our archers and how easily men could be sent up to attack them. We were leading our horses back the way we'd come, when there was the scrape of boots on the rough ground ahead of us.

One of the two men approaching us was Shahin. 'You say His Majesty has seen my report?' he asked in an anxious whine. 'That means he knows the actual situation in Constantinople. I do urge him to reconsider his plan for tomorrow. Alaric was in total control when I left Constantinople. The only way he could have been here was at the head of a Greek army. That means everything must be known to the Intelligence Bureau. I suggest we should cut the ceremony. Why not let me hand everything over tonight in private? We can then keep moving cautiously forward.'

'Be silent, Shahin!' the Grand Chamberlain trilled. 'The Great King knew that Alaric was lying from the moment he arrived here. At

454

no time was His Majesty deceived. He was but playing with the blond barbarian.' Not moving in the shadows, I hoped the horses would keep quiet. The Grand Chamberlain was passing by in his chair not a dozen yards away. Shahin hobbled along beside him. The guards were heavily armed and looked as if they were expecting trouble.

The big eunuch twisted round, making his carriers stagger a little as they fought to keep the chair steady. 'The Great King has been assured in a dream that Alaric came alone and that there is no Greek army. If His Majesty believes us to be perfectly safe, will you dare say otherwise? I think not!

'Now, I have delivered your instructions for dawn tomorrow. I will not advise you to follow them to the letter, regardless of your own misgivings. I take it for granted that you know this already. I also will not carry back such misgivings as you may have expressed. You may regard this as a personal favour for which I shall, in due course, expect a return.'

With that, he motioned Shahin to stop and reached forward to prod his carriers to hurry him on to the main camp.

Rado was keeping the horses remarkably quiet. But it was soon plain that Shahin wouldn't simply turn and traipse back to his own camp. For a while, he stood unmoving in the middle of the pass. Then, instead of going away, he walked over and looked up to the far side.

'Alaric,' he shouted, 'I know you're up there!' He looked quickly to where the Grand Chamberlain might still be in hearing. He switched into Greek. 'Alaric, the silver cup has given me heightened awareness of all things. I can feel that you're up there. You've got the girl. There's nothing more you can do here. Take yourself and your household slaves back to Constantinople. Go now, or you'll get us all killed!'

For a while longer, he continued looking up into the darkness. At last, with a loud sigh, he turned and began walking slowly away to the right.

As soon as everything was silent, we got ourselves to one of the gentler slopes. 'What was that all about?' Rado whispered as we paused halfway up.

'I think Antonia was right about his being touched in the head,' I replied. 'Other than that, Shahin was uttering a convenient lie. Since he's unable to produce her as a trophy, he's decided to suppress any mention of Antonia. That means he needs another reason to explain our presence. Either he admits that we did follow him out here, or he puffs up the efficiency of our intelligence services and says I'm here with an army. As for Chosroes, he's keen to save face – even to the point of bending reality to fit his image of himself.' I sniffed. I looked at Rado in the darkness and hoped he was aware of my smile. 'That's a frequent weakness of those at the top, by the way. It's never easy to get the truth out of people who are scared of you. Add to that an unwillingness to see things as they really are, and you explain the trouble with any form of settled government but a constitutional republic.'

But this was no time for lectures. I took the reins of my horse again and waited for Rado to go ahead. There was little I could tell him about the military arts. One thing I did know, however, better than most generals I'd met. But perhaps he'd long since guessed one of the chief reasons behind my liberal scheme of household management. Between attacks of cold feet, my opinion of General Rado was rising into the sky.

67

Our reconnaissance along the top of the pass took us above the Persian camp. The army had moved forward a couple of miles since the dying away of the rain, but looked as chaotic as ever. It was getting late and the moon was already far up in the sky. The front part of the camp was ablaze with light. The singing eunuchs showed no evidence that they'd soon be going to bed.

As you might expect of Chosroes, the evening entertainment was mostly executions. In defiance of his people's established worship of fire, he was roasting men alive in iron cages suspended over bonfires. Search me who the poor buggers were. Prisoners brought back from the foraging raids? The engineers who'd made such a balls-up of his night palace? Human offerings to the shade of Urvaksha? Young Babar and anyone else who'd upset him in the past few days? You decide. The cages were a fair distance away and there wasn't much to be seen through the smoke but the occasional glimpse of a thin, capering body. The screaming was enough, though. Not even the thousand eunuchs could obliterate that. His Majesty had to be down there in one of the better viewing positions – roasting alive was one of his favourite punishments – but I couldn't see him.

Rado was marching up and down, now peering over the edge, now stamping his feet near the edge. The path along the top was narrower than on the other side. Looking up, there was nothing to be seen in the dark. But I knew some of the high points rose a couple of hundred feet above where we were standing.

'Here, what are you doing?' someone called in Persian from the shadow of an overhanging rock. He stepped out, pulling his clothes down and wafting a shitty smell through the night air. He hadn't seen Rado – he was busy in what looked like the act of embracing a boulder – and stepped closer to me. 'State your business, stranger,' he said in the tone of a customs officer.

'I'm Alaric,' I said earnestly. 'You may know me as the barbarian spy who nearly murdered your King the other night. I've come back to spy on you.'

Honesty's a fine policy, especially when it shocks a man into not going at once for his sword. I took hold of his shoulders and head butted him in the face. I lifted him into my arms as if he'd been a sleeping child and tossed him over the edge. With the general racket down in the pass, no one could have heard his scream. No one seemed to notice his impact on the now dry floor of the pass.

I stepped away from the edge. There was another burst of cheering and a long wail of despair, as I suspect a new victim was hoisted into position over one of the fires. 'How much more to do?' I asked, raising my voice. I suspect Rado hadn't noticed it, but I felt moderately pleased with my latest kill. All the same, where one had been there might be others.

'All done,' came the reply. 'I've got everything I needed.' I wasn't sure what I'd been expecting. I only knew it was more than this. In the next few hours, we'd be making a frontal assault on this lot with a pitifully small and untrained force. And Rado was giving his preparations less time and apparent detail than I'd seen from actors testing the acoustics in a theatre they knew. I swung abruptly from worship of my military hero to the fringes of panic over the madness of what we were doing.

If Rado picked anything up from my tone, it didn't show. 'It's done,' he said. 'We can go back and try for some sleep. I want everyone in his place an hour before the dawn.'

I scratched my head. What *places* was he talking about? He'd spent the remaining hours of light mumbling on and off in bad Greek over one of his pebble maps. Every so often, one of the half dozen young men listening had asked a question that bore no obvious relation to anything Rado was trying to say. Even with Antonia to interpret where his Greek failed him, the answers in turn bore no relation to the questions. And this had been *before* the pair of us had come out to see the topography for ourselves. Granted, those half dozen young men had gone off looking mightily pleased and had then visibly raised every spirit in the sections they were appointed to lead. Everyone had been cheered still more when Rado got us running about in groups while he shouted at us to move left and right. That was part of the reason for my depressive speech. Everyone was eager for the dawn. On the other hand, did anyone know better?

'Is there any chance,' I asked on our way back to the camp, 'that you could get a couple of the bigger men to take Antonia back to where we camped last night?'

'Not really,' he said. 'She's the Emperor's niece and everyone thinks she brings good luck.' He sighed. 'However, I have told Eboric to keep a close watch on her tomorrow morning. If things go wrong, he'll get her to safety.' He coughed, I think to cover a smile. 'You do realise, though, that nothing will go wrong tomorrow?'

I tried for a smooth answer but gave up. Rado laughed softly. 'You'll be surprised,' he said. 'What I realise more and more is that everything in my life has been a preparation for this moment.'

Oh dear! It's when someone comes out with this kind of lunatic remark that sensible men start looking round for an escape. But there could be no escape. I was the complete author of this madcap raid. All I'd needed to do was get the militias to guard the paths round the mountain. They could have fought defensive actions, on their own ground, against little bands not really inclined to push their luck so far from base. Instead, I'd called for another Marathon and was most likely to get another Thermopylae, though without actually buying time for a real defence. A further thought came into my head. Some of our horses were captured from the Persians. They could be expected to charge into battle. What about the others? What about *mine*?

I was halfway down a spiral of misery when I heard a clomping of feet on turf somewhere on my right. Rado was already off the path and picking up speed. I drew my sword and waited. The moon was presently behind a cloud. There was nothing I could

459

see, though what I heard suggested no serious problem. It was a faint squeal, followed by a louder cry of fear and then a savage laugh from Rado and a mouthful of obscene abuse in Slavic.

'Is that Theodore?' I asked.

It was.

'Don't let big Rado kill me, Father,' he cried in Greek, as he was tossed on to the path before me.

'Don't kill him unless you have to,' I said. I thought quickly. 'Take him back to the camp and wait for me there,' I added. I turned my own horse off the path and cantered into the darkness. 'Priscus!' I cried softly. 'Priscus! I know you're out here. Why won't you show yourself?'

I fell silent. I bit my lip. I waited. I thought of riding back to the path. Then I heard the gentle stamp of a hoof behind me on the right. 'So eager for my company, dear boy!' he called mockingly. 'If only that had marked our friendship from the beginning, how much better things would now be for all of us.' He laughed. 'Still, it's never too late to mend.' He laughed louder. 'Any chance of a drink? That boy of yours is a rotten thief.'

'The order was for dimmed lamps only,' I said. From the illumination showing through the walls of our tent, Antonia had inherited something from her father.

She ignored the rebuke. 'Who's that man with you?' she asked in Latin, nodding towards the open flap of the tent.

'That's the demon I told you was living with us,' Eboric said, crossing himself. He went placidly back to letting Antonia comb his hair.

Priscus stepped fully inside. 'I am delighted, Madam, finally to have made your acquaintance,' Priscus said in Latin. How bowed. 'I am Priscus, former Commander of the East, among much else.'

Antonia raised her eyebrows. 'I was under the impression you'd been dead for a year. Are you the swine who was spying on me in Alaric's palace?'

'It's *our* palace,' he replied with a smile – '*our* palace, please be aware.' He sat on the ground and reached for a jug of the local red.

I scowled at the pathetic dribble he'd left for me. He laughed and finished that as well. 'Am I right in my suspicion, dear boy,' he asked, 'that you are proposing to lead an army of shepherds and beekeepers into action against the main Persian army? If so, you've gone fucking mad.' He smiled at Antonia. 'The young lady will, of course, pardon my Syriac.'

'Oh, don't worry about that, My Lord,' Eboric said helpfully. 'Rado's in charge of everything.' Antonia nodded and pushed him down again, to continue with the bow she was tying in his hair.

Priscus grunted and put the jug down. He looked about for another. I hoped there was none. 'Well,' he finally said, 'Alaric's not as completely stupid as he often looks. If he's let Rado take over, you've some chance of being alive and at liberty this time tomorrow.' He reached into his sleeve and took out a lead pill box. 'But where is the young hero?'

'If you're speaking of me, My Lord, I'm here.' Rado stood in the doorway of the tent. 'How long have you been following us?'

Priscus got up and bowed again. 'Not long at all,' he said. 'When I discovered that Shahin's reception party was somewhat larger than we'd expected, I had the same idea as Alaric to snuff out the top man. Sadly, I've had no more success.'

'That's all very well,' I broke in. 'The idea now is to scare them into a retreat. Rado will give you a listing of our forces. If you want to inspect them for yourself, we'll get everyone out of his tent.'

Still on his feet, Priscus looked at Rado. 'I don't think we need to disturb men on the eve of battle,' he said. He walked across the tent. 'Let's go for a walk. We can discuss everything in private.'

I made to get up. 'I wasn't speaking to you, my fine and pretty bean counter,' he sneered. 'You just wait in turn for your hair to be done. We'll be back when we're ready.'

I broke the long silence that resulted. 'I didn't realise Priscus bothered much with the household slaves,' I said.

'Rado was always his favourite,' Eboric explained. 'They used to spend hours together when you were working or having sex.' He twisted round and smiled shyly at Antonia. 'My Lady will forgive me?' She patted him on the shoulder and took up a mirror to show him with his finished red bow. He spent an age admiring himself, while I tried not to fidget. But he did finally put the mirror down. He kissed Antonia's hand. 'Yes, they always got on ever so well,' he took up again. 'They'd sometimes talk all night about war and fighting. It was Priscus who gave him the idea of building his muscles up until you would think of letting him go into the army.'

I tried my best not to notice how Antonia shook with laughter.

It seemed like half the night, though it probably wasn't that long, before I heard them walking back together. They shared a quiet joke in Slavic outside the tent, before the flap was opened wide and Priscus poked his head in. 'Come out, Alaric,' he said in Greek. 'It's time we had an honest word in private.'

68

The moon was out once more from behind the clouds and its dim light shone over the quiet stillness of the plain where we'd set our camp. Priscus led me up a small hill and sat down on the grass. I sat beside him and refused the pill he offered – for what was to come in just a few hours, I needed my natural wits about me. Together, we looked for a while at the distant glow of the fires in the pass.

'Rado's plan is sound,' he said abruptly. 'That's not to say it will work. But what he's cobbled together to meet your strategic requirements is the best one for the circumstances. I suggested one change in a matter of detail – an important detail, I'll grant – but you've no need to outrage the boy by asking me to take charge. Believe me that he's the best man to do the job you've set him.'

I said nothing. My earlier panic was over and I now felt ashamed. I patted the short grass, and thought of the hills in Kent. There was nothing for me to say. Priscus had brought me here for him to do the talking. It was for me to listen.

'Do you recall how, when I was banged up in that monastery, I wondered if I hadn't been reserved for some final achievement?'

I nodded. 'Something that would get you a better place in the histories than you were likely to get,' I said.

He sniffed. 'On second thoughts, I think the histories can look after themselves. But I did spend a lot of time in the attic you gave me, thinking about one last thing I could do with myself. The trick with the silver cup seemed exactly the thing. I heard about it on one of my night wanderings. That was a while after I'd discovered that Shahin was sniffing about with Eunapius and Nicetas. I approached the old loons who had it and told them I had a commission from Heraclius himself. I got the box made, covered it with lies and got word to Shahin about its wondrous qualities. After that, it was largely a matter of letting events unfold without further intervention. I stole the cup and dumped it with you when something you don't need to know about went wrong. It was somewhat ungrateful of me. But, so long as you keep telling yourself that the end justifies the means, you can't deny that everything went absolutely swimmingly. By the time he took sail with the thing, Shahin had no reason to believe other than that we were desperate to keep it out of Persian hands. I could hug myself, thinking that I'd saved the Home Provinces and sent the Persian elephant charging at Egypt instead.

'Then it all began to unravel. I should have expected you'd work out part of the truth about the box. I was hoping Eunapius didn't know quite as much as he did. When you left earlier than I expected, I had to come after you and stop you from interfering with Shahin.

'But you got here faster than I ever expected. By the time I'd realised that, of course, the box and its contents had been made largely irrelevant by some turn of the Royal Mind in Ctesiphon. So I decided to take out Chosroes. But he was too well guarded, even for me. I suffered the humiliation of learning from useless bloody Theodore that you'd nearly got there instead – and that you would have got there but for his own insane jealousy for the girl, or the boy, or whatever he had fixed in his diseased mind.'

Priscus stopped. 'Something I can't work out is why you let me think you hadn't got the real secret of the box. Did you want me to come after you?'

I smiled. 'Would you have let me come out here if you'd known the truth?' I asked. 'Even without the invasion, there was a chance I'd fall into Persian hands. Could you risk that I'd talk under torture? You let me go because, if I were taken, you thought I'd only reinforce belief in the magic cup and its *true* message of our strength in the Home Provinces. In the end, I suppose you followed me anyway, to see what would happen.'

'Would you believe I followed you in case you needed to be saved?' he asked. 'You and somebody else?' That thought hadn't crossed my mind. I fell silent again.

464

'I can't recall how many times in the past I used the phrase "We stand or fall together",' he continued. 'Too often, you took it as ironic. Perhaps it often was. I mostly uttered the phrase before or after trying to stitch you up. The Empire needs a genius to defend it and a genius to make it worth defending. It doesn't matter who's the Emperor, so long as those two are agreed on what needs to be done. You are the reformer – sound money, low taxes, honest government, quiet toleration of religious and other differences. I can't be the defender. But I do ask you to look after young Rado. When he first tried to make me get up in the morning and wash, I saw he had unusual qualities. He's shown these pretty well in the past few days. If he survives this battle, take him back to Constantinople. Get him into the Military Academy. Make Heraclius promote him as illegally as he promoted you. Give him five or six years of carving up the Lombards. Then turn him loose again on the Persians. He'll astonish the world.'

I pursed my lips. 'That depends on my standing with Heraclius,' I said.

Priscus sniffed again. 'There's no doubt of that, dear boy. Before I left, he'd renamed a square after you and announced your marriage to his niece. He's extended your land law to every province not under occupation and declared non-compliance punishable as high treason. He's even sent an army to your assistance, such as that may be. It might be here within another ten days. Win tomorrow and you'll go home as quite the golden boy.'

'And what of you, Priscus?' I asked.

He stood up and looked harder at the continuing glow from the bonfires. 'Oh, I'll get my final achievement,' he said. 'General Rado's idea was to concentrate most of his forces on the frontal assault. He did put some aside for a preliminary sideways attack – to cause panic and pull defenders away from the site of the main attack.' He laughed. 'Imagine digging a hot needle into a caterpillar's side. It rears up and twists about. The problem with Rado's original plan was that his needle wasn't hot enough. He's now agreed to group all the survivors of some Persian atrocity under my command. I'll be leading them down into the pass. We'll make it look as if we're going for the True Cross. That should put Chosroes in a sweat.'

465

'And how will you get men on horseback down the slopes?' I asked.

He sniffed louder still. 'Who mentioned horses, my dearest? We're going down on foot.'

There was an obvious answer. I still asked the question. 'How will you get out again?'

'Dearest Alaric,' he laughed, 'you'll just have to make a success of the frontal assault.'

I got up and stood beside Priscus. Together, we watched the glow from the pass. Every so often, there was a snatch of voices lifted in rapturous song and of wind instruments.

'Do you remember how we first met?' he asked.

'It's not something I'm likely to forget,' I answered. 'It was my second day in Constantinople. I was enjoying myself in a restaurant with Martin, when you walked in with half a dozen of your Black Officers. You clubbed someone to pulp while arresting him and finished him off in private when you discovered you'd got the wrong man. You arrested the pair of us and took us off to be tortured to death. It was a stroke of luck I'm still here.'

'Oh, Alaric,' he said, 'I've always wished we could have got off to a better start. But who was it said "When error is irreparable, repentance is useless"?'

'Thucydides,' I said automatically.

'Oh, such scholarship!' he mocked. 'And such a contrast to the battle speech you've taught to young Rado.' He let his voice fall back. 'Still, must be getting along. You won't believe the work Rado and I have on our plates before dawn.' He put his hand out. 'Will you wish good luck to an old comrade?'

'With all my heart,' I said, taking his hand. As ever, it was cold and dry. He smiled and withdrew it.

And that was it. He walked quickly away from me in the direction of Rado's tent. I watched until I saw the faint brightness as the flap was opened and closed again. I stood a long time in thought. Still thinking, I walked back to my own tent. Antonia would be up and waiting for me.

466

69

The sky promised a fine day. But it was cold at dawn. I don't think anyone had slept in the end. I'd spent the rest of the night talking things over with Antonia. Rado and his deputies may not have once looked up from their urgent fussing over heaps of pebbles. Everyone else had gone through the later hours of darkness in a long religious service. With all the kissing and pawing, I could be surprised there was any paint left on our icons. And now the moment was coming inescapably forward. Almost before the eastern sky was pink, we set out for the junction of the two passes. We arrived as the pink was glowing brighter and brighter.

With Rado, I poked my head above some bushes and watched Shahin's slow procession to the appointed place. Still in its open box, I watch the cup glinting in the grey light. Right at the front, it was carried by Shahin himself. I spotted Simon beside him and a limping and somewhat slimmer Timothy close behind. At a distance of about ten paces, they were followed by what may have been their whole armed band. All were dressed in white. None was visibly armed. That surely meant they were to be ushered, at some point in the proceedings, into the Royal Presence.

Once they'd all gone past and vanished round the last turn in the Larydia Pass, it was time for the scouts to go after them for a good look. It wasn't long before they were waving up at us that everything was clear. At a signal from Rado, all of us who weren't with Priscus, or waiting overhead, bows at the ready, dismounted and followed him. Still leading our horses, we crept forward till we were at the edge of the smooth ground. The right-angle turn that led to the junction of the passes was just over four hundred yards ahead.

'Stay here,' Rado ordered. 'No one must move till I give the signal.' The two of us moved silently forward on horseback. Fifty yards before the turn, we dismounted again and walked the rest of the way. Unlike nearly everyone else, I'd squeezed myself into some captured chainmail. It was heavier than any Greek armour I'd known, and, though it was the biggest I'd been able to find, was slightly too small for easy breathing. I did consider asking for help to pull it off again. But Antonia, in one of her own moments of the jitters, had made me promise to keep it on. It was probably for the best, all things considered, to keep the promise.

'Let me take first look,' I said. Except that no one watching us could have been in any mood to be amused, what happened next had its funny side. Replacing my helmet with a grey cap, I pressed myself against a wall of smooth rock and slithered a few feet to the right. I was met, as I pushed my head out, by a blast of sound that had Rado and me straight into each other's arms. It was the eunuch choir, you see. I'd been looking round the corner of the rock wall so briefly, and then been so shocked, that I'd taken in nothing that made sense. It was only as the eunuchs got into their stride, and were joined by an army of trumpeters and cymbal players, that I was able to put things together.

A quarter of a mile away, the eunuchs were spread out, several deep, in a semicircle that brushed both sides of the pass. Behind them were the musicians. Behind them, glittering in the first reflected rays of the sun, were the spear points of the Royal Guard. The semicircle was broken in the middle. Here, somewhat recessed, were the gorgeous robes of the main court functionaries. Right in the middle, Chosroes was looking out from his public security cage. Of soldered iron plates on three sides, this was protected in front by a double bronze grille of the sort I've already described. A hundred yards closer to us, Shahin had everything set out on a low table and was waving his arms about in the manner prescribed for court presentations.

Now joined from far back by all the military bands, the noise swelled in both volume and cacophony. I put my head round for another look. Yes – what mattered was that the Royal Guard was

468

blocked both front and back. I pulled back and let Rado see for himself. He looked round at me, relief plainly on his face. We both looked up at the sky. It would soon be time. Rado took a few steps back along the pass and raised his arms. Two hundred and fifty men climbed on to their horses. The priests began their last round with their icons. Far behind, ready to bolt if need be – that much I'd got Eboric to promise – Antonia was presently out of sight.

We both looked again at the presentation ceremony. Shahin had placed a white cloth over the box and Chosroes had opened a small flap in his grille. The eunuchs were simmering down – though they'd once caused part of a ceiling to collapse in Ctesiphon when the Great King broke with precedent and stepped right out of his security cage. At last there was a moment of silence. Then seven trumpeters came forward and blew seven fanfares that were loud even at this distance. A dozen eunuchs stepped forward from the choir and drew breath.

'What, O slave,' they screeched in unison, 'hast thou brought unto His Majesty, the Lord of All Creation, from the City of the Greeks? Let it be displayed for the whole universe to behold.'

Shahin went into another waving of arms.

He stopped.

High up, and from half a mile back along the big pass, two steerhorns blared out. Their sound cut through the rising warble of the eunuchs. It was followed by a long roar of hate and then by a muffled clash of arms. After that, it all seemed to go quiet. Arms frozen in mid-contortion, Shahin stood still. One of the court officials stepped out of line and looked uselessly round. I looked at Rado. He looked at me. I smiled nervously.

Suddenly, Priscus was shown right in his metaphor of the pricked caterpillar. It really seemed as if the whole army had reared up and turned back on itself. With a rising babble of shouts, the Royal Guard and the soldiers behind them were spilling forward to shove the eunuchs aside and make their way to where the terrified screaming was concentrated. The front of the crowd was both thinning out and moving forward. Chosroes was lost to sight. I could hear, and almost see, the wave of panic spreading out from where our hot and very sharp needle had been thrust into the beast's side.

Rado lifted his right arm. Behind us, another steerhorn sounded. It was time for our archers to let fly their opening volleys. Panic turned to chaos, and almost every Persian had his back to us.

We got on to our horses. Rado beckoned everyone forward. 'Remember,' he said calmly – 'no prisoners; no looting; pull back when you hear the trumpet blast.' We arranged ourselves into a column, fifteen wide by sixteen deep. Rado and I were at the front, our standard bearer just behind us. We moved forward at a slow trot. We rounded the corner and looked fully on the spreading chaos before us. I heard the flutter of our unfurled standard. One of the priests had suggested we should fix an icon recovered from a smashed church to a spear. I'd overruled him, insisting instead on the formal *chi-rho* of the military – the first two letters of Christ's name superimposed on each other. It was a crude thing of charcoal on an altar cloth we'd rescued, but it gave us the proper military look. Everyone gave a loud cheer. I held tighter on to my reins. No one in the main crowd seemed to have noticed we were coming straight at them but Shahin was looking round at us. His mouth fell open, he clutched at the box. Simon clutched at him. I saw Timothy scuttle towards the cover of an old rock fall. 'God with Us!' Rado cried. With a great answering roar of 'God with Us! God with Us!' we drew our swords and went into a gallop.

Everyone did now see us. The front of the crowd dissolved into a terrified blur. I distinctly heard Shahin's wail of terror as he took to his heels. He stumbled forward, still holding his box aloft. We skirted the table. We ignored Shahin's unarmed and useless flunkies. The last sight I had of him, he was vanishing into a crowd of court officials. The box was empty.

Just yards before smashing into the crowd, Rado shouted the final command. When he'd got us practising the move on foot the previous afternoon, even he was dubious of its success. Now, on horseback, we might have been professional cavalry. Like a hunter's net, unfolding as it's thrown, a column sixteen deep became a row five deep. At the very last moment, it became two separate rows. We struck in a loose line that filled half the big pass. No longer scared – no longer thinking very much – I knocked the unarmed eunuchs out of my way and struck at the first Royal Guard in reach. With a recoil that moved me on my saddle, I got him above the collar bone. He went down, screaming and spurting blood. Shouting in a mixture of English and Greek, I moved to the next, and then to the next. For a moment, I was aware of Rado beside me. His face shone with the sort of exaltation you see when a relic is held up in church. On my left, I had a brief sight of our standard bearer. With his free arm, he was slashing all about him. Then, someone in leather armour thrust a spear at me. It caught on one of the rings in my chainmail and nearly pulled me down. But I managed to stay on my horse. I took hold of the spear in my left hand, ramming the pommel of my sword into its bearer's face.

I'd been worrying about how my horse would take the noise and movement of a battle. After a few signs of alarm, it soon appeared to be enjoying things more than I was. We darted here. We darted there. For the first time since I'd climbed on its back, the creature was doing as I asked.

When you're writing the history of a war, battles are easy to describe. The hardest part of describing them to my mind – at least, it is in Latin – is keeping to the right sequence of tenses in the exaggerated *oratio obliqua*. You start with a silly speech, such as no winning general ever gave, and proceed through accounts of attacks and counter-attacks in which the individuals present might as well be counters on a gaming board. It may be, as I keep pointing out, that I have no feel for military things. But my general recollection of this battle – as of every other in which I've had to take part – is the moving from one brutal kill to another. Once or twice, there was the inevitable dawning fear that a tickling in my side was first warning that I'd been done for, or, when splashed in the face with someone else's blood, that I was blinded. But this was less a battle than a slaughter. If we'd gone at them in the rain, they'd have put up more of a fight. When we'd struck, everyone armed had been drawn up on parade and was squeezed on every side by the unarmed. What little fighting order had remained was then erased by the continuing deathly hail from our archers. After the first wild slashing and stabbing, my own problem was finding anyone remotely worth killing. I think most of those I killed would have had trouble hurting a mouse.

One notable event, though, I must record. I was formally in charge and this would have been the ultimate in what the Romans of old called the *spolia opima*. I'd finished carving up someone in a fancy robe, whose beard turned out to be a falsie, when I saw Chosroes himself. Well, I saw his public security cage. A dozen eunuchs were pulling and pushing frantically at its wheeled base to get it from a fighting zone that was spreading along the pass almost as fast as they could move. Spurring my horse, I raised my sword and made a dash towards it.

'Die, fucker!' I shouted in Persian, taking the head off one of the eunuchs. That got the others out of the way. I knew the cage would be locked on the inside. The weakest point would be the front grille. Though doubled, this was only of bronze. I snatched at the spear I hadn't yet bothered using and rammed it at the grille. Straight in it went, passing through something soft before it jarred against the iron plates behind. I heard a bubbled scream for mercy that included my own name. I hadn't struck a killing blow – but the next one might kill. I pulled on the shaft of the spear. The head stuck fast in the bronze bands.

And that was the end of my second chance to end the Persian War in one stroke. Before I could do more, a whole mass of armed foot soldiers were driven at me – desperate to get away from three berserk farmers on horseback. By the time I was able to cut my way through them, the wheeled iron box was gone. In its place, hundreds of eunuchs were on their knees, arms outstretched to create the impression of a thicket of human flesh.

I wheeled round just in time to parry a big man who was riding at me with levelled spear. The tiniest delay and it was an attack that would have driven a spear right through my chainmail. I'd no sooner scared him out of reach when a blow from behind knocked me sideways. Nearly dropping my sword, I clutched at an increasingly maddened horse. I found myself looking into the face of another big man whose battleaxe looked inescapably directed at one of the less well-covered parts of my body. I pushed myself upright and tried to raise my sword. The blow never came. Even as he began to swing at me, the man dropped his axe and settled into a position on his horse held only by the rigidity of his armour. An arrow had gone in through one of his temples and was poking four inches out through the other side of his face.

I gave the briefest look to where the arrow must have originated. I nearly fell off my horse again. Halfway down one of the slopes, I saw Antonia and Eboric on horseback. He had a bow in his hands. She seemed to be directing him where to shoot. From what little I could see, they both seemed remarkably pleased with themselves. If I hadn't got into a viciously unequal fight with some footmen, I'd have been straight up there to give the pair of them a good hiding.

But one of the younger men was now beside me, pulling at my reins. 'My Lord, My Lord!' he shouted. 'Can't you hear the signal? Withdraw and regroup.' I might have heard it. For sure, I hadn't paid it any attention. But this was the order and we picked our way together, over ground that was thick with the dead, to where Rado and the standard bearer were waving everyone into position behind his appointed leader. Two dozen of the younger men got behind me. At the renewed steerhorn blast, we rode back into the battle. When I looked again, Antonia and Eboric had withdrawn to the top of the pass and he was taking aim at someone deep within the swirling mass of the enemy. The archers had now run out of arrows and had joined us on horseback. Even the priests were joining in. Clubs in hand, they hopped from pocket of resistance to another.

But it was no longer a battle. Over the vast expanse of the fallen that lay before us, there could be no repeat of our first charge. Nor, when we caught up with the fleeing, shoving camp followers who separated us from the actual fighting men, was there any more killing than took our fancy. Fifteen deep into the retreating mass, the fighting men could have thrown us back into the Larydia

Pass and far along it. These were the real soldiers of the army that had fought its way through the streets of Jerusalem. But they never got to us. Even as they cut a path through their own people, they were overwhelmed by the stampede. It was less an assault than a mounted herding of two-legged cattle.

Simply because they couldn't get to us, I can't call the Persian regulars cowardly. But any chance they might have had to stand and fight now vanished for good. In one of his last revisions to the battle plan, Rado had incorporated a stepped descent about a mile into the big pass. I'd stared wonderingly at the six rows of pebbles one of the locals had placed far into the pass – far, far beyond the marked point of our own engagement. One row after another, the Persian regulars fell backwards over the first of these steps. It was rather like watching foam carried down the rapids of a stream.

That was the end of resistance. Regulars, camp followers, eunuchs in what had been golden robes, useless cavalry in their heavy mailed armour – all were swept backwards and lost. Far ahead of us, trumpeters blew their lungs ragged. They were barely heard above the pandemonium of screams and clashing of metal on metal and of breaking wood. No one obeyed the orders they tried to pass on. Our horses stepping carefully over multiple layers of the dead and dying, we picked our way down each of the big steps. We pushed and sometimes hurried forward, killing and killing and killing until we'd run out of energy to lift our swords. I stopped for what seemed a moment and leaned forward over my horse. When I looked up, the closest Persians were already fifty yards ahead of me. This low in the pass, the floodwaters hadn't yet finished receding. If we continued forward, the bodies underfoot would be floating. But there was no need to continue. Roaring with fear and pushing and stabbing and slashing at each other not to be at the exposed rear, and increasingly falling over in the stinking water, the Persians wouldn't be back.

I sat up straight and stared at my notched, slippery sword. Rado was beside me. 'Are you wounded?' he asked.

The bruises I'd got from that battleaxe and a few cuts on my forearm didn't count. But I suddenly noticed how my arms were

474

red with gore. If the rest of me was like this, he'd only have been able to tell me from my size. 'I don't think so,' I said. 'How about you?' He shook his head. I turned my attention to the now distant enemy. 'I could prose on about ancient and largely forgotten battles, like Gaugamela and Magnesia. But did you ever listen to Father Macarius and his sermons about Samson and his jawbone?'

'Not really,' said Rado. 'You see, you always slept through services. So did everyone else out of respect for you.'

I couldn't think of any answer to that. So I sat up straighter and stretched out my hand. 'General Rado,' I said very loudly, 'the day is yours.' There was a ragged cheer behind us. Not turning, we both looked again at the fleeing wreckage of what had to be one of the greatest invasion forces in history.

Someone spoke behind me. 'As a full participant in the battle, the Lady Antonia claims her right to share in the booty.'

70

However they disgust you at first, you soon get used to the carrion birds. The noise of their flapping and squabbling was the chief sound in the vastness of the dead that stretched as far as the eye could see. I won't mention the flies. You can take them as read. So far as it could be done, the throats of the wounded enemy had been cut, and some beginnings had been made on gathering in the immense booty that had fallen to us. But that, we'd agreed, would have to wait properly until help could be procured from the far side of the mountain.

Rado coughed behind me. 'If you please, My Lord Alaric,' he said softly. I turned and saw him with one of the priests. Rado himself was illiterate. This was something we'd have to see to when we got home. A bloodied priest held out a big square of parchment ripped from a Persian book. On the clean side, he'd scrawled the answer to my question.

'A hundred and fifty more or less uninjured,' I read. 'Ten badly injured and like to die before evening. Fifteen bodies found so far. The rest unaccounted for.' They both nodded. I looked at the sky. The sun would soon be going down on this day of slaughter. Those unaccounted for almost certainly meant we hadn't been able to tell our own dead from the multitudes of enemy dead. Of the men we'd led into battle, I'd have to accept that we'd lost nearly half. Was this good or bad as these things went? I didn't know. Rado's own experience didn't stretch to casualty rates. In my view, it was a hundred and fifty men too many.

Of course, it was worse than that. I turned and continued looking at the dead from the flank attack. These hadn't enjoyed our luxury of almost permanent insulation from anyone who could hit back. From the Persian dead who lay all about, they'd rushed down upon one of the regular army units. If any of them had got out alive, I hadn't yet seen him. Add a hundred to my previous figure, and make it a fraction of our whole little army. Bearing in mind we weren't talking about exact numbers, I could take it that we'd lost three-fifths of everyone we'd led here. What would Priscus say about that?

I'd never find out. His body had been pulled out from beneath a mound of the Persian dead. I hadn't seen him in proper light for about eighteen months but I'd not seen him this dark and shrivelled. It was as if he'd been burned up in the sunlight. I recognised him only from his lower face. Even in death, he kept that look of amused contempt for the world. But he was pushing seventy and it must have been a difficult journey from Constantinople.

He'd been a bastard in life. Oh, he'd been more than a bastard. The words might not exist to describe the beastliness of his life, or the misery he'd inflicted on the world. But he was now gone from the world. And, if a strict moralist might have thrown up his arms in despair at the recitation of his sins, and announced there could be no set off against a tenth of them in any Divine Court of Justice, I could say he'd made some atonement. Without that unsung and unsingable repeat of Thermopylae, the rest of us might easily not have lived to behold the mournful joys of victory.

A few feet closer to the high wall of the pass lay the boy who'd run all those miles to us. I hadn't learned his name. I hadn't so much as spoken to him. I'd thought he was about fifteen. In death, he looked younger. I looked away, and found I could still see his dead face. I swallowed and clenched both hands into fists. These had been volunteers among volunteers, I told myself. Leave Priscus aside, this was atonement of their own for having lived after everyone dear to them had died.

I'd been faintly aware of a voice babbling insanely away on my left. 'Vanity of vanities, all is vanity,' Theodore cried in Syriac. 'So proud and boastfully squirting in life – all now burn in the lake of black fire that awaits us!' Not up to walking, he crawled from body to body, calling indiscriminately at our dead and those of the enemy. It would have been easy to give the order. A dozen swords would have rasped from their sheaths, to be buried in that twisted body. But he'd spoken in Syriac. The only insults to the dead worth punishing are those heard by the living.

'Fuck off, Theodore,' I said wearily. 'I'm putting you straight into a monastery when we get back. If I ever have to see you again, I'll put a black mark against the day it happens.' A look of mad cunning spread over his face. He raised one of his hands in a gesture of malediction but crawled out of kicking distance. The last I noticed of him, he was propped against a smashed cart, his arms about knees that he'd drawn up to his chin.

Rado touched me on the shoulder. I turned and saw a group of perhaps thirty horsemen picking their way towards us. Each wore full armour and carried a long spear. I looked at our own men. They were still knocked out. But the man at the front of the group climbed down from his horse and began picking his way towards us. He was wearing yellow boots and had to keep stepping aside to avoid the pools of jellied blood. I waited till he was a dozen yards away before bowing. 'Greetings, Shahrbaraz,' I said in Persian.

He gave me one of his dead looks. 'The customary agreement in these circumstances,' he said without bowing, 'is that we should be allowed to watch over our dead till the seventh hour of the night.'

'Then let it be as the custom prescribes,' I replied. I could explain later to Rado that the Persians don't bury their dead, but leave them to be devoured by wild beasts. Shocking to any Western sensibility, this had its convenient side. Burying that lot, in a place without earth, would have been out of the question. Even our own small number of dead I'd decided to leave till help arrived.

Shahrbaraz was looking at Priscus. 'So the old fox was alive after all,' he said thoughtfully. He looked away. 'Am I right in believing a barbarian boy, even younger than you, did this to us?' he asked. I nodded and put my arm about Rado. For a long moment, Shahrbaraz stared in silence. Then he bowed gravely. 'The young man is to be congratulated,' he said. 'But you shouldn't take this as a victory. If today's battle is over, I need only pick out a few hundred veterans of the Syrian War and lead them against you tomorrow. You'll not be so lucky then. I've seen your numbers. Or are you going to lie to me that this is only the vanguard of a Greek army of defence?'

'Where is Chosroes?' I asked.

Shahrbaraz reached up to stroke his beard. 'Alive,' he said cautiously. 'His Majesty was wounded in his right shoulder by your most disrespectful spear thrust. He is being carried back in all haste to our own territory to secure the appropriate medical treatment for a wound sustained on the field of battle. After that, he will return to Ctesiphon.'

I smiled. 'Then you can drop your silly talk of coming back for second helpings.' I walked over to a large stone beside the wall of the pass. I pushed a dead Persian from it and sat down. 'Let me put a case to you, My Lord General.' He came and leaned against the wall. His men were a long way off. No one was able to follow us here, so I kept my voice loud and steady.

'Either you've been defeated by the vanguard of a Greek army, or you've been routed by a local militia. The former is an occupational hazard, the second a disgrace that can lead only to the impaling stake. If you ignore this plain consideration and press forward, you won't get much deeper into the Home Provinces. This isn't Syria. Between here and Constantinople, every farmer is now also a soldier. You can forget supply lines. Your zone of occupation will be measured in the square inches that each of your men is standing on at any particular moment. Never mind whether we beat you in a regular battle, you'll be lucky to make it back to Chosroes at the head of a hundred men. And, with no army to your name, how long before His Majesty decides he doesn't like the sour expression on your face?'

For the first time that day, I was almost enjoying myself. 'So let's agree that there *is* a bloody great army hurrying along the Larydia Pass. Why not take my offer of continued truce and go back to the Euphrates? We won't harry the retreat. You can blame everything on Shahin. He was working for us all along. He led us here. The Horn of Babylon was a fraud he made up with us for the

479

purpose of murdering Chosroes. Its silver body was covered in a poison that could turn a man to grey slime in three days.'

'And how will the Lord Shahin be persuaded to admit to so dastardly a betrayal?' came the obvious question.

'You'll take his signed confession back with you, of course,' I said with a smile. 'You can present him with a choice between the discomforts of being flayed alive and the mercy of the sword. He'll sign. Take his head back with the confession. So long as you've an army for invading Egypt next year, or the year after, Chosroes will decide to believe you. My understanding is that he made no official announcement of the invasion. This being so, there's no need to announce its defeat. I promise that Heraclius won't celebrate his victory.'

Shahrbaraz rested his eyes on the body of Priscus. 'Will Heraclius be told about the part played by a man who died in disgrace over a year ago?' he asked. It was a feeble threat. But I'd let him get away with it.

'I understand that your affairs are somewhat embarrassed by the confiscation of your brother's estate,' I said, repeating some gossip I'd picked up a few days earlier while my legs were being shaved. His eyes narrowed. 'There's a Jewish banker in Damascus called Josiah ben Baruch,' I continued. 'If you go to him in confidence, you'll find him a most generous subject of the Persian hegemony.' I paused. 'His brother runs a bank in Constantinople. I've always found the whole family *very* confidential in their management of funds.'

Shahrbaraz stood up and brushed dirt from his sleeve. 'We need till the seventh hour of the night,' he repeated stiffly. He began walking slowly back across the sea of his own dead. Almost out of hearing, he suddenly turned. 'Shahin has a Greek with him called Simon,' he called over. 'Would you like me to send him back to you for punishment?'

'I thank you for the great kindness of your suggestion,' I answered. 'However, you might find that executing him in the manner of your choosing might awaken Shahin all the more to the joys of literary composition.'

I watched until he and his men were gone. A polite cough from within a low crevice reminded me that there was yet more unfinished business for my attention. 'You can come out of there, Timothy,' I said. 'I won't kill you. I know you've been on our side all the time – or enough of the time not to make any difference that counts.'

He *had* lost weight! He stood looking at the body of the only man who could possibly have made him seem pure by comparison. 'He liked you a lot, you know,' he said. 'I knew from the start you'd given him refuge. Priscus wasn't the sort of man to die in some random Avar swoop on the suburbs. Since there was no one else mad enough to take him in, he had to be with you. He told me everything on the night of Leander's big recitation. Or perhaps he didn't tell me everything – Priscus never did that.'

Timothy paused and looked into my face. 'By the way, where is that silver cup? I do believe Shahin dropped it. He never let me see it properly on the way here and I feel some obligation to look at the proximate cause of all our troubles. But for that, we'd none of us be here and our lives would not have been so *amended*. Forgive me if I confess to a somewhat philosophical interest.'

He had a point. I looked vaguely about. The thing could be anywhere. With all the human movement over this ground, it might still be half a mile away. Or it might be here, under one of the bodies, or lodged in one of the rocky clusters. Doubtless someone would find it and claim it as loot. But none of us would see it again. For good or ill, an object which had burst into our lives, transforming them in unexpected ways, had now, just as abruptly and mysteriously, vanished.

Timothy brought himself back to more pressing matters. 'I trust you'll put in a word for me with Heraclius. And, if you have gone through the motions of confiscating it, I want my property back. Above all, though, I'd like to go home. I'd really like that, Alaric. Indeed, I'd like to go home much more than you must.'

I frowned. 'How do you arrive at that, my dear Timothy?' I asked.

481

He creased his face into an oily smile. 'Because, my dearest friend in the world, when I get back to Constantinople, I'll not find unanswered correspondence flowing out of my palace into the street.'

Will you think less of me, Dear Reader, if I say that I joined him in laughing till the tears ran down my cheeks?

EPILOGUE

Canterbury, Wednesday, 9 September 688

I've done it. I've told the story. And let's end it here. Rado's at the start of a career as glorious as Priscus had guessed it would be. Shahrbaraz is already counting his bribe. Shahin will soon have an offer put to him that he can't refuse. And Simon has two or three days of wishing I'd got lucky with the lamp I threw at him on board that ship. Timothy ends rather well – though that isn't revealing much: Timothy is a born survivor and will soon return to his accustomed size.

Eboric will be beautiful to the last, fancied by all who saw him, loved by all who knew him, unable to think ill of anyone. More important, he'll be happy to the last. Lucky the man who is that.

What of Antonia? Well, we did get back to Constantinople. Heraclius was as good as his word over the marriage. Even before then, and never mind her growing belly, we were hard at work, fucking each other's brains out. We were still at it fifty years later. My only regret is that I didn't go first.

I don't think I need talk about the Empire. It's still there, now having good times, now bad. It will outlast me. I'm reasonably sure, Dear Reader, it will outlast you.

But you may have noticed, I still haven't made it back to Jarrow. The reason for that is complex and may be the starting point of another story. I'll only say that, with Theodore far advanced into a second, though assuredly no more happy, childhood, the English Church needs someone to hold things together in his name. Somewhere in the mass of papyrus I've generated, I mention killing, lying, scholarship and ruling. Well, it seems that I'm back, for the moment, to doing all these things. We'll see how long that lasts.

Oh, and the cup – the fabled Horn of Babylon. Before the catalogue of his library was entirely wiped, Theodore said having the thing back would make me as unhappy as he'd been. Of course, that was a sign that he was on the way out. It's a lump of silver, no more, no less. This being said, I did pass it straightaway to Good King Swaefheard. You'll not imagine how grateful he was. He said he'd have it made into a crown and that, in one form or another, it would be possessed forever by all who ruled Kent, or even the whole of England.

Perhaps the speed with which I handed it on tells you something about me that I don't choose to admit. But, when you get to my age, you really can't be too careful.